STORM'S FURY

AMELIA STORM SERIES: BOOK ONE

MARY STONE

AMY WILSON

Mary Stone

To my readers, who are the best ever. You mean the world to me. Thank you from the bottom of my grateful heart.

Amy Wilson

To my one and only, my husband and best friend, and the best boys a mother could dream of, who all worked with me to make this story possible.

DESCRIPTION

Some storms destroy. Others clear a path.

Military veteran Amelia Storm returns to her hometown of Chicago when her beloved police officer brother is killed in the line of duty. Now she is a special agent with the FBI. No longer a scared girl, she vows to avenge her brother and do what she can to end the city's deep wells of corruption.

A television documentary puts a spotlight on a four-year-old kidnapping. Amelia and her colleagues in the Organized Crime Division know there's more to the girl's case than meets the eye.

The twelve-year-old wasn't just abducted. She was targeted by a human trafficking ring.

As Amelia falls deeper down the rabbit hole of Chicago's criminal hierarchy in search of the girl, she finds herself uncomfortably close to the people she left behind so long ago. This time, though, she won't run. Now, she is the storm that will unearth the city's long buried secrets. Or die trying. After all, she has nothing to lose.

From the wickedly dark minds of Mary Stone and Amy Wilson comes Storm's Fury, book one of the Amelia Storm Series, where you'll be reminded that Mother Earth is wild, but humans are the most dangerous creatures.

1

Leila Jackson's stomach growled as she poured what little of the off-brand shredded wheat cereal was left—crumbs and all—into her plastic bowl and sank a partly melted plastic spoon into the dry mix. As per usual, there wasn't any milk to go with the cereal. There was never milk.

In fact, pretty much everything Leila wanted was either unavailable or a sad approximation of what a real family would have in their kitchen. Their home. In this den of sin, as her grandmother would've called it, any remotely valuable dishes or silverware would grow legs and walk away.

The men in charge of the house didn't care about the squalor surrounding them, though Leila felt sure that the use of plastic cutlery and dishes was a tactical move on their part. Sure, the men weren't willing to put in the money for anything better, but more than that, they wouldn't dare risk one of the girls using a broken plate as a makeshift weapon. Not that any of them would have had the guts to do such a thing.

To avoid the hassle and hard stares, Leila and the others normally ate with their hands. Which wasn't often, since they rarely had much to eat. Try as she might, Leila couldn't remember the last time she'd eaten a proper meal off a real plate. Most of the women who lived in the house had turned to drugs to escape the hunger and degradation that was their reality.

Leila wasn't that far gone...yet.

From the corner of her eye, Leila spotted a flicker of movement as a tall man in a black leather jacket strode through the arched doorway. His presence jerked her from the moment of reverie, and every system in her body seemed to halt.

The quiet chattering from girls on the other side of the room stopped. It was almost as if a mage from one of Leila's beloved fantasy novels had cast a spell over them, freezing time.

She had only been at the rundown Victorian mansion for just over a week, but Leila recognized the man's flat brown eyes and five o'clock shadow. Women who lived outside of this house might have considered him handsome, with his sleek hairstyle and muscular stature, but to Leila, he was every bit as disgusting as the perverts who had frequented the last house she'd been kept in.

Leila squared her shoulders and met his stare. Not with a look of defiance. She'd learned over the last four years that insubordination caused more problems than it solved. She might be new to this particular house, but she wasn't new to the world of sex trafficking and forced prostitution. Nor was she new to the men who controlled her every move.

For the better part of four years, she'd been kept captive in a brothel where sleazy men paid to have their way with underaged girls. Now that her body had matured, and she fit the coveted "barely legal" category, she'd been sold and trans-ferred to this house, with the expectation that she'd make double the profits on the streets.

But just because the scenery had changed, it didn't mean the men in charge were different. They were all the same brand of twisted, and they all wanted the same thing.

Obedience. Subservience. Complete and total control. So, yes. She knew all too well where defiance would get her.

Despite the relentless cadence of her heart against her ribs and the sweat that dampened her palms, she met the man's stare with a look that displayed as much emotion as a stone. Best not to react...negatively or positively. That would draw unwanted attention, which was the last thing she needed.

She got it anyway.

The floor creaked beneath his booted feet as he closed the remaining distance. Though Leila's stomach churned at the scent of his cologne mingled with the smell of stale cigarettes, she maintained her dispassionate façade even as her pulse pounded in her ears.

His hand snapped forward without warning. The movement was a blur, like the strike of a deadly snake. Leila's charade fell away as she let out a squeak and leapt backward, colliding into the edge of the counter. It bit sharply into her spine.

Try as she might, Leila couldn't help but wince as tears welled up in her eyes. Adding insult to injury, trapped against the cabinets as she was, Leila had nowhere to run.

The corner of the man's mouth turned up, clearly enjoying her sudden display of fright. He lifted his hand once again, and it was only then that she recognized the articles of clothing dangling from his finger. Whore clothes. Swallowing hard against the churning bile threatening to erupt from her mouth, Leila hesitantly pulled the outfit from his outstretched hand.

"I know it's your first night working out on the street, but this..." his hateful smile widened as he plucked at the flimsy fabric of her t-shirt, "this isn't going to work, doll. I got you something to wear, courtesy of The Captain."

Leila tried in vain to back away from his touch, but the counter only dug deeper into her spine. If she hadn't already given herself a bruise, she had one now.

His eyes bore into hers as he cupped her chin. "What do you say?"

Though Leila wanted nothing more than to rake her long nails over those soulless eyes, she merely tightened her grasp on the skimpy outfit—a pair of Daisy Dukes and a backless halter top that would barely cover her chest. June in Chicago was hot and humid, but the clothes were so tiny that Leila couldn't help but think she'd freeze as soon as the sun went down.

Her knuckles had turned white by the time she finally managed a nod. "Th-thank you."

She hated herself for saying those words. He didn't deserve her gratitude. She wanted to punch him in the throat, but she shoved those thoughts of retribution to the back of her mind.

Lashing out at the creep wouldn't get her away from here. She had to remember that.

The smirk took on a devious edge as he trailed his hand down to grasp her waist. Leila knew that look. It was an expression she'd seen more times than she should have in a hundred lifetimes, much less in her meager sixteen years.

When a man donned that expression, the outcome was never good.

"Let's try that again." His voice was quieter and bordered on sultry. "This time, how about you show a little gratitude, huh, doll?"

Leila's thoughts swirled like a vortex, equal parts rage and fear, or perhaps rage inspired by fear. In the wild, when an animal was cornered, violence was the typical outcome. And at that moment, she *was* a cornered animal.

She should have gone along with his request. After all, today wasn't the first time she'd been in such a scenario. She could have faked a small smile and forced her voice to remain even as she tacked an affectionate nickname to the end of her "thank you."

That's what they all wanted—to bathe themselves in the illusion of being desired and worshiped by beautiful women.

According to other girls who'd been in the house for a while, he acted like he owned the place. Leila didn't know his name, but she knew if she gave into him now, she'd regret it for the rest of her time in this part of town.

Wherever this part of town even is.

"Well?" A twinge of impatience edged into his tone.

Lifting her eyes up from the clothes, Leila met his expectant stare. She willed as much moisture to her mouth as she could manage, and before she could think through the action, she spat in his face.

His head snapped sideways as if she'd slapped him.

The air was sucked out of the room. Over the rush of her pulse, Leila barely made out the slight gasps of the two women at the other end of the kitchen.

Leila wouldn't have dared to do such a thing to The Captain—the Main Man in Charge. He scared the living hell out of her. She still couldn't believe she'd been bold enough to do this to his minion.

Did she have a death wish?

Shadows moved along the man's unshaven face as he clenched and unclenched his jaw. With one hand, he brushed the spittle from his cheek and the side of his nose. She was prepared for an outburst or even a physical blow, but the low chuckle in his throat unnerved Leila more than an overt act of violence.

He glanced down at his fingers, and the hateful smirk reappeared. "You know, I always did like them with a bit of fire. But this…" he returned his unsettling gaze to Leila and held up a hand, "this isn't going to fly, sweet thing."

A surge of adrenaline raced along Leila's spine. Her mouth was even drier than it had been at first, and she had to fight to keep the expression of sheer terror off her face. From the corner of her eye, she spotted movement as the two older girls slunk out of the kitchen.

Leila managed a slight shake of her head. "I—"

His hand clamped down on her throat. "Save it, sweetheart." It was Satan's voice, she knew. He'd come to take her from this living hell to the eternal one far below.

Horrified, she tried to swallow, but his grasp was too tight.

This was it.

The split-second of defiance was the last act Leila Jackson would ever make. Maybe she should have been terrified, but if she went out swinging at one of these sick bastards, then she was a warrior. Like the Vikings she'd watched on television in her previous life, she'd meet Odin in Valhalla.

Only those who fell in battle went to Valhalla, and what was Leila's life if not a constant battle?

The hand tightened even more, and her life flashed before her eyes.

She remembered her tenth birthday, the first time her parents had been able to afford to rent a party room at a pizza and arcade place back in her hometown of Janesville, Wisconsin. She'd beaten her older brother at *Street Fighter* for the first time that evening. Her friends—even her parents —had all stepped up to challenge her after she'd bested Pierce, but Leila had still been undefeated when they went home.

Did her parents still think about her? Her brother? He

would be twenty soon. Had he gone to college, joined the military, or had he become an electrician like their father?

As the tall man's fingertips dug into the sensitive skin of her neck, Leila was sure she'd never learn the answer to her questions. She'd never see her family again…all because she'd been foolish enough to believe a hysterical woman begging for help with her unresponsive toddler.

Leila had been warned all her life about the importance of avoiding strangers, from her parents and from school, but no one had ever told her that the danger might come in the form of a desperate mother. Of course, Leila knew now that the whole encounter had been an act. There was never any toddler—the woman probably didn't even have any kids. It had all been a ruse to lure her into a stranger's van and knock her unconscious.

Like she was going unconscious now.

All at once, the pressure at her throat lifted. The air along the raw skin felt like a cool breeze, though she hadn't moved from her spot in the kitchen.

Leila would have dropped to the dingy tiled floor if it hadn't been for the cabinets at her back. She lost her grip on the skimpy clothes as she grasped at the edge of the counter. Her other hand flew to her neck as she took in a violent breath.

She was still here, for better or worse, in this shoddy house with sixteen other girls and the men who guarded them. A stone sank in her stomach as a new realization hit her.

There was no Valhalla. There was no Odin. There was only Leila and this leather-jacket-wearing creep.

Leering with malevolence, he rapped his knuckles on the worn countertop. "I'd bash your face into that counter until your own mother wouldn't recognize you, but lucky for you, you're worth a lot more if you're pretty."

Leila sucked in a breath. "G-go ahead." Her throat was raw, but she forced the words out. "I've b-been gone for so long, my m-mother wouldn't recognize me, anyway."

His soulless eyes bore into hers as he held up an index finger. "Mark my words, you little whore, this ain't over. If you think you can pull some shit like that and get away with it, I'll show you just how wrong you are. You're headed out to the street soon, but you'd best believe that I'll be here waiting when you return."

Bile stung the back of Leila's throat. Of course that's what he wanted. He was just like all the others. So hungry for power that he wouldn't hesitate to exert his control by forcing a helpless girl to have sex with him.

He stepped back, snickering victoriously at her inability to respond to his implied threat, and his gaze lowered to the cereal Leila had poured only moments ago.

With another malicious twist of his lips, he swiped the bowl off the counter. Plastic smacked against the linoleum with a resounding clatter, sending chunks of shredded wheat skittering across the floor.

Leila jumped at the sudden disturbance, and his faint smile escalated into mocking laughter.

He held both hands out at his sides as he backed up toward the door. "Just looking out for your figure, doll. I'd hate for you to go and ruin that smoking hot body of yours, you know?"

Leila didn't let her eyes leave him until he disappeared through the arched doorway.

Clutching her throat with one hand, the other covering her mouth, she leaned all her weight against the cabinet. As she slid down to sit on the sticky linoleum, she bit her tongue to stave off the tears she knew were coming. Even though her throat felt like she'd swallowed glass, she wasn't crying for the brutal treatment of the pervert who had just left the room. He wasn't the first violent man she'd dealt with, and she doubted he'd be the last.

That was the real reason for her tears. This life. These soulless monsters. The cutthroat girls and women who never looked out for one another. This was her life, and now, she'd make it official by working as a prostitute on the streets of Chicago.

And when she returned to the house...

Bile clawed its way back up her throat as her stomach lurched. Clamping a hand over her mouth, Leila leapt to her feet and sprang to the sink. Hunched over and struggling to keep strands of ebony hair from her face, she emptied her stomach into the stainless-steel. Acid stung her throat while tears blurred her vision. She heaved until she was certain the nausea had passed.

After she drank a few handfuls of lukewarm water from the tap, Leila leaned heavily against the counter and turned to the spilled cereal. Glancing from one piece of shredded wheat to the next, she covered her mouth and squeezed her eyes closed. The only meal she was allocated for the entire day had been scattered over the pockmarked linoleum.

She'd been told by one of the other girls to turn her mind to happy memories when she felt overwhelmed, but any time Leila tried to heed the advice, she only felt more defeated. Though none of the women trapped with her in this house were here due to favorable circumstances, Leila had come to realize that not all of them had fallen victim to the traffickers quite like she had.

That was to say that most of them hadn't been kidnapped at age twelve and sold into prostitution.

Even now, she couldn't believe four years had passed. She hadn't even known what sex was back then, and in the snap of a finger, all her innocence had been forcibly erased.

Stripped of her dignity, she'd been tossed into a closet of a room and told to "do whatever the men want."

She cried a lot in those early days. But tears didn't matter. Often, it only made things worse.

Most enjoyed that sense of power they had over her. The consequences of an unsatisfied man were far worse than her feelings, anyway. When men didn't get their way, the response was always violent. Eventually, she learned to close her eyes and just accept the constant stream of men visiting her room. She lost count of how many she'd serviced over the years, but the lesson stuck. Doing whatever disgusting thing a man demanded, without question, made life a lot easier.

She wasn't sure how long she stood in front of the sink, her blank stare fixed on the crumbs of cereal at her feet. As the minutes ticked away, she knew she had to prepare herself for the night ahead. Her makeup was a mess, and she still had to change into the barely there outfit she'd been given by Leather Jacket Creep.

A shadow moved at the edge of her vision, and Leila jerked away from the counter. She was sure that her tormentor had returned to claim his retribution early.

She wasn't ready for that. She had expected to have the entire night to steel herself for the confrontation.

To her relief, the newcomer was a different soldier. This one had the same tall, muscular frame, but he looked younger. Though his dark eyes lacked the same malice as his counterpart, the expression on his clean-shaven face seemed as if it had been carved from stone. As he brushed the strands of jet-black hair from his forehead, the waning sunlight caught the polished chrome of the handgun holstered beneath one arm.

Leila's relief was short-lived. As soon as she spotted the weapon, she froze. "Did he send you in here to kill me?" The question came out in a rush, and she wasn't sure which answer she hoped for.

The newcomer frowned. "What? Who? What are you talking about?"

She swallowed past the tightness in her throat. "The guy who just left. The guy who did this." She gestured to the cereal.

With a groan, the man shook his head. "Giorgio. 'G,' as he prefers to be called. Is that who you're talking about?"

Leila swallowed again. "I don't know his name."

The soldier scratched his temple. "Yeah, Giorgio's a real piece of work. Just because he's The Captain's cousin, he thinks he can do whatever the hell he wants."

Leila flashed a paranoid glance around the room. Was Giorgio listening? If she agreed with this man, would he pop out from one of the cupboards like a twisted jack-in-the-box and put a bullet in her skull?

"He's not in here." Although the soldier's reply was flat, Leila caught a twinge of a sentiment she couldn't immediately place. Was it sympathy?

No. None of the men in this godforsaken place are capable of genuine human emotion.

Leila lifted her chin and met his gaze. She was sick of being scared. Sick of it all.

He spread his hands and took a step forward. "Look," his voice was almost a whisper, "I know it's your first night working the street. I'm not going to pretend to know how that feels, but honestly, it doesn't matter. You don't have a choice. Now that you're here, it's their way or a hole in the ground."

Tears pricked the edge of Leila's vision, but she clenched her jaw to will them away. "What's to stop me from just leaving while I'm out there tonight? Why wouldn't I just have one of the Johns take me somewhere outside the city?"

Did I really ask this stranger these questions? Maybe she did subconsciously hope to die.

Instead of putting her out of her misery, the man frowned, though the look was more resigned than menacing. "You can't. Too many of the women who come through here think they can *Pretty Woman* their way to freedom. You can't."

Anger and frustration warmed her skin. "Why not?"

He took a step closer. "Because they'll find you. They'll find your family. You ought to know by now that there's nothing to stop them from getting who or what they want. Not even the cops. They *own* the cops."

Leila's stomach sank. *Pretty Woman* had been her mother's favorite movie. But the soldier was right, at least as far as Leila could tell. The world of prostitution was nothing like Julia Roberts's portrayal in the iconic film.

As defeat weighed on her shoulders, Leila took hold of the countertop. She still had one option left. "Fine. I'll just kill myself."

She could almost feel the sweet release of letting it all go, of sinking into the nothingness of death. Was she brave enough to do it herself or could she goad this man into doing it for her?

"If you do, then *I'll* be the one who pays for it." He tapped his chest with an index finger.

"I don't care." Leila's voice was scarcely above a whisper. Her vision blurred again, but she held his gaze. "You're just like all the rest of them, anyway."

Through her tears, she could have sworn he winced at the callous remark. "I'm not like them."

Her laugh was filled with bitterness. "Then why are you here? Trying to play like you're one of the nice guys? I've got your number. I've been seeing nice guys like you for the last four years."

She took a step toward him, the cereal crunching under her foot. The sound added to her fury.

"Now look where I am!" She waved her hands at the squalor of the room. "Being forced to walk the streets. Like that's supposed to be some kind of upgrade from waiting in a bedroom for the next man to do whatever he wants."

"I—"

She held up a hand. Now that the words had started, they didn't seem to want to stop. "I never had a choice, but you do. Like you said, if I try to leave, they'll kill my family. But you, you can just walk out that door any time you want. You can go home to your family, your warm bed, and your nice house."

The muscles in his jaw twitched as seconds ticked away in silence. Leila half-expected him to turn and march back out the door. Or wrap his hands around her throat and finish Giorgio's job.

Kill me. The thought was like a whisper in her ear.

Instead, he blew out a long breath and raked a hand through his hair. "You'll be leaving soon. You need to hurry and get ready."

Her shoulders sagged. There would be no reprieve today.

Leila glanced again at the spilled cereal. "I still have to clean this up."

He held up a hand to stop her before she dropped to her knees. "I'll clean it up. You really need to hurry."

She bit down on her lip to keep her voice steady. "I haven't eaten today. This is all I have."

Muttering a slew of four-letter words under his breath, along with at least one mention of Giorgio, the man reached to the back pocket of his dark wash jeans.

Leila flinched at his sudden movement.

"Here." He held out a five-dollar bill and a handful of ones. "There's a gas station close to where you're going.

When you get a break tonight, go get yourself something to eat."

Even as Leila mulled over his words in an effort to discern whether he was setting a trap, she reached out to accept the offer. "Why are you giving me this? Why are you doing any of this?"

He pressed the cash into her palm as his brown eyes met hers. "Because I'm *not* like them."

Leila glanced at the money and back to him before shaking her head. For the last four years, she'd been conditioned to interpret any gesture of kindness as a trap.

She swallowed hard. "I don't know if I can pay you back."

"It's okay. This isn't a trap. Just take the money and get something to eat tonight. I'll beat nine dollars out of Giorgio if I have to. He might be the boss's cousin, but I'm still in charge of that idiot."

In a different world, Leila might have laughed at the comment. But as she pocketed the cash and scooped up her skimpy outfit, she honestly couldn't recall the last time she'd made a sound that even came close to sounding like joy.

❄

LEILA'S FIVE-INCH heels clacked against the pavement as she stepped over the curb and onto the street corner. Clasping the strap of her small handbag, she glanced over her shoulder to watch the black Town Car pull away.

The drive hadn't taken long, but even if she'd been inclined to make a break for freedom, she didn't have the first clue where she was. The other girls had told her they did the majority of their work in a community called West Garfield Park, but Leila couldn't identify the location on a map if her life depended on it.

Before her kidnapping, she had only been to the state of

Illinois once. Her hometown, Janesville, was a good-sized city, but it was a speck compared to Chicago.

The sun hung just over the city skyline, and streetlights buzzed with life. The street she had been given to work was home to a handful of vacant lots and a poorly maintained expanse of grass, which the *house girls* referred to as "Needle Park." It didn't take much deduction for Leila to figure out why it had earned that nickname.

The soldier pulled into an empty parking lot and pointed toward a group of girls standing under the glow of a street-lamp. "This is where you work and will be picked up at the end of your shift."

"What am I supposed to do?" Leila's stomach churned with anxiety.

"Watch and learn." The soldier nodded at a car as it slowed to a stop beside the street corner.

A thin blonde in six-inch heels and shorts that were almost as revealing as Leila's sauntered over as the driver rolled down his window. Over the distant hum of traffic and the rush of her pulse, Leila couldn't make out the dialogue, but the body language said enough.

Blondie's hips swayed hypnotically as she bent forward to speak to the driver. She moved her hands as she spoke, drawing attention to her breasts and her lips. All the areas men loved to covet. And finally, with a sultry smile, blondie nodded, made her way around to the passenger side door, and got in the vehicle. Before she'd even closed the door, the driver took off so fast, his tires chirped on the street.

"Is that what I'm supposed to do?" Leila asked the soldier. "Just supposed to hop in the car with some creep and hope that he doesn't kidnap or murder me?"

"Hop in the car with a paying customer, yes." The soldier met her eyes in the rearview mirror. "Someone will be nearby to keep a watch out. Stay close. Find somewhere quiet and out of the way to do your job and have them drop you back here when you're done. There's a payphone nearby. You have the number to call if there's any trouble, and the watcher is busy with something else. Someone will be back to collect you when your shift is done."

Watcher. Leila shuddered at the word.

Someone was always watching...waiting...

"That's it?" She didn't want to get out of the car and hoped that stalling might buy her at least a few more moments.

"Clock's ticking, and you've got a quota, so get out there."

Swallowing against the onslaught of nausea, Leila clasped her handbag and exited the car.

The soldier rolled down the window and turned to face her. "A word of advice. Stay close enough to the girls who are working. At least for tonight. They know how to spot a cop if one comes by. But don't get too friendly. They are your competition."

The soldier drove off, leaving her alone and exposed. It was one thing to know men were coming to screw her in a private room. But now, she was being put on display, side-by-side with the competition, who were vastly more experienced.

What if she didn't make her quota? Leila was so focused on reigning in her mounting anxiety that she didn't notice the attention she'd gained until she turned to find a woman staring at her.

By Leila's best guess, she was at least in her mid-twenties. Her ebony hair was pinned atop her head in a messy bun, and her outfit—stilettos, a skintight black miniskirt, and a semi-sheer halter top—was just as skimpy as Leila's.

Her high cheekbones and smooth, tan skin were memorable, but Leila was sure she'd never seen her before.

Whoever the woman was, she ran in a different circle than Leila.

The woman lifted a sculpted brow as she held out a tin of Altoids. "You straight, kid? You look like you're about to puke."

Leila pressed her hand against her stomach. "I'm...queasy, I guess. I've never done this before."

The other woman's honey-brown eyes didn't leave Leila as she popped open the mints.

"First night? No wonder you look shook. Here, get some. These mints will fix your stomach right up." The tone of her voice was amicable enough, but Leila didn't miss her carefully guarded expression.

Leila managed a small smile as she picked out two mints. Without hesitating or even caring if they were laced with poison, she popped them in her mouth. "Thank you."

"Baby girl, you're gonna have to get straight real fast if you want to survive out here." She gestured to a group of girls milling about less than a block away from them. "Ain't none of us picked this work, but we're all in the same business, with bosses to keep happy. You wouldn't be out here if you didn't have the assets, so work what you got. If you don't..." her eyes met Leila's as she shrugged her thin shoulders, "then you'll be out here for the rest of your life."

Leila wasn't sure what the woman expected her to say, so she nodded absently as she crunched on her mints. She was already bound to this work for the rest of her life, and she knew better than to think she'd ever be able to make this so-called job work in her favor.

A spell of silence descended over them, though the sound of traffic along a major street nearby was steady. Shifting from one foot to the other, Leila glanced back to her companion.

She forced a slight smile to her lips as she stuck out a hand. "I'm Leila. Thank you for the mints."

With unabashed skepticism alight in her eyes, the woman accepted Leila's awkward handshake. "Ain't no problem. And the name's Angel." She stepped backward, and the glow of a streetlight caught the polished silver of a cat-shaped pendant at her throat.

Leila's smile came a little easier as she touched her own cat necklace. "We have something in common."

"Yeah, I guess so." Angel didn't seem impressed.

"My mom gave this to me when I was eleven." Leila gingerly clasped the silver cat—the last piece of her former life. "The next day, she took me with her to the shelter so we could adopt a cat. We had a dog too, but I think my mom secretly always wanted a cat. I thought I was going to get a kitten, but there was this sweet calico cat I loved. All her kittens had been adopted, so I just knew it was time for her to go home too."

Angel's gaze remained fixed on Leila, but the older woman's countenance changed little.

Though the threat of tears loomed behind Leila's eyes, she forced herself to smile. "I named her Hup, after the hero in a show called *The Dark Crystal*. I hope my parents still have her. I hope they didn't get rid of her after…I…was gone."

Angel responded with a meager nod, and Leila wished she could vacuum up all the words she'd just uttered. Angel clearly didn't care about Leila's old life, and for all Leila knew, Angel's life might have always been the streets. She might not have even *had* a mother to look out for her.

Leila tugged at the hem of her too-short shirt. At least the threat of puking had subsided. "Hey, um, Angel?"

Angel lifted a brow as she angled her head back toward Leila. "Yeah?"

"I don't know this part of town well…at all, actually. Is

there a gas station or something close by where I can get something to eat?"

With an impatient sigh, Angel pointed to the abandoned grocery store kitty-corner to where they stood. "Go past that old store. There's one at the other end of that block. But you'd better get over there fast."

Leila readjusted her handbag over her shoulder. "Why?"

"All the businesses around here close up by nine."

"Nine? Why so early?"

Angel shifted from one foot to the other and slapped a hand down on her hip. "You're in West Garfield Park, kid. This ain't exactly a place for law-abiding citizens after the sun goes down."

Before Leila could speak, a silver coupe pulled up to the curb. Angel didn't even bother to glance back at Leila as she strode over to the driver to strike up a conversation. After a quick exchange, Angel sauntered around to the passenger's side.

"West Garfield Park," Leila muttered to herself.

She waited for Angel and her client to pull away before hastily crossing the street. Headlights flashed on, and she wasn't surprised when the watcher followed her from a distance.

Maybe the gas station would have a map of the city so Leila could start to decipher the treacherous puzzle that was Chicago.

2

Special Agent Amelia Storm popped a piece of cheese tortellini in her mouth as she squinted at her computer. The machine might have been official FBI property, but she hadn't hesitated to download Netflix to pass the time during her breaks. She hated watching shows on her phone's tiny screen, especially when she had a nineteen-inch monitor right in front of her.

Tonight's dinnertime feature was a new documentary series that honed in on a handful of missing persons cases that had grown cold across the United States. Even though Amelia worked in law enforcement, she was still a sucker for a good crime show. She especially liked to watch for accuracy and rail at the actors when they did something wrong.

Propping her elbows on the laminate desk, she stabbed another tortellini and scooted closer to the computer. An episode about a girl who had been abducted at twelve had just finished, and Amelia carefully watched the short summary at the end.

Heart squeezing for the child, Amelia glanced at the

calendar. She'd been gone for four years now, almost to the day.

The chances of her still being alive were abysmal, and a small part of Amelia hoped that death had claimed her quickly. That the young girl was now resting in peace instead of enduring forty-eight months of unknown cruelty and torture.

There were things worse than death. Much worse.

And the families...she didn't want to think of the hell they'd been through.

All four cases in the series had been placed on the proverbial back burner once the trail of evidence dried up. Initial suspects had been ruled out due to alibis, and all the leads had been investigated and dismissed one by one.

Law enforcement agents who were responsible for the cases could store the evidence away and move on with their duties, but it wasn't so neat and tidy for the victims' families.

Amelia could sympathize.

Two years earlier, her brother had been killed in the line of duty as a detective for the Chicago Police Department. Trevor had been following a case lead when a routine stop to pick up a person of interest turned into a shootout. The case had been what some would call a slam dunk, closed with all its files archived after the suspect was tried and convicted.

But just because the box of evidence had been tucked away somewhere in the basement of the Chicago police department, that didn't mean Amelia and her family had the same ease in storing away their grief.

She pushed the thoughts from her mind and returned her focus to the monitor. The show was called *Vanished*, and that was exactly what all four of the victims had done.

The cases featured in the ten-episode series were from different cities across the country—Boulder, Tacoma, Miami, and Janesville. There were no signs of violence, no indications of a break-in, just *nothing*. Each victim had disappeared without a trace.

Amelia reached the end of her leftover pasta as the credits rolled across the screen. Blowing a few strands of dark hair from her face, she leaned back in her chair and brushed her fingertips along the braid that started at her temple and ended in a wavy ponytail. For good measure, she double-checked the piece of hair she'd wrapped around to cover the elastic tie.

It had grown many inches in the two years she'd been out of the military, and her hairstylist sister-in-law often hinted about "shaping it up." Amelia had no time for that. Besides, she liked it long. Liked the ease of pulling it back as well as the security of running the thick rope of it through her fingers when she needed to think.

From around the corner of her cubicle, she spotted the Special Agent in Charge of the Chicago field office, Jasmine Keaton.

Her glossy black hair was pulled away from her face in a neat ponytail, and her white blouse and gray slacks were crisply pressed, as always. Her silver hoop earrings caught the overhead fluorescence as she tilted her head to point at one ear.

Amelia took the cue and pulled out her earbuds. Aside from the drum of raindrops against the row of windows at the other end of the room—a reminder of Chicago's unpredictable summer weather—the Organized Crime Division's corner of the sixth floor was quiet.

Amelia pushed away from the desk. "SAC Keaton. You're here late."

Jasmine shrugged as she glanced at Amelia's computer. "More true-crime documentaries? This is what you watch in your spare time, Storm?"

With a grin, Amelia returned the shrug. "Hey, it seemed work appropriate."

Jasmine Keaton's dark eyes moved to Amelia's two monitors as she leaned against the edge of the desk. "Have you ever thought about watching something that isn't so depressing?"

Amelia sucked in a breath through her teeth and made a show of leaning farther back in her chair. "Have I thought about it? Yes. Have I acted on it? Also, yes. Just not at work. I could throw on some *Brooklyn Nine-Nine*, but I'd be a little out of place if I was over here cackling at my desk in the middle of the FBI office."

From the other side of the partition separating Amelia and her neighbor came a quiet snort of laughter.

SAC Keaton crossed her arms and turned her attention to the chuckling agent. "What about you, Agent Palmer? Do you watch murder and cold case shows on your break?"

Like a gopher emerging from underground, Special Agent Zane Palmer stood to his full six-two height. His slate-gray eyes were alight with mirth as he glanced between the two women. Though his sandy brown hair was styled with whatever mystery product he used, he'd discarded his black suit jacket and had rolled his sleeves up to the elbows.

Scratching the side of his face, he made a show of pondering the SAC's question. "No, I can't say that I do. I usually go sit in my car and play solitaire on my phone." Though faint, there was enough of his native Jersey accent to confirm that he wasn't from the Midwest like Amelia and Jasmine.

The SAC drew her brows together. "You spend your break in your car?"

Palmer clicked his tongue as he pointed a ballpoint pen at the SAC. "I smoked for fifteen years, from the time I was sixteen to a few weeks after I turned thirty-one. Since smoking bans kept popping up while I was working in the D.C. office, I'd drive around on my breaks and chain smoke. I haven't had a cigarette in three years, but by now, I'm so used to driving around during my lunch break that it's weird *not* to do it."

Glancing from Agent Palmer to Amelia and back, Jasmine shook her head. "So, *you* drive around in Chicago traffic, and you watch cold case documentaries…for fun."

Zane held up a hand. "No, I *used* to drive around on my breaks. I don't hate myself enough to spend my free time in Chicago traffic. Now, I just go sit in my car. Maybe do a few laps in the parking garage."

Amelia crossed her arms. "See? At least I'm indoors watching television like a normal human being."

"*Normal,*" Zane mouthed, wiggling his fingers to add air quotes.

Even as Amelia rolled her eyes, she couldn't suppress her amusement. Ever since the great pizza debate—Chicago versus New York—Amelia and Zane took every opportunity to throw sarcastic jabs at one another.

The pretend spat was all in good fun. With the universe of dark details that came with their jobs as FBI agents, a little sarcastic humor was necessary for the sake of their sanity.

Amelia just wished that everyone she worked with had the same sense of humor.

Especially her fellow agent, Joseph Larson.

Try as she might, Amelia hadn't been able to convince her friend and frequent case partner that the interactions between her and Zane were harmless. Though Larson wouldn't vocalize his concern, Amelia was convinced that he suspected that Zane was trying to get into her pants.

At that thought, a snort of laughter slipped from her lips, earning Amelia curious looks from Jasmine and Zane. She waved them away. "My show's over. I've got work to do."

With a little salute, the SAC continued on her way to the breakroom while Zane lifted a shoulder and offered her a quick grin. "Normal is boring anyway."

Amelia flashed him a thumbs-up before he disappeared behind the partition. She stared at the empty space he just occupied, wondering if Joseph Larson might possibly be right.

Not that it mattered. If Palmer's intent was to woo Amelia to his bed, he was sorely out of luck.

Ever since the borderline traumatic breakup with her high school sweetheart ten years earlier, Amelia hadn't the faintest interest in a romantic engagement. Her career in the Army hadn't allotted her the free time to fret over boys, and neither had her new career in the Organized Crime Division of the Federal Bureau of Investigation.

Her work and her family were all she needed.

Her beloved sister-in-law, niece and nephew, and her now-sober father were why she'd moved back to Chicago. Joanna had been widowed when Amelia's brother was killed two years before, prompting Amelia to leave her military lifestyle behind. She'd returned home to help her sister-in-law juggle her ventures as a small business owner and a newly single mother of two.

Trevor...

She closed her eyes as a flash of pain shot through her. She still couldn't believe that her brother was gone.

"Focus," she muttered to herself. It was too easy to fall into the quicksand of sadness and grief.

But even as Amelia went back to finishing the paperwork for a case they'd recently wrapped up—the drug traffickers who had nearly killed her fellow agent Fiona Donahue—she struggled to keep her thoughts focused.

She'd been a morning person for the better part of her adult life, but for the past few months, she and Zane had adjusted their shifts to cover for Fiona while she recovered from the brutal beating she'd received at the hands of a group of Irish gangsters. Since Fiona worked nights and weekends, that meant Amelia had been forced to flip her sleep schedule to hours she hadn't kept since high school.

The buzz of her cell rattling against the desk snapped her from the lazy contemplation. Before it could vibrate itself to the floor, she snatched it up. The area code was from Wisconsin, that much she recognized. At close to midnight, a call from an unknown number usually meant one thing—her younger sister, Lainey, needed money.

Lainey hadn't bounced back from the rough upbringing like Amelia and Trevor had. She was the youngest, and Amelia suspected that the downward spiral of events after their mother's death had impacted Lainey more harshly than it had Amelia or Trevor. Lainey, much like their father, had taken to self-medicating as early as her freshman year of high school.

Amelia shook off the unwelcome thought of her troubled sister and answered the call. "Agent Storm."

"I'm glad I got ahold of you, Agent Storm," a woman with a distinctly folksy Wisconsin accent chirped through the phone. "I was worried I might not reach you so late at night."

Amelia connected the dots almost immediately. "Detective Schauss. Yeah, I've been working some night shifts lately, so you actually caught me in the office."

"Oh good. I'm glad I didn't wake you." The detective's voice was upbeat. She was clearly used to working these nocturnal hours.

Come to think of it, when she and Joseph had worked with Schauss on one of Amelia's first cases in the Chicago field office, the detective had been upbeat and chipper with every interaction. Not even Irish drug traffickers could dampen the Janesville detective's perpetual positivity.

Stifling a yawn, Amelia reached for a pen and pad of paper. "Nope. You sure didn't. What can I do for you, Detective?"

"Well, I'm in a bit of a pickle right now, and it's looking like this might be something we ought to hand off to you guys down there in Chicago."

"What kind of pickle?"

She could have sworn she heard the hushed sound of Zane's laughter.

"You know that new Netflix show about those four cold cases that just came out yesterday? Well, technically late at night the day before, but anyway, I digress."

"Right. I actually just finished watching the fifth episode on my lunch break. Well, dinner break, I guess." Amelia propped her elbow on the armrest of her chair. "What about it?"

"Oh, good. That saves a lot of explanation." Detective Schauss chuckled quietly. "Well, you know how there was one on there about a girl from Janesville?"

The poor girl who'd been snatched four years ago.

"Janesville, yeah. I remember her. Leila Jackson, right?"

"That's her, yep. She's been missing for about four years, it looks like." The detective's chipper voice darkened. "She disappeared when she was twelve, and no one's seen hide nor hair of her since. We used that new federal age progression software to generate a picture of what she'd look like now."

Amelia pulled up the Netflix show again. "Right, and they showed it next to the picture of her when she was twelve."

"They put the phone number for a tip line at the end of the broadcast. I didn't really expect anything to come of it, but, well…we just got a call from someone who says they saw her."

"Really?" Propping the phone against her ear with a shoulder, Amelia pulled up the FBI's case database.

The only information she knew about Leila Jackson's disappearance was from the television show, and those details were often hyped up for dramatic appeal. Amelia's fingers flew over the keyboard as she typed Leila's name into the search bar. Scanned copies of statements, photographs, and interview transcripts popped up from the initial investigation four years earlier.

"Here…I'll shoot you an email real quick with the recording." Furious keyboard clicking followed. "You can have a listen, though you probably know the places he talks about better than I do."

As Amelia dragged the photos and documents over to her second monitor, a pop-up in the bottom corner of the screen showed she'd received a new message from Detective Schauss.

"Thanks, Detective. It says here that her disappearance was investigated by the Janesville PD. At the time, they didn't think there was any evidence to suggest she'd crossed state lines, so they didn't involve the Bureau."

"That's right. Case went cold after a few months, and not much has been added to it since. But the call we got tonight was from a gentleman who says he saw someone who looked an awful lot like Leila there in Chicago."

Amelia scrolled through the old case report. "When did the caller say they saw Leila?"

"Tonight."

Amelia sat up straighter, the case going from cold to crucial with the single word. "How long ago?"

"Couple hours. Said he saw her in West Garfield Park, but I'll be honest, I don't really know where that is."

"West Garfield." Amelia tabbed down to the bottom of the report. "Yeah, I know that park. It can be a tough place."

She left out her intimate familiarity with "tough" places. For close to ten years, Amelia had called Englewood her home. Year after year, the Englewood community area turned out some of the highest rates of violent crime in all of Chicago.

"One more thing." Uncertainty was plain in the detective's voice. "Just so you know, the caller said that she was a working girl."

Amelia hated that she wasn't surprised. "Okay. Yeah, that's going to be our jurisdiction. It looks like we've got most of the case file already in our database but send me anything else you've dug up. Oh, and anything on the Jackson family too."

"Will do. Let me know if there's anything else I can do."

"I will. Thanks, Detective Schauss. Take care."

"You too, hon."

As Amelia set the phone back on her desk, she replaced her earbuds and pulled up Detective Schauss's email to play the recording of the phone call.

"Janesville Police Department anonymous tip line."

"Hey, yeah." The caller—a young male—cleared his throat. *"So, I think I might have seen one of those missing people...from a Netflix show. See, we were slow at work tonight. I work at a gas station on Madison Street. I was watching that new cold case show between customers."*

Amelia chuckled. She'd known she wasn't the only one.

"One of those girls, the one from Janesville. Leila Jackson...that was her name, I think. Well, I saw a girl come in here who looked a hell of a...sorry. A girl who looked an awful lot like that age progression picture they put up on the screen. She came in to get some soda and chips. She paid cash, and the whole time she was looking over her shoulder like someone was following her or something. I don't know. It was weird, you know?"

Amelia mentally shrugged. From what she remembered, most people looked over their shoulder in that part of town.

"I kept an eye on her after she left, just to make sure that no one"

jumped out at her or anything. And I mean, I don't judge, but she was dressed like a working girl, you know? Seemed like she was a little young for that, but I keep my nose out of that stuff. I stepped out for a smoke after she left, and sure enough, she was walking back over to where those working girls like to hang out."

Though the caller gave a rough estimate of the last location he'd seen the woman he thought might be Leila, he provided neither his name nor the name of the gas station. Amelia couldn't say she blamed him. She'd lived in neighborhoods like West Garfield Park and had a keen memory of how residents viewed law enforcement.

After typing a short explanation, Amelia sent the recording to SAC Keaton. Leila had been spotted a couple hours ago, and if Amelia was lucky, she might still catch the girl.

As she stood, Amelia grabbed the black zip-up hoodie she'd draped over the back of her chair. Though outdoor temperatures that week had hovered around ninety degrees, the FBI kept their building about as cold as a meat locker. Even on the hottest summer days, she still came to the office prepared to freeze her butt off.

Tonight, she donned the hoodie more to make herself look less like a federal agent than to ward off a chill. Even this late at night, temperatures still hovered in the low eighties.

Before she had shrugged into the first sleeve, Zane rose from his chair. "You bailing out already? It's not even midnight."

Amelia zipped up the hoodie. "If bailing means searching for a missing girl in our least savory part of town, then yeah, that's exactly what I'm doing."

Zane headed her way. "What girl?"

"The Janesville PD got an anonymous tip about a girl who matches the age progression picture of Leila Jackson from the cold case show, *Vanished*. The one who disappeared four years ago."

He scratched the side of his nose. "So, you're going to Wisconsin?"

She scoffed. "Yeah, Palmer. I'm going to drive to Wisconsin at quarter 'til midnight on a Saturday."

His confused expression relaxed into a sarcastic grin. "Then where?"

"The caller said they saw her in West Garfield Park, somewhere around Madison Street. I'm going to drive through the area and see if I can locate her."

Amusement drained from Palmer's face. "You're just going to drive through West Garfield Park in the middle of the night...by yourself?"

With an exaggerated eye roll, Amelia lifted the hem of her hoodie, revealing her holstered Glock. "I'm a big girl."

"I'll go with you." He shot her a matter-of-fact look as he scooped a set of car keys from his desk. "I'll drive while you look for her. Unless you've grown an extra set of eyes I don't know about, I don't see how you'd spot anything this late at night while trying to navigate those dark streets."

Though Amelia had been prepared for him to protest on the grounds that West Garfield Park was a treacherous neighborhood after sunset, his actual suggestion, sarcastic though it may have been, made much more sense.

Amelia shrugged. "Good point. Sure. It's basically like a break for you anyway, right?"

Zane snorted as he stepped away from his desk.

Amelia held up a hand. "Hold on. That's what you're wearing?"

He glanced down at the white dress shirt and shiny blue tie. "Good point. I look like a Fed." He jerked his tie off and tossed it on his chair.

Amelia pressed her lips together, trying not to laugh.

After a second, she gave up. "Wow...that's a real transformation. I almost didn't recognize you."

Zane shot her a double middle finger before pulling a hoodie from a drawer. "Better?" He did a little twirl to give her the full affect.

She applauded. "Much."

They set off for the parking garage attached to the building. Zane's music preferences were a refreshing change from Joseph Larson's. If Amelia was forced to listen to "Old Town Road" one more time, she wasn't sure she could be held accountable for her actions.

Though Amelia considered Joseph to be a friend, their tastes in music couldn't have been more different. Joseph had grown up in rural southern Missouri, whereas Amelia had been born and raised in the heart of Chicago.

In fact, the more she thought about her frequent case partner, the more she wondered if they had any commonalities aside from the fact that they'd both been in the military.

Not that the differences were a bad thing. Before her death nearly twenty years ago, Amelia's mother, Bonnie, had told her that having friends who were different from her made for an enriching experience.

Well, Mom, if you could see my friend now, you'd know that I followed your advice to a tee. A corner of Amelia's mouth turned up at the thought.

As she and Zane pulled onto West Madison Street, Amelia reached for the dial to lower the music's volume.

Zane shot her a curious glance.

"It helps me concentrate," Amelia replied to the unasked question. "I turn down the radio when I'm trying to find a new place too. It's a thing. They did a whole piece about it on NPR the other day. Something about not having enough cognitive resources to devote to all the sensory stimuli around you." She waved a hand. "Or something like that. I'm not a psychologist."

The light turned green, and Zane spread his hands along the steering wheel, chuckling softly. "Okay, okay. I believe you. Just thought for a second there that you hated my music."

Amelia shook her head. "No. You have no idea what I have to put up with when Larson's driving. I don't know what we were just listening to, but it's a vast improvement from songs about blue jeans and trucks."

Zane's quiet chortle turned into full-blown laughter. "I'm going to tell him you said that."

"Wouldn't be anything I haven't said to him before." She tapped the screen of her iPad and searched for Leila's file. "Okay, enough of that. We're looking for Leila Jackson. The guy who called into the anonymous tip line said that he worked at a gas station on West Madison Street in West Garfield Park."

"I don't suppose he said *which* gas station?"

Amelia scoffed. "Nope, but he mentioned the last place he'd seen Leila. We can start there. It wouldn't hurt to look through the area around that block too."

As they pulled up to another red light, Zane leaned forward, glancing around the intersection. He nodded in the direction of a vacant lot across the street. "There's a lot of people out and about, but I'm not seeing anyone who looks like our girl."

He was right. A group of young men milled about near the corner. Amelia didn't miss the side-eyed glances or the way they closed ranks around one another. Though there were other cars on the road, the number was small, and Amelia suspected the new make and model of Zane's Acura stuck out. More than likely, the neighborhood residents thought they were either tourists who'd gotten lost, or cops.

Various groups of young men, boys, and even some women stood in clusters. They congregated around street corners, in vacant lots, and huddled under the glow of outdoor lamps of closed businesses. Zane cruised up and down various streets north and south of Madison, but Amelia didn't see any working girls who remotely matched Leila Jackson's description.

Zane's gaze flicked over to Amelia as he prepared to turn around to head back to the FBI building. "Nothing?"

Tapping her index finger on the doorframe, Amelia squinted to look deeper into a dark alley. "Nothing. If Leila *is* a working girl, maybe some John picked her up, or maybe her pimp had her move. Something could've spooked them. The anonymous tipper might have looked a little sketchy. In his call-in, he said he had been watching her for safety."

"True. Hard to tell." Zane stepped on the accelerator as they neared an on-ramp for the interstate. "What's next? Is this even our case?"

"I'm claiming it." Disappointed, Amelia sat back in her seat. "If the girl the gas station clerk saw was actually Leila, then that means she's part of an underage prostitution ring, and that's definitely in our wheelhouse."

Zane craned his neck to check the blind spot before he merged onto the highway. "Okay, then we need to go back to basics, pull up all the case files, get a little history here, and try to trace the steps. Maybe I should take a look at that cold case show too. I don't even know what the girl looks like."

"Detective Schauss said she was sending everything over to the Bureau. I had a chance to look at the original case file a bit, but you're right. It wouldn't hurt to shake the dust off that whole thing. I think I'll circle back to the parents, get their statements again, and see if anything's changed since the initial investigation."

"You're going to drive to Wisconsin?" He reached to the

cup holder for his coffee. "Maybe you should get started on that drive right now."

"No." Amelia popped a stick of gum into her mouth. "The report says Leila's parents moved to DeKalb about six months ago. It's only an hour away."

"Great." Zane finished off the last of his coffee. "When are we leaving?"

"We?"

"Does Chicago have different rules than D.C.?" He arched an eyebrow. "Doesn't the FBI like to have more than *one* field agent present when interviewing a witness?"

Shit. It was Saturday. The past few weeks had been a blur.

"Right, I keep forgetting this is the weekend. I figured I'd have to suffer through Larson's Spotify playlist again, but he's out of town until Monday morning."

Zane held up his coffee thermos like it was a glass of expensive champagne, ready to pour yet another cup. "Guess it's you and me then, partner."

3

Leila glanced over her shoulder as the black Town Car idled at the curb, the driver watching her with narrowed eyes. In the middle of the night, the house where she and the other girls were kept reminded Leila of a haunted mansion she'd visited during her childhood. The roof arched in dramatic angles, and the lights glowing in each window were mismatched shades of different colors.

Leila tightened her grasp on the strap of her handbag. Her tired legs felt heavy with each step, and the point of her heels clacked against the worn sidewalk, like they were announcing her arrival. She cursed her luck as fear sent her heart racing with each step toward the rickety front porch.

You mark my words, little whore. This ain't over.

Giorgio's words echoed through her mind, drowning out the gentle drone of the sleepy city around her. Leila hesitated as she reached the tall wooden door.

Maybe she could avoid him. He might not be home or even remember the threat he'd made earlier that evening. The kinder soldier had told Leila that Giorgio was known for his hostile behavior. Maybe he'd found a new target in the passing hours.

Her stomach clenched at the thought. As much as she wanted Giorgio to forget that she existed, she didn't want her relief to come at another young woman's expense. She doubted the other girls would feel the same. In the short time she'd been in that house, she'd seen how the others, the women especially, approached their peers with cutthroat animosity.

Despite her situation, Leila had been taught better. Her mother had told her that girls needed to look out for each other, have each other's backs. That lesson might prove to be her undoing, but if she didn't hold on to at least some part of her old self, she'd become a shell, just like the rest of them.

Swallowing the bitter taste in her mouth, Leila finally forced herself to push open the heavy door. Faint echoes of women's voices drifted over to her as she glanced around the foyer and nervously stepped inside.

She used one hand to guide the door closed, trying to make as little sound as possible. With another paranoid glance around the wood-paneled foyer, she knelt to remove her heels. The floors of the house were perpetually dingy, but she needed to avoid drawing attention to herself.

The thundering rush of her pulse rendered the voices in the background indistinguishable. She forced herself to take in deep calming breaths and cautiously approached the short hallway.

All she had to do was make it to the stairs at the other end of the common area, and then she could hurry to her room. As long as Giorgio didn't spot her along the way, he might not know she'd returned.

With another steadying breath, Leila peeked around the corner. To her left, the dim hall led to the common living area, and to the right was a den the soldiers used to congregate and smoke. The door to that room was almost always closed, but a slat of golden light pierced through the gap at the floor. Muffled voices filtered out to the hall, but Leila couldn't be sure of the men's identities.

The longer she stood at the edge of the foyer, the more certain she was that Giorgio was among them.

Though fear crept along Leila's spine, she sprinted through the living area, pausing briefly to nod a greeting at the two women lounging on a raggedy sectional couch.

In the relative quiet, the clatter of a door opening rang out like a gunshot. Leila didn't bother to look back to confirm that the sound had come from the den. Her blood was ice, and goose bumps prickled along her forearms as adrenaline surged through her veins. She took the steps two at a time.

Make it to the end of the hall, and you'll be home free.

As the floorboards betrayed her with every step she made, unease churned in the pit of her stomach. Any moment she'd be caught. In reality, the sound of her footfalls was quieter than any other disturbance in the house, but to Leila, each step might as well have set off an air horn to announce her presence.

She was ready to collapse into a heap when she finally reached her door. With one trembling hand, she twisted the brass knob. Safe at last. Hot tears welled in the corners of her eyes as she slid into the relative darkness of her room.

She wanted a shower, desperately needing to wash off the lingering feeling of the men she'd let have their way with her that night. Most were old enough to be her father, and some doubled that generation gap. Leila felt physically and mentally filthy.

The men in charge of the house kept the water temperature lukewarm to avoid the girls using unnecessary resources on hot showers, but at that moment, Leila would gladly bathe in a bed of ice. Tempting as that was, unless she wanted to risk running into Giorgio, cleanliness would have to wait.

Leaning her back against the door, she dropped her stilettos and slid down next to them on the floor. Tears streamed down her cheeks with the weight of the emotions she'd kept buried all day. Emotions better left buried.

She scrubbed at her face. Crying didn't solve anything. All it did was mess up her makeup and being pretty was the only thing that had kept her alive all these years. She tucked her face into her knees, trying to squeeze all the emotions back inside, and stifled her sobs.

Even if she'd managed to avoid Giorgio, tonight had been one of the worst nights of her life. At the brothel, she'd had little choice but to stay in her room and accept whatever came her way.

Tonight, though, felt different. She'd walked up and down that sidewalk on her own two feet. She'd approached cars. She'd negotiated a price and opened the door to slide into the passenger side. What she didn't do was run, and she was disgusted with herself.

The thunderous blows of a fist against the door sent vibrations through her spine like shock waves. She barely managed to clamp a hand over her mouth before crying out in surprise.

The man banged his fist a few more times, and Leila held her breath. Her heart hammered a merciless cadence against her ribs, but she remained perfectly still.

Time slowed to a crawl. If she remained silent, maybe he would go away.

The muffled sound of a man's laughter cut through the still night air, and Leila knew all her effort had been for naught.

"I know you're in there, sweet thing. You can keep pretending like you're not here, but it's only going to make it worse for you. Hell, maybe you'll like it. You know what I mean? Maybe you like a little pain. You wouldn't be the first broad who wanted this dick after I gave them a taste."

Bile stung the back of Leila's throat as her stomach clenched.

Please go away.

"Tell you what, doll face. You open that door and let me in by the count of three, and I'll go easy on ya. But if you keep trying to act like you're something special and don't have to pay up on what you owe, then I'm going to bust this door open and—"

Before he could finish his colorful threat, Leila swiped the tears from her cheeks and sprang to her feet, determined to get this over with and take her hard-earned shower.

Rip off the band-aid.

Leila knew this was going to happen one way or another, and she might as well just get it over with. This wasn't anything new. She'd been dealing with perverts like this for the last four years. Let him think he's having his way and just be done with it.

With one last sniffle, she pulled open the door. "Sorry." Leila's voice was a cracked whisper.

Sweat dripping down his temple, his dark eyes fixed unerringly on her. "Not as sorry as you're going to be, you little bitch."

So much for placating him with her surrender.

Swallowing in an effort to return a little moisture to her mouth, Leila stepped back to give him room to enter. She just needed to numb herself, let her mind take her to another place and time.

His booted feet stomped loudly against the hardwood, and Leila's surge of adrenaline finally receded, leaving her legs heavy with fatigue.

As she sat down on the edge of the twin-sized bed, she

noticed movement over the creep's shoulder. *Please, no. Not two of them. Not tonight.*

The newcomer was an inch or two taller than Giorgio, but they had the same dark brown eyes and jet-black hair. He was still clad in the same shirt he'd worn when he came across her in the kitchen earlier that night. He cleared his throat...loudly.

Giorgio spun around to face the other man. "Adrian? What the hell are you doing?"

Adrian's expression was stony, but the seething rage in his glare was unmistakable.

Giorgio waved a hand at Leila and then at himself. "You mind? I'm in the middle of something here."

Adrian let out a derisive snort. "In the middle of what? Pulling your wallet out? Because I know you wouldn't be stupid enough to take advantage of The Captain's girls. Is this an authorized transaction?"

Giorgio's face twisted into a mask of hatred, but the other man cut him off before he could spew his vitriol.

"She's worked her shift for the night. And since I don't see any cash in your hand..." Adrian pointed to the hallway. "Get the hell out of her room. Go back downstairs and do your job."

"Or what?" Giorgio sneered.

The newcomer's expression turned deadly. "You were given an order. Do I need to remind you of the penalty that comes with insubordination?" He moved his arms just enough so that the dim hallway light would catch on the handle of his holstered weapon. "Have I made myself clear, G?"

As glad as Leila would be to be rid of Giorgio, she couldn't help but wonder what the alternative would be. Was Adrian chasing Giorgio away because *he* wanted to screw her? Or was he trying to impress her so she'd be *willing* to have sex with him?

If there was anything she'd learned in this life, it was that no one got a free lunch. No act of kindness came without a stipulation, and no good deed went unpunished.

Muscles popped in Giorgio's clenched jaw.

"Tell you what, G. I'm going to give you to the count of three to pull your head out of your ass and start acting like a contributing member of this organization." Adrian took another step closer. "Or…you know what? Maybe I don't want you to man up. I haven't beaten your ass in a while. This is just the kind of excuse I need to work out a little aggression."

"Fuck you, Adrian." Giorgio jabbed his index finger at Adrian's chest and slowly backed away, inching toward the hall. "That little bitch needs to be punished, and—"

"That's not your call," Adrian shouted over Giorgio's rebuttal.

"No, and it ain't yours, either." For all his bluster, Giorgio inched into the hall. "You wait, you asshole. Wait until my cousin hears about this shit you're pulling."

"Keep talking," Adrian replied coolly. "This is all going in my report to The Captain tonight."

The flush on his face and the wild flicker in his eyes insisted Giorgio wanted to add more to his veiled threat, but despite all the posturing, he turned tail and stormed off down the hall.

Leila's eyes were so wide, she wondered if they'd fall out of their sockets. The nausea had passed, but her heart still pounded against her chest like the drumline to a Marilyn Manson song.

"Are you okay? He didn't hurt you, did he?" Adrian's quiet voice cut through her hazy disbelief.

Leila nodded but didn't meet his gaze. Clenching both

hands until her nails bit into her palms, she gritted her teeth against the pain keeping her grounded.

She should have been grateful. She should have been glad that Adrian had come to her rescue. He'd humiliated Giorgio and sent him scurrying back downstairs.

But there was no such thing as a free anything. Not in this world.

Biting down on her tongue to stave off more tears, Leila shook her head. "Why did you do that?"

The old hinges squeaked as Adrian closed the door. "He was going to rape you."

Leila met his gaze. Though she was briefly taken aback by the concern in his expression, she pushed past the sentiment. "So? You think it'd be the first time or something? It's business as usual."

He froze in place. "What?"

She barely kept herself from rolling her eyes. "They took me when I was twelve. What the fuck do you think they've been doing since then? Did you think I chose to be here? That I wanted to be a streetwalker, sleep with people for money, and put up with assholes like G?"

Clenching his jaw, he reached up to rub the back of his neck. His shirt rode up, reminding her of the handgun holstered beneath it. "How old are you?"

Leila was surprised by his question. She'd been passed around to so many men over the years, they all blended into one misogynistic entity. But she wondered if the men who guarded the house and the men who watched the girls on the street were different groups.

She searched his expression for a reaction as she said, "I'm sixteen."

It might have been the low light playing tricks, but Leila could have sworn some of the color drained from Adrian's face.

Seconds ticked away in utter silence. Leila tugged at the hem of her too-short shorts. She wanted nothing more than to shower and go to sleep.

Based on Giorgio's flair for the dramatic, Leila figured The Captain would know all about her transgressions within the next few days. What wrath would The Captain bring down on her? Leila wasn't sure she wanted to find out.

After what felt like an eternity, Adrian heaved a resigned sigh. "I doubt I have to tell you this but stay away from Giorgio. I'll make sure he leaves you alone otherwise."

Leila managed a slight nod. "Okay."

"I'm sorry."

She frowned as she met his eyes. Those were two words she hadn't heard in an eternity.

He sighed again as he reached for the doorknob. "I didn't know what else to do. I couldn't let him do that."

The hinges groaned in protest as he let himself out into the hall.

Maybe he wasn't like the rest of them. Maybe one of these men had a soul, after all.

No. If he had a soul, he wouldn't be working in this house to begin with. He wouldn't know men like The Captain or G.

She knew better than to believe Adrian's good intentions would save her. Nothing could save her now.

4

A t a little past nine in the morning, Amelia arrived in a picturesque neighborhood on the outskirts of DeKalb. She had drunk an entire large iced coffee, complete with two extra shots of espresso, on the trip down to the quaint town, and still, Amelia felt sleep calling her name.

She'd intended to go straight home to get some sleep before the early morning trip but stayed at the FBI office, poring through Leila's old case file. She'd hoped to uncover a piece of information that might create a new lead but found nothing helpful.

Before she and Zane had departed the field office, Amelia phoned the Jacksons to make sure they were home. Without revealing the reason for her visit, she'd informed them of the change in jurisdiction regarding Leila's case and that the FBI would be handling it going forward. The paperwork had been processed overnight.

Stifling a yawn, Amelia pushed her aviator sunglasses up to rest on top of her head as she glanced around the quiet street. She'd become so accustomed to the hustle and bustle of the city, she forgot that people actually lived in quaint suburbs with lush lawns, wide sidewalks, and red brick mailboxes.

Zane killed the engine, and the lively chirps of nearby birds filtered through the car's windows. Almost every house on the street boasted a lush and colorful flowerbed. The Jackson's garden was no exception.

Amelia couldn't help but wonder if Leila had grown up in an equally picturesque home when she and her family were in Janesville.

Distinctly middle-class, the entire neighborhood gave off a wholesome Mayberry vibe that left Amelia feeling like an intruder. She'd grown up in the inner city of Chicago and abandoned her poverty-stricken roots in favor of combat zones when she turned eighteen. Even with all the strides she'd made to distance herself from her past, she still felt out of place. Like a mud-covered swamp monster about to stumble onto crisp white carpet.

Swallowing the uncharacteristic bout of trepidation, Amelia turned her attention to the driver's seat. It might have been a product of her imagination, but she could have sworn she spotted a hint of that same anxiety in Zane's gray eyes.

As much as Amelia wanted to ask if he also felt out of place, she bit her tongue. It wasn't like her to open up to a man, especially one she'd only known professionally for a few months.

Instead, she shook the melting ice cubes in her nearly empty latte cup and took a final watered-down sip.

Zane pulled his gaze away from the single-story house. "I'm not going to lie. That drive felt like it took four hours."

Amelia rolled her head on her shoulders, stretching out the tight muscles in her neck. "If you didn't drive like an eighty-year-old woman, we might have made it here faster."

Shaking his head, he pulled the keys from the ignition. "Uh-uh. No, I was doing five over the entire way here."

"We got passed, like, fifty times."

"Too bad we're not cops. I'd have ticketed them for going twenty over." He huffed in feigned exasperation. "If you keep criticizing my driving, I will personally text Joseph and ask for his playlist."

Amelia leveled an accusatory finger in his direction. "I'll call that bluff. You wouldn't put yourself through that."

Zane shoved his door open. "Okay. Yeah, that's true. You're right."

Even though Amelia wouldn't admit it, she was grateful for their banter. The back and forth stopped her from dwelling on the fact that she stuck out like a sore thumb in this suburban paradise.

She eased the car door closed behind her as she slipped into the morning air and set her sights on the gently sloping driveway. The garage door was closed, and a blue Hyundai had been parked in front. A host of colorful blooms sprouted from a bed of mulch beneath the picture window, and a row of ferns graced the shady side of the covered porch.

Amelia smoothed the pastel blue fabric of her dress shirt and straightened her cardigan before she and Zane started up the sidewalk.

Once they were beneath the shade of the front porch, Amelia noticed that the interior wooden door had been left open. Through the panes of glass that comprised the storm door, she could see the foyer, and beyond that, the distant kitchen.

Amelia knocked on the doorframe. "This is Agent Storm with the Federal Bureau of Investigation."

A woman with shoulder-length ebony hair and bright blue eyes appeared in the foyer. Amelia recognized her from the handful of DMV photos she'd looked through the night before.

With a reassuring smile, Amelia raised her badge for the

woman to see. "Joy Jackson? We spoke on the phone about an hour and a half ago. I'm Special Agent Storm, and this is my partner, Special Agent Palmer."

On cue, Zane flashed his badge. "Morning, Mrs. Jackson."

A glint of recognition brightened Joy's eyes. She smiled politely, opened the storm door, and waved them both inside. "Come on in, Agents. The coffee just finished brewing, if you'd like a cup."

Amelia nodded eagerly. "That would be great, actually. Thank you."

Joy led them into the house and gestured to the living area, just off the foyer. "Please, have a seat. I'll just bring the coffee pot in with some mugs. Shoes off, if you don't mind. The carpet in there is still brand new."

Joy's request reminded Amelia of her mother. While Bonnie had been alive, the Storm house had been immaculate.

Bonnie had been a neat freak, and she'd passed the knack on to her oldest daughter. Soon after her mother passed, though, the Storm household fell into disarray.

Amelia tried to emulate her mother's cleaning routine, but she'd been the only one committed to keeping the house spotless. She'd resented her father and two siblings for nearly a year after her mom's death, pissed at their unwillingness to help her keep the house as tidy as Bonnie had.

She remembered back to the day her brother had come home late from an outing with his friends and left a handful of dirty dishes on the dining room table. In a fit of rage, Amelia had stormed into Trevor's room that next morning, demanding he clean it up.

He responded in typical teenage fashion. "Who cares?"

That was when she snapped...hard. Not her proudest moment.

She snorted silently at the memory, stepped out of her black flats, and followed Zane into the spacious living room.

Zane dropped down on the center cushion of the couch. Amelia took a seat at his side and immediately spotted the six by eight framed photo of a young Leila on the end table. Leila's grin was wide, and her blue eyes—the same shade as her mother's—seemed to sparkle.

In the photo, Leila appeared to be seated in a restaurant booth with a giant milkshake on the table in front of her. A leopard print headband kept her hair off her fair face, and a cat-shaped pendant rested at her throat.

To the side of the photo, a mason jar candle burned, giving off a sweet scent of summer berries. The candle's glow was dwarfed by light streaming in from the picture window. Underneath it, a loveseat had been positioned, creating a cozy place to sit and read.

Across from where Amelia and Zane sat, a television was mounted above a wooden entertainment stand. It seemed that the whole room had been thoughtfully put together and decorated.

A gentle *mew* pulled Amelia's attention away from the entertainment center. She turned toward the sound and met a pair of bright green eyes.

"Hello there, kitty." Amelia extended a hand, and the little calico meowed again.

Zane leaned forward, rubbing his fingers together to draw the kitty's attention. "I love cats."

Amelia arched an eyebrow at her partner. "I thought you were a dog person?"

He grinned. "Two things can be true."

Once the cat finished sniffing Amelia's fingers, she allowed the human to pet her. After a few pats on the head, the calico rolled over, purring loudly. The vibration from its small body ran up the leg of Amelia's slacks.

Joy's quiet voice drifted in from just beyond the arched doorway. A male voice followed, and Amelia assumed that she was speaking to her husband.

Joy emerged from the kitchen a moment later, coffee pot in hand. She offered a strained smile as she stepped onto the carpet and gestured to a lanky fellow with a neatly trimmed beard and a full head of dark brown hair.

"This is my husband, Wendell. Wendell, this is Agent Storm," Joy waved her free hand at Amelia, "and this is Agent Palmer. They're from the FBI office in Chicago."

His green eyes flicked from Amelia to Zane before giving them both a curt nod.

Amelia rose to her feet and extended a hand to Wendell. "Thank you for opening up your home to us. I know it's a little early for a weekend, but we appreciate you taking the time to talk to us."

Zane followed Amelia's lead, offering Wendell a warm smile and his hand to shake.

The long-haired calico, no longer the center of attention, trotted over to her owner. She mewed for attention and rubbed up against Joy's leg. That small gesture seemed to ease some of Joy's tension.

"I see you've met our fur baby." She scratched behind the cat's ears. "This is Hup. She was Leila's cat, but Wendell and I fell in love with her as soon as Leila brought her home. We had to put our dog to sleep a couple years ago, and Hup must've known how sad we were. She's always been a friendly cat, but it seemed like she just turned into a cuddle machine for a few months."

Amelia could have sworn that a specter had reached into her chest to squeeze her heart. She hardly knew the Jacksons, but they reminded her so much of her own family that Amelia felt as if she'd been in their lives for years instead of hours.

Her own mother's cat, a tortoiseshell named Ripley, passed away a mere three months before Bonnie herself finally succumbed to the cancer ravaging her body.

Amelia gave herself a mental shake, forcing her focus back to the present.

Once coffee had been poured into each of the four ceramic mugs, Amelia and Zane resumed their seats on the couch. The Jacksons took the love seat under the picture window.

"Thank you again for the coffee." Amelia raised her mug. "You can never have too much caffeine this early in the morning."

The corners of Joy's eyes creased as she smiled, but Amelia noted the strain the woman was trying to hide. "Of course. You're very welcome. What was it you wanted to talk to us about this morning, Agents?"

A quick sip of the steaming liquid warmed Amelia's throat. "Well, a couple things. To start with, we're here to let you know that the FBI has taken over Leila's case."

Wendell's brows furrowed. "Why's that? Is it because it was a cold case for so long?"

"No." Amelia softened her voice, knowing she was about to turn these sweet people's lives upside down, not for the first time. "Last night, the Janesville PD contacted us after they received an anonymous tip from someone who claims to have spotted a young woman matching Leila's description. As the sighting happened here in Chicago, we have picked up the case for further investigation."

Joy and Wendell's mouths gaped open. Wendell reached for his wife's hand and squeezed, but neither of them pried their gaze away from Amelia.

Wendell broke the stunned silence. "You...you mean Leila's in...in Chicago? Sh-she's alive?"

Amelia kept her expression carefully blank. "We cannot

confirm anything yet. We are, however, taking this investigation seriously, and will be addressing all possible leads."

Wendell's Adam's apple bobbed as he swallowed.

Joy set her mug on the end table at her side and reached over to pat her husband's hand. "So, you don't know for sure yet if they were telling the truth?"

"We have no reason to believe," Zane jumped in before Amelia could respond, "that the anonymous tip was made under false pretenses. However, before we make any broad assumptions, we need to verify that the girl they reported was Leila and not someone who *looks like* her."

Joy sniffled and swallowed hard before replying. "Of course. Of course, yes."

Zane shifted his focus between the couple, as if searching for the right words to say before he opened his mouth again. "Look, we don't want to give you any false hope here, but at the same time, we believe this is a solid lead worth following. We'll be as transparent with you as we can as the case develops, but for now, we have to keep your expectations realistic. We are not at a stage to promise any results just yet."

Wendell lifted his gaze and nodded. "We understand."

Joy wept silently as Amelia explained the reason for the change to federal jurisdiction, though she purposefully left out the part of the call that insisted that Leila was a prostitute.

Between the tears and stifled sobs, it was painfully clear that the Jacksons still grieved deeply for the loss of their daughter.

Amelia felt their pain acutely. And though talking to them seemed to make it worse, she had to do this part of the job if she hoped to save them from further pain.

Zane continued the conversation while Amelia took a gulp from her cup. "We were hoping to pick up where the previous investigation left off. Now, we know you've probably heard some of these questions before, but we'd still appreciate as thorough an answer as you can give us."

Joy squeezed her husband's hand as if needing some of his strength to reply. "Of course. We'll help as best as we can."

Amelia recognized the slight loosening of Zane's jaw as he worked to keep his expression neutral. "In your initial statements, you told us that Leila was on her way home from a friend's house."

"That's right." Joy pressed a tissue under her nose. "She never made it home."

Zane's face was a picture of sympathy. "You also said your family didn't have any enemies or anyone who wanted to cause you harm. In the time that's passed, has anyone or thing else come to mind? Anyone you may not have thought of before?"

Joy tapped a finger against her lips, the strain of their conversation deepening the wrinkles around her mouth. "No. Not me, not Wendell, not Pierce, and definitely not Leila."

Zane pulled out a notebook and pen from his pocket. "And Pierce, he's playing baseball at Northern Illinois University now, isn't he?"

"Yes, he is." Joy's expression brightened a little at the mention of her son. "He's got a full academic scholarship to play ball there. We just wanted to be close to him in case he needed anything. He's out of town for a game right now, though."

Zane quickly jotted a note about Pierce. "And back around the time Leila went missing, were there any of his friends who might have shown any unusual interest in Leila? Any of them who maybe seemed a little too forward with her, or who might have acted inappropriately around her?"

Joy and Wendell exchanged sidelong glances as their expressions darkened. "He had one friend, yeah. Jesse Yates.

Jesse was four years older than Pierce. They became friends when Pierce was a freshman and Jesse was a senior."

Amelia lifted an eyebrow, remembering the name from Leila's file. "Jesse Yates? The state pressed charges against him four years ago, correct?"

Joy offered a solemn nod. "Yeah. The charges didn't make it past the grand jury, though. There wasn't enough evidence."

Amelia leaned forward, propping her elbows on her knees as she focused on the couple. "Did you notice Jesse behaving in a way that seemed inappropriate toward Leila?"

Wendell scratched his bearded chin as he turned his gaze to the ceiling, as if searching for the right memory. Amelia waited silently, scrutinizing the couple, searching for nonverbal clues.

Minutes went by before Wendell slowly shook his head. "Well, I mean, I wouldn't say that we saw anything inappropriate. Leila always liked her brother's friends, and that included Jesse. Pierce and his buddies would drive around town blasting rock music like Marilyn Manson and stuff, and that was the same music Leila liked. She'd always ask Pierce's friends to send her their Spotify playlists and stuff like that."

Amelia wasn't surprised to hear that Jesse's behavior had been normal. During her read-through of the case file, she'd gotten the impression that the investigation into Jesse Yates had been rushed. Either that or the original detectives had missed a significant piece of information about him. More than likely, they had just been barking up the wrong tree, which was why the charges were ultimately tossed out.

Zane refilled his mug and held it up in a silent *thank you* to their hosts before chugging it down. Apparently, he needed the caffeine just as badly as Amelia. "And what exactly was it about Jesse that made you think he might've had something to do with Leila's disappearance?"

Wendell heaved a sigh and leaned back in his seat. "Well, like I said, he was one of Pierce's friends. He was nineteen at the time, and for the most part, he seemed like a normal kid. He was starting college, studying computer science or programming, something like that. But, well…" he scratched his bearded cheek again, and his gaze shifted briefly to his wife.

Joy sat, plucking at the hem of her t-shirt, absently shaking her head. "A couple weeks before Leila went missing, Jesse Yates was on trial for rape. We couldn't get ahold of much of the details, but it had to do with a sixteen-year-old girl. The timing…it just seemed like it couldn't have been a coincidence, you know?"

As she swallowed her skepticism, Amelia laced her fingers together. "What happened with Jesse Yates?"

Joy took in a shaky breath. "Nothing. There wasn't any evidence, or at least that's what the police said. They got a search warrant for his house, but they didn't find anything related to Leila. The detectives interviewed him multiple times, but he'd always say he didn't have anything to do with her disappearance."

Amelia nodded. "We'll make sure to go through those interviews. Where is Jesse now?"

Wendell draped an arm around Joy's shoulder and pulled her in close. "He wound up on the sex offender registry after he was convicted of statutory rape in that other case. The state pressed charges against him for kidnapping Leila at about the same time that happened, but it never went anywhere. We've kept an eye on his whereabouts ever since the grand jury dismissed the charges against him. He's in Sheboygan, Wisconsin now."

If Wendell had said "Chicago," Amelia might have been able to quell the nagging doubt in the back of her head.

But Sheboygan? Not so much.

After a few more procedural questions, confirming their belief that Leila did not run away—and another cup of black coffee—Amelia handed the Jacksons her business card. She and Zane said their goodbyes and headed back out to the car.

As she fastened her seat belt, Amelia blew out a long breath.

Zane shot her a quizzical glance as he turned the key over in the ignition. "What was that?"

Amelia pulled her aviators down to block the glaring sunlight. "I don't know. Does something about Jesse Yates seem off to you?"

Shifting the car into reverse, Zane pulled out onto the street, using his backup camera instead of being forced to crane his head to peer out the rear windshield. "What do you mean by off?"

"If Yates had anything to do with Leila's disappearance, why would she show up in Chicago when he's in Sheboygan?"

"Yeah, that didn't make much sense to me, either. Maybe we're missing something about Jesse Yates, something that the Janesville PD missed too." Zane threw the car into drive. "But, honestly, I doubt they missed anything when they were looking into him. From the sounds of it, they were relentless toward that kid."

Amelia nodded half-heartedly. "They were, but the grand jury *still* dismissed the charges. You know, maybe this is a little presumptive of me, but I don't think Yates is connected with Leila's disappearance."

"Yeah, me neither."

At the succinct response, Amelia slumped down in her seat. Part of her had almost hoped that Jesse Yates would once again be their prime suspect. If Leila had run away with him, or even if he'd kidnapped her, then they would have a cut-and-dried case to work.

But if Jesse *wasn't* involved, then Amelia suspected the case could easily lead them into the spiderweb filled corners of Chicago. Places that normal human beings avoided at all costs.

If there was no personal motive behind Leila's kidnapping, that could mean only one of two things: they were dealing with a serial killer, or they were dealing with human traffickers. And since Leila had been spotted, the prospects for the former looked grim. Serial killers worked quickly, but traffickers...

Traffickers were anything but.

Their tendrils permeated so many aspects of the communities in which they operated that removing them was akin to excising a malignant tumor.

If Leila had been abducted by traffickers, then they were in for a long ride.

❄

THE WOODEN PEW squeaked as Gabriella Hernandez shifted in her seat. The sun had climbed higher in the sky over the last half-hour, sending rays of light piercing through the elaborate stained-glass windows, directly into Gabriella's eyes.

Blinking to clear her vision, Gabriella turned her attention to the priest behind the lectern at the front of the room.

The church was well over one hundred years old, but only about half the stained-glass artwork was from the original construction. In this part of Chicago—North Lawndale —churches had to make do on limited budgets.

As the priest came to the end of his prayer for a young pregnant woman who'd recently been ordered on bed rest, his dark eyes shifted toward Gabriella and her mother, Martha.

"And last but certainly not least." The man raised one robed arm to gesture to Martha and Gabriella. "Our beloved Martha Crowley, who has been a part of this congregation for longer than I've been here. I know that she means so much to so many of us."

Martha brushed aside a wavy strand of hair as she smiled back at the priest.

The wavy locks weren't Martha's hair, however. Gabriella had purchased a wig for her a few months back. In addition, Gabriella had used an eyeliner pencil to fill out Martha's thin brows.

Even as the chemotherapy ravaged her mother's body, Gabriella did her best to ensure Martha could still look and feel good about herself.

After a few claps and a chorus of *Amens*, the priest, Father Fredricks, held up a hand to quiet the congregation.

"And let us not forget about Martha's wonderful daughter, Gabriella. She's been at her mother's side for every step of her journey through chemotherapy, from the time Martha received the dreaded breast cancer diagnosis. And we know she'll be there to support her mother both emotionally and financially as they continue to travel forward into the unknown. So, for Martha and Gabriella, let us take a moment to pray."

With a gentle smile, Martha squeezed her daughter's hand as best as she was able.

Gabriella bowed her head and tightened the purple cardigan around her shoulders. At least the church kept the air-conditioner set to high during the summer months. The cool temperature kept Gabriella from having to worry about sweating like a whore in church.

Tears sprang to her eyes as the fleeting thought hit much too close to home.

No one, not even her mother—*especially* not her mother—

knew how Gabriella made the money she used to support them both. Didn't know of her second identity.

Angel.

After Martha's husband—Gabriella's stepfather—died, Gabriella was the only source of financial stability for her mother. The insurance company was only willing to cover so much, but Gabriella would do whatever was necessary to ensure that her mother received the care she needed.

She'd only been in her second year of college when her mom received the breast cancer diagnosis. She hadn't been an outstanding student, average really, but if she'd applied herself, she could have done much better.

Her path of study was political science, but she knew the road to even a mid-grade job in the field was a long one that would require an advanced degree. As soon as she learned that her mother had cancer, Gabriella knew she had to do whatever it took to help.

Working two or three minimum-wage jobs wouldn't cover the hospital bills. Of that, Gabriella was certain. But Angel, as she was known in certain circles, had connections with jobs not listed in the classifieds where she could earn double, or triple, in a single night's work what she'd make slinging burgers.

Her motivation might have been a bit selfish, but she could be selfish and still support her mother. She'd always told herself that there was an expiration date for her street-walking days, but lately, with all the bills piling up, that end seemed farther than it had ever been.

After the quiet moment of prayer, the congregation rose for one last hymn before Father Fredricks bade them farewell. The church was a significant part of Martha's social life, and she and Gabriella always lingered in the front reception area to chat with other parishioners.

Her mother's friends and acquaintances showered

Gabriella with compliments and well-wishes, but the words rolled off her like raindrops rolled off a slicker.

None of them knew the *real* Gabriella. None of them knew the number of wedding bands she'd ignored as she accepted a John's money. None of them knew how she'd flashed an illegal handgun when a handful of those same men refused to pay her.

The parishioners at Blessed Mother Church didn't live in Angel's world, and no matter how much time she spent interacting with them, she would never be convinced she lived in theirs.

Even though she stood close to a head taller than her mother, Angel felt short without her five-inch heels. With one hand on her mother's shoulder, she put on her most convincing warm smile and braced herself for the compliments she didn't deserve.

5

Barely a third of the way through the latte in her hand, Amelia stifled a yawn and squinted against the irritating brightness of the sunny conference room. She blinked a few times, allowing her tired eyes to adjust as she pulled the door closed behind her and hunted for a place to sit that might allow her to stretch her legs while she shook off the remaining fog of sleep. Never mind that it was almost noon on a Monday.

Fiona Donahue would be back at work in a couple weeks, and Amelia could hardly wait to return to her normal sleep schedule.

The circular table in the center of the room could seat up to four, but Amelia wasn't inclined to squeeze into the empty chair between Joseph Larson and Zane. She chose instead to plop down on the cushioned leather bench beside the window.

As Joseph shuffled through a handful of papers on the shiny tabletop, his pale blue gaze flicked over to Amelia before landing on SAC Jasmine Keaton. "Well, it looks like you guys were busy while I was out of town."

Amelia toyed with a lock of hair before tucking the stray piece behind her ear.

In the twenty-some hours since she and Zane had visited the Jacksons, Leila's case—along with the others included in the documentary series—had exploded. She could only assume that Jasmine had convened the three of them in the pint-sized conference room so they could lay out the groundwork for their newest investigation.

Pushing open a matte silver laptop, Jasmine nodded. "*We* weren't busy, but plenty of others were. Mostly the press, honestly." She turned to Zane and Amelia. "I caught Agent Larson up on the Jackson case, and we've already had a few developments this morning."

The announcement pushed the lingering haze of sleep from Amelia's mind. "Developments? What kind?"

Jasmine shook her head slightly. "Not *that* kind of development. Press related. Earlier this morning, a few different celebrities posted about Leila Jackson, and the topic took off on social media. There's a fundraiser to get money for the Jacksons to hire a private investigator. There's even a trending hashtag. Actually, two of them." She wiggled her fingers for air quotes. "'Where is Leila' and 'Justice for Jesse.'"

"Jesse Yates." Amelia arched an eyebrow as she cocked her head toward Zane. "The state pressed charges, but they were thrown out by a grand jury."

Joseph scratched his temple. "The grand jury didn't indict him? Their evidence must have been pretty weak. But why would the D.A. take a case that far if they didn't have enough to convict?"

Amelia cleared her throat, drawing the room's attention to her. "Well, if any of you had actually *watched* the episode, you'd know that a lot of it focused on Jesse Yates. The cops in Janesville had tunnel vision, and they went after that kid like he was Jeffrey Dahmer."

Zane's lip twitched with amusement. "I watched it when I got home last night, thank you very much."

Joseph cocked an eyebrow. "So, you don't think Yates had anything to do with it?"

"No, I don't." Amelia didn't have any suspects to offer at that time, but she felt certain that the Yates boy had been a red herring.

The amused smile faded from Zane's face. He shrugged, having nothing else to offer.

Skepticism narrowed Joseph's gaze. "We're picking up this case all because of one anonymous tip from a guy who works at a gas station in West Garfield Park? With all due respect," he turned to address their SAC with a polite nod, "this doesn't seem like a case for Organized Crime. Even if that girl *was* Leila, why exactly would *we* take the investigation? Seems more like something for Violent Crimes."

Maybe it was the lack of sleep, or perhaps she felt somehow connected to this case, but hearing Joseph's dismissal had Amelia's hackles up. She scooted to the edge of her seat. "Because Leila Jackson is sixteen, and the witness said she was a working girl. A prostitute. And if a sixteen-year-old girl is working the streets after she disappeared without a trace *four years ago*, then there's more at play here than what the Janesville PD found."

Larson opened his mouth to reply, but Jasmine cut him off with an upraised hand. "This is Federal jurisdiction now, and I'm assigning Organized Crime because agents in VC are up to their eyeballs in open cases right now. We've got a media shitstorm knocking at our door. They're busy scrutinizing the Janesville PD, but you know where they'll turn next. And when they do, we'd better have something to show for it."

A faint hint of indignance passed over Joseph's face, but he kept whatever thoughts he might be having silent.

Over the past few months, Amelia had gotten to know Joseph as more than just a colleague. She'd come to think of him as a friend and a damn good agent. He'd been in the Organized Crime Division of the FBI for almost a decade, and he tended to look out for the bigger picture.

One missing girl from Janesville wasn't the bigger picture.

Joseph was a good man at heart, but he'd been at this job so long, he sometimes acted as if he were the SAC and needed to be punted off his high horse.

They worked the cases that came across their desks, period. Whether the investigation involved one missing teenager or an entire neighborhood, they made their best effort to put the pieces together to solve the case.

The loud squeak of Zane's chair as he leaned back broke the awkward silence that had enveloped the room. "Those episodes dragged the Bureau pretty hard for not stepping in to do something to help find Leila Jackson. Apparently, four years ago, someone at the Wisconsin office must've had a conversation with their SAC that went a lot like this. And, well..." Zane's gaze shifted to Joseph as he held out his hands in feigned helplessness. "Leila's still missing, isn't she?"

And there he went, tumbling from his high horse.

Amelia fought to keep her expression neutral as laughter bubbled in her chest. As her niece and nephew would say, *shots fired*. No wonder those two didn't get along.

Narrow eyes shot daggers in Zane's direction, but Joseph kept whatever angry retort he was chewing on silent.

Slapping both hands on her thighs, Amelia pushed herself off the cushion and up to her feet. Three sets of eyes turned to her, but she ignored their scrutiny.

"Great. Why don't we meet back in here in a few hours?" She waved at a wall-spanning whiteboard. "We can use this room to compare notes and start visualizing this case a little better."

Jasmine was the next to stand. "Agent Storm, you'll take point on this. Agent Palmer, Agent Larson, you're both on this too. Like Palmer said, the Bureau in Wisconsin got raked over the coals for not doing more to help Janesville find Leila. I don't want that kind of press at my doorstep. This office has enough to deal with as it is. Dismissed."

Amelia had admired Jasmine Keaton's commanding presence right from the start. Other agents around the office might have found the woman borderline terrifying, but Amelia was routinely impressed by her no-nonsense demeanor.

She resisted the urge to offer Jasmine a crisp salute as they dispersed.

Amelia set her latte beside the second monitor at her desk and flopped into her seat. Her eyes drifted away from the screen to the porcelain cat figurine that rested between the two monitors.

The white cat had one paw raised beside her face, the other atop a gold coin at her feet. Marked with Japanese writing, the coin was crafted to resemble currency used in Feudal Japan.

Maneki-neko, known as the Lucky Cat in English, was a common fixture among Japanese businesses and homes. For Amelia, it had a special meaning.

Her father had been in the Navy when she was a little girl, and one of his tours had taken him to Japan. He'd been gone for six months before finally returning home. When he did, he brought back a Lucky Cat figure for Amelia's mother, along with a second and third cat for Amelia and Trevor. Lainey hadn't yet been born or they'd have owned four, Amelia was sure.

Since they were still small children at the time, their cats had been carved from durable wood, whereas their mother's gift had been cast into an exquisite porcelain cat and now sat on Amelia's desk.

For weeks, maybe even months after her father had brought home the Lucky Cats, Amelia begged her mother, nightly, to tell the story of the *Maneki-neko* before they went to bed. Each time, Bonnie would add a new detail or a new side story. Now, more than twenty-four years later, Amelia could hardly remember them.

The decision to bring such a personal memento of her mother's to work had been spur-of-the-moment. Amelia hadn't wanted to risk accidentally damaging the delicate figurine during her move, and at the time, the least chaotic place for the Lucky Cat was her desk.

Shaking herself from the recollection, Amelia straightened and took a long drink of her lukewarm coffee. Maybe the Lucky Cat would bring her good fortune for this investigation.

Over the following half-hour, Amelia downed her latte as she studied the Janesville PD's original case file. Once the expensive drink was gone, she went in search of more caffeine. She hated the free coffee in the breakroom, but if she stirred in a little hot chocolate mix and French vanilla creamer, it wasn't so bad.

If nothing else, it kept her going through mindless and obligatory office small talk, searching and printing copies of important case documents, and the deep dive into background checks on the people who'd been closest to Leila. The list wasn't too long, but it still took a while to go through them all; her parents, brother, friends, brother's friends, teachers, anyone mentioned even fleetingly in Leila's file.

Aside from Jesse Yates's placement on the sex offender registry, she couldn't find red flags in anyone else's background. One of the teachers had popped with a citation for driving under the influence of alcohol about a year ago, and one of Pierce Jackson's friends had been caught with marijuana in his possession, but those minor infractions were the only highlights of Amelia's search.

By the time Amelia had collected her notes and headed back to the conference room, she was certain none of the friends or acquaintances of the Jackson family had been involved in Leila's kidnapping.

To her surprise, Zane was already seated at the circular table as she let herself into the room. His gray eyes flicked up from the screen of his laptop as she eased the door closed.

The shift change had drastically affected her caffeine intake, but Amelia had noticed a different effect on Zane. Ever since the two of them had taken over Fiona's shift, Zane had all but ignored the stubble sprouting from his chin. Though he'd grown lazy with shaving, he still maintained his neatly styled hair and smart attire.

After she dropped her freshly gathered papers on the polished wooden table, Amelia made her way to the whiteboard.

Zane gestured to the folder. "Excuse me. I thought this was an environmentally friendly work office."

Amelia rolled her eyes. "There are recycle bins every four feet around this office. Plus..." she tapped the whiteboard with the capped end of her marker and flashed him a sarcastic smile, "we can't fill a murder board with flash drives and spreadsheets."

He hitched a shoulder. "Can we even have a murder board if no one was murdered?"

"Well, there are still people who call a refrigerator an icebox, so I think we can."

Zane opened his mouth to reply, but the clatter of blinds smacking against the glass door as Joseph Larson stepped into the room stole his thunder.

The ill will between those two men was palpable.

Amelia tried to ignore the sudden tension. They were both grown men, federal agents, no less, and she didn't have time to play mediator. A sixteen-year-old girl was missing, and the scrutiny of hundreds of thousands—maybe even millions—of social media users was about to shine on their office.

Amelia cleared her throat, drawing the attention of both men. "Let's start with Jesse Yates, unless either of you found someone else worth noting?"

Joseph dropped to sit—opposite Zane, of course—and shook his head. "No, I didn't. Learned a lot about all those people, but I didn't find anything that makes me think a single one of them might be our suspect."

Zane tapped a couple keys on his laptop. "Jesse Yates. Nineteen at the time of Leila's disappearance. Now, twenty-three. Lives in Sheboygan, Wisconsin, probably because he wasn't allowed to move out of the state after he was put on the sex offender registry."

Amelia scrawled Jesse's name toward the top of the whiteboard. "Let's start with that. When was he added to the registry?"

After another short series of clicks, Zane responded, "Leila disappeared four years ago on Thursday, the twenty-sixth of May. Jesse was convicted of statutory rape on Friday, the thirteenth of May. Less than two weeks before Leila vanished. She was on her way back from a friend's house, but she never made it home."

With a nod, Amelia wrote down the dates. "And the grand jury threw out the indictment for Leila's kidnapping on the twenty-second of June, less than a month later."

"That's a pretty fast indictment," Joseph added.

Amelia used the marker to gesture to herself and then the two men. "Well, if we can rule out just about everyone in the Jacksons' lives in an afternoon, I don't imagine it took too long for the Janesville PD to go through them too."

"True." Zane twirled a ballpoint pen between his fingers. "I looked back through the statements, and it's safe to say that none of the Jacksons had any enemies. Joy had an ex-husband, but he's been living in Hawaii for the last twenty years."

Amelia fiddled anxiously with the cap of her marker. "Which takes us back to Jesse Yates."

Joseph flipped over a sheet of paper. "I looked into the case that landed him on the registry." He gave her a sidelong glance. "It's completely baseless. The kid got screwed by the system. The girl, Tara Crismore, didn't even want to press charges. She told the cops that she and Jesse had been dating for over a year and that they loved each other. It was her parents that wouldn't let it go. They hated Jesse, claimed that he listened to all kinds of satanic music and that he was corrupting their precious angel."

Amelia rolled her eyes. "So, they ruined the kid's life because they don't like Marilyn Manson?"

Zane snorted.

Joseph crossed both arms over his chest and leaned back into his chair. "It would appear so."

Amelia bit back a remark about where exactly Joseph Larson's taste in music would land him. If Zane hadn't been in the room, she would have let the friendly jab fly, but she had no desire to add to the make-believe rivalry between the two men.

"In Tara's statement, it was noted that she wanted her parents to drop it," Joseph said. "But they didn't. Jesse's mother passed when he was a kid, and it was just him and his dad. His dad didn't have much formal education, but he worked construction and they made ends meet. On the other hand, the Crismores live in a million-dollar house and vacation in the Swiss Alps every year."

Amelia didn't bother to hide her angry scowl at the way that family had destroyed Jesse's life. "So, they could afford to keep the legal machine rolling, but Yates couldn't."

"Exactly." Joseph dropped his notebook on the table. "Jesse wound up pleading. Instead of fifty years on the registry the D.A. had pushed for, he agreed to fifteen. The plea deal said three months in prison, but he was out on good behavior after a few weeks served."

Amelia twisted the cap back onto her marker. "So, the entire reason he was a suspect is basically invalid. He was nineteen, and his sixteen-year-old girlfriend's parents didn't like him. Usually, that's just grounds for an awkward dinner conversation, not fifteen years on the sex offender registry."

Propping both elbows on the table, Zane scanned the mostly empty whiteboard. "We've got no family enemies. No ties to shady people. No suspects. Just a twelve-year-old girl who disappeared without a trace when she was walking home from a friend's house."

"Traffickers." Amelia said the word slowly. By the lack of reaction, she could tell that the idea was also in the forefront of their minds.

Zane nibbled the end of his pen cap. "Yeah. That anonymous tip just about proves it. Her parents said she wouldn't run away from home, and all her friends backed that up. By all accounts, she was a happy pre-teen who was looking forward to wearing makeup and learning how to drive."

Amelia's expression went stony. "I worked a case on some traffickers out in Boston while I was there. They were backed by the Russian mob, and they'd get a lot of their girls from nearby towns. Places where people didn't keep their kids locked up quite as tightly as they did in the city."

"I grew up in southern Missouri." Joseph rubbed his

temple. "My graduating class was forty kids, and no one locked their doors at night. Granted, that was almost twenty years ago, but not much has changed since then."

"Exactly," Amelia said. "It's the same concept. Kids in smaller towns and cities will be easier prey. Then, they take them back to wherever their operation is based, and no one ever hears from the victim again."

Zane closed his laptop. "Unless Netflix makes a documentary about them."

Amelia fought against the smile teasing the corner of her lips. This was not a time for levity. "Which brings us to our anonymous tip."

Joseph lifted a finger. "A tip that we still need to corroborate before we decide for sure that this girl was abducted by traffickers."

Leaning forward, Zane met Amelia's gaze. "We go back to West Garfield Park. Back to Madison Street and check if anyone around there has seen her."

Amelia's shiny ballet flat barely made a sound as she tapped her foot. "No one in that neighborhood talks to the cops or the Feds. If we went in there flashing our badges, chances are whoever's pimping Leila out would go underground or relocate."

Zane lifted a shoulder. "Then we don't go in flashing our badges."

To Amelia's surprise, by-the-book Joseph nodded. "Plainclothes. We can act like we're worried parents and ask the working girls if they've seen her. It wouldn't be the first time a frantic parent came through to ask those women questions while they're looking for their kid, and I doubt it'll be the last."

Amelia and Zane exchanged glances before they turned back to Joseph.

Dragging a hand over his face, Joseph heaved a sigh. "And

based on the way you're staring, I'm going to be the worried parent, aren't I?"

With a faint smirk, Zane spread his hands. "You and Leila both have blue eyes. I don't look a damn thing like her. And I'm thirty-four, but it's a stretch to look at me and think I've got a sixteen-year-old kid."

"Are you telling me I look old, Palmer?" Joseph huffed, but the exasperation was largely feigned.

Zane's lips parted in a wide grin. "Not at all, Larson. You look great."

Glad to see the two getting along, Amelia replaced the marker. "You can't just start asking questions about who sent Leila out there to work the street, so if any of the girls know about Leila, we'll have to bring her in for a conversation. Palmer and I can post up somewhere nearby and watch from a distance. You let us know if you find a witness, and we'll figure it out from there."

Joseph brushed his hands along his black suit jacket. "Guess I'd better get to making myself look like a soccer dad."

❄

ZANE WATCHED with amusement as Amelia futilely swiped at a fly that had been buzzing around her head since they'd stepped into the abandoned apartment building. Amelia had done away with her usual slacks and button-down dress shirt in favor of attire that would be less conspicuous in a neighborhood like West Garfield Park.

In the three months Zane had been in Chicago, he'd only seen her outside the office once or twice. But she had never looked so strangely casual. A blue, gray, and white oversized flannel over a white t-shirt concealed her service weapon. Gray shorts and a pair of blue-gray canvas shoes completed the look. She had done her homework and looked inconspicuous enough to fit in with the rest of the neighborhood, whereas he'd opted for a black zip-up hoodie and jeans.

As the temperature climbed into the mid-nineties, he regretted his decision.

Debris crunched beneath his booted feet as he followed her to a window. Well, it would have been a window if construction on the building had ever finished. Though the contractors had stripped the interior of the small apartment building down to the studs, somewhere along the line, they must have lost funding.

What little drywall remained had been decorated with colorful graffiti, some of which was artistic. The rest, however, was decidedly not. Broken beer and liquor bottles littered the main hallways, and Zane spotted a couple hypodermic needles in the midst of the debris. Cigarette butts, dried leaves, and dirt had been swept into drifts against the walls.

Kicking at the floor to make a clear space, Amelia gingerly set her tote beneath the splintered window frame.

She held out a pair of binoculars for Zane. "You do know it's June now, right? You're going to broil up here."

He swiped at a trickle of sweat rolling down his temple. "How about you offer fashion advice *before* we're creeping through abandoned apartment buildings." He leaned against the wall at the edge of the window.

They were a few blocks from Agent Joseph Larson, who was making his way down Madison Street. Knowing the neighborhood had a reputation for being spooked by law enforcement, they'd opted to keep their distance. No reason to take the unnecessary risk of being spotted if they could avoid it.

Amelia's smile was decidedly sarcastic. "Is this your first time hanging out in a condemned building?"

Zane's brow furrowed before he raised the binoculars to his eyes. "I take it this is *not* your first time?"

"Nope. This is the type of place I used to party in back in high school."

"Weird venue choice, but okay." Zane focused the lenses until he had a clear visual of the neighborhood.

As if on cue, the buzz of Amelia's ringtone cut through the humid air of their third-story perch.

She knelt to retrieve the smartphone from her gigantic handbag. Larson had been fitted with a wire so they could hear him through a radio, but they had no inconspicuous way to fit him with an earpiece. If he wanted to hear Zane and Amelia, he had to call them.

The method of communication was a bit disorganized, but in a pinch, it worked.

As Amelia swiped the screen, Larson's voice filled the space. "You guys ready yet? I'm sweating my ass off out here."

Zane unzipped his hoodie. "You and me both."

Though Larson might not have heard the remark, Amelia grinned. "Yeah, we're in place. The sun's about to go down, and I'm seeing some women start to show up. None of them are our girl, though."

"That figures. It's never easy, is it?"

Zane studied one girl's face more closely. Damn, she looked so young. "If it was easy, we wouldn't be here to begin with."

Larson sighed. "True enough. All right, I'll start making the rounds. Maybe we'll get lucky, and Leila will be out here tonight."

The tone of his voice insisted that even he didn't believe in casual optimism. As Amelia wished Larson luck, Zane brought the binoculars up and scanned the block until he spotted the agent.

Clad in a button-down plaid shirt and a pair of well-worn

jeans, Joseph Larson looked every bit the part of a rural Missouri transplant.

"So, do you actually think we're dealing with traffickers, or were you just agreeing with me earlier because we don't have any other leads?" Amelia's voice drew Zane's attention from the binoculars and back to the ramshackle room. Her eyes were fixed on him, her expression equal parts curious and skeptical.

Zane leaned his shoulder against the wooden window frame and rubbed the stubble on his chin. "A little of both, probably. I think we're dealing with traffickers *because* there aren't any other leads."

Amelia nodded as she pulled the cap off the long-distance camera lens in her hands.

Zane tilted his chin at the camera. "That's a serious setup you've got. Something tells me the camera and that lens probably cost more than any electronic device I've ever bought in my life. You do a lot of photography?"

She shot him a quizzical look. "You don't have to be a photographer to take the pictures we use. I don't think anyone in a courtroom is going to complain that the lens aperture for one of the photos is off or that the lighting doesn't give the subject enough contrast."

Damn. Amelia was a smartass, but it was one of the things he liked most about her. "No, that's not what I meant. I meant that operating a camera like that is like trying to work a machine at NASA or something."

"Maybe it is the first time you use one, but after that, it's pretty easy. I'm not trying to take *good* pictures. I'm just trying to take *clear* ones, so it's not nearly as complicated." She held the camera up to her eyes and peered out over the neighborhood. "I zoom, I make sure the image is clear, and I take the picture. That's only three things. Easy peasy."

Zane would have to take her word for it. She seemed to

know what she was doing, so he was happy to let her do it. "Guess I've never really been on photo-taking duty. Not from a distance like this, at least."

She shrugged. "I was always the designated photographer while I worked in the Boston office. Guess they thought that since I was a sniper for ten years, I'd be able to take good pictures."

Zane tried to make the connection. "How does being able to hit a target from five-hundred meters away translate to photography? Aside from the lens and scope, the mechanics are pretty different."

Amelia shrugged. "I'm not trying to calculate wind interference, angles, or distance, so it's not exactly the same. But I do need to get a clean sight, so maybe there is some correlation. I just kind of like being on photographer duty."

Larson's staticky voice came to life over the radio, prompting Zane and Amelia to return to their vigilant surveillance of the neighborhood.

Age progression photo of Leila in hand, Larson approached a blonde woman who stood at the corner of a vacant lot. The agent scratched the back of his neck in feigned nervousness as he held up the photo for the blonde to see. "Hi, um, I'm sorry. I'm not here for, uh, you know."

Zane was impressed. "He's pretty good at this whole awkward soccer dad thing, isn't he?"

Amelia made a sound that some people might even call a giggle. It made him smile.

Though the sentiment probably bordered on unprofessional, Zane had to admit that he liked to see her happy. Then again, it was normal to enjoy seeing a friend or colleague happy, wasn't it?

From what he'd gathered in the few months they'd worked together, Amelia had been given a tough lot in life. Zane's upbringing had been far from peachy keen, but he hadn't spent his teenage years in poverty in a crime-ridden Chicago neighborhood.

His parents were flawed as any, but at least they'd been loaded—a fact he preferred to keep to himself.

Dealing with a drug-addicted father was difficult enough when finances weren't strained. He couldn't imagine what his life would have been like if his parents had struggled to make ends meet on top of everything else.

He pulled himself away from the contemplation and refocused the binoculars as Agent Larson made his way down the sidewalk to another pair of working girls—a redhead and another blonde.

Both women's postures stiffened as Larson neared. Clearly, they weren't used to being approached by men on foot.

Larson held up both hands and paused about six feet away from the women before his voice crackled to life over the radio.

"I'm sorry. I'm not trying to weird you out or anything. It's just, I'm looking for…" he held out the picture of Leila, "my daughter. She's been missing for a couple weeks, and my wife and I." He blew out a long breath. "We're worried she might've run away, and well, you know…"

The blonde and the redhead exchanged skeptical glances.

Larson took a tentative step forward. "Please, it'll just take a second. I just want to know if you've seen her."

The redhead's voice came faintly through the speaker at Amelia's feet. "Sorry, man. Can't help you. I ain't in the business of looking after missing kids. We're all out here to make money. Ain't no room for babysitting."

"I'm not asking for any of that." Joseph waved the picture for emphasis. "Just one quick look, please? Here, I'll even pay you for it."

At the mention of cash, both women seemed to snap out of a trance.

The redhead eagerly extended a hand. "Twenty, and we'll look at your picture."

"Money talks," Zane grumbled under his breath. He hoped Larson had withdrawn enough money at the ATM on his way there.

Passing the photo of Leila to the two women, Larson dug a couple bills out of his back pocket. The blonde moved to take the cash, but he jerked his hand away before her polished fingertips made contact.

"First, tell me if you've seen her."

The redhead cackled as she handed the picture to her friend. "Guess you ain't that stupid after all, are you?"

Zane could only imagine the death glare the woman had earned with her comment. On more than one occasion, he had been the recipient of that same disappointed scowl.

It was the kind of glower a father might use on his son, after watching him come home drunk, puke in a potted plant —a gift from his saintly grandmother—and then stumble around until the little shit broke his favorite lamp.

"Have you seen her?" Larson's voice warbled, but even over the comms system, his irritation was clear.

Shaking her head, the blonde returned the photo. "No, she doesn't look like anyone I've seen around here."

Larson hung his head in mock disappointment as he handed her one of the bills. "What about you?"

The redhead shrugged her thin shoulders. "I've seen a couple girls who look a little like her, yeah. Can't say for sure if they were her, but there's been a couple around here with black hair and light skin like her. Never got close enough to get a good look at them, though."

Larson offered a stiff nod as he placed the second bill into the woman's waiting palm. "Thank you."

The faint click of a camera shutter drew Zane's attention back to Amelia.

"What's our play if no one recognizes her?"

Amelia blew out a long sigh and lowered the camera. "I don't really think we *have* a play. Other than heading to the Chicago PD and digging through their files, I mean."

He brought the binoculars back to his eyes as Larson made his way across a battered street. "At least we've got a good visual on the street from here. We ought to thank whoever decided not to just knock this building down."

"Perfect. When we get back to the office, I'll see if the FBI will let us send them a fruit basket."

As Zane pictured Amelia delivering a basket of assorted fruits to a slumlord to thank them for the decision to forgo demolition of a condemned apartment building, he smiled.

Dusk settled over the Chicago skyline as Larson made his way to a handful of other working girls loitering along the street. Like the first few women, none of the others had been willing to share their knowledge free of charge.

A couple others remembered seeing one or two pale women with black hair, but they hadn't paid enough attention to the girls' appearance to say for sure whether one of them was Leila.

Though the lack of confirmation was frustrating, the lack of information was itself a lead. If multiple women who frequented Madison Street and the surrounding area didn't recognize Leila, or if they hadn't seen her close enough to recognize her, then Leila must have been new to this part of the city.

Or she'd never been here at all.

Zane clenched his jaw as he watched Joseph near a lithe woman with ebony hair and sun-kissed tan skin.

Ruddy orange streetlight caught the fabric of her tight black miniskirt as she pivoted on her heel to face Joseph.

Even through the binoculars from blocks away, Zane could tell this woman was a different caliber than her peers farther down the block. Whatever her reason for working the streets of West Garfield Park, her story was different.

As best as he could tell, her skin was clear. He focused the binoculars on her arms to check for track marks but found none. Though thin, her body was toned, not malnourished.

She fidgeted with a silver pendant at her throat as Larson neared her position. "Something I can help you with, sweetie?"

The agent went through his usual motions—he held out both hands to show he was no threat, paused several feet away, and advised that he wasn't there to ask her for sex. For emphasis, he even pointed to the silver wedding band on his left ring finger.

"Please, could you take a look at her picture and just tell me if you've seen her? I'll pay you. I just need a second of your time. Please."

A pang of sympathy flashed behind the woman's dark eyes. "Yeah, okay. Let me see the picture."

As Larson handed over the photo, he retrieved another bill.

Zane expected the same song and dance that had occurred with each previous encounter. He was just about to heave a resigned sigh and suggest he and Amelia take a water break when the woman nodded before returning the picture and accepted payment.

"Yeah, I've seen her. Last night."

Larson's mouth dropped open. Either he was just as shocked as Zane, or he was a great actor.

After a moment of stunned silence, Larson collected himself. "You've seen her? You're sure? Last night?"

The woman's head bobbed once more. "Yeah. It's the first time I've seen her here, though. I don't know if she's going to be here tonight. She, uh…she said her name was Leila. It could be a fake name, though, I'm not sure."

"Holy shit," Amelia uttered breathlessly, followed by a rapid-fire *click-click-click* from the shutter of her camera.

"Oh my god." Larson's eyes grew so wide they risked rolling out of their sockets. "Thank you, thank you so much. My wife and I have been searching for *weeks*, trying to find out where she might've gone. Here." He held up a hand as he reached back into his pocket for a handful of cash. "Take this, please."

Though the woman accepted the payment, a hint of skepticism had settled in beside the concern on her face.

"You're welcome. I hope you find her."

Larson's extra payment had been their agreed-upon signal. It was an expensive signal, but an effective one, nonetheless.

"We might have a problem." Amelia's quiet proclamation snapped Zane out of the celebratory cloud. "There's a man coming toward them. He looks pissed."

Zane adjusted the focus of his binoculars as he searched for the man striding toward Larson.

Clad in a black leather jacket and dark jeans, the man's status was clear—he wasn't a wandering homeless person or a drug addict. This was an authority figure.

"Shit," Zane muttered. "I didn't see him drive up."

Amelia shook her head. "He didn't drive up. He just came out from behind a building. He must've been parked close by, which means he's probably not alone."

Muttering a string of four-letter words, Zane zoomed out to get a wider picture of the area.

The woman near Larson took a step backward as she stuffed the money into her handbag, but she didn't remove her hand from the purse.

As Larson spun around to face the approaching man, he

held both hands out wide. He was armed with his service weapon and badge in case the situation deteriorated, but they'd all decided that revealing his status as a federal agent was an absolute last resort.

The entire reason he'd donned the role of soccer dad was so people who were forcing Leila to work the streets wouldn't catch wind of their investigation.

If the newcomer forced Larson to draw his weapon and present his badge, their cover would effectively be blown, and so would the promising lead they'd just found.

The man jabbed a finger in Joseph's direction. "Who the hell are you, huh, buddy?"

Larson stepped back, hands still out wide. "I-I'm sorry. I'm looking for my daughter. She's been missing for—"

The leather-clad man closed the remaining distance between him and Larson and stuck his index finger in the agent's chest.

"I don't give a shit! What the hell do you think you're doing out here talking to these girls, distracting them from doing their damn *jobs*? Huh?"

Shaking his head, Larson gestured to the woman on the corner. "I paid her—"

"I don't give a shit about *her*. She doesn't make *me* any damn money." His dark eyes flicked up to the woman before he returned his glare to Larson. "You've talked to four of my girls, and you've been keeping them from making *my* money. Give me one good reason why I shouldn't shake you down right here, right now."

Zane was sure that Larson was using every bit of self-control he possessed to keep from shoving the thug out to arm's length so he could draw his weapon.

"I'm sorry." Larson's voice was strained, but his tone didn't suggest fear. "I'll leave, okay? I'll leave right now, and you'll never see me again."

The gangster shoved Larson, sending him crashing down on the pavement. The dull thud of the blow echoed through his hidden mic all the way up to Amelia and Zane's perch.

This was it, Zane thought. This was the moment that had the potential to define the rest of their investigation. If the angry gangster closed in again, Larson would be more than justified to pull out his weapon.

With a sneer, the man spat on the concrete at Larson's feet. "You'd damn well better. Now get the hell out of here and don't come back."

Zane didn't realize he'd been holding his breath until a sharp pang shot through his chest. As Joseph hurried across the street and through a vacant lot, Zane took in a deep breath and lowered the binoculars.

He could feel Amelia's expectant gaze burning into the side of his face and slowly turned to meet her sarcastic grin. He heaved a sigh and sent a hand up to rake his fingers through his hair. "What?"

"Oh, don't go getting all relieved just yet. We've still got to get that girl to the FBI office so we can get some *real* info from her."

Zane gnashed his teeth.

Amelia was right. They'd only just scratched the surface of their investigation, and it was going to be a long night.

❄

ANGEL REMAINED on high alert even after the man in the leather jacket disappeared. The adrenaline had receded, and her hands no longer shook, but she couldn't help looking over her shoulder at every tiny noise.

On a normal night, she kept her distance from other groups of girls. But after the altercation between the mafioso and the man who had been searching for his daughter, Angel felt she needed the safety that came with numbers.

She tuned out their chatter as she sent another paranoid glance around the vacant lot.

Leaves on the trees across the street rustled in the humid summer breeze. Neon lights from the nearby businesses mixed with the ruddy orange of the streetlamps. The combination created an eerie shadow that made Angel feel like she was in a video game.

If she had to guess *which* video game she'd be stuck in, it would have to be *Grand Theft Auto*.

Tonight wasn't the first time a desperate father had made rounds to ask about his missing daughter—at least that's what she'd picked up from the other women. The parents were often chased off by a man who oversaw the street workers, and more often than not, the encounters were nonviolent.

Despite the knowledge, the predatory glint in that gangster's eyes as he'd threatened the missing girl's father had Angel convinced she was about to witness bloodshed.

And she wasn't so convinced the fight would have been one-sided. She'd seen the military tattoo on the inside of the father's arm, and she hadn't missed the cold confidence as he stared the gangster down.

She'd never seen the mafioso before, but he had a presence that left a lasting impression.

Angel readjusted the handbag on her shoulder and breathed a quiet sigh of relief at the reassuring weight of the chrome forty-five tucked safely inside.

She'd only ever had to brandish the weapon once, and she never wanted to point it at another human being again. She liked to shoot at cans, but firing at a living person? That was a whole different ballgame.

Most of the girls in this part of West Garfield Park were

beholden to pimps who were affiliated with one organized crime group or another, and they weren't permitted to carry handguns. They were kept on a tight leash, expected to hit a nightly quota, and when they left, they didn't return home like Angel did.

She still wasn't sure *where* the girls lived, but each night they were picked up and dropped off by the same men.

Angel worked for a pimp too. Every girl on the street did. But her relationship with her boss was far more akin to a business agreement than the typical pimp-and-working-girl dynamic.

Then again, that was because she'd started out as an escort, and she'd only shifted to the streets in the past few months.

Taking in a deep, steadying breath, Angel forced her focus back to the pockmarked asphalt. She'd been out for close to an hour without a client. There was only one reason for her to be in West Garfield Park, and that was to make money.

Her mother's breast cancer was gradually improving, but the insurance only paid so much for her lifesaving medication. If Angel didn't close the gap, the treatments would stop, and she'd lose the only family she had left. Her big brother had been killed in Afghanistan four years ago.

Right now wasn't the time to think of the pretty girl with the long black hair and bright blue eyes. The *girl* who couldn't have been any older than seventeen. The same girl whose father had come searching through the neighborhood only the night after Angel had first seen her.

Her next breath came sharper. She straightened her back and pushed the image of that poor girl out of her mind.

She was here to make money.

She'd gotten lucky when the girl's father had given her close to a hundred dollars for her tiny sliver of information, but she needed to stay at the top of her game if she wanted to have a productive night.

After a couple of the other girls had left with their own clients, a pair of headlights swung around the corner. Blinking to clear her vision, Angel stepped up to the edge of the curb, hands on her hips.

A silver Acura crept close to her, and the driver lowered the window.

Angel fought hard to keep herself from visibly balking at the man behind the wheel. His dark blond hair was disheveled, and despite his black hoodie and gray t-shirt, he held himself with the air of a man of high status.

Though she'd been visited by clients of all shapes and sizes, the number of conventionally attractive men she encountered was quite small.

And in her experience, the more attractive a man was, the more violent he could be. They were the ones who viewed the lives of working girls as expendable. They felt entitled to every piece of the women they hired.

The single time she'd been forced to draw her chrome forty-five, she had been with a particularly handsome man in his late forties. He clearly hadn't grasped the meaning of the word no. After encountering Angel, however, she was sure he'd gotten the memo.

Swallowing down her trepidation, Angel stepped off the curb to make her way to the car. She swung her hips as she walked and offered him a playful wink for good measure.

Arrogance dripped from his lips as he smiled. The combination of streetlights and the glow from the car's gauges made his eager gaze appear almost eerie.

Odd. Normally, men's attention went straight to her chest.

For the second time, she pushed aside the bout of anxiety.

"Hey, honey, you looking for a date?" She leaned forward,

putting her best assets on display, and gave him a sweet smile.

He showed her a few more teeth. "As a matter of fact, I am."

He had an accent she couldn't quite place, but the entire scenario suddenly made much more sense. As she sauntered around to let herself in the passenger's side door, she decided he must be an out-of-town executive looking for a little entertainment in his downtime.

Shifting the car into gear, he turned down the radio but didn't speak.

Great. He's one of those men.

The drive only lasted five minutes, but in the awkward silence, it felt like an hour had passed. Once he pulled the car into a spot at the edge of a shadowy parking lot, she turned her full attention to him.

As he reached into the pocket of his zip-up hoodie, she expected him to produce a condom. But the blue light from the car's dash glinted off a vaguely familiar polished gold shield and eagle.

Angel sucked in a sharp breath.

Behind a protective laminate screen above the badge and eagle was an identification card that bore a small photo of the man. His expression looked more akin to what she'd expect from a mugshot, but the badge and ID card both read FBI.

Snapping the leather case closed, he met her wide-eyed stare. "I'm Special Agent Zane Palmer with the FBI. I'm not here to hurt you, hopefully not even to arrest you, so do me a favor and set your handbag in the back seat."

Before she opened her mouth to protest, he held up a hand.

"I know you're carrying a weapon. This is just for my safety, okay?"

Angel swallowed hard and made sure to keep her movements slow as she set her bag on the floorboard behind her seat.

When she straightened, she rubbed both hands over her bare arms. She wished she had real clothes, and not just because the air conditioner of the car was chilly.

"Am I under arrest?" Her voice trembled despite her attempt to keep a level tone.

With a slight shrug, he pocketed the badge. "That depends on you. My guess is that weapon in your purse is unregistered, and the serial number's probably been filed off too. That's a felony, but not what I'm interested in. At this moment, you are a witness, so I need your help."

Angel shook her head. "A…a witness? To what? That fight I saw earlier, the one between the guy looking for his daughter and some…" Aside from gangster or mafioso, she couldn't come up with an apt word to describe the other guy.

The FBI agent rubbed at the stubble on his chin. "Sort of. It's more about the girl that the man was looking for. Leila."

Though Angel wanted to maintain a cool expression, she couldn't keep her eyebrows from shooting up at the girl's name.

"Her? What about her?"

"She was kidnapped four years ago, and we're trying to find her."

"Oh my god." Angel rested a hand over her rapidly beating heart.

How could this be real? How could she have been *that* close to a missing kid without knowing it?

He tapped the steering wheel with a thumb. "I need you to come and answer some questions. I'm giving you the benefit of the doubt here, and I won't try to hold anything over your head unless you force my hand. If you're uncooperative, then, well…"

Angel bit her bottom lip to stop the quiver. "No, you don't have to do that. I'll answer your questions."

She'd been told repeatedly not to talk to cops, but the man behind the wheel of the Acura wasn't a normal cop. He was a *federal agent.*

And he wasn't here to ask her about her occupation or who she worked for. He was here to investigate a kidnapped girl.

Plus, if she was popped with the weapons charge he'd mentioned, how exactly would she help her mother pay for her cancer treatment?

The answer seemed obvious enough.

She wouldn't.

6

Zane made good time returning to the FBI office with Gabriella Hernandez in tow. He set her up inside the interrogation room while Amelia relieved Joseph for the night. The altercation had left an impression on Agent Larson, and Amelia felt that his edgy demeanor might spook their witness.

She assured him she and Zane were more than capable of interviewing Gabriella by themselves, and he accepted her offer to head home for the night.

With Joseph taken care of, Amelia quickly changed into more professional attire—swapping her shorts for a pair of black dress pants—and fixed her hair into a neat braid before heading toward the conference room. Zane met her at the door, having taken the opportunity to swap the hoodie and t-shirt for a more FBI agent standard white button-down and tie. He appeared to be busily tapping out a message on his smartphone as she approached.

Amelia rested her hand on the metal handle of the interrogation room door. "You ready?"

"Yeah." Zane pocketed his phone. "Shouldn't be a big production, though. She seemed willing to help."

"Okay. Let's see what she knows."

Gabriella was seated at a rectangular table in the center of the room. Her honey-brown eyes shifted toward Amelia as the door opened, and she immediately straightened her posture and tightened a gray FBI sweatshirt around her shoulders.

"Evening, Ms. Hernandez." Amelia offered her a quick smile and then gestured to Zane. "You've already met my partner. I'm Special Agent Storm."

Gabriella's expression was a mask of restrained nerves, but she managed a polite nod. "Hello. I...I understand you have some questions for me? Your partner, Agent Palmer, he told me you guys were looking for someone."

Amelia took a seat directly across from Gabriella and dropped a folder on the laminate tabletop. "That's right."

Zane perched on the corner of the table as Amelia flipped open the manila folder and spun it around to face Gabriella.

"Have you seen this girl?" Amelia pushed the folder toward the other woman.

Her eyes widened with obvious recognition. "Oh, you poor baby girl." She did a double take, blinking a few times as she inspected the original and age-enhanced images. "Leila, right? That's the name I remember hearing. Most girls don't use real names, though."

"That's correct." Amelia folded her hands atop the table.

Zane reached out to tap the age-progression generated image of Leila. "We need confirmation. This is the girl you saw, correct?"

Gabriella licked her lips. "Yeah, that's the girl whose dad was looking for her earlier."

Zane's gaze turned expectant. "And you've met her? You're sure it was her?"

Gabriella took one more look at the pictures. For several quiet moments, she studied them. "Yeah, it was her. This one on the left looks more like her."

Amelia gestured to the other photo—Leila's school picture from the year she went missing. "She's who we're looking for. The other picture is an age progression generated photo. Basically, it's an image that an algorithm spits out based on an analysis of her facial structure and images of her parents. So, technically, you're not looking at a real person. It's an approximation."

As Gabriella's mouth formed an O shape, her knuckles turned white from where they gripped the hooded sweatshirt.

Amelia gestured from the real picture to the age progression one. "That being said, it's an *accurate* approximation. But the fact remains that it's an image that was shown along with her name on a Netflix documentary that's become pretty popular. So, we're going to need a bit more information from you, some details to confirm that you actually saw Leila and aren't just someone who might've seen that show."

The likelihood of a coincidence seemed small, but based on the increasing popularity of the documentary, Amelia wasn't willing to take any chances. She wanted to know with absolute certainty that Leila Jackson was in Chicago, and not just a similarly aged doppelganger.

Moreover, they had to make sure Gabriella was telling the truth. They had to rule out the possibility that she'd made up the entire story for an easy paycheck after she'd seen Joseph paying other women for the same information.

After a quiet pause, Gabriella replied, "Okay. What can I tell you?"

Zane pulled out his notebook and pen. "Just walk us through your interaction with her."

"Okay...um...let me remember." Gabriella pinched the

bridge of her nose and squeezed her eyes closed. "That was yesterday. I'd just gotten to Madison Street. I hadn't been there for more than ten minutes when she showed up. A black Town Car dropped her off."

Amelia tugged the cap off a pen and flipped open a legal pad. "Can you describe the driver?"

As Gabriella blinked repeatedly, she shook her head. "No, not really. I didn't see. The windows were tinted pretty dark. I just saw a silhouette. I could tell that much. She got out of the back seat."

Of course. Didn't every criminal tint their windows?

Amelia scribbled down the description. "Okay. What happened next?"

"She came over to where I was, all nervous and twitchy. Maybe on drugs. I don't know. Some girls use. Helps them deal, know what I mean? Anyway, she looked out of it, like she was going to puke. I gave her some mints since they've always helped me when I'm nauseated."

Zane scrawled the words quickly in his notebook. "You said she introduced herself. What did she say?"

As she fidgeted with the hoodie's drawstring, Gabriella glanced back and forth between the photos. "She told me her name was Leila and that it was her first time out on the street. I told her a little bit about what was going on, that all the girls worked for different people. Just really basic. She thanked me for the mints and told me her name. And then…" Gabriella blew out a long breath.

"No rush," Zane said. "Take your time. Try to remember as much as you can."

His tone was so reassuring that even Amelia felt more at ease.

Gabriella touched the silver pendant at her throat. "She saw my necklace." As if she'd snapped out of a trance, she looked up from the pictures to meet Amelia and Zane's gazes. "She had a cat necklace too. She told me that she had a cat or that her mom had a cat. A cat named...um...what was that damn name? Something from *The Dark Crystal*. Hup! Yeah, that's it. My stepdad loved that movie."

Amelia fought to keep the surprise off her face as she scribbled down a few more notes on the yellow legal pad.

Zane scooted closer to Amelia and showed her the note he'd written.

The Jacksons' cat wasn't mentioned in the documentary series.

That detail was more than enough to suggest that Gabriella had interacted with Leila.

Gabriella's eyes flicked from Zane to Amelia and then back. "It's her, isn't it? That girl I met, that was Leila Jackson?"

Zane nodded. "Yeah, it appears so. Look, we need to ask you some questions that you've probably been given explicit instructions *not* to answer. But I want you to keep Leila in mind, okay? She was abducted while she was on her way home from a friend's house four years ago when she was twelve."

The color drained from Gabriella's cheeks. "So, she really is...sixteen?"

"Yeah, she's sixteen. Which means," Zane tapped a finger on Leila's school picture, "that whoever's pimping her out is part of an underage prostitution ring."

"Oh, no. Hell no!" Gabriella's face contorted in what appeared to be genuine shock. She shook her head emphatically. "I'm not part of that shit. Nu-uh. I stay away from that. Look, I'm out there to make money, but not like that. I'm trying to help my mom while she's going through chemo. I'm not trying to make a career in organized crime."

She pushed her chair back from the table, growing more hysterical with each word she uttered.

Amelia leaned forward. "It's okay. You're—"

"There's just no legit way to pay these doctor bills, okay? My...the guy I work for used to run an escort service. The cops took down a lot of it, so..." She crossed her arms and shrugged. "I did what I had to do. Went...freelance."

The mention of Gabriella's mother struck a sympathetic chord in Amelia's heart. She held up a hand. "We aren't accusing you of anything. You're here because we're asking for your cooperation and your help. As far as any of our dealings with the public go, you'll remain completely anonymous. But we need to ask you what you know about the pimps who operate around that area, okay?"

"Okay." The word was little more than a squeak.

Zane set down his notebook and rested his arms on the table. "Start with the man who showed up and chased away the guy who'd been asking about Leila earlier today. Do you know who he is?"

She fidgeted in her seat and picked at the edges of her fingernails. "I'd never seen him before today. I was listening to some of the other girls talk afterward, but none of them mentioned who he was."

Zane held the young woman's gaze as he asked his next question. "You said that you don't deal with *child* prostitution personally." He was going to call it what it was...child, not underage. "But what about the man you work for? Your pimp?"

"No, that's not what he deals with. He's a club owner, and he used to run an escort service. He tries to keep his businesses as legal as he can." She paused, chewing on her bottom lip, as if struggling with what to say next.

As the wheels in Gabriella's head turned, Amelia and Zane let the room lapse into silence. Neither of them pressed her for an answer.

So far, the young woman had been cooperative, and Amelia didn't want to start throwing around charges. The threat of a felony conviction sometimes worked to coax information out of unwilling witnesses, but there were also plenty of instances where the tactic backfired. Gabriella Hernandez was street smart, and Amelia wasn't about to risk alienating their best lead.

And to be honest, Amelia sympathized with Gabriella's plight more than she wanted to admit. Had a few aspects of her life played out differently, Amelia could have wound up in Gabriella's shoes—venturing into the city's underbelly to make money to pay for her mother's cancer treatment.

Before Amelia could prod for an answer, Gabriella took in a deep breath. "I've heard my boss and one of the bottom girls around the area mention some guy named Marshall Grove. I don't know much about him, just that he goes to my boss's club, Evoked, every Tuesday and Thursday. From what I've heard, he deals in drugs and all kinds of other shit. Word is, he does business all over the world."

Amelia jotted down the name. "Like he's a jack of all trades?"

Gabriella nodded. "Exactly. That's how he sounds, anyway."

"What makes you think he might be connected to Leila?" Amelia made sure to keep her tone strictly inquisitive and non-accusatory.

Gabriella slumped down in her chair and pressed her fingertips to her temples. "I don't have anything hard, really. But Marshall Grove's pretty new around the area. I only started hearing about him a couple weeks ago. And since Leila's new too…" She finished with a hapless shrug.

"This club." Zane spread his hands. "Evoked is what it's called?"

"Yeah."

"Have you ever been there?"

Gabriella went to bite her painted fingernail but stopped

at the last second and set her hand in her lap. "I've been there, yeah. I work there sometimes. On Tuesdays and Thursdays, the days that my boss and the girls say Grove is there, they section off the lower level for the," she lifted her hands and air quoted, "exclusive members."

Amelia's phone buzzed in her pocket, but she was too close to putting everything together to worry about answering it. She wrote down the name of the club. "It's reserved for pimps and girls, correct?"

Gabriella tugged on the drawstring of her sweatshirt and shrugged. "Something like that, yeah. It's almost like a messed up job fair. The 'members' come in looking for something, and they talk to whoever's there to see if they can get it. Whenever I work there for that, I just serve drinks. Those people, they're..." She appeared to search for a word. "They're too far *into it* for me. I don't want to get any closer to them than I have to."

Zane arched an eyebrow. "How do people get up there to begin with? What's the selection process?"

"There's a password. It changes every week. My boss doesn't have much to do with it. He just provides the venue, and then these people all show up. I know someone has to refer the people to get them put on the list. Just so there's no one down there that they don't know."

Zane followed up with a handful of other procedural questions while Amelia continued to scribble down any detail that sounded important. Her phone vibrated again, distracting her for a minute as she fished around blindly to decline the call.

Gabriella's information all seemed to be on the level, and by all accounts, she'd given as much as she could about the other prostitution rings operating in West Garfield Park.

When Amelia's phone buzzed in her pocket for the third time, she handed Gabriella a business card and excused herself. All the questions about Leila had been covered, and all that was left was for Zane to set up a way for them to get to the club's VIP section.

Once she'd closed the door of the conference room, Amelia dropped her notepad and the manila folder onto the polished wooden table. Heaving a sigh, she flopped into an office chair.

For the last few hours, she'd been avoiding a text message she'd received from an unsaved number. The same number had attempted to call her a couple times before it sent the message, and Amelia didn't have to be an investigator at the FBI to figure out who was behind the communication attempts.

Blowing a few strands of hair from her eyes, she swiped the pattern to unlock her phone.

Sure enough, the author of the message was her estranged younger sister, Lainey. Though Amelia was tempted to ignore her communication, she pulled up the message on the off chance that Lainey needed help that wasn't financial.

As Amelia scanned the text, she sighed.

Hey, Amelia, it's Lainey. This is my new number. I tried calling you, but you didn't answer. I know it's been a while since we've talked, but I really need your help. My boyfriend kicked me out of the house, and I don't have anywhere to go. Could you call me? I really need some money so I can get a place.

"Right," Amelia muttered to herself. Locking the screen, she dropped the smartphone onto the table with a clatter.

Lainey might not have been lying about her boyfriend kicking her out, but Amelia already knew that any money she sent to her younger sister would go straight into her and her boyfriend's veins.

She'd cut Lainey off years earlier, back when she'd been in the military. But as soon as Lainey had realized that Amelia wouldn't help her, she'd turned to Trevor. Then, once

Trevor died and Lainey learned their father was sober, she turned to him.

Absently twisting a lock of hair around her index finger, Amelia couldn't help but think that any outreach Lainey made to their father was a threat to his three years of sobriety. As many times as Amelia told her dad to ignore Lainey, that she was manipulating him and lying to get money, Amelia knew there was no way she'd ever break the bond between Jim Storm and his youngest child.

The sharp sting of hair almost ripping away from her temple brought Amelia's attention back to the conference room. She untangled the hair from her finger and tucked it behind her ear. Their so-called murder board was sparse, and the lack of evidence made her want to sigh all over again.

At ten 'til midnight, chances were good that Joseph Larson had already settled into his nice warm bed.

Must be nice for him.

Sleep wouldn't come for Amelia anytime soon. She pushed aside her documents and flipped open a second manila folder.

In the time that it had taken Zane to grab Gabriella and bring her to the FBI office, Amelia had printed out a number of the photos she'd taken earlier in the day.

As she shuffled through a few of Joseph in his plaid shirt and jeans, she came to the image that had piqued her curiosity.

The man who had come out of the woodwork to threaten Joseph.

There was no guarantee that the man was involved with the same people who'd forced Leila out to the streets, but the photo of the man with his black leather jacket and designer jeans raised the hairs on the back of Amelia's neck.

Holding the photo up to the light, she leaned back in her

chair and studied his features. She didn't recognize the man, but she could tell he was Italian.

There were two major Italian crime families that dominated the underworld of Chicago—the Leóne and D'Amato families. Though there were other so-called satellite families, Leóne and D'Amato were by far the two largest and most powerful.

Amelia's knowledge of the Italian crime families didn't come from her tenure with the Bureau, nor did her understanding come from her brother's time as a detective in the Chicago PD.

Her history with the Italian crime families, specifically the D'Amato family, was far more complicated and personal.

She'd been a fifteen-year-old high school sophomore from a poor neighborhood in Englewood when she fell head over heels for a boy who would permanently alter the course of her entire adult life.

While she worked at a movie theater to try to help her family make ends meet, he was a handsome young man from an incredibly wealthy family.

Even though she'd known who he was and how his family made their money, the idea of dating the son of a mafia kingpin was the Cinderella story of Amelia's neighborhood friends.

Waving the picture of the Italian man, she slowly shook her head. "Dammit, Alex. This better not have anything to do with you."

Her knee-jerk reaction was to reassure herself that the D'Amato family was more honorable than those who would force an underage girl into prostitution. And when she'd been around them, they had indeed shunned human trafficking.

She could only hope, more than a decade later, that still rang true.

The blinds clattered against the glass door as Zane opened it, spooking Amelia and nearly sending her springing from the chair.

Zane grinned as he held out his hands to show he was unarmed. "Hey, wow. Didn't mean to scare you. Did I wake you up or something?"

Amelia would never admit her fright in a million years. "No, I was just thinking. Trying to tap into some supernatural psychic energy to tell me who this guy is." For emphasis, she dropped the photo to the table.

Zane pulled out a chair to sit, and with a resigned sigh, he met Amelia's gaze. "And here I was hoping that you'd just know this guy. I mean, how long did you live in Chicago? Are you sure you didn't go to school with him or something?"

"You know, if I didn't know you, I would have no idea you were being sarcastic just now." Amelia shook a finger. "It's impressive, honestly. Well done."

Her dismissiveness was only partly untrue.

As far as Amelia was concerned, she'd left that part of her life behind when she'd stepped into an Army recruiter's office at eighteen years old. Emulating her brother hadn't been the only reason she'd joined the military.

At the time, she'd wanted to get as far away from this city as humanly possible. If the option to be stationed on the moon had been available, she would have taken it.

Shaking off the unbidden memories, she stood and made her way to the whiteboard.

The weight of Zane's stare couldn't be ignored. It was as if he were trying to look straight through her. Sometimes, the man was *too* observant.

"What do you think about going to the club tomorrow?"

A smile tugged at the corner of Amelia's mouth as she hung the Italian man's photo on the murder board. "I've been waiting for you to ask me that since SAC Keaton introduced us on my first day here."

Zane's brows furrowed. "Wait, really?"

With a laugh, Amelia picked up a blue dry-erase marker. "Not really. I'm not usually a nightclub type of person. I went to plenty of them back when I was in high school."

He scratched the side of his unshaven face. "High school? Wow, Chicago really must've been a lot different than Jersey City. We couldn't get into clubs there until we were eighteen or twenty-one."

Amelia pointed the marker at him. "Fake ID, Palmer. Improvise, adapt, and overcome."

Again, her recollection was only partly false. The bouncers had never checked her ID when she was with a D'Amato capo's son, but she'd *had* a fake ID.

With an "ah," Zane snapped his fingers. "That's what it was. We didn't improvise enough, so we couldn't adapt and overcome. Probably because I wasn't in the military."

Amelia fought to rein in her goofy expression. "That must've been it."

As he rested his arms on the polished table, Zane flashed her one of his trademark grins. "I've got to say, you might've had one of the most interesting high school careers of anyone I've ever worked with. Partying at vacant condemned buildings, going to nightclubs with fake IDs. What *didn't* you do?"

Oh, wouldn't you like to know?

Waving a hand as if the motion would wipe the discussion clean, she pulled the cap off the marker. "Okay, I know we're tired, but let's get back on track. You're talking about going to Evoked, right?"

With a quirk of his lips, Zane looked like a mischievous boy who knew more than she was letting on, and for a split-second, Amelia wondered if he was psychic.

He clasped both hands together. "Yeah, that's what I was thinking."

Amelia scrawled the name of the club on the whiteboard. "Gabriella said that people who wanted to get downstairs needed a referral and a password, right?"

Zane rapped his knuckles against the table as his easy-going expression returned. "She did. She knows Thursday's password, and she said she'd get us put on the list as soon as we've got aliases to use."

Tapping a pensive foot, Amelia pursed her lips. "A club VIP section full of pimps and mafiosos. What could go wrong?"

Zane stretched both arms above his head. "I guess we'll have to find out."

With one more glance to the picture of the man with the slicked-back hair and leather jacket, Amelia hoped that none of the ghosts from her past were frequent fliers at Evoked.

7

The door creaked as Emilio eased it closed behind him. All the doors in the house were made of solid wood, not like the flimsy hollow ones so often used in newer constructions. Even the hardwood floor beneath his feet was part of the original build. With nine bedrooms and four bathrooms, the home was practically a mansion.

With a little remodeling, Emilio could easily sell the place for millions, but for the moment, it was profitable as a whorehouse.

Pausing beside his sturdy oak desk, Emilio parted the window blinds, allowing a shaft of late morning sunshine into the room. The light glittered off dust hanging in the air and highlighted various dings and dents in the floor. He might need more than a *little* remodeling to make this place worth selling. Nicotine stains streaked along the upper portion of the drywall, and a layer of grunge also seemed to coat the floor, no matter how many times he'd had the girls scrub it away.

With a frown, he let the blinds fall closed.

There was a reason he was compelled to take a shower every time he left.

Emilio straightened his button-down shirt as he made his way to the cushioned office chair behind the desk. Though he and his fiancée had returned from their vacation the previous day, she had convinced him to take his time before he went back to work.

She didn't have the faintest idea what he did at work, and as long as the money kept rolling in, he suspected she wouldn't care.

Ileana Piliero—Emilio's fiancée for the past six months— had grown up around the mafia lifestyle. She knew her place in Emilio's world, didn't ask questions, and was perfectly content to spend her days fraternizing with the other mafia wives and daughters.

As he leaned back in the chair, Emilio fished in the pocket of his black slacks for a mostly emptied pack of cigarettes. He hadn't even taken the first drag when the creak of footsteps from the hall was followed by a light knock.

He grumbled at the interruption. "Who is it?"

"It's me, boss," Antonio Piliero replied.

Of all the voices that could have been on the other side of that door, Emilio was relieved to hear Tony's—Ileana's older brother and his right-hand man.

"Come in, Tony." Emilio tapped the cigarette against a glass ashtray. Other than a computer monitor, keyboard, mouse, and a notepad, the desk was empty.

Tony closed the door behind him before offering Emilio a respectful nod. "Morning. How was the trip?"

Exhaling a cloud of smoke, Emilio shrugged. "Fine. Typical Vegas, you know?"

Tony shot him a knowing grin before sinking into a chair. "Yeah, I'm familiar."

Ever since Emilio had been granted the lofty status of

Capo—The Captain—of the Leóne crime family, Antonio had been at his side. Tony was only a few years older than Emilio, but like his sister, he'd grown up in the lifestyle.

From birth, Tony had been raised to be a loyal Leóne soldier. Over the years, his advice had proven invaluable.

In the ensuing silence, Tony's hazel eyes shifted to the window as he crossed his legs, resting an expensive leather boot on his knee.

"Did anything happen while I was gone?" Emilio took another drag.

Tony turned his attention back to Emilio as he scratched at his temple. In the low light, the flecks of silver in his jet-black hair were all but invisible.

Stubbing out the cigarette, Emilio straightened. "Based on that look, I'm assuming the answer is yes."

"Yeah, you could say that." As he let out a quick grunt of exasperation, Tony reached into the pocket of his dark jeans to retrieve a smartphone. Scooting to the edge of his seat, he tapped a few buttons before placing the device on the polished oak.

Emilio lifted an eyebrow, but he accepted the phone as Tony slid it across the desk. "What's this?"

"Tweets." The response was cryptic.

Emilio bit back a petulant response as he scrolled through the series of messages. "They're about a show? Some documentary series called *Vanished*?" Brows furrowed, Emilio glanced up from the screen. "What does this have to do with anything?"

Tony gestured to the phone. "Tap on that one."

Although he wanted straight answers, Emilio complied. As a photo of a school-aged girl with raven-black hair and bright blue eyes loaded, he shook his head. "Is this supposed to mean something to me?"

"Scroll down."

If Tony gave him one more cryptic instruction, Emilio might just toss that damn phone across the room. But he swallowed the surge of irritability and scrolled to a second photo—the same girl, but several years older.

Before he could demand an explanation, Tony reached forward and zoomed in on the image.

"That show, *Vanished*, it's about cold missing persons cases. And she." He held up the phone. "She's the subject of episodes two, three, and four. And also our newest street worker, brought here last week from the brothel."

The weight of the revelation pressed down onto Emilio's shoulders. "How many people have seen this show?"

Tony's expression turned stony as he pocketed the phone. "A lot. You saw those tweets, right? Those were all about that girl, Leila. That show is taking off like it's the next *Making a Murderer*. There're celebrities tweeting about her, donating to the cop shop in the town where she used to live. Her parents set up one of those crowdfunding things, and it's already gotten close to ten grand since yesterday."

With a groan, Emilio dragged a hand over his face. "You've got to be shitting me."

"Wish I was, boss. That, and…" Tony rubbed his chin.

Emilio turned the full force of his intent stare to his right-hand man. "And?"

Tony shook his head. "Your cousin, Giorgio. I don't know what happened exactly, but he was telling me yesterday how that girl was acting up."

At the sound of Giorgio's name, Emilio's teeth gritted together. "Acting up, how?"

"No one else saw it." Tony casually rolled his shoulders. "But I've got no reason to think he's lying. Here, I'll go get him and let him tell you what went down."

Though fewer than five minutes had passed before Giorgio shuffled into the room, Emilio was tempted to light up another cigarette. Ileana had asked him to quit, but business snags were always a test of his patience. If he didn't have nicotine to fall back on, there was no telling how many heads he'd be tempted to crack open in a day.

Giorgio glanced around nervously, his gaze shifting from Tony, who was blocking the doorway with his big broad shoulders, to Emilio, waiting impatiently at the desk.

Propping an elbow on the armrest of his office chair, Emilio fixed his gaze on Giorgio. "Tony tells me you had an issue with one of the girls. Care to explain?"

The Adam's apple in Giorgio's throat bobbed with a hard swallow. "That little bitch from Saturday, that's who you're talking about, right?"

"Unless you had an 'incident' with another girl?" Emilio's tone dared him to say yes.

Giorgio's Adam's apple was getting quite the workout, Emilio noted, not liking this at all.

"No." G, as he liked to be called, shook his head as if to emphasize the word. "Just that one. I came into the kitchen to give her some clothes, right? The stupid whore didn't even thank me. I had to *tell* her to thank me, and then, you know what she did?"

"No." Emilio's voice was as dry as a desert.

Unperturbed, Giorgio let out a low chuckle that sounded closer to a growl. "That little slut spat in my face."

Emilio's expression remained stony. This wasn't the first time that a new street worker behaved out of line, and Emilio suspected it wouldn't be the last. He had methods in place to correct such behavior, and he had to admit there was a part of him that looked forward to the corrective action.

The angry fire still burned in Giorgio's dark eyes as he raked a hand through his hair. "And that asshole, Adrian, he stuck up for her!"

Adrian Vallerio was new to the house and the prostitution ring, but he was a tried-and-true Leóne soldier. His ties to the family were generations old—almost as old as the Leónes themselves. But even so, maybe Leila wasn't the only one needing a behavioral adjustment.

Though Emilio enjoyed breaking the girls when they misbehaved, he didn't relish in the instances where he had to beat one of his men back in line.

Clenching one hand into a fist, Emilio glared at Giorgio. He suspected there was more to the story. More than Giorgio was willing to divulge. "Tony, go grab Adrian Vallerio, would you?"

Tony spun on his heels and took off down the hall.

Giorgio shifted to the door as if he intended to leave, but Emilio halted his movement with a snap of his fingers. "Where are you going?"

Jerking a thumb over his shoulder, Giorgio opened his mouth to answer, but one look at Emilio's icy expression silenced any excuses he wanted to give. Giorgio pocketed his hands. "Nowhere. Sorry."

In the ensuing silence, the house's air-conditioning hummed to life. Boards creaked above their heads, water rushed through pipes, and the faint murmur of women's voices filtered down through the air vents.

A flicker of movement at the other end of the dim hall drew Emilio's attention away from his cousin. Adrian Vallerio stood a couple inches taller than Tony's five-eleven, and though his short-sleeved button-down shirt displayed his muscular forearms, he didn't quite match Tony's barrel-chested frame.

At the door, Tony paused to gesture for Adrian to enter the room before he followed and shut them all inside.

Adrian scowled as his eyes fell on Giorgio.

Unsurprisingly, Giorgio responded to the obvious animosity in kind.

Emilio straightened his back and cleared his throat. "Adrian. My cousin was telling me how you were 'sticking up,'" Emilio air quoted the words so Adrian would know the verbiage wasn't his, "for an insubordinate girl after she spit in his face."

Adrian turned to Giorgio with a look of dark amusement. "I don't know what exactly happened with her. I didn't witness the spitting incident, but I know this asshole made it personal. He followed the girl up to her room after she got back from working the street. I knew he'd threatened her earlier, but I didn't know what else he had planned for her."

Giorgio moved to respond, but Emilio snapped his fingers again to cut him off. "What do you mean, 'you didn't know what he was going to do to her?'"

"She's an investment, right?" Crossing both arms over his chest, Adrian glanced to Giorgio and then to Emilio. "She's pretty, and those girls don't come cheap. I'm willing to bet that whatever this prick had planned wouldn't have done anything positive for her value. Hell, he might've even killed her if I hadn't come upstairs when I did. He'd practically beaten down her door when I got there. Poor girl was shaking like a leaf."

Emilio clenched his hand into a tight fist and met his cousin's disbelieving stare. "Is that true?"

"I was just—"

Emilio brought his fist down on the wooden desk with a resounding crash that rattled the nearby ashtray.

"I don't give a shit what you were *just* doing!" He used the same hand to push himself to stand. "Adrian's right, and I know you know that. That girl wasn't cheap! This is a *business*, Giorgio. Do you understand that? And in a business, you don't break the fucking merchandise when it hurts your feelings!"

Despite his six-foot-plus frame, Giorgio seemed to shrink

to a fraction of his size. "I…I'm sorry, boss. It won't happen again."

Emilio hardly waited for him to finish. "No! It won't! Because if it happens again, I'm going to ship you off to refine opiates with the damn laborers!"

Giorgio's gaze shifted to the chair at his side, to the floor, anywhere other than to his cousin.

Clenching and unclenching his fist, Emilio shifted his gaze to Tony. "Is she here right now?"

Tony hooked a finger toward the door. "She's in her room, far as I know."

"Good. You two." He gestured to Giorgio and Adrian. "Get back to work. And thank you, Adrian, for looking out for my business interests while I was gone."

"Of course, boss," Adrian replied stiffly.

Once the two men made their way out into the hall, Emilio gestured for Tony to close the door. "The fewer people who know about Leila Jackson's appearance on a Netflix documentary, the better off we'll be. The last thing I want is for the men around here to be gossiping about how there's a celebrity in the damn house."

Tony scratched his jaw. "What do we do about her?"

Emilio tapped a finger against the wooden desk, thinking through his options. "She needs to be thoroughly trained by someone who knows what they're doing, not someone like my cousin who's just there to get himself off. This seems like a good enough time to do it. It'll keep her away from the streets and the rest of the house for a while. By the time she's ready to go back, the craze over this show will hopefully have died down."

Truly, breaking the girls and bending them to his will was an art form. If he used too much physical force, he'd irreparably damage a substantial investment, but if he didn't use enough force, then he got what they had here today.

He got a girl like Leila.

"Good timing," Tony agreed.

As much as Emilio hated the financial loss that came with taking a girl away from their work on the streets, this needed to be done right.

Now was as good a time as any to remind pretty little Leila of her place.

❄

LEILA WAS ONLY HALFWAY through a page of her latest read—a battered paperback version of the iconic science fiction novel *Dune*—when the floorboards of the hall outside her door creaked. Taking in a sharp breath, she snapped the book closed and jammed it beneath the pillow of her twin-sized bed. She still wasn't sure if reading was prohibited at the house, but she wasn't in a position to test her fortune.

As the metal doorknob began to turn, she held her breath. She'd caught a couple glimpses of Giorgio since he'd been chased off the night before last, but the man had merely pretended to ignore her existence. His disregard would have been a relief if she weren't sure the fallout from her act of defiance was coming.

By the time the door swung open, her knuckles had turned white from her death grip on the edge of the mattress.

The slat of sunlight piercing through the room's only window fell over the man's unshaven face and gave his eyes a menacing amber color. The sleeves of his dress shirt had been rolled up to the elbows, exposing the lean muscles of his forearms and the expensive silver watch on his right wrist.

But the sunlight or the price of his watch wasn't what sent the cold rush of adrenaline up Leila's spine.

She was taken aback by the malice his gaze promised.

Pure, unadulterated fury, and beneath that rage, a sentiment she'd learned to fear even more.

Glee.

Though she didn't remember rising, Leila stood beside her bed as he crossed the room in a few long strides. She backed away from his sudden advance, trying in vain to place his face. She *knew* she'd seen him before, but she couldn't recall where.

When Leila's shoulder met the wood paneling beside the window, a shiver ran from her neck all the way down to her bare feet. Her retreat had been more reflexive than anything.

She couldn't get away.

Swallowing against the sudden bitter taste on her tongue, she opened her mouth to ask him why he was here.

The words died in her throat as he snapped out a hand to take a fistful of her hair. Instead of a coherent question, all she managed was a yelp of surprise.

With one gruff tug, he pulled her flush against his hard body.

His breath was hot on her neck as he jerked her head to the side. "Do you know who I am, little girl?"

As much as Leila hated the pitiable whimpers that slipped from her lips, there was little she could do to stop the sounds. Tears blurred the edges of her vision as she made an attempt to shake her head.

His hand moved down her body. "I own this, and I own *you*. You know what you say when I tell you to jump? You ask me *how high*. And you know what you do when one of my men tells you to jump?"

Scalding tears streaked down Leila's cheeks as her eyelids droop closed.

Tightening his grasp on her hair until her scalp stung, he

leaned in until his lips brushed her ear. "You ask them *how high*. Do you understand me, little girl?"

Trembling, she fought to stay perfectly still. It took everything she had to summon her breath and reply, "Yes. I understand."

His low chuckle reverberated against her skin. "No, see, that's the thing. I don't think you do. You're too smart for that, aren't you? I think you're just telling me what I want to hear, and I think I'm going to have to *make* you understand."

Bile stung Leila's throat.

She had to have known this was coming. She had to have known she couldn't defy one of the soldiers in the house and expect to skate away consequence-free just because another, higher-ranked soldier had taken pity on her.

"P-please." The word was little more than a whisper. "Please, you don't have to do this. I'll do anything you want. I'll…I'll have sex with you however you want. I'm sorry."

He clucked his tongue. "I know that already. I know you'll do whatever the hell I tell you to do because you're *mine*."

Leila finally dared to open her eyes. "Yes. I'm yours."

As her heart continued its relentless cadence against her ribs, she hoped that he would just get it over with. But when he took a step away, he didn't relinquish his grasp.

Strands of hair ripped away from her scalp, and she hurried to follow him into the hall. She took hold of his arm with both hands and twisted herself until she was walking forward. Her grip on his arm was merely to keep the distance between them as small as possible so she could ease the pain caused by his iron grasp.

Though her gaze was turned down to the floor, she spotted the shapes of a few of the girls in her periphery as the man dragged her down the hall to the stairs.

Tears dripped from her face by the time they stepped off

the downstairs landing. She had no idea where the man was taking her—maybe he was dragging her outside to shoot her and put her out of her misery, like a rabid dog or a lame horse.

He pulled her into the kitchen. Through the hair that had matted to the sides of her face, she spotted Adrian, and her heart sank.

Both muscular arms were crossed over his chest as he sat scowling. Though it might have been her imagination, she thought she saw another sentiment behind the ire—a look more akin to resignation or sadness.

She was left no time to ponder the expression as the man unceremoniously jerked her out of the kitchen and into a mudroom. Rather than open the back door to drag her out onto the lawn and shoot her like an animal, he flung open the door to the basement.

"Oh my god, no, please." She hated the sound of her high-pitched voice. More than that, she despised the fact that she would have done anything he wanted just to get him to turn around and send her back upstairs.

The scent of musty wood wafted up to greet them as he pulled her down each rickety step into the gloom below. A fluorescent fixture illuminated the dingy floor and the crumbling concrete of the foundation, but the light was dim compared to the early afternoon sunlight from which Leila had just been pulled.

A sharp rock, or at least she hoped that's what it was, bit into the sole of her foot, causing another yelp of pain.

When he finally relinquished his iron grip, she dropped to the floor, gasping for breath. Pieces of dirt and concrete debris cut into her knees. Blinking repeatedly to clear her vision, Leila sniffled and brushed the matted strands of hair from her face.

She snapped her head up at the metallic clink of a latch.

To her horror, she'd been deposited directly in front of a rusted metal dog crate.

As he hunched down to bring himself eye level with her, the man none-too-gently took hold of her chin, forcing her to look at him.

He gestured to the filthy kennel. "This is where you'll be staying until I can figure out what to do with you."

Leila opened and closed her mouth, but she couldn't so much as form a single word. Defeated, she merely shook her head.

His expression remained stony. "You forced my hand here, little girl. I can't have someone like you going around in front of the other girls, spitting in the face of my man, can I? If you hadn't done that..." he snickered softly, "well, we wouldn't be here, now would we? How quickly you get out of here is up to you. You'll have to prove, with more than words, what a good girl you can be. Do you understand?"

All Leila could do was swallow as she fixed her blank stare on the kennel.

In the four years she'd lived in this world, she had yet to be shoved into a cage meant for an animal. At the old house, she'd been locked in a makeshift cell, a stiflingly hot room, even out in a backyard during a downpour. But an animal crate. Never.

Though she'd thought it impossible, she found herself in an entirely new era of domineering cruelty.

When she didn't reply, he tightened his grasp on her chin to force her focus back to him. The sympathy on his chiseled face was undoubtedly feigned, but part of Leila wanted desperately for the feeling to be genuine.

With his free hand, he pointed at the crate. "You can get in yourself, or I can put you in."

The warrior she thought she was would have told him to do his worst.

That warrior would've said a prayer to Odin before she spat in this man's face too. The warrior would've let him kill her. In death, there was peace, but in this world, there was nothing but despair.

But as it turned out, even his pathetic offer was only the illusion of a choice. Reaching beneath her long hair, he clamped down on the nape of her neck and dragged her forward.

More tears fell, but Leila offered little resistance as he pushed her into a kennel designed for an animal less than half her size.

With her knees tucked up to her belly, Leila tried to adjust herself to relieve the bite of the metal grate on her shoulders and back.

The effort was for naught. She wasn't sure she'd be able to move at all, much less turn around.

After snapping a padlock into place, the man stood to his full height. His tall frame blocked out much of the fluorescent light, but the shadow was only a slight taste of the darkness that was to come.

He held up a silver key. "There's only one copy of this key, and it's mine. I'll be back at some point to make sure you're still alive. Otherwise, try to use this time to think about what you'll be doing differently if I decide to let you out."

"Please," she whispered. "Don't do this. I'll be good. I'll do anything. I swear."

He snorted, shaking his head as he turned to leave. The crunch of his black dress shoes against the dirt and debris of the floor grew quieter as he reached the stairs. Then, after the creak of a few steps, the entire basement was bathed in darkness.

Squeezing her eyes closed, Leila did the only thing she could think to do. She cried.

8

B lowing out a long sigh, Alexander Passarelli combed his fingers through his long shaggy locks. It had been a while since his last trip to the barber, and until someone complained, he'd let it grow. Long hair was in vogue these days, anyway. He leaned back, pressing his full weight into the chair. Metal squeaked in protest as he let his head fall back to gaze sightlessly at the beams and pipes crisscrossing the ceiling of his high-rise condo.

The walls on one side of the place were brick, while the other held floor-to-ceiling windows. Alex had always been a fan of the industrial feel that came with many of Chicago's older remodeled buildings. His five thousand square foot condo located on the twenty-second floor of a high-rise overlooking downtown was a perk of the job.

Then again, whenever he was home, he was usually working. Rare were the days he was able to enjoy the luxurious property that cost him a small fortune to live in.

As he scratched the stubble on one cheek, he glanced out over the city's skyline. A mass of hazy gray clouds had moved in to obscure part of the sunlight. The forecast didn't call for storms. In fact, the last time he'd checked the weather report, the temperature was slated to soar over the next few days.

Straightening, he returned his focus to the spreadsheet he'd pulled up on one of his two monitors. Today's task was to reroute the funds earned from their counterfeit and cyber-crime efforts.

Alex's specialty.

He'd never been keen on the old-school ways. Sure, there were plenty of traditions he honored in his role as a D'Amato capo, but his life as a commander in the Italian mafia was a far cry from the average Joe. Since earning his master's degree in business finance, with a special focus on mathematics and statistics, Alex had made it his mission to bring the family into the digital age.

When the business was doing well, he spent more time in front of a computer screen than he did shaking down the local thugs for their allegiance. In fact, screen time had become the measure of the family's financial success.

If he was posted up in front of a computer, it meant the D'Amato family was making money.

From the corner of his eye, he spotted the flash of his prepaid phone's screen before the first vibration rattled against the matte black desk.

Clearing his throat, Alex snatched up the device and flipped it open. Though he didn't recognize the number of his lunchtime caller, he pressed the green key and raised the phone to his ear.

"Yeah?" His greeting was curt, but to those who called the disposable phone, it was business as usual.

"Alexander Passarelli?" The man's voice was deep but hushed.

Try as he might, he couldn't place the caller's identity. Whoever he was, he wasn't part of the D'Amato family.

Alex was immediately suspicious. "Who is this?"

"Look." The faint sound of a sigh followed. "I don't have a ton of time, so I'm just going to get right down to it. We both know no one's listening to this line, and chances are no one ever will. I'm using a burner, and I know you are too."

Pulling the phone away from his face, he jotted down the number on the screen. Maybe one of his contacts would get lucky and ping the man's closest tower. "Okay, fine. Who are you, and what do you want to talk to me about?"

A whoosh of air created static on the line, suggesting his caller was outside. "We don't know each other personally, but I'm sure you've heard my name before. I'm Adrian Vallerio."

For the second time, Alex pulled the phone away from his face. This time, he looked at the screen in disbelief. "Adrian Vallerio?" he echoed. "Emilio Leóne's guy?"

Getting a call from a rival family's lieutenant was unprecedented and broke all the rules of protocol. If anyone from the Leóne family called him, it would be a capo, like himself. Not some lowly lieutenant.

Alex's intuition demanded he drop the call right then and there, but curiosity piqued his interest. "What do you want?"

"I have an offer for you."

Drumming his fingers against the desk, Alex shifted in his chair. "An offer? Forgive my skepticism here. I'm not really sure what kind of offer I should be getting from a Leóne lieutenant."

He'd heard of Adrian before. It was standard practice to familiarize one's self with the noteworthy soldiers of a rival family. The Vallerio family had been part of the Leóne's for almost as long as the Passarellis had been with the D'Amato family. But that bit of knowledge didn't give him any additional clues as to why this particular soldier would break protocol to call him personally.

A heavy exhale from Adrian's end of the phone line broke

the awkward silence. "Look. I know this is unusual. Our families have a nice little 'don't step on our toes, and we don't step on yours' policy that goes way back."

"More or less, for the last decade, yes."

Over the past decade, the D'Amato family had divested from the drug empire to put their considerable financial might into the counterfeit industry. The profit margin was almost too high to believe, and the risk to the family's affiliates and the members who peddled the product was minimal.

Cops didn't give two shits about a guy selling fake Louis Vuitton handbags from the back of a van when there was another gangster nearby who was peddling crack or heroin.

All in all, the D'Amato family operated like a business. Higher profits meant more money went to the ground-level workers, which meant a higher tier of loyalty than the family had ever seen.

They'd kept the policy of leaving the Leónes alone simply because they had matured and grown into more profitable business ventures. It had little to do with keeping the peace, though that did have its benefits too.

"Are you going to get to the point anytime soon, or am I to guess the reason for you calling today?" Alex growled, growing more impatient by the minute. Adrian had grown a pair enough to call him, but since connecting the call, the Leóne lieutenant had done little more than mumble.

Adrian cleared his throat. "This is a sensitive matter. I hope you understand that. Our families have not always been so civil and—"

"Then why in the hell are you trying to change that now?"

He could almost hear Adrian's teeth grate together through the phone. "I'll tell you why, but not like this. I have an offer for you, one that needs to be handled face-to-face.

No cops, no one else from the family, just you and me. You pick the place and the time, but it has to be today."

Alex's fingers stopped mid-drum. What the hell was going on? Curiosity was getting the better of him as he considered the lieutenant's request and potential consequences.

Adrian cleared his throat again, hinting at his urgency for an answer. Alex finished the drumming motion of his fingers as he made his decision. "Fine. Meet me at Riverbank Park in an hour. It's north of the city. About a forty-five-minute drive this time of day."

"Okay. I'll be there."

"One quick thing." Alex paused to be sure the other man was listening. "Like I said, this is a forty-five-minute drive. You'd better not be wasting my time, you understand me?"

"Don't worry," Adrian replied flatly. "I won't."

❄

ALEX HAD USED Riverbank Park as a meeting place for sketchy business deals in the past. Located on the outskirts of Chicago, the park was at the end of a long, straight patch of road. If anyone had followed him, he would have seen them long before he pulled into the gravel parking lot that overlooked the park's focal point—a lake that was nestled among the hilly landscape.

A number of old trees shrouded much of the grounds in shade, though the sun still hadn't emerged from behind its blanket of clouds. At the edge of the parking area, a grassy outcropping sloped gently toward the southern shore of the lake.

He stepped out of his gunmetal Infiniti and glanced around the immediate area. The gravel lot was one of several, but in addition to his vehicle, only two others were parked nearby. A woman, her husband, and their two children had just stepped out of a forest green SUV. Alex doubted that the beat-up little Saturn two spaces down from him was the Leóne lieutenant's car.

Midway through the drive, Alex had sent a text message with instructions to meet him at the southern parking lot. He was also confident that he'd left Chicago early enough to be the first to the meeting. He preferred it that way, especially considering the company he'd be keeping.

A warm summer breeze rustled the leaves of the trees as he set off toward a gazebo at the other end of the picnic area. Other than a group of teenagers seated at one wooden picnic table, the only people Alex could see were specks on the distant walking trail around the lake.

He focused on the grassy area behind the gazebo, but aside from birds in the trees, nothing stirred. The high ground of the southern recreation area was another aspect of Riverbank Park that suited him well during questionable meetings.

Pulling his smartphone from the pocket of his black slacks, Alex sat on a wooden bench, giving him a clear view of the parking lot. As he shifted to get comfortable, he felt the reassuring weight of the forty-five tucked into his pants.

According to his phone, he'd only been waiting for five minutes before movement drew his attention to the narrow road that led to the parking lot.

Like Alex's Infiniti sedan, the approaching car was nice, but still reasonably inconspicuous. He'd never been much of a car person. He preferred to dabble in cutting edge technology rather than vehicles that could accelerate from zero to sixty in point-three seconds.

Muted daylight glinted off the polished black car as it pulled in to park a couple stalls down from the family and their SUV. Though Alex watched the tall figure that stepped out of the sleek sedan, he made sure to glance around to ensure that the Leóne lieutenant had truly arrived by himself.

On his way to the gazebo, the man, who could only be Adrian Vallerio, smiled politely at the couple and their children. The little family returned the courtesy as they took off for a walking trail that would lead them around the lake.

Well, at least he has some basic manners.

Alex almost scoffed at the thought. The bar for the Leóne family had been set so low, it might as well have been a hole in the ground.

He watched the Leóne lieutenant close in, strolling past the last picnic table. By appearance, Adrian looked to be a couple inches shorter than his height of six-three, but the Leóne lieutenant made up the difference in his broad-shouldered, muscular frame.

To be sure, Alex maintained a rigorous workout regimen and was in far better shape than an average thirty-one-year-old man. But if this interaction came down to an arm-wrestling contest, he wasn't so sure he'd emerge victorious.

Alex nodded slightly as the Leóne lieutenant made his way up the three steps to the floor of the modest gazebo. "Afternoon." He kept his voice smooth and unreadable.

Brushing off the front of his shirt, Adrian took a seat at the picnic table in the center of the circular space. "Likewise."

At the lessened distance, Alex could finally make out the fish shapes decorating the Leóne lieutenant's pastel green shirt, though he fought to keep the curiosity from his face at the realization.

Adrian glanced down to his shirt and shrugged. "It was a Father's Day present from my kids. They know I like to fish, so they thought I must like to wear them too."

Alex was unsure of the appropriate response and brushed

past the remark altogether. "What was it you wanted to meet with me about today, Mr. Vallerio?"

The shadows along Adrian's clean-shaven face shifted as he clenched his jaw. "I'm sure you barely know who I am, but I know who you are. And believe it or not, I respect you. So, I'm not going to waste your time with filler and needless conjecture."

"Fine by me." Alex propped his elbows on his knees and leaned forward. Though he wouldn't admit it aloud just yet, he was impressed by the Leóne lieutenant. "What's this offer you've got for me?"

Adrian laced his fingers together on his lap. "I'm offering to give you information about the Leóne family's human trafficking ring."

Alex narrowed his eyes to keep the expression of surprise from his face.

The family he served had once dabbled in the more traditional mob enterprises—trafficking drugs, guns, prostitutes, underground gambling, and extortion. These days, thanks in no small part to Alex and others who shared his vision for the future, the D'Amato family had ventured away from the riskier aspects of organized crime, distancing themselves from guns, drugs, and human trafficking.

The family he served had never truly been involved in the despicable industry, though they operated their fair share of high-class brothels in the city.

But, in true D'Amato fashion, the escort services were run with a certain air of professionalism. Alex personally oversaw the operation to ensure none of the workers were mistreated. In the rare event they were, he took pleasure in dealing with the perpetrators himself.

But the Leónes...they were a different story. Like remnants of the days of Al Capone, they embraced all forms of organized crime. If it made them money, no matter how despicable, they dabbled in it.

Their two families were like the Hatfields and McCoys. Once upon a time, they'd been on the same side, but societal change had sent them off in separate directions.

Sure, Alex was a mafia captain and dabbled in illegal acts on a daily basis, but he and all the affiliates of the D'Amato family knew where to draw a line.

As far as the Leóne family was concerned, there was no line.

Despite the uneasy ceasefire, the two families hated one another.

The peace they'd lived in for the last few years had been tentative. And though none of them mentioned the sentiment aloud, all the D'Amato commanders were waiting for the day their flimsy façade of neutrality would be shredded.

Knowing key information about the other family's operations would certainly tip the balance of power to the D'Amato side of the scale.

One question demanded an answer, and though Alex would have normally tried to deliver it diplomatically, he couldn't stop it from spilling out like an accusation. "Why?"

Anger simmered behind Adrian's stony expression. "Like I said, Mr. Passarelli, you have my respect, so I'm not going to spend time on bullshit. I'm a happily married man. Been so since I was eighteen. My wife and I have two kids, both girls, eight and six." He plucked at his fish shirt. "They're great kids. They're thoughtful, smart, and funny. Everything you'd ever want your little girls to be. And my wife, well, I think she's where they get it from. She's amazing."

Alex held back from responding, allowing the pause to lapse into silence. He clenched his jaw and turned his gaze toward the distant lake.

"I've been in this life since I was born." Adrian shifted in his seat. "My pops was a Leóne capo, and I always assumed that one day that's what I'd be too. I looked away from all the despicable shit *the family* did to make money because I thought, someday, I'd be the one in charge. That someday, I'd be able to scrap all this nasty shit and run something a little more like a real business."

The flicker of anger in Adrian's eyes turned into an inferno.

Alex began to suspect where the conversation was headed and opened his mouth, ready to end this meeting.

Adrian beat him to the punch. "How am I supposed to watch someone like Emilio, or his dipshit cousin, treat those poor women, those poor *girls*, like that and then go home to my family at the end of the day?" A mirthless chuckle escaped his lips before he continued. "A couple of the guys who work around that house are raging alcoholics, and honestly, I can see why. I always thought we were supposed to be more honorable than that, you know?"

No, I don't know. Alex stared unblinking at the Leóne lieutenant, waiting for him to continue.

"I'm sick of it." Adrian's voice sharpened as determination overtook his anger. "And that's why I'm here today. I know how the D'Amato family works. I know you run it like a business, and I know you're all disciplined. Anymore, it seems like the Leóne family is just a free-for-all. They've needed to clean house for a long time, but I guess I'm the first one who's actually thought to do anything about it."

"What exactly do you expect me to do about it?" Alex growled in frustration. "Why aren't you talking to a capo from your own family if you think Emilio's mismanaging his operation?"

Adrian snorted. "Emilio's a Leóne. The command is his right by birth, not merit. If he's left to his own devices, he'll be the underboss before he turns fifty. And then..." he shrugged, "who knows? Chances are, Emilio or one of his kin in charge will mean open war against the D'Amato family, against the damn Russians, against whoever happens to look at Emilio wrong that week."

Alex crossed his arms over his chest. He'd had the displeasure of meeting Emilio Leóne. The man had a short fuse, and he viewed the world in black and white.

Either you were Emilio's friend, or you were his enemy. There was no in-between.

"I don't doubt you're sincere." He pinned the Leóne lieutenant with a hard stare. "But I'm more curious about the *how* of this entire proposition. How do you suppose I'll manage to wipe out their trafficking ring without bringing a full-on war to my front door?"

"I don't know." Adrian spread his hands, his expression unreadable. "But I figure that's for you to figure out, not me. I'll give you the information so you can make a plan. That's what I'm offering."

Alex and his damn curiosity was piqued again. "What information, exactly?"

"Whatever you need."

Alex leaned forward. "And what, specifically, do you want in return?"

Adrian's expression softened. "I want Emilio gone and his trafficking ring crippled. I don't give a shit how you do it. Send him to prison or end his existence, as long as he's out of the picture. The only stipulation I have is, you can't hurt any of the girls. If you can do that, I'll give you routes, suppliers, locations, whatever you need."

As another silence descended on them, Alex kept his scrutiny on the Leóne lieutenant turned informer.

He didn't doubt Adrian's sincerity. At least not so far.

Tapping a finger against his leg, Alex straightened. "I'm going to have to think about this."

Adrian's jaw clenched. "It's going to have to be fast. One of the girl's life is at stake right now, Passarelli. Maybe that doesn't mean anything to you, but time is of the essence right now." He pushed himself to stand. "You know how to get ahold of me. Three days, that's how long I'll give you. I just hope that's long enough for this girl."

9

As I descended the last few metal stairs, the musty scent of damp concrete drifted up to greet me. Wrinkling my nose, I glanced around the area.

Everything from the concrete floor to the ceiling—crisscrossed with structural beams, vents, and pipes—was a drab shade of gray.

At the beginning of June, a warehouse basement fifteen miles south of Washington, D.C. was among the last places I wanted to be.

Summer was the perfect time to take my luxurious yacht, *Equilibrium*, out for a cruise along the Florida coast. With a length of just over one-hundred-thirty meters, *she* was one of the sixty largest yachts in the world.

And when the weather was favorable—as it often was in the month of June—I much preferred to spend my time out to sea.

However, a trip out to sea wasn't complete without a pretty young plaything to pass the time and warm my bed at night.

Glutton for punishment that I was, I had an addiction to

girls with a little spirit. I wasn't happy without a challenge and couldn't feel satisfied unless I had someone to break.

Though I'd developed an effective method over the years, it still needed a bit of tweaking. Especially when dealing with a particularly fiery challenge, like pretty little Maribel. My god, it had been years, but I still missed Maribel.

Those sparkling blue eyes, that porcelain skin, and raven black hair that hung almost to the small of her back, she had been the embodiment of beauty.

What a waste! Maribel's delicious body had no doubt been a feast for the marine life out in the volatile waters of the Atlantic Ocean. I wasn't one to live with regrets, but if I could go back in time and change how I'd handled things that day…Maribel might not have wound up as fish food.

I guess that's why they called me The Shark, though that was a term usually reserved for lawyers, and I'd never practiced law a day in my life.

With a quiet breath to shake myself from the memory, I turned to the man at my side as we reached the bottom of the short stairwell. Mark, my long-time friend and right-hand man, angled his head toward a couple men standing beside a cement column.

I recognized the taller of the two men—Ivan, if memory served—and though I was sure I'd seen the shorter man before, I couldn't place where.

As Mark and I approached the pair, I extended a hand. "Evening, gentleman."

The short man accepted the handshake.

"It's always a pleasure." Ivan spoke with a prominent Russian accent, though he'd lived in the United States for most of his adult life.

Mark's expression changed little as he went through the standard pleasantries.

I rarely attended these meetings in person, but recent

dealings with the Russian trafficking rings operating along the east coast had required a more personal touch.

Ivan stepped to the side and waved a hand to a dark-haired young woman. The harsh fluorescent lights glinted off the tears streaking down the sides of her face. She strained against the zip ties binding her to a metal chair, each movement causing it to scrape and screech against the concrete floor. No doubt cursing as she struggled, her words were muffled by a bandana tied around her mouth.

Her cheeks flushed deliciously with the heat of her anger. She glanced back and forth between Ivan and his shorter companion. Her eyes were bloodshot, but the blue of her irises stood out in striking contrast.

Since birth, I'd been red-green colorblind. Protanopia was my official diagnosis. Over the years, I'd learned that, compared to others, my view of all other colors was faded and washed-out.

Blues, however, were vivid.

She was pretty, but I couldn't help the sinking sensation in my stomach as I looked her up and down. Then again, with Maribel so recently in my thoughts, it was no small wonder I was disappointed. Maribel had been perfect.

I pushed past the pang of regret as I met Ivan's gaze. "Can she stand?"

Ivan reached into his olive drab jacket, turned to the girl, spat out a few words in Russian, and brandished a pocketknife.

I didn't speak Russian, but the girl's meek gaze flicked up to me as Ivan cut the first zip tie.

I tapped the corner of my mouth. "And the gag too."

With a nod, Ivan untied the bandana and dropped the cloth to the dusty floor. He gave her another command in Russian before folding both arms over his broad chest.

The girl's eyes were fixed on her painted red toenails as she rose to stand on thin, shaky legs.

Buttoning my black suit jacket, I stepped forward, closing the distance between the girl and myself. As I reached out to remove the matted hair from her cheeks, every muscle in her body froze.

Her fear amused me. With a low chuckle, I brushed the dark brown locks over her shoulder before I took hold of her chin.

I lifted her face to check the smoothness of her neck and then dragged my finger down her collarbone to tug at the semi-sheer fabric of her white camisole. Though the see-through material didn't leave much to the imagination, it had become a routine for me to check for scars that might have indicated plastic surgery.

I turned to face Ivan. "Does she speak English?"

The Russian gangster's countenance was as unremarkable as if he was standing in line at the supermarket. "She is immigrant, but speaks plenty English to follow basic command."

My balls tightened as ideas came to mind of exactly the commands I wanted to give, but that would come later. I refocused on the girl. "Good. Now, lift up your shirt."

Tears shimmered in her eyes as her gaze shifted between Ivan and me before she pulled the thin fabric up, revealing her stomach. She hesitated briefly when she reached her breasts but rebounded quickly, tugging the shirt up to her collarbone.

I kept my expression blank as I studied her abdomen to look for scars. As expected, her skin was flawless—aside from a few nasty bruises that would heal. Her breasts hadn't been augmented, and I saw no other signs of a surgical procedure having been performed on her thin body.

After a quick circle around to finish my examination, I

turned my attention to Ivan. "Where did you say you found her? Who is she?"

Ivan shrugged as he produced a toothpick from his front pocket. "Her father owed money and did not pay. We take daughter as payment." He popped the toothpick in his mouth. "Then we kill him. She is no one."

The girl's breathing picked up at the mention of her father, but she remained silent.

I moved the dark brown hair away from her shoulders. "No scars, that's good. She's thin, though she honestly might be a little *too* thin. I don't know why the girls I look at are always so damn *thin*. Didn't her father feed her?"

Ivan snorted and leaned his shoulder against the cement column.

Once I'd circled back around to face the girl again, her eyes were glassy. I ignored the display of emotion as I took hold of her upper lip. A tear slid down her cheek as I lifted it to inspect her mouth.

"Her teeth are a little crooked. Guess her father couldn't afford to feed her *or* take her to a dentist."

"He was poor man. Spent his money on booze." The observation came from Ivan's shorter companion. Though still prevalent, the man's accent wasn't as pronounced as Ivan's.

I nodded to myself. "Is she a virgin?"

More tears welled up, threatening to spill over her cheeks. She'd understood my question. Good.

As I turned to the Russian men, Ivan shrugged again. "I don't know. Ask her."

I pinned her with an intent stare. "I know you understood me. Are you a virgin?"

She opened and closed her mouth as a new round of tears streaked her face, but no sound escaped her lips. Dropping her gaze to the floor, she shook her head.

"Good." The sentiment might have been considered bizarre among other men who ran in the same circles that I did, but I'd never been a fan of untouched girls.

Despite the one positive mark in her favor, there was still much about the young woman that was inconsistent with Ivan's description on the phone.

With a sigh, I took a step backward and crossed my arms.

"Crooked teeth, too thin, oily skin." I rounded on Ivan. "My friend, I dare say you've misrepresented your product."

Irritability flashed across Ivan's face but faded just as soon as it had appeared. "We had old photos of the girl. She is thinner maybe, but same girl."

Shaking my head, feeling less than stellar about this transaction, I turned to Mark. "Emilio always found the best girls, didn't he?"

Mark smirked as he scratched his bearded chin. "He did. Seemed to have a knack for it, if you ask me."

"Always the perfect age. Slender, but not too thin." I heaved a wistful sigh. "God, I miss Emilio's girls. It makes me almost wish I'd taken better care of some of them."

Mark replied with a hapless shrug.

I turned back to Ivan. "How old is she?"

Pulling the toothpick from his mouth, he pursed his lips as if deep in thought. "I don't know."

"Fair enough." I spun to face the girl. "How old are you?"

A few strands of dark hair fell in front of her face as her eyes riveted to the cement floor.

I took another step closer. "I know you understand me. How old are you?"

More silence.

Well, at least she had the fire. That, I liked. Now, I just had to hope her willfulness wouldn't prove to be an insurmountable hurdle.

Without warning, I slapped her across the cheek. The dull

crack as my hand connected with her face reverberated up my arm.

She cried out in pain-filled surprise.

Clenching and unclenching my fist, I glanced to the back of my knuckles. "One more time. How old are you?"

She lifted a shaking hand to cover the darkening mark on her cheek. She swallowed hard but still didn't meet my gaze. "I'm twenty."

I didn't even attempt to hide the rage from taking ownership of my face. Ivan knew that my preferred age was closer to fifteen or sixteen.

"Twenty?" I shot Ivan an exasperated look. "She's twenty? You said high school aged."

Ivan lifted his shoulders in a semblance of a shrug so weak I wanted to break his arm. "Information from girl's father was old. We expected young girl."

I looked back to the girl, letting the space lapse into silence as I scrutinized every inch of her thin frame. "She's thin, which isn't usually what I like, but I think if we wax her underarms, legs, and between her legs, she'll seem young enough."

Looking relieved, Ivan waved a hand at the girl. "You will buy her, yes?"

By now, the tremors that wracked her body were plain to see. If it turned out she was epileptic or suffered from another neurological disorder, I would make sure I got every damn dime back from Ivan.

I narrowed my gaze. "I'm a businessman, my friend. It'd be poor form to commit to a purchase and back out at the last second. Then again, it's also poor form to misrepresent the product you're selling, but I'm willing to take the high road this time around. How much are you asking for her?"

"I will make good for misrepresentation." Ivan made a

show of weighing his hands. "We cut three thousand from asking price. Fifteen thousand U.S. dollars."

Fifteen grand was pocket change. But that didn't mean I accepted shoddy deals just because I had the capital. I'd learned better at the University of Chicago Booth School of Business.

Aside from today's slipup, Ivan's prices were fair, and he had owned up to the mistake.

After a moment of silence, I nodded. "Fifteen thousand it is."

Until another girl like Maribel came along, I'd have to make do.

Even the expendable girls had their uses.

10

As much as Amelia hated how hot and humid the summer days could get in the Midwest, she was glad for the heat that lingered after the sun sank below the horizon. If the temperature dipped too low, she'd have a rough time waiting in line for the nightclub.

She'd dug deep in her closet to find one of the few remaining dresses she hadn't donated to secondhand stores. More than eight years had passed since she'd last worn the jade green halter dress, but to her surprise, the material stretched to hug her figure like a glove.

The thump of the bass was muffled from where she and Zane stood in line, but as they crept closer to the bouncer and the door, the volume gradually increased. Regretting her choice of heels, Amelia shifted from one foot to the other. The skin-hugging fabric of her dress shimmered with subtle hints of purple and gold as she moved.

According to the tag, the dress had been made by Chanel, but she hadn't the faintest idea how much it had cost. She hadn't been the one to buy it. It had been given to her by Alex Passarelli.

Alexander Giuseppe Passarelli, the son of Luca Passarelli, a highly regarded capo of the D'Amato crime family.

By now, Amelia was sure Alex had ascended to his own position of authority in the D'Amato family. Though they didn't share the D'Amato surname, the Passarellis were still mafia royalty.

As she glanced around to the other well-dressed patrons in line, the entire scene struck her with a haunting familiarity that sunk a stone in her stomach.

When she'd left Alex and Chicago more than a decade ago, Amelia had made a clean break. Though she'd been tempted on a couple occasions, she'd never stalked Alex over social media, nor had she used her abundant resources at the Federal Bureau of Investigation to watch him.

Scanning the men and women in line behind her and Zane, she wondered if she would have been wise to brush up on Alexander Passarelli before she'd come out to a club that was frequented by the members of the city's various criminal organizations.

Then again, even if she'd discovered that Alex was a frequent flyer at Evoked, what would she have done? Would she have divulged her decades-old secret to the entire FBI office, or only her department?

She almost snorted aloud at the thought. No, the people who populated her new life didn't need to know about the ghosts from her past.

For all she knew, Alex had completely forgotten about Amelia Storm from Englewood.

Turning to Zane, she resisted the urge to tug down the hem of the short dress as she forced her thoughts back to the present. She'd caught his gaze lingering on her a few times so far that night, but she couldn't say she blamed him. Whenever she caught a glimpse of herself in the shiny stone of the building's exterior, she was taken aback too.

To say Amelia didn't get out much anymore would be an understatement.

As his eyes met hers, Zane pushed to his full height from where he'd leaned against a metal rail. The five-inch heels of her strappy gold stilettos narrowed the difference between her five-eight and his six-three to a mere couple inches.

White fluorescence from a nearby streetlight caught the polished silver band on his left ring finger as he circled an arm around her waist.

Rather than back away from the overly familiar contact, Amelia eased into the warmth of his body. Her adjustment to the lessened proximity had taken all their time in line, plus the initial drive downtown, but she'd finally taught herself not to flinch away from his touch.

She liked Zane, and so far, she trusted him, but Amelia valued her personal space. Physical contact beyond a handshake with anyone who wasn't a part of her immediate family elicited a cringe on a good day, and a callous rebuff on a bad one.

Tightening his grasp on her hip, Zane leaned in until his nose brushed her cheek. "Did you see something? For a second there, you looked like you saw a ghost."

As he straightened, she rested her cheek on his shoulder. If she had to forgo her trepidation at close physical contact that night, then she'd at least take advantage of the situation to catch a whiff of the mystery product he used to style his dark blond hair. She was too embarrassed to ask for the name of what made him smell so divine, but someday, she would find out.

She brushed her fingertips along the buttons of his shirt. "No, I'm just jealous. You get to dress like you're going to work, but I had to spend an hour making sure I didn't look like a slob."

She didn't include the extra time they'd both spent at the

FBI office to make sure their hidden microphones functioned.

The gold feather pendant at Amelia's neck and the silver watch on Zane's right wrist both contained tiny microphones. They knew they'd be patted down at the door, so smuggling in weapons and badges was a no-go.

Though their hidden mics could technically be used as a method to collect evidence, the devices' primary function was to allow Joseph Larson and Spencer Corsaw—the Supervisory Special Agent of the Organized Crime Division—to monitor them from a surveillance van parked in a nearby garage. If the situation deteriorated, they could signal for backup.

Zane kept his arm around her as they moved forward in line. "Well, you *definitely* don't look like a slob."

Amusement tugged at Amelia's lips. "Yeah, I know. That's because I spent an hour making sure I didn't."

As Zane chuckled, one of the bouncers beside the entrance ushered them forward.

After a quick pat down, Zane reached into the pocket of his black slacks to produce their IDs. Apparently, Amelia's formfitting attire exempted her from the obligatory search.

The burly bouncer flicked on a miniature flashlight and gave each license a cursory glance. "Mr. and Mrs. Kantner. Enjoy yourselves."

"Thank you." Zane pocketed his wallet.

Amelia linked arms with her date and smiled politely at the bouncer as she headed inside.

The interior of the club was every bit as sleek and polished as the exterior. As the room opened up, a polished concrete path surrounded the perimeter of a sunken lounge area that was dotted with circular tables, backless chairs, and a handful of leather booths. Panes of plexiglass spiderwebbed with cerulean fairy lights divided the lounge into four distinct sections.

Overhead, the tall ceiling was dotted with a litany of twinkling blue lights, creating a nighttime sky aesthetic. Illuminated icicles, in the same shade as the glass dividers, hung in regular intervals like shooting stars.

The whole scene was ethereal, like walking through a dream. Amelia blinked a few times and forced her focus away from the enchanting glow and to the man at her side.

A voice in the back of her mind insisted that Zane, with his lean, muscular frame, flawless hair, and boyishly disarming grin, was no less mesmerizing than the upscale club.

Brushing away the sentiment, she gently elbowed him in the ribs to get his attention.

As his gaze snapped over to her, she angled her head toward the bar at the other end of the room. "We should get drinks. We'll look weird walking around without 'em."

He grinned. "Fair enough. Looks pretty busy here tonight."

Amelia shrugged her bare shoulders. "Rich people can afford to go to the club on a Thursday." She glanced to the women in sparkly dresses and men in designer suit jackets and slacks who were situated throughout the lounge. "I doubt anyone here is on that nine-to-five grind, you know?"

Zane snorted out a laugh. "You've got a point."

As they approached the sleek granite bar, Amelia kept a possessive hand on Zane's arm. He waved to the bartender and ordered a couple mojitos. A set of steps near the entrance to the adjoining room—the dance area—led to an exposed second floor, but Amelia knew the real VIP section was in the basement.

The balcony style second floor had a clear view of the lounge and the dance floor, but the people Amelia and Zane were searching for were the kind who did not want to be seen. The club owner, however, had to maintain appearances, and what was a nightclub without an upper-level VIP section?

Once they each had a drink in hand, Zane left the bartender a generous tip, and they set off in the direction of the stairs.

According to Gabriella Hernandez, the entrance to the basement was on the other side of the wall.

Amelia scanned the crowd as she and Zane strode through the wide, arched doorway to an even larger room. Half of the space was devoted to a lounge similar to the front room, and the remaining area was open to the club's dancers.

As a new song started, fog rolled out from under the raised platform that held the DJ booth. The man and woman behind the mixers both threw their hands up in the air, and a cheer followed from the dance floor.

After taking a long pull from her mojito, Amelia reminded herself to hold Zane's hand to keep up appearances. He seemed to be shocked by her sudden familiarity, but as she angled her head toward a sectioned off area past the lounge, he smiled with understanding. Taking the lead, he guided them both toward the shadowy doorway beyond the fairy lights.

A bald man clad in all black sat beside the plexiglass. His observant gaze zeroed in on Amelia and Zane as they approached. Muscles strained against the fabric of his uniform as he straightened on his stool and put away his phone.

Like a predator ready to pounce, he regarded the two of them cautiously. "Can I help you two?"

With a disarming smile, Zane gestured to Amelia. "My wife and I should be on the list."

Baldie retrieved a sleek tablet from a podium at his side. "Names?"

Amelia cleared her throat. "Harley Kantner."

Zane draped an arm over her shoulders. "Aaron Kantner. That's Kantner with a K."

Amelia's stomach clenched as she watched the bald man tap a few buttons and scroll down the screen. She nervously twirled a lock of hair around her finger as she waited to see if Gabriella had come through with registering their aliases on the VIP list.

Though Zane had attempted to quell her nerves before the mission, they'd never received a true confirmation that the request had gone through. Partygoers to a shady section of an already shady club didn't exactly register through Ticketmaster.

With a nod, the bouncer looked up from his tablet.

Rather than heave a sigh of relief, Amelia took another drink of her mojito. They'd only cleared stage one. They still had to hope that the password hadn't changed.

The bouncer waved them into the closed-off area before the doorway.

A second darkly dressed man, with a head full of thick brown hair, rose from his stool. "Password?"

Still curling her hair around her index finger, Amelia kept the sweet smile on her lips even as her heart threatened to punch a hole through her chest. "Dandelion."

Echoing Amelia's expression, the man stepped aside to allow them to pass. "Thank you very much. Have fun."

Zane circled an arm around her waist as they strode through the doorway. A blue-green glow outlined each step, while above them, more of the same twinkling lights hung from the ceiling of the rest of the club.

At the top of the stairs, Amelia paused. With a final

anxious glance at Zane, she gulped back her nervousness and chased it with another swig of her mojito.

It was showtime.

✳

AMELIA SPENT the next two hours faking smiles and laughter as she sidled up next to her pretend husband.

They'd spent the afternoon rehearsing their respective roles, and their diligence had paid off. Conversations with the other VIP lounge patrons flowed effortlessly.

Waitresses, with skimpy dresses that made Amelia's look like a ball gown, weaved through the crowd with trays of champagne. Keeping up appearances, Amelia allowed herself to indulge and plucked two glasses from a tray as the waitress came up to her. The young woman acknowledged Amelia politely before continuing to snake her way through the crowd as she headed back to the bar.

The color of the lights embedded in the ceiling and behind the bar gradually changed as the hours passed, transitioning from blue to a soft violet. Evoked might have been owned and operated by an alleged pimp, but his lighting designer was brilliant. Through the course of the night, Amelia repeatedly felt like a character in a science fiction film.

The purple glow caught the respectable diamond on her left ring finger as she handed one of the champagne flutes to her fake husband.

She kept her movements measured as she took her seat beside Zane. She rarely went out, and as a result, rarely wore dresses of any shape or size, much less as short as the jade green halter she'd picked for the night. If she weren't careful, she'd be the subject of an embarrassing wardrobe malfunction.

She and Zane both knew that building a rapport with the shady characters in the VIP lounge would take time. They had to fit in perfectly. So, for what felt like half an eternity, Amelia clung to Special Agent Zane Palmer, batting her eyelashes, smiling flirtatiously, and giving an Oscar-worthy performance as she pretended to be the trophy wife of Mr. Aaron Kantner.

Fortunately, if she needed a laugh to come across as genuine, all she had to do was picture Zane's face earlier in the day when he'd asked her why she picked the name Harley.

"Because your name is Zane." Amelia chuckled at her own wit. "Harley...Zane. Get it?"

Before he'd groaned and covered his face with both hands, his expression had been a cross between resignation and outright shame.

Afterward, Amelia had gone on a ten-minute spiel about the memorable traits of Harley Zane in her animated series, all of which undoubtedly went in one of Zane's ears and out the other. When she looked back on the tangent, she realized how comfortable she'd become around Agent Palmer—her willingness to ramble on about fictional comic book characters was a testament to that.

Across from Zane and Amelia was a second cushioned bench, and between the benches was a short, circular table.

Another man, Eli, and his wife had asked them to sit after learning of Zane's fake occupation as a hedge fund manager. At least for the two men's conversations, Amelia didn't have to play dumb. She genuinely didn't understand half of what they'd said so far that night.

Eli's wife, Sara, had just flagged down a friend to join them, and the topic of discussion seemed like it might finally shift.

Aside from a couple mentions of Marshall Grove,

including the fact that he was much more small-time than he made himself seem, she and Zane had yet to broach the real reason for their visit.

Gesturing to the woman at her side, Sara beamed at Zane and Amelia. "Hey, y'all, this is Viv, my friend. Viv, this is Harley and Aaron." With her Southern drawl, sun-kissed skin, and platinum blonde locks, Sara was the embodiment of a Southern belle.

Viv offered them a polite wave as she came to join them. Her black hair drank in the purple lighting, but the sequins on her strapless dress glittered as she took her seat.

Unlike Sara, Viv's porcelain skin was even fairer than Amelia's. Together, the two women made a perfect yin and yang.

As Amelia carefully crossed her legs, Zane reached a hand to clasp the exposed skin of her thigh. After their hours at the club, Amelia thought little of the physical contact. They had to sell the idea that they were a sexually adventurous couple, and they couldn't do that if they sat at arm's length from one another.

"So." Eli pushed his glasses up. "What brings you two here?"

Zane stroked Amelia's leg. "Well, I've got it on good authority, from a friend of mine back home in New York, that this is the place to go if you're looking for…" He trailed off as he turned to Amelia.

She mirrored his devious expression before she glanced back to Eli and Sara. "For a little fun. The type of fun some people might think is, you know, taboo."

Sara rolled her honey-brown eyes. "Prudes."

Raising her glass of champagne, Amelia gave the woman an appreciative wink.

Eli sipped at his whiskey. "What're you into? Do you guys swing?"

Amelia almost spit out her drink, forgetting, for a moment, how *forward* these people were expected to be.

When Eli's gaze shifted to Amelia, a suggestive glint flickered to life in his pale eyes. "Because, you know. The offer's there."

Even as Amelia forced her expression to remain amiable, she scooted closer to Zane. As if he could sense her unease—and maybe he could—he tightened his grip on her leg.

With his trademark disarming grin, Zane shook his head. "No, but I do appreciate it. I'm just..." His gaze turned possessive as he slowly turned toward Amelia. "I'm not great at sharing."

Eli's expression said he more than understood.

Though the man seemed unbothered by Zane's rejection, Amelia's gut told her he didn't act the same way to a woman's rebuff. Eli was reasonably attractive and easily fifteen years Amelia's senior. He was taller than average, with a strong jawline, and appeared to be in good physical shape.

Despite his good looks, Amelia hadn't missed the predatory spark in his gaze. But unless he was Leila's pimp, Amelia wasn't here for him. Even though Marshall Grove was shaping up to be a dead-end, Amelia was determined not to leave empty-handed.

Amelia painted a flirtatious smile on her face. "We're looking for a woman. Young, pretty. Someone we can have a little, you know, fun with while we're in town. But... someone who won't bother us after we're gone, you know?"

Eli and Sara chuckled knowingly.

Zane leaned forward to set his emptied champagne flute on the polished table. "My friend said that Marshall Grove would be able to help us out on that front."

To Sara's side, Viv waved a dismissive hand. "Sounds like your friend got Grove mixed up with someone else. Marshall

Grove's good if you want an unregistered Glock or a brick of coke, but he's not going to get you laid."

Amelia's laugh was mostly genuine. Part of her appreciated Viv's candid tone and no-nonsense explanation. If Amelia had been part of a criminal organization, she could see her and Viv becoming friends.

Zane lifted an eyebrow. "What about you?"

With an upraised finger, Viv shook her head. "No, sorry, honey. I've got a man at home already, and he's not good at sharing either."

Laughing, Zane nuzzled his nose in Amelia's hair. "No, I'm sorry, that's not what I meant. I should've phrased that better. I meant, do you know someone who might be able to help us out?"

Viv covered her face with one hand as she let out an embarrassed laugh. "Wow. Way for me to assume. You know what they say about assuming, right?"

Amelia grinned, thinking of the quote her father used at least once a week. "That it makes an ass out of you and me. It's okay, though, really." She waved a hand as if the gesture would alleviate Viv's trepidation. "Don't even worry about it."

Fanning herself with one hand, Viv drained the remainder of her champagne flute. "I do have someone that can help you guys out, though. It sounds like she's going to have exactly what you're looking for.

Zane nodded eagerly.

Viv set her glass on the table and pushed herself to stand.

With an outstretched hand, she beckoned Amelia and Zane to follow. "Yeah, I've got someone who can help you out."

Zane offered Eli and Sara a parting handshake. "It was good talking with you, man. Next time we're back in Chicago, we'll have to swing by here again."

"I hope to see you again sometime, my friend." Eli's unsettling gaze shifted to Amelia. "You and your beautiful wife have a good night. Have some fun, okay? You're on vacation."

Rather than the scowl she would normally give a man as creepy as Eli, Amelia smiled brighter and finished with a flirty wink. "Oh, we intend to."

After another quick round of farewells, Amelia and Zane followed Viv to a cluster of round tables set up in a corner across from the bar. Four of the tables were vacant, but the sole occupant of the fifth was a tall, thin woman.

As Zane and Amelia approached, Viv placed her hands on her hips. "This is Dawn. She's got the connections I think you guys are looking for. Really pretty girls, all very professional too." She mouthed the word *discrete*.

On cue, Dawn's bright eyes snapped up from where she'd been focused on her phone. The colorful lights lent her golden blonde hair a pink tinge. Her halter dress hugged every curve of her body as she rose to stand.

With a wide smile that revealed her straight white teeth, Dawn offered a hand first to Zane, then to Amelia. "Wow, Viv's been keeping me busy." Stepping to the side, she gestured to her table—the only table in the little cluster that boasted cushioned booths as seats. "Have a seat. Thank you, Viv."

Viv flashed the "okay" sign before she turned to leave.

Once Amelia and Zane had taken their spots opposite Dawn, the blonde woman folded her hands. "What can I help you two find tonight?"

With the way the words rolled off the woman's tongue, Amelia could have fooled herself to think she was shopping for car insurance, not a living, breathing human being.

Amelia swallowed the bitter taste in her mouth. "Well, we're looking for a little company." She curved her lips into a playful smile before glancing at Zane.

He echoed Amelia's expression and offered a hand to Dawn. "I won't go into any of the details unless you want me to, but we're looking for a young woman to have some fun with. We're from New York, so it's easier just to, you know, pay for it." He shrugged. "Like my wife says, this way, we make sure we get a clean break when we leave. No phone calls or anything like that."

Dawn scooted forward. "Absolutely. You're looking for a young woman, right? How young?"

Swallowing her distaste, Amelia didn't miss a beat. "Well, we prefer a girl who's got a little experience, you know? Preferably someone who's done this a few times. But still young or, at least, young looking."

Dawn took a quick sip from her cocktail. "What about physical characteristics? Any turn-ons or turn-offs?"

Tilting her head at Zane, Amelia made a show of contemplating Dawn's question.

Zane shrugged. "I'm not the one who's particular about her appearance. That's my wife's territory."

Amelia wanted to punch him in the arm, but instead, she batted her eyelashes adoringly at Zane's manufactured deference. "Yeah, that's true, I suppose. Well, you know, for starters, I like a girl with fair skin. Porcelain, that type of complexion. And black hair, even better if it's naturally black so it has that sexy shimmer." Pursing her lips, Amelia drummed her fingers on the table as she feigned pensiveness to give herself a moment to catch her breath. Damn Zane for putting her on the spot like that. "Oh, and I absolutely love blue eyes. Like yours, Dawn."

Dawn's face lit up at the compliment. "Oh, well, thank you." She held up a hand as she reached to pull a tablet from the handbag at her side. "I think we have a young lady who'll work just perfectly. We actually have some pictures of the girls. My boss likes to make sure that our clients are getting exactly what they pay for, so I keep the pictures with me when I come here."

Amelia's pulse quickened. She'd described Leila as well as she could without pulling out the age progression photo and asking Dawn to match the girl's features. Fair skin, blue eyes, and naturally black hair wasn't a common combination, at least not in Chicago.

Seconds felt like minutes as Dawn typed out the unlock code to bring the tablet to life. The glow of the screen reflected off the whites of her eyes as she tapped a few more buttons.

Finally, after an eternity, Dawn spun the tablet around to face them. "We have about sixteen women at this location. They're all legal, and they've all got plenty of…experience." Dawn giggled softly.

As Amelia swiped through the photos, Zane leaned forward. "Now, I hope this isn't an issue at all, but we prefer to be as private as we can. Is there any chance that this place is like a brothel?"

Dawn's expression turned mischievous. "As a matter of fact, that's something we're happy to accommodate. You'd need to make an appointment, but we can set that up right now."

Swiping past a photo of a blonde girl who appeared much younger than eighteen, Amelia lifted an eyebrow. "How soon? I'm afraid we aren't, um…you know, in town for very long."

"We're heading out tomorrow afternoon, actually," Zane added. "I'm more than happy to pay to expedite the process if it's necessary."

At the mention of a larger payment, a sly grin curled Dawn's lips. "That's certainly something we can accommodate, yes."

Though fleeting, the woman's sneaky expression told

Amelia that she was more than just a working girl who had been commissioned to solicit clients at a seedy nightclub. She probably took a small cut of each transaction, and more than likely, she knew just how her so-called boss operated.

Pushing the sudden spark of anger from her mind, Amelia turned her focus back to the pictures while Zane and Dawn discussed payment.

Many of the girls were blonde, with a couple brunettes and redheads included in their ranks. A few of the young women wore slight smiles, but for the most part, the photos were like mugshots. In fact, she wouldn't be surprised if these were the same pictures that Dawn's boss had used for each of the girl's fake ID.

By the time she swiped to the thirteenth of sixteen photos, Amelia's hopes of finding Leila had been all but dashed. One young woman she'd passed had black hair and fair skin, but the lustrous ebony color was clearly the result of dye.

Just as Amelia was about to make a show of heaving a resigned sigh, the fourteenth picture loaded onto the screen.

The icy caress of excitement lifted the hair on the back of Amelia's neck as she peered down into a familiar pair of vivid blue eyes. Leila's face was expressionless, her raven black hair splayed over her bare shoulders, and a familiar cat-shaped pendant at her throat.

Amelia swallowed the sudden rush of anticipation to take in a steadying breath. As she pulled her awestruck stare away from the picture, she scooted the tablet over to Zane.

Twirling a piece of dark hair around her index finger, Amelia painted a sultry smile on her face. "She's perfect. What do you think, babe?"

If Zane was surprised when he spotted Leila's picture, he did a damn fine job of hiding the sentiment. With an approving wink to Amelia, he slid the tablet back to Dawn.

"She's exactly what my wife is looking for. And, you know what they say." That disarming grin spread across his face. "Happy wife, happy life."

Rather than giggle at Zane's comment, Dawn dropped her chin into one hand and sighed.

The woman's countenance turned Amelia's blood to ice. Were they too late? Was Leila gone? Was she *dead*?

Amelia furrowed her brows and tempered her look of concern. "What? What's wrong?"

Glancing over her shoulder quickly and then back to Amelia, Dawn scooted forward in her seat.

"I probably shouldn't tell you guys this." The volume of her voice dropped so low that Amelia had to lean in to make out her words over the music filling the air.

As Zane snaked a hand beneath Amelia's hair to touch the bare skin of her back, he shrugged. "Well, we aren't going to tell anyone."

Dropping her hand back to the table, Dawn sighed again. "I'm sorry. I should've taken her picture out of there. It's just...there's been a little shake-up at the house these last couple days." She gestured to the photo of Leila. "I wasn't there, but from the sounds of it, this one has been a bit of a handful. A little *too* feisty, if you know what I mean."

"No." Amelia continued to fidget with the same strand of hair, twisting it around her finger. "What does that mean?"

Lips pursed, Dawn shook her head. "Between you and me, I think my...*our*...boss is planning to get rid of her."

A rush of anger brought warmth to Amelia's cheeks. "Get rid of her? Like what? Fire her!" She knew that wasn't what Dawn meant, but she wanted to hear the woman say the words herself.

Drumming her fingers atop the table, Dawn shrugged. "My boss has been doing this for a while, so he has a few methods to correct this sort of behavior. But, well, it really depends. This is business, so he has to take everything into consideration. When it comes to losing money, he's got to decide if he wants to invest to make things profitable again, or if it's better to sell early and cut his losses."

Zane, truly embodying his fake persona as a hedge fund manager, arched an eyebrow eagerly. "So, your boss is thinking of selling her? Any idea what his asking price might be?"

Amelia channeled her anger into another devious smile. "It's not something we've really considered before, but…" she turned to Zane and gave his hand a gentle, suggestive stroke, "maybe it's time to, you know, try something new."

Her proposition seemed to reignite the fire of interest in Dawn's eyes. "Really?"

Zane shrugged as if the notion of purchasing a human being was nothing new to him. "If the price is right, it's something I'd be interested in discussing with the boss, of course. But that being said," he kneaded his fingers against Amelia's back, "we're still looking for something tonight."

Dawn's sly smile returned. "Of course. But just a word of caution." She rested her arms on the table and leaned forward. "If you're interested in buying her, you might have some steep competition. Like I said, my boss has been doing this for quite a while, and he's well-connected. Word has it that he's even got connections with The Shark."

When Amelia drew her brows together, her confusion was genuine. "The Shark?"

As Dawn's lips formed an O, she patted the air with one hand. "That's right, I'm sorry. I forgot you're from New York. I'm not sure who he is exactly, but from what I understand, he's got quite the appetite for pretty young girls. If he's involved, we won't hear from that girl again."

An ominous shroud accompanied Dawn's revelation.

Before their table could lapse into silence, Amelia waved

a dismissive hand. "We can talk more about that with someone at the house, can't we?"

Dawn's expression brightened. Clearly, the woman was glad to be off the subject of The Shark…whoever he was.

"Of course. That would be best, actually. I'm not usually the contact for that sort of thing. Now, did any of the other girls catch your eye?"

"As a matter of fact." Amelia gestured to the tablet. "There was one other."

If she could help it, Leila would never so much as hear of The Shark.

And if she could help it, Dawn would go down right along with everyone else in charge of that house.

11

E milio's phone buzzed and vibrated against the nightstand like a jackhammer boring into concrete. The noise jerked him from his tentative slumber. He had downed a few fingers of bourbon before bed that night, but even with the booze, he was still a light sleeper.

As the prepaid phone vibrated for the second time, his eyes snapped open. He shot straight up in bed and snatched the device off the faux driftwood nightstand.

A soft moan drew his attention away from the flip phone. Clenching the device in one hand as it buzzed a third time, he balanced himself on the plush mattress and eased down to brush his lips against his fiancée's bare shoulder.

Blue light from the nearby alarm clock cast a soft glow over her smooth skin, her hair a dark halo beneath her head. As he planted a gentle kiss on her shoulder, she shifted in place.

"Go back to sleep, Ileana," he murmured.

She pulled the comforter up to her chin. "Mm-hmm."

As she rolled onto her side, Emilio swung his legs off the bed. A few purposeful strides took him off the plush rug and onto the cool hardwood. Stepping into the shadowy hall, he eased the door closed.

"Yeah?" His greeting was terser than he'd intended.

He had to remind himself that his people knew better than to contact him in the middle of the night unless the matter required his urgent attention. Scrubbing one hand over his face, he set off toward the kitchen.

"You need to clear out your house."

That voice. It froze him in place.

He knew that voice. It was not one he ever wanted to hear in the middle of the night.

The Leóne family had snitches all over the city, but the late-night caller was among their most valuable. He'd saved them more grief in the past seven years than Emilio even wanted to consider.

If he said there was a problem, then Emilio knew damn well there was a *big* problem.

Emilio swallowed to return some semblance of moisture to his mouth. "My house?"

"Your whorehouse." The unspoken urgency in the man's clipped tone told Emilio that he didn't have long.

Clasping the granola breakfast bar with one hand, Emilio straightened his back. "Why? How was the location compromised?"

"The club. Your girl, Dawn. She's a little too chatty. A little too eager to close a sale. The Feds are breathing down your neck, Leóne. You'd better get your ass in gear."

The line went dead.

Emilio squeezed his eyes shut and rubbed the bridge of his nose. Snapping the phone closed, he blinked away the blurriness in his vision and glanced at the green glow of the microwave's digital clock. Quarter 'til one in the morning. *Great.*

He raked a hand through his disheveled hair. "Shit!"

Only the hum of the condo's air-conditioner greeted him in response.

Spinning around on one heel, he reopened the phone and dialed Tony's number.

First Leila, and now the Feds. Emilio didn't believe in coincidences, but now wasn't the time to ponder the reason for the sudden scrutiny. Even if he drove straight to the house and shot Leila in the head, he couldn't undo the sudden interest in his prostitution ring.

He had to act. Now! Get his ass in gear, or he and his most profitable business venture would go down in flames.

He could get rid of Leila once they'd relocated the rest of the girls, and his investment was secure.

❄

IF LEILA HADN'T BEEN SO exhausted, she might have noticed the sudden increase in footsteps stomping on the floor above her head. How could she be so tired when she'd barely moved for...how long had it even been? A day, *two days*?

Though she'd initially thought to keep track of the meager sunlight that infiltrated the narrow windows high up in the walls, she stopped caring before the first day ended. An unfamiliar man had come down to provide her water at some point, but through the pounding in her head, Leila couldn't recall much of the interaction.

Of course, he hadn't been kind enough to give her a bottle or a cup. The only hydration she'd been offered since she was dragged down here was a *bowl* of tepid water. Changing position to so much as manage a sip had taken more effort than the drink was worth. Getting out of the cage to use the bucket she was provided was the most movement she was allowed.

As the footsteps above continued, Leila tensed and

relaxed her calf muscles, then her arms, and then, as well as she could, her back.

In one of the fantasy books she'd read, the main character had used the same technique to keep the blood flowing through his muscles. She still wasn't sure how effective the tactic had been, but it was better than doing nothing.

A light tickle along the top of her foot jerked her attention away from recalling the fantasy world. Gritting her teeth, she flicked her ankle to displace the insect.

The first time a bug had crawled over her, she'd nearly hyperventilated. Now, she almost thought of the creepy crawlies as companions. If left down here much longer, she'd start talking to them like some sort of twisted Disney princess.

In all honesty, if it hadn't been for the cage and the dehydration, Leila would have preferred the company of spiders, beetles, and centipedes to the men and women upstairs.

If I ever get out of here, maybe I'll be an entomologist.

Ever since the stranger had given her the bowl of water, her mind oscillated between sheer terror and outright lunacy. Her thoughts might as well have been part of a fever dream. Maybe she'd crack and go insane before the Man in Charge sent one of his men to check on her.

Her eyes stung as she sniffled, but she was so thirsty, she didn't understand how her body could produce tears.

There were stories—both fictional and real-life—of children whose parents locked them in basement cages as a form of punishment. Before being kidnapped, Leila couldn't imagine such an abhorrent act. Now, it was her existence.

When the door at the top of the stairs clattered open, she wasn't sure if the sound was part of her imagination or if it had occurred in the real world. After a faint click, the overhead light fixture sputtered to life.

Her visitor was real.

Fear pushed aside the ache that pounded behind her temples. Her eyes snapped open as quiet footsteps crunched against the dust and debris.

A familiar voice spat out a string of four-letter words.

Leila's eyelids felt like they'd turned to sandpaper as she blinked to clear her vision. "A-Adrian?" The vocalization sounded like it had come from a frog. Coughing in an effort to clear her throat, Leila turned her frightened gaze to the tall man.

He looked stricken. "Yeah, kid. It's me."

His quiet response offered more emotion than she'd heard in the last four years combined. Even as he tempered the worried expression, the glimmer of concern remained in his dark eyes.

The entire display might have been in her head, but her eyes burned from tears she couldn't cry.

He dropped to a crouch and set a plastic bag at his side before unclasping the padlock that held the cage shut. Flinging the door open with a metal groan, he beckoned for her to crawl out.

Her muscles creaked in protest, but Leila gritted her teeth and ignored the pins and needles as blood rushed back into her arms and legs. As she scooted away from the kennel, she took in a shuddery breath and rubbed at the parts of her skin that had been pressed against the metal grate.

Even though the motion felt like it was ripping the muscles from her bones, she couldn't recall a stretch that had ever brought her such relief. As much as she wanted to stand, she wasn't so sure her wobbly knees would support her.

The plastic bag rustled as Adrian dug around inside it. He withdrew his hand and offered her a bottle of water. "Here, drink this. I brought you some clothes to change into."

Uncoordinated as the blood returned to her limbs, Leila reached out and snatched the bottle from his hand a little rougher than she'd intended. With another clumsy jerk, she twisted the top off. The water was room temperature, but in that moment, it was the best beverage she'd ever had. Without pausing for breath, she drained half of the contents.

Adrian gestured to the bag. "Come on, get changed. We need to leave."

Leila took another swig of water before his words registered completely. "Leave? Why?"

He shook his head. "Don't worry about it. We just need to go." As he rose to his full height, he held out a hand to help her to her feet.

Try as she might, Leila couldn't force herself to focus on any singular thought. Why was Adrian here and not the Man in Charge? Why were they leaving? Was *everyone* leaving, or just her?

His eyes were glued to her as he pulled away his hand. "Can you stand?"

She managed to squeak out the word, "Yeah."

He stepped backward to give her space. "I'm going to turn around so you can change. I—"

Leila had her t-shirt over her head before he finished the thought. "Don't worry about it. Modesty is a luxury I lost a long time ago."

He kept his gaze averted as a response.

Finding a small box of wet wipes, she cleaned the filth from her body the best she could before pulling on a fresh pair of leggings next, and glanced to one of the narrow windows. "It's dark. What time is it?"

When Adrian raised his hand to check the time, she caught a glimpse of the chrome handgun holstered beneath his gray jacket. "A little after one in the morning."

The hairs on the back of her neck stood on end. At one in the morning, there were only two possible reasons she would be moved from the basement. Either the cops were onto them, or Adrian was about to take her away from the house to be killed.

Despite downing the bottle of water, Leila's mouth was dry again. Blinking back tears, she turned to face him. "Are... are you going to kill me?"

For a split-second, he appeared to be considering it.

"No. But you're right to be worried. You're on the boss's shit list, kid. You need to listen to him, and you need to watch what you say when his guys are around."

Leila swallowed against the sting of bile. The next words tumbled from her lips before she could think them through. "Maybe they should just kill me and get it over with."

Adrian clenched his jaw. Seconds dragged away in silence as his dark eyes bore into hers.

"They will kill you, but they won't just 'get it over with.'" His expression blanked of emotion. "*They* won't even be the ones to do it. The boss paid a lot of money for you, and he's not going to throw that away. Trust me. I've known him for most of my life."

All Leila could do was stand there blinking stupidly.

His eyes were cold, but an unmistakable fire of anger glimmered behind the practiced countenance. "He'll sell you to someone who will kill you, but not until they're through with you. They'll do things to you that I can't even imagine. And once they've used you up, then they'll kill you. Have you ever heard of a snuff film?"

Leila's stomach turned. Of course she had, but she'd never realized how close she might have been to such a grisly fate.

With a sniffle, she brushed away the tears before they could spill over her cheeks.

A set of pronounced footsteps above snapped Adrian back into action. "Grab your stuff. We need to leave."

Fighting against her sobs, Leila knelt to scoop her dirty clothes into the bag. "What about my room?"

"I got it already. Come on."

Biting down on her bottom lip, Leila followed him to the base of the stairs. If Adrian was trying to scare her into submission, the tactic had been successful.

Death was the ultimate threat to most people, but most people didn't realize that there were fates much, much worse.

12

As Zane slowed the car to a halt at a traffic light, its red glow accentuated the jade green fabric of Amelia's extremely short dress, turning it a shimmering purple.

He had to force himself to keep his attention on the road, especially as his eyes drifted toward her shapely legs.

They had made it two blocks from the club when Amelia pulled out her phone to call Joseph Larson.

Over the course of the night, he'd done plenty of ogling in the interest of pretending to be Amelia's fake husband. The whole ordeal had left him feeling like a creep. He doubted he'd shake the sentiment until he had a chance to take a long, hot shower. Still, he dared to tempt a look at her once more, curious to see her response to Joseph's tinny voice.

"Yeah, we'll be there in fifteen or twenty, depending on traffic." She fidgeted with the hem of her black-and-white striped cardigan. "Okay. Yeah, I'll tell him. You too. Later."

Amelia ended the call and set her smartphone down in the cupholder. "Larson said that SAC Keaton is getting ahold of a judge friend of hers to sign a warrant to search the address that Dawn gave us."

Zane's brow furrowed as the light turned green. "So... back to the office?"

She glanced down to her halter dress and sighed. "I guess, yeah."

He let out a quiet chuckle. "What was that for?"

"A few weeks ago, I used the change of clothes I keep at work after I had that mishap with the fountain drink I got from the gas station." She exhaled loudly. "You know the one I'm talking about."

"Oh, I remember. You picked it up by the lid and spilled fruit punch all over yourself. The best part was that you had to be in court later that day. Is there still a red stain on the carpet under your chair?"

She huffed, but he didn't have to look at her to know the exasperation was feigned.

That was one aspect of Amelia's personality he'd appreciated from the get-go. She rarely took herself seriously. Fluent in self-deprecating comments himself, Zane appreciated another person who used that humor liberally.

One of her chandelier earrings glittered as she brushed the stray hairs from her face. "Okay, for starters, it wasn't just fruit punch. It was mixed with Sprite." She waved a dismissive hand. "But I'll look past your oversight. Yes, that's what I'm talking about, and no, there's not a stain under my desk anymore. The cleaning crew at the FBI office does *not* cut corners."

Laughter continued to bubble up Zane's throat as he switched lanes. "I spilled chili on the carpet in the breakroom once, and when I was trying to clean it up, one of the cleaning crew came in and..." he held up a finger and glanced at her, "I shit you not...they shooed me out like I was a civilian wandering around a crime scene."

She shifted in her seat and yanked at the hem again. "I told you, they don't mess around. But, anyway, yeah, I used my change of clothes a few weeks ago and keep forgetting to bring in a new set. I guess I'll just walk around and execute a search warrant looking like I'm a Bond girl or something."

"You sure you're not violating the FBI's dress code?"

She flashed her middle finger, and Zane nearly choked on his laughter.

"Okay, okay." He patted the air with his free hand. "How long do you suppose we've got on that warrant, anyway?"

Amelia shrugged and tightened the cardigan closer. "I don't know. Guess it depends on SAC Keaton's judge friend. Probably a half an hour, maybe longer? Why?"

He checked his blind spot before merging onto the interstate on-ramp. "You live in Lincoln Park, right? That's not out of the way by much. Traffic's light anyway, and I've still got to prove to you that I don't drive like a grandma."

Zane half-expected her to protest. Instead, she looked relieved. "Okay. I can be in and out of my apartment in a couple minutes." She tugged at the hem of her dress for the millionth time. "I mostly want to put on some pants. Hell, I'd settle for leggings right about now."

He clenched his jaw to keep from blurting out a reflexive compliment about her appearance. She might have been his work friend, but that relationship, being totally professional, might be jeopardized if his words were taken out of context.

The conversation lapsed into silence.

No matter how many times he tried to dismiss the notion that he'd behaved like a creep all night, the feeling persisted. In his logical mind, all their close contact, suggestive touches, and sultry looks had been part of an act.

Why, then, was guilt gnawing at him?

Was it because there was a part of him that had enjoyed being so close to her?

Clearing his throat, he brushed away the thought. "Hey,

I'm sorry. For the…" He gestured awkwardly between the two of them. "For all the…touching."

She remained quiet, and every second of silence cranked his anxiety up another degree.

"Actors do it all the time, right?" She toyed with a stray strand of hair, twisting it around her index finger. "It's not like we had to, you know, do a sex scene on camera or something. We were just putting on an act for a bunch of rich perverts so they'd, you know, think we were just like them."

He kept his gaze firmly on the road. "I gather you don't like rich people very much, do you, Storm?"

With a snort, she propped an elbow on the doorframe. "I don't know what gave you that impression."

He gripped the steering wheel tightly and sent her a sidelong glance. "Not all rich people are terrible, you know."

Amelia shook her head. "Maybe not all of them, but definitely the ones who have more than enough money to wreak havoc on us commoners."

As much as he wanted to change the topic, his curiosity had been piqued. Clearly, she had a story to tell.

"You sound like you speak from experience."

He caught the flash of anger in her expression, and he wished he could retract the comment.

The ire vanished as soon as it had appeared, and the next time he glimpsed her, Amelia had turned her gaze outside of the car. Absently staring into the distance as she toyed with a strand of hair, she appeared detached. No…defeated.

As he turned back to the road, Zane held up a hand. "Sorry, you don't have to say anything to that if you don't want to. I wasn't trying to pry."

"It's fine." She sighed. "My mom died from lung cancer when I was ten. I don't know all the technical terms, but it had something to do with her being exposed to carcinogenic pesticides when she worked in agriculture."

"Agriculture?"

Amelia nodded. "She was an immigrant from the USSR. Her parents, my grandparents, brought her to the States when she was a teenager, a few years before the Iron Curtain fell. I never met either of them. I think they were deported. I'm not sure. Neither of my parents talked much about that side of the family."

"Wow." He wanted to say something more profound but couldn't summon any coherent words.

"Yeah. Mom didn't get official citizenship papers until she was in her early twenties, so she had to work some sketchy jobs to pay the bills. My guess is that the bosses didn't give a shit if their laborers got cancer from the chemicals they used on the crops."

Zane didn't bother to hide his scowl. "No, probably not. I know it's a little late, but I'm sorry about your mom." He scratched the side of his face as he mulled over his next words. "I can't even imagine it, honestly. Not going to lie, I was a mama's boy. Still *am*. But that's what you get when you're raised by a single mother for a few years, I guess."

Finally, a faint smile made its way to her lips. "Yeah, I can imagine."

Zane shot her a quick glance. "I gather that's not all there is to the story, though?"

She sighed and leaned back. Lips pressed tightly together, she shook her head.

Their conversation lapsed into silence once more. He was fully prepared to let the subject rest, to move on to a discussion about Frisbee golf or some other sport that neither of them played.

When he'd made a casual observation about Amelia's distaste for the wealthy portion of the populace, he hadn't anticipated such a heavy response. Truth be told, he hadn't expected an *honest* response.

Maybe they were closer to *personal* friends than he'd thought. After all, they had just spent the night pretending to be a married couple.

They were just pulling up to the intersection at the end of the off-ramp when Amelia finally broke the silence. "Sorry. You asked me a question, and I just started whining. Not really how I meant for that to go."

"Don't worry about it," he replied softly. "And, for what it's worth, it didn't sound like you were whining."

She let out a deep breath, sending rogue strands of hair away from her face, and shrugged. "Well, either way. Thanks for listening to me ramble." She raised a hand to point to an upcoming intersection. "Take a right up here."

He followed Amelia's instructions to a tall brownstone building at the corner of a street of row houses. Though the vintage area wasn't ritzy, the classic architecture and tall trees lent the neighborhood an air of sophistication.

True to her word, Amelia emerged from a door at the other end of the grassy courtyard less than four minutes after she'd hopped out of the car. She'd exchanged her strappy gold stilettos for a pair of canvas sneakers, and the dress with a pair of dark jeans and a concert t-shirt.

As she pulled open the passenger's side door, he squinted to read the text on her shirt. "You've seen Kendrick Lamar live?"

She smiled brightly as she fastened her seat belt. "It's probably the last social event I went to. Right when I got out of the military, but before I started at Quantico. I visited home for a bit, and my friend from high school took me to a show."

"Ah-hah," he said, drawing out the words as he nodded.

A crease formed between her sculpted brows. "What?"

Shifting the car into gear, he grinned. "Nothing. It's just

that you and Larson clashing over music makes a lot more sense now. That guy *hates* rap music."

She snorted as she reached down to her tote. "Oh, believe me, I know. Don't get me wrong, there's a lot of garbage out there. But, honestly, that's the same for every genre."

"True." He glanced in her direction as they pulled out of the neighborhood. "You and Larson must be pretty good friends if you can overlook the fact that your musical tastes are diametrically opposed."

She shrugged and checked her phone for messages. "His music taste is atrocious, but he's a good guy. Larson and I worked on a drug trafficking case together back in Boston. That's how he found out I was from Chicago. I mentioned that I wanted to transfer, and he offered to listen for any spots to open up."

The light turned green, and Zane hit the gas. He wasn't so sure he agreed with her assessment that Joseph Larson was a good guy, but he had learned during his time with Amelia that she was a shrewd judge of character. She'd known Joseph for a year longer than he had, so perhaps there was a redeeming aspect to that man, and his often abrasive personality, he'd yet to see.

Or maybe Larson behaved differently toward Amelia because he had an ulterior motive. Though the sentiment seemed odd, Zane hoped that Joseph's ulterior motive was based on a physical attraction and not something more sinister.

He shook himself from the thoughts.

Sniffing out potential red flags wasn't their goal that evening, and Zane still wasn't sure he'd even *seen* any red flags, though he wouldn't discount the thought outright. Something he would need to keep a watch on as he worked with both of them.

The fact that he didn't care for Joseph Larson's abrasiveness wasn't a warning sign. There were plenty of personality types that Zane preferred to avoid. What mattered most was how well they did their job. And that was the only thing he would base his assessment on, going forward.

Once they were safely back on the interstate, Zane turned his attention to Amelia. "Good work tonight, by the way. You mentioned earlier that you hadn't done a ton of undercover work, but you nailed it."

The confusion on her face was evident, even glimpsing it from the corner of his eye. She opened and closed her mouth before finally pushing the words out. "Oh. Well, thanks. You probably don't need me to tell you this, but you did great too."

Guilt slammed at him again. He'd enjoyed each and every moment. "Thanks. Even though I've done my fair share of undercover work back in D.C., it's still nice to hear a compliment."

Her expression brightened. "How do you know so much about being a hedge fund manager, anyway? I didn't even have to play dumb. I genuinely didn't understand half of what you and that guy Eli were talking about."

As he double-checked the blind spot, he felt his amiable countenance falter. She'd just revealed her disdain for the wealthy elite. How could he possibly reveal his family's financial status?

He shrugged dismissively, hoping that would be convincing enough. "My mom worked in the financial industry."

Turning back to the road, he didn't have to look at Amelia. The burn of her unflinching stare was fixed to the side of his face. "Well, so does my friend, but you guys were talking gibberish, not dollars and cents. What did your mom do?"

Aw, hell.

He considered lying to her. It would be easy enough to say that his mother had managed a bank or that she'd worked in a more obscure department. But Amelia was smart, and even if he convinced her, he'd be lying to someone he considered a friend.

He gripped the steering wheel tighter and sucked in a deep breath. "She was a hedge fund manager."

Anne Palmer hadn't just been a hedge fund manager, she'd been one of the best in a field dominated by men. She'd carved out a place for herself, and then some.

"She was...wait, she was a-a what?" Amelia gawked at him. "Wait, really? Are you trying to, you know, psych me out right now?"

He chuckled, but the sound was more nervous than amused. "No, it's true. She retired before she was fifty, but yeah, she made a killing during her working years."

"Oh my god." Amelia leaned back, slapping a hand over her face. "I'm sorry. You know I didn't mean *all* wealthy people, right? Just...you know...the bad ones. I'm sure your mom is great. I mean, you're pretty cool, and she raised you, you know?"

His laugh came easier this time. "Thanks, Storm. You say 'you know' a lot when you're nervous, by the way." He flashed her a cheeky grin. "Something to, *you know*, remember next time you're undercover."

She groaned. "Yeah, duly noted, Agent Palmer."

He couldn't keep a straight face as he held out a hand in a gesture of concession. "It's okay. Don't worry, I didn't take it personally."

Though her eyes narrowed skeptically, Amelia accepted the handshake. "Fair enough. Let's change the subject then. Here, I've got something to lighten the mood. What do you call a group of rabbits hopping backward?"

"I'm going to regret this, aren't I?" Zane groaned. "What?"

A devious smirk tugged at her lips. "A receding hare line."

His second groan was louder than the first. He gestured to the passenger's side door. "When we get to the intersection at the bottom of this exit ramp, I need you to get the hell out of my car."

Amelia lapsed into a fit of giggles, trying unsuccessfully to stifle them with her hand. "Come on, that was a good one!"

"You know what? I'm just going to pretend that didn't happen, okay?" Even as he fought to keep his expression neutral, Zane shook his head. Amelia Storm didn't *look* like the type of person to crack dad jokes and make ridiculous puns…or giggle…but his overreaction to her corny jokes had become a routine part of their back and forth.

He slowed the car to a stop at the traffic light. "We're about ten minutes from the office, probably more like seven at this time of night. Any word on the search warrant?"

Amelia was still chuckling as she checked her phone. "No, not yet. It hasn't been that long, though."

Tapping a pensive finger against the steering wheel, he growled a few choice words under his breath. "And we're still not sure who runs this house, are we?"

She shook her head. "No, we're not. There wasn't much Larson could dig up on Dawn, considering we didn't have her last name. Same with Viv. Eli and his wife weren't anything special on paper. Larson just sent me a text to say he's still looking at who owns the house at the address Dawn gave us."

Zane pressed down on the accelerator when the light turned green. "Probably won't find much. If these girls are being pimped out by any group that's even close to being a big fish, they'll have put the registration to the house in a fake name. Or a stolen identity. They did that all the time out in D.C. They really like to use dead people's names on the deeds to their property."

"That's about what I figured." Amelia chewed her bottom lip. "We'll serve the warrant with the tactical team. Better to have them with us and not need them than to need them and not have them."

He nodded. "Exactly. With fifteen or sixteen girls there, there's bound to be plenty of goons around the place to keep them in line. But we don't exactly have the luxury of time to stake the place out. From what Dawn said, Leila's got a target on her back."

Leaning against the headrest, Amelia let out a long breath. All the amusement from moments earlier seemed like a distant memory. "True enough."

A glimpse at the digital clock told Zane that they'd left the club only twenty minutes ago. The FBI—not to mention he and Amelia personally—had moved quickly on the information they'd gleaned from Dawn.

For the time being, they would have to hope that their swift reaction would be enough for Leila.

13

A melia had expected the house to be a veritable hive of activity, but when she stepped out of the black sports utility vehicle, the air was quiet. The rickety mansion stood on the corner of the street. A vacant lot separated the house from its closest neighbor—a condemned three-story Victorian.

A humid breeze rustled Amelia's ponytail. Despite the warm temperature that persisted into the late hours of the night, the hairs on the back of her neck stood on end.

"No lights," Zane observed softly.

His voice jerked Amelia from her moment of paranoia. She focused on what could be seen while taking a mental note of what couldn't. "No cars in the driveway, either. I can't hear anything."

"I don't think anyone's home."

Amelia wasn't buying it. She steeled her courage as she turned to face her partner. Where she was determined, he appeared somehow concerned. "What?"

He readjusted his Kevlar vest. "You okay? You look...I don't know. *Intense.*"

She pursed her lips. "It might be a trap."

The cadence of her pulse picked up as the first chill of adrenaline rushed through her body. She'd expected to arrive at the house to a handful of men or women milling about the perimeter, cars picking up or dropping off working girls, and shouts of panic as the occupants realized what was about to happen.

Instead, they were greeted with a still silence, the likes of which was rarely present in a city the size of Chicago.

And to Amelia, unexpected quiet only ever meant one thing.

Tonight wouldn't have been the first time she'd come upon a clever trap.

For a split-second, the faint scent of car exhaust and wet concrete was gone—replaced with the dusty odor of desert sand.

As her thoughts snapped backward in time, she wasn't wearing a Kendrick Lamar concert t-shirt, jeans, and a pair of Vans. She was wearing dusty, sweat-stained camouflaged fatigues. In her hand wasn't a Glock nine-mil, but the Barrett fifty-caliber rifle she'd so often used to back up her fellow soldiers when they forged into the unknown.

The mental image lasted only a fraction of a second, and when she snapped herself away from the reverie, her heart knocked against her ribs like a snare drum.

Not right now, she told herself. *Not in the middle of serving a search warrant. Come on, Amelia. Pull it together. It's a house in the middle of Chicago, not a bunker in the desert of Afghanistan.*

Swallowing past the tightness in her throat, Amelia slowly inhaled a deep breath through her nose. She'd never been shot or gravely injured in combat, but no one left a war zone unscathed. Concentrating on being in the moment often helped her fight against the nerves that might betray her. In and out. One breath after another. Focus.

"Are you sure you're okay?" Zane's tone softened.

Amelia gulped again and forced her lips into a neutral line. She took another breath before responding. "Yeah, I'm fine. I just haven't, you know, eaten anything yet today. With everything that was going on, I just forgot about it."

The excuse wasn't untrue. She *hadn't* eaten, but that wasn't the reason for the overwhelming sense of trepidation flooding her mind as she kept her gaze fixed on the shadowy mansion.

Zane's expression turned quizzical. He reached beneath his vest to retrieve a handful of papers. "Should've said something back at the office. I've got a stash of candy bars at my desk."

Amelia wrinkled her nose. "Candy bars? Are you expecting trick or treaters or something?"

He snorted. "No, but when you forget to eat all day, a candy bar can be a good way to get your blood sugar back in check."

His casual tone worked wonders to ease the tension that had been building in her chest.

She wasn't in the Middle East anymore, and this wasn't a raid on some fortified enemy bunker. This was the FBI issuing a search warrant to the suspect in a kidnapping case that had turned into a human trafficking investigation.

To a layman, the difference wouldn't have seemed soothing. But to Amelia, the latter location was a vast improvement over the former.

With a sigh, she shook her head and turned her gaze back to Zane. "I'm not sure that's how that works, but props for trying, at least."

As Zane opened his mouth to reply, Amelia noticed a shadow move. She swiveled around to face the oncoming threat, finding Joseph Larson instead.

They'd all been outfitted in standard-issue black Kevlar.

However, Joseph's addition to the uniform, an old Saint Louis Cardinals baseball cap, made him stand out from the team. It shadowed his face from the ruddy orange streetlights.

Additional black-clad figures approached from a second SUV, each of them sporting an M4 Carbine and a full tactical vest. They hadn't expected a firefight, but as Amelia had become fond of saying, she'd rather have the tactical team at her back and not need them than need them and not have them.

When Amelia spotted a familiar face, a little more of her anxiety dissipated.

"Agent Harris." Amelia extended a hand to the fellow veteran.

For the first few weeks she'd been at the Chicago field office, Amelia had wondered if Tom Harris was actually an android. Each word the man spoke, every movement he made, and every step he took seemed meticulous. Planned and executed without error.

Then, one afternoon, she'd walked into the breakroom to the tall, muscular man arranging a row of blueberry lemon muffins he'd baked the night before. The more she thought about it, the more the detail-oriented nature of baking seemed like a perfect fit for someone as particular as Agent Harris. Before the end of that day, Amelia had obtained the muffin recipe and sent it off to her sister-in-law, Joanna.

"Storm. Haven't seen you in a while." Harris accepted the handshake. "We're executing a search warrant tonight, yeah?"

"That's right." Amelia gestured to Zane, who waved the paper copy of the warrant for emphasis.

Harris lifted an eyebrow. "It sounded like we expected to run into some trouble when we got here, but I don't see a single light in that house that's on."

"No, I haven't seen one either." Trepidation clawed its

way back to Amelia's thoughts. Clearly, she wasn't the only one who had noticed that the scene in front of them was disconcerting.

Readjusting the rifle in his arms, Harris glanced to a clean-shaven man with dark eyes and jet-black hair. Rather than an automatic rifle, the agent held a matte silver battering ram.

"No worries." Harris smirked. "I think Agent Lopez has the key."

Zane snickered. If battering rams were keys...sure.

First, the muffins, and now Agent Harris was making jokes. *Definitely not an android.*

After Harris issued a few more directives to his small team, Amelia, Zane, and Joseph followed the tactical agents to the covered front porch. Splintery boards creaked beneath the booted feet of a half-dozen FBI agents as they took up their posts to either side of the wooden door.

Zane's easygoing expression had all but disappeared. In its place was the laser focus and cool determination that had no doubt propelled him along in his FBI career.

As Zane raised a fist to pound against the wooden door, Amelia glanced at the tactical agent at her side. Ruddy orange streetlight glinted off the glass of his rifle's optic. She gripped her trusty Glock in both gloved hands, wishing she'd taken the couple minutes to obtain her own M4.

The sudden volume of Zane's voice snapped her from contemplation. "This is the Federal Bureau of Investigation. We have a warrant to search the property. Open up."

As Agent Lopez inched closer, battering ram at the ready, Zane beat his fist against the door again.

"FBI, open up!" With the same hand, he grasped the door-knob and tried in vain to turn it. "You've got until the count of three, and we're breaking down the door." Zane's hand hovered near the wood, but he didn't knock again.

Amelia's pulse rushed in her ears. Did Zane have the same suspicion—thinking they were about to walk into a trap?

No, you're just being paranoid.

As Zane started the countdown, Amelia straightened her back against the wall. At the slight contact with the siding, a flake of beige paint fluttered to the ground beside her foot. A faint sheen of sweat beaded on the brow of the man at her side, but he kept his attention fixed on Zane, Lopez, and the door.

Time crawled as seconds morphed into minutes. Amelia was aware of every little detail in her surroundings. Everything from the rustle of paper as Zane tucked the warrant away and stepped to the side.

Agent Lopez arced the battering ram backward. Amelia controlled the urge to flinch at the resounding crash as metal collided with the aged wooden door. On the second strike, the hinges creaked, and the door burst inward.

In the time it took Amelia to blink, Agent Harris had slipped through the shadowy doorway. Lopez was close on his heels. The second pair of tactical agents strode in after Lopez and Harris, their rifles at the ready.

Finally, Amelia made her way into the murky darkness of the house. She could scarcely make out the built-in wooden shelves on one side of the foyer, but a slat of orange light pierced through the doorway, illuminating the tarnished planks of the floor. A threadbare rug, littered with dead leaves and a few twigs, was splayed across the entryway.

Clenching her jaw, Amelia pressed a button to bring her tactical flashlight to life. A light switch was mounted on the wall just before the built-in shelves, but ever the paranoid one, Amelia wasn't willing to risk flicking switches in a house that might have been occupied by career criminals.

With a quick glance to Zane, she gestured to a hall that branched off to the right.

Joseph Larson stepped past the two of them and pointed to a short corridor and the living area beyond. "I'll check this way."

The plan was for the tactical agents to conduct the initial sweep of the premises, calling out as they cleared each room. In the meantime, Amelia and her colleagues would make their way through the space to look for items that might be useful to their investigation. Last but certainly not least, the crime scene techs were on standby to conduct a more thorough examination.

Honestly, Amelia wasn't sure what to look for. They wanted a sign to indicate that Leila had been there or that she was still alive, but they'd planned for the house to be occupied.

Now that there weren't any suspects to question, what exactly was she supposed to find?

She pushed away the cynical thoughts as the first "Clear" echoed through the house.

Zane tilted his head at her flashlight and then gestured to the light switch. "Why don't you just turn on the light?"

Amelia clenched her teeth. *It might be rigged.* The sentence made perfect sense in her head, but she couldn't bring herself to vocalize the words. Though Zane had worked for the Bureau for more than a decade, he didn't have the same type of military experience as she and Joseph. And, in turn, he didn't have the same type of paranoia.

When Amelia didn't immediately answer, Zane fixed her with a curious look. "Do you think it's booby trapped?"

Rather than answer, she shifted the beam of her flashlight to the hall.

To her surprise, Zane shrugged. "Well, we don't know who we're dealing with yet, do we? You know, the Mexican drug cartels do shit like that. They'll rig explosives to stuff like light switches or tripwires."

Keeping the light trained on the hall, Amelia gawked at Zane with uncertainty. "Wait, you don't think I'm just being a lunatic?"

He shook his head. "No, not really. We know there's a cartel presence in Chicago. Hell, there's a cartel presence in most major U.S. cities. Can't really be too careful if we don't know who we're dealing with."

Amelia nodded slowly. "Right. I mean, I'm mostly thinking of what we used to run into when I was in the military."

Zane followed behind her as she started down the hall. "Some cartels use military tactics, so that's not a bad mindset to have, honestly."

"Thank you," Amelia replied, though the words felt awkward for a reason she couldn't explain.

Drawing his brows together, Zane met her gaze. "What for?"

She blew the stray strands of hair from her eyes with a quiet sigh. "For letting me know that I'm not completely insane."

"Not completely," he quipped. "Honestly, I'm more worried about what ridiculous pun you're going to make next."

Amelia couldn't stop the snort from blaring from her nostrils. "Don't worry, Palmer. I've got plenty of them left. The hare line one is one of my favorites, though."

As they reached the end of the hall, Amelia pointed the flashlight on a set of wooden double doors. One of them had been left open, and a beam of streetlight fell over the dingy wooden floor.

Satisfied that the tactical team had already swept through the room, Amelia flicked the beam of the flashlight around the space as she and Zane stepped through the doorway. A picture window stood at one end of the room, and opposite that, a built-in bookshelf had been converted into a bar. The harsh white glow of the tactical flashlight reflected off shards of glass in front of the makeshift liquor cabinet.

The rest of the room was in similar disarray. Cables dangling from outlets along the walls indicated that electronic devices had been abruptly unhooked and taken away. On a matte black desk, shapes in a thin layer of dust revealed where a monitor, tower, and keyboard had once been. On the other side of the room, wall mounts for computer monitors were bare, their cables dangling along the drywall.

Amelia lowered her Glock and swiped her hand over her sweaty forehead. "They're gone. We aren't going to find anyone here."

"From the looks of it, they left in a hurry." Zane paused to sniff the air. "You smell that?"

As she took in a deep breath, Amelia narrowed her eyes. "Cigarette smoke. Someone was smoking in here. Not long ago by the stench."

Zane's expression darkened. "No ashtrays, though. They took all the butts with them, probably worried we'd run DNA on them or something."

Amelia scoffed. DNA analysis was expensive, tedious, and not as easy to obtain as it appeared on popular television shows. Then again, whoever had taken the cigarette butts was right to do so. Just because DNA tests couldn't be conducted with a proverbial snap of their fingers didn't mean they wouldn't have run the analyses.

Paranoia was always founded in some truth.

As they turned to an open door at the other end of the room, another "Clear" drifted over to them. Amelia kept her Glock at the ready, but her pulse slowed at hearing the confirmation.

"How long do you think they've been gone?" She trained the light on the entrance to the kitchen.

"Hard to say. An hour, maybe."

"An hour?" She hated to think they'd been that close.

"I smoked for sixteen years." He met her curious stare. "That was recent. Someone was *just* in there."

Muttering a string of four-letter words, Amelia stepped onto the pockmarked linoleum and flicked the flashlight around the spacious kitchen. The empty cupboards had all been left in a state of disarray. Rust speckled the handles and hinges, and the white paint had cracked in spots.

In another lifetime, the kitchen might have been luxurious. Now, it was hardly a relic.

Amelia shook her head. "I can't tell if they cleaned out the cupboards or if this is just what this place always looks like."

"All clear!"

Despite her focus and her attention to the environment, Amelia nearly leapt into the air at the sudden pronouncement. She'd expected to hear one of the tactical agents give the *all clear*, but not so close.

Tom Harris stepped into the kitchen from a door that presumably led to the basement. His gaze zeroed in on Amelia and Zane. "We've cleared the house. There's no one here, but we'll have some of the specialists come in to make sure whoever owns this place didn't leave behind any nasty surprises. Once they're done, you can send in the crime scene techs."

Amelia replaced her Glock in the holster beneath her arm. "Thanks, Agent Harris." She pointed to the shadowy doorway from which Harris had just emerged. "That's the basement?"

Harris looked over his shoulder. "Yeah. Not much down there, though. Just some old furniture and a dog kennel."

"A dog kennel? Just one?"

Harris nodded. "It's the only one I saw, yeah."

Zane shrugged. "Guard dog, maybe."

Amelia's gut didn't think so. "Maybe." Without preamble, she picked her way past the island in the center of the room.

Nestled in the corner of a mudroom adjacent to the house's back door, the entrance to the basement was cloaked in as much shadow as Amelia would have expected. Training the beam of light on the narrow steps, she carefully descended into the gloom.

With a click, a second beam of light came to life at her back. "Damn. You see the foundation down here? No wonder the floor upstairs is like walking around in a funhouse."

Once she stepped onto the cement floor, she glanced to the wall in question. Sure enough, the concrete and cinderblocks used to support the house had long since begun to crumble.

Amelia trained her light on an especially saggy area. "Well, if they're running an under-aged trafficking ring, I doubt they're about to hop onto Angie's List and find the best foundation specialists to fix this mess."

"Exactly." Zane pointed to a metal pole not far from the decaying foundation. "Those aren't supposed to be permanent. Contractors use them when they're working on houses, but they aren't a substitute for an actual structural fix."

Though Amelia considered asking him how he knew so much about home repairs, the halo from her flashlight illuminated the metal rungs of a kennel. Well, it resembled a cage more than a kennel.

As she neared the crate, the flashlight caught another metal object on the ground beneath the cage.

"What's that?" Zane asked before Amelia could even form the question in her head.

"I don't know." She dropped down to crouch in front of the kennel. As she trained the light on the silver object, she heard herself take in a sharp breath.

Zane's flashlight snapped to the same spot. "What?"

Its delicate chain caught in the grate, a silver, cat-shaped pendant rested on the dusty concrete beneath the cage. "Holy shit." Amelia's voice was barely above a whisper. "Hup. Leila's cat. The necklace she was wearing in that picture, the same necklace that Gabriella saw when she met her. That's it."

Zane sucked in a quick breath through his teeth. "Shit, it is. That means she *was* here."

With a gloved hand, Amelia pointed to the kennel as she looked up to him. "She was here. *Here.* In this damn dog kennel." She didn't need to look into the bucket at the side to know that it'd been used for a toilet.

Poor, poor girl.

Zane's expression turned stony. "Dawn said that she was on her boss's shit list. Something about her potentially being sold."

Amelia rose to her full height, not wanting to disturb the scene. She would make sure that the first place the crime scene techs examined was this dingy basement.

A whirlwind of thoughts whipped through Amelia's head as she and Zane returned to the kitchen.

Where was Leila now? Had their conversation with Dawn hastened the move?

Worse…was she even alive? Had she been killed after the occupants of the house fled?

If she hadn't been killed tonight, then her hours were numbered. Amelia couldn't place the source of the knowledge, but she was certain that Leila's life was in peril.

At this point, the only real question was how long did she have?

Through the two doorways that led out of the room, flashlight beams flickered as the specialists from the tactical team spread out through the house.

Joseph Larson's attention snapped to Amelia and Zane as they entered the room. "Find anything?"

Even as Amelia met his gaze, Joseph's expression was unreadable. "Yes. Leila was definitely here, and what Dawn said about her being on the boss's bad side is true."

Joseph hooked his fingers in his Kevlar vest. "This place hasn't been empty for very long. They had to have known we were coming."

Amelia had been so wrapped up in the intensity of the search, anxious about improvised explosives, she hadn't allowed herself to fully think through all the reasons for the sudden vacancy. "Someone tipped them off? Dawn?"

Though slight, he shook his head. "No, not like that." He sighed and lifted the Cardinals cap from his head. "I don't think they've got a watchdog in the FBI, but…"

As Larson ran a hand through his hair, Amelia narrowed her eyes. "But what, Larson?"

He replaced the cap and rubbed the back of his neck. "Someone made you."

"What?" The vitriol in Zane's exclamation came as a surprise. "You're saying someone at that club *made us*, but we still got out of there without so much as a sideways glance?"

Joseph held his arms out at his sides. "They didn't have to make you while you were there. They might've made you after you left."

Zane was already shaking his head before Larson finished. "No. Nuh-uh. No fucking way. No one *made* us. Something else tipped these assholes off, and then they ran. It *wasn't* us!"

Amelia's first inclination was to agree with Zane. If they'd been made, Dawn wouldn't have gone through the girls' photos with them. But right now, arguing over how the traffickers had been notified wouldn't change the fact that Leila's life was in danger.

Before Joseph could open his mouth to reply, Amelia snapped up a hand. "Maybe. We don't know. We'll figure it out, but first, we need to figure out where Leila is before they kill her. If they haven't already."

"They won't kill her." Joseph shook his head. "She's worth too much."

"Same difference." Amelia's gaze shifted between Joseph and Zane. "Either way, she ends up dead. Right now, that's what we need to focus on. There are too many question marks. We don't even know who these people *are*."

"And if they took the cigarette butts, I doubt they left anything that's going to tell us."

Zane was right. No matter how it happened, the traffickers had been alerted and had disappeared like the wind. They'd still go through the place with a fine-tooth comb, but Amelia already knew Zane was right.

They wouldn't find out who their suspects were—not with the evidence they had. Leila's days were numbered, but only if she was still alive.

Realization sank like a stone in her stomach.

Amelia knew who would have the information she needed. He'd been front and center in her thoughts for more than half the night.

Ever since she'd made the decision to return to Chicago, she should have known that an encounter with him was inevitable. But if she couldn't avoid the contact, then the least she could do was make it happen on her terms.

Clearing her throat, Amelia clicked off her flashlight. "I've got one more thing I can look into."

Before either man could prod her on the cryptic proclamation, she strode past Joseph Larson and out of the room.

If anyone could point her in the right direction, it was Alex Passarelli.

14

Alex had just finished fastening the top button of his white dress shirt when the rattle of knuckles against the front door jerked him from his silent contemplation. He'd spent much of the afternoon in the personal gym of his spacious condo, beating mercilessly on a heavy bag as he considered Adrian Vallerio's proposal.

Today was day three—the day Adrian expected an answer.

As Alex stepped off the plush rug in the center of his bedroom, he glared suspiciously at the front door. He'd just gotten out of the shower, but he hadn't missed any calls or text messages to advise him that he would soon have a visitor.

His stocking feet made little more than a whisper of sound against the rich hardwood floor as he strode over to a nightstand to retrieve a wood and steel finished forty-five. After he tucked the weapon behind his back, the visitor knocked a second time.

"Just a second!" He shouted the words to be sure the visitor would hear him from the other end of the condo.

Curiosity prickled at the back of his neck as he made his way out of the master bedroom, down a short hall, past the kitchen, and into the foyer.

Each step was measured and silent, and when he arrived at the heavy wooden door, he held his breath in an effort to avoid detection. With one hand along the grip of his concealed weapon, Alex stood to the side as he squinted through the peephole.

All at once, the air burning his lungs escaped in a hiss.

Of all the women who'd come in and out of his life, he'd never expected to see this one again. She'd spent the better part of the last decade haunting his dreams and nightmares.

Had he overdone his workout? Alex blinked a few times and double-checked to be sure he wasn't hallucinating.

There she was.

Though her head was turned down and the hood of a black sweatshirt covered much of her chocolate-brown hair, there was no mistaking her for anyone else.

As if she could read his thoughts, her forest-green eyes flicked up to stare into the peephole.

Though Alex wanted to pause to ask himself *how* or *why* she'd gotten here, he stepped back, flicked the deadbolt, and pulled the door open.

She straightened her back, but she made no move to push down the hood of her sweatshirt.

Her beauty hadn't faded in all those years. She'd always joked about how the Storm family aged well, and how she hoped she wouldn't still be carded at bars when she was thirty.

She was twenty-nine now. He wondered if she still had to show her ID to get into a bar.

But even though she looked the same, all the familiarity stopped at her eyes.

Where once there had been an exuberant sparkle, now

there was the same type of paranoid scrutiny Alex would expect from a seasoned mafioso.

She'd run off to join the military after she left Chicago, and he had secretly followed her life from afar. She'd seen and been through a lot during her time overseas. Clearly, it had made a lasting impression.

Gone was the flirty, carefree spirit. She'd become Amelia Storm, a soldier.

"Alex." Her voice was quiet but firm. As she extended a hand, the recessed light overhead caught the polished gold of an eagle and a shield.

He wouldn't admit it out loud, but when she flipped that FBI badge open, a cold rush of adrenaline streaked through his veins. As she returned the badge to her back pocket, he caught a glimpse of the Glock holstered beneath her arm.

Clearing his throat, Alex mentally reached up in a desperate effort to pull his head from the clouds. "Amelia. It's…been a long time."

The ghost of a smile played across her face. "It has."

He waved a hand at the foyer. "Do you want to…come in?" Summoning words to his lips had suddenly become a Herculean task.

She nodded. "If you don't mind."

Alex stepped aside to make room for her to enter. "No, not at all. I've…uh…got some lemonade and soda. A few beers, maybe. Do you want anything to drink?"

She eased the door closed behind herself. "Sure. Lemonade sounds good."

He smiled half-heartedly as he turned to lead her out of the foyer. After the short hall, he ushered her around the granite breakfast bar to the open-air kitchen.

With both hands jammed in her pockets, Amelia glanced around the sunny space. "Wow. This is nice."

"Yeah. I've lived here for about five years now." He

opened a cherry wood cabinet to retrieve two glasses. "Barring any unforeseen circumstances, I don't plan to move."

"I can see why."

Ice clattered as he prepared the drinks. He spun around and held one out for her.

She accepted politely.

"I made it myself." Alex gestured to his drink for emphasis. "Fresh lemons, even."

What the hell was wrong with him?

"So, it's not the powdered stuff?" After a sip, she offered him an approving smile. "No, definitely not the powdered stuff."

Alex wagged a finger at her. "The powdered stuff is good. Don't hate, Amelia."

She snorted but failed to hide the sound behind her hand. "No, of course not. No hate here."

The subtle upward quirk of his mouth and the ease of their banter gave the impression that they'd only been separated for a couple weeks instead of the decades-worth of distance between them. He'd heard of such a connection—friends apart for years who picked up right where they left off.

But he wouldn't have guessed that an interaction with *her* would go so well.

He'd been heartbroken when she left the city. From the day of that tearful breakup and all the years that had passed since, he had never been able to shake himself from the spree of self-destructive behaviors. When he'd learned she joined the military, the knowledge only added to his confusion and hurt.

Despite his father's reassurances that he was better off without a so-called outsider like Amelia, the ache had taken years to even begin to subside.

Never mind that he'd been ordered into an arranged

marriage with Salvatore D'Amato's only child—a daughter ten years Alex's junior.

The thought left a bitter taste in his mouth. He returned his focus to Amelia as he drowned his sorrows with a long drink of lemonade.

Her keen eyes were already studying him. "I'm assuming you knew about me before I got here, right? Me, meaning my badge."

There was no reason to lie. "Yeah, I knew."

A flicker of indignation twisted her lips into a scowl. "You've been keeping up on me over the years then, huh?" She took another sip of her drink.

Based on the determination in her voice and the steel in her gaze, there was no point in lying. She'd always had a knack for seeing straight through people, Alex included.

"To make sure you were safe," he agreed solemnly.

She chuckled into her glass. "I was in a war zone, Alex. You didn't do a very good job."

Though part of him wanted to be offended at the sarcastic remark, he surprised himself by laughing. As he shook his head, her grin widened.

"No." He combed a hand through his hair. "No, I guess I didn't."

Another silence enveloped them, but some of the tension had left the air, at least.

He'd never taken her to be one to wear black nail polish, and he found himself mesmerized by the dark gloss as she tapped an index finger against the glass. "How have you been?" Her gaze flicked up to take in the luxurious kitchen. "It looks like you're doing well. Financially, anyway."

A coy smile spread across his face. "Yeah. Pretty well."

"How about Gianna? I bet she's raising hell now, isn't she?"

At the mention of his little sister, a hand of ice reached in to grasp Alex's heart. Swallowing the imaginary cotton balls that had been stuffed into his mouth, he weakly shook his head.

Amelia's amused expression faltered. "Oh, no." Her mouth opened and closed a few times. "I...I'm sorry. Obviously, you kept up with me, but I neglected to return the favor. Is she...what happened? Unless you don't want to talk about it."

He set his glass on the granite counter, giving himself a moment to prepare to share the terrible news. "It's okay. It was..." Damn. Would the pain of his sister's loss never end? "Right after you left. She went to visit a friend, and then...we just never saw her again."

When he looked back to Amelia, her knuckles had turned white from her grip on the edge of the counter. Though she'd always had a fair complexion, she was pale as milk.

During his and Amelia's four-year relationship, she had always adored Alex's little sister. Amelia's own sister, Lainey, was only a couple years older than Gianna, so she'd frequently arrange time for the two girls to hang out, watch R-rated movies, and talk about their social lives.

Alex cleared his throat. "How about Lainey? How's she?"

Squeezing her eyes closed, Amelia rubbed her forehead. "She's not great. I'll just leave it at that."

He already knew better than to ask her about Trevor. When Trevor Storm had been killed in his job as a Chicago Police Detective, Alex had seen the headlines printed across newspapers throughout the city.

Once those headlines were printed, Alex suspected Amelia would return to Chicago. He just didn't know how long it would take.

Two years, apparently.

He shook himself from the thoughts. "I'm sorry about your brother, by the way."

She touched her fingertips to her temples. "Thanks. I'm sorry about Gianna too."

One more thing they had in common. Alex might have come from money, but he'd been raised more by the Passarelli family's staff than either of his two parents. His mother was a closet alcoholic, and his father was a domineering ass.

Luca Passarelli had toned down his overbearing presence as Alex had grown older, but as far as Alex was concerned, Gianna had been his only actual family member. Luca was more boss than a father.

In the silence that ensued, Alex steered his thoughts back to Amelia's sudden appearance.

She was right. He *had* known about her position in the FBI before she'd arrived. More than a year had passed since he'd learned of her career choice, and in that year, he'd come to terms with the fact that they were on opposing sides of the law.

"So." The sound of his own voice drew him back to reality. "Mind if I ask why you're here? Are you here on FBI business, or just to catch up?"

She shrugged, and a little color returned to her cheeks. "A little of both, I guess."

Anger and something else he couldn't name made his voice come out sharper than he'd intended. "Start with the FBI business."

Opposing sides of the law or not, he doubted he could bring himself to treat her with the same curt demeanor he usually reserved for law enforcement agents. If she started to ask questions about the D'Amato family, though, he'd have to ask her to leave.

Maybe he should just ask her to leave right now. Maybe he shouldn't have ever let her in the front door. Maybe he shouldn't have even *answered* the door when he saw her.

His heart clamored against his ribs as he waited for her to respond.

Holding up a hand, she set her drink on the counter and reached to the pocket of her hoodie. A dozen what-if scenarios raced through his head as she produced a sheet of paper.

Was it a search warrant? A warrant for his arrest? A warrant for someone else's arrest?

As his pulse spiked, Alex wished he'd dumped half a bottle of rum into his lemonade.

With a slight rustle, Amelia unfolded the paper and slid it across the granite counter. "I'm trying to figure out who he is. He looks Italian, and well," she shrugged, "we aren't having any luck finding him. Nothing in any database, and as far as I can tell, he probably doesn't have a criminal record."

Alex scrutinized the printed photo of a muscular man with a venomous look in his eyes. But the picture wasn't one of his own. He blew out a relieved breath.

"Sorry." He met Amelia's expectant gaze. "He's not a D'Amato guy."

Whatever anxiety he had just released transferred to Amelia's face. "Do you know who he is?"

Alex picked up the picture and peered at the angry man more closely. He didn't have to examine the photo for long before recognition finally came.

"Yeah, actually." He handed her the paper. "I do. He's a Leóne soldier. A cousin of one of the Leóne capos, if I remember right. Giorgio…something." He snapped his fingers. "Giorgio Delusso. That's him."

Rather than relief, paranoia narrowed Amelia's gaze. "Leóne? You're sure?"

"Positive."

Amelia grimaced as she folded the paper and pocketed it. "I took that picture. We're looking for a missing girl, and we were observing the area where she'd last been spotted. Hold on, I've got a flier."

She produced a second paper and handed it to Alex.

As he unfolded the sheet, he was met with a pair of bright blue eyes and a wide smile. The girl in the picture couldn't have been older than twelve or thirteen. Next to what appeared to be a school photo was the same girl, but several years older.

"Leila Jackson." Alex scanned the rest of the text. "Missing for four years? So, this is an age progression picture, right?"

Amelia nodded. "She went missing in Sheboygan, Wisconsin. There's a new Netflix documentary series called *Vanished*, and it's been getting a lot of attention. She's one of the four victims featured. Someone called the tip line and said they saw her in a gas station in West Garfield Park. They said she was a working girl. That's where I took the picture of that guy, Giorgio. He was on guard duty for the working girls around the area."

His anxiety faded. Amelia wasn't here to try to interrogate him about the D'Amato family. She was here to try to find a missing girl.

"If you saw Giorgio there, then that means Leóne runs that spot." Alex leaned against the counter. "They aren't good at sharing. If that's their territory, then they won't let anyone else do business there. If this girl was working around that area, then that means she works for Leóne."

Amelia groaned low in her throat. "We found the house where they'd been keeping her. If I gave you the address, do you think you could tell me if it's in Leóne territory?"

"Yeah, definitely." Alex took a quick drink from his depleting glass as Amelia fiddled with her phone.

She handed the device to Alex, and he zoomed in to the area on the map that she'd pinned.

He returned the phone almost as quickly as he'd accepted it, meeting her eyes with certainty. "Yeah, that's their territory."

As if a spell had broken, her cool veneer crumbled as she spat out a string of obscenities that would have brought a flush to a sailor's cheeks. "We're looking for an organized trafficking ring. I knew it."

"Sex trafficking has been the Leóne family's bread and butter for years." Alex shook his head in distaste. "They're pretty secretive about the operation, but I can't say I'm all that surprised to hear that they're kidnapping little kids in different states so they can pimp them out here in Chicago."

A scowl further darkened Amelia's expression. "No, I can't say I'm surprised, either. I've always hated those slippery bastards."

Alex fought to keep the proud smile from showing.

"One more thing I was wondering about." She held up a finger, punctuating her statement.

Though he wasn't sure he wanted to address another question, he nodded. "Sure."

She tugged at the ends of her dark hair, hesitating as if trying to figure out how to ask her next question. "We heard something from a woman who works for them, some woman named Dawn. I never got her last name, but that's not important. She said that this girl, Leila, had been... misbehaving." Amelia looked as if she'd tasted something bad. "She said that the man who ran that house was planning to sell Leila to someone called The Shark. I've never heard that moniker before. Have you?"

Alex felt like he'd taken a blow. "Yeah, I've heard of him."

She licked her lips, excitement creeping back into her expression. "He? He's real?"

Alex scratched the side of his unshaven face. "Yeah, he is.

We…" he tapped himself on the chest, "don't deal with him. At all, for any reason. I don't even know who he is, and I don't think anyone else in the D'Amato family does, either."

Amelia kept her skeptical gaze fixed on him.

In answer to her unasked question, he held up a hand. "Believe me, if I knew who he was, I'd tell you. Some of the stories I've heard about him." He met her gaze full on. "He's dangerous, and his pockets are deep. He gets off on torturing and raping women, or at least that's what I've heard. If this Dawn woman said that the Leónes planned to sell Leila to him, then you need to find her as soon as you can."

Pinching the bridge of her nose, Amelia exhaled a loud groaning sigh. "They were gone when we got to that house. Somehow, they knew we were coming."

Probably because they have someone on the inside. Alex kept the thought to himself.

She blinked and glanced back at him. "Do you have any idea where they might have taken the girls in that house?"

Alex was shaking his head before she'd finished the question. "No, I don't. I only knew that address was in Leóne territory because they've been in that area for decades. They keep a low profile, though. I wouldn't have guessed they were running a prostitution ring around there. But aside from the areas where the Leónes actually sell their…product, territorial lines are pretty blurry."

"Shit." She brushed the hair over her shoulder. "Okay. Thank you. And don't worry, I'll make sure none of this comes back to you. I kept my face out of view of the cameras in this building too."

Beautiful and smart too. He allowed a ghost of a smile to cross his face. "Thanks, Amelia. Just let me know if you need anything else. And I doubt I need to tell you this, but…watch your back. You know how ruthless the Leónes can be."

"Believe me. I was more relaxed in the mountains of Afghanistan than I have been since this case picked up."

He wanted to laugh at the comment, but at the same time, he wanted to wrap her in a bear hug to make sure she stayed safe.

They said their goodbyes after Amelia gave him her business card. Though the parting words were markedly less awkward than their greeting, he still felt like a part of his brain had been activated after it had sat dormant for years.

Ever since Gianna had disappeared, Alex hadn't worried about anyone other than himself. Sure, he had a handful of friends, but they were all hardened D'Amato soldiers.

He had to remind himself that Amelia wasn't just an FBI agent, nor was she a grizzled mafioso. She was a ten-year veteran of the United States Armed Forces.

The various criminal syndicates across the country often used the word "war" when they described a period of contention amongst themselves, but Amelia had seen *real* war.

The carefree, bubbly young woman he'd known more than a decade earlier had become a hardened soldier.

As Alex sunk into the center cushion of his sectional couch, his vacant gaze fixed on the dark form of the television.

He wanted to know why she had left in such a rush. Why she'd ended their relationship out of the blue. She'd left Chicago a day after ripping his heart out. Had there been something else forcing her hand?

Scrubbing a hand over his face, Alex groaned. That was a conversation for a different day. Right now, he had a certain Leóne lieutenant to contact.

Though he'd been unsure how exactly he would have used Adrian's information to dismantle the Leóne trafficking ring, he'd now been provided with a solution.

By himself, or even with the help of the D'Amato family, the Leónes would have been difficult to take down.

But now, he knew someone who could. Someone who had a vested interest in seeing Emilio Leóne and his miserable family's heads on a pike.

15

I'd spent most of the day walking the deck of the *Equilibrium*, discussing party details with an event planner I'd hired many times in the past. The young man was enthusiastic but not overly chipper. His demeanor was cool and professional.

Truth be told, I could swear I saw a little darkness in him. Maybe he could sense the darkness in me, and that was why he didn't hesitate to fly out to the Florida coast from his home in Saint Louis.

Maybe he was just keen on the zeroes at the end of his paycheck. Either way suited me just fine. Darkness or not, I wasn't about to invite him to any of my *real* parties.

At the thought, I chuckled quietly to myself. After draining the rest of my iced tea, I gazed out over the sprawl of the Atlantic Ocean. The sun hung low in the horizon, lending the shifting waves a golden orange quality, like topaz strewn across a dark velvet cloth.

The clatter of a glass against the wooden tabletop reminded me that I wasn't alone.

Lifting an eyebrow, I glanced at my old friend. "Is everyone gone?"

Mark leaned back against the cushioned booth. "The event planner will be back tomorrow so we can wrap things up. You said tickets sold out, right?"

Smiling, I nodded. "Right. We're toning it down from your usual fundraiser. That way, we can report a higher percentage of funds donated and make Stan's competitor look like a damn liar."

Mark's smile turned devious, matching my own. "Well, statistically speaking, it's already an uphill battle for a challenger to beat an incumbent in a senatorial primary race. Stan's making it seem like this Ben Storey guy is a big deal, but I looked him up. He's a small fish."

I rattled the ice cubes in my glass. "He is a small fish. And, well...you know what they call me, right? The Shark."

Mark's laugh sounded closer to a snort. "Just what we need to take a nice big bite out of Storey and make sure Stan's got another term serving the great state of Illinois."

I grinned. "Speaking of Illinois, you had news for me. Something from Chicago?"

Mark straightened in his seat. "Right. I almost forgot, yeah. Emilio Leóne reached out to me and asked if you could get in touch with him. It sounded like he had a girl you might be interested in."

"Really?" I shifted in my seat to retrieve the burner phone from the pocket of my black slacks. "Weren't we just talking about Emilio the other day?"

Amusement glittered in Mark's eyes. "We sure were. When we met with those Russians."

I snapped my fingers. "That's right. What about that girl? Is she still refusing to eat?"

"Yeah, she is. She's acting like a wild animal."

"I had a feeling I'd regret buying her." Pissed that I hadn't followed my instincts, I scrolled through the numbers in my prepaid phone.

Then again, I'd been preoccupied since unloading her in the lower level. Perhaps she was only being obstinate because I hadn't taken the time to properly introduce myself.

Tonight was as good a time as any. I hadn't spent any quality time with my playthings in almost a week. The three girls had one another, but I needed to make sure they didn't get any ideas while I was busy.

As I selected Emilio's number from the list of contacts, I shifted in my seat and crossed my legs to hide the bulge I knew was growing. With any luck, the call with Emilio would be quick.

In the middle of the second ring, the line picked up.

"Yes?"

Emilio's familiar voice brought the smile back to my face. I'd never met Mr. Leóne in person, and even though I questioned plenty of his decisions, I appreciated the man's tenacity. "Emilio, it's been a while, hasn't it?"

There was a slight pause before he replied. Perhaps he had shooed someone out of the room. "Mr. K, it has been a while. You got my message?"

"I did. My chief of staff just passed it on to me. What do you want to discuss?"

Mark shoved himself up to his feet and gestured to the wooden deck before he flashed me a thumbs-up.

The hand signals were vague, but I knew what he meant. Apparently, I wasn't the only one who wanted to spend some time below decks.

As Mark bounded down a set of stairs, I turned my attention back to Emilio. "Good news, I hope," I added as an afterthought.

Emilio's dry laugh reminded me of a couple of rocks grating together. "Yes, it is good news. Well, I hope you'll see it as good news. Bad news for me often means good news for you, you know?"

"I follow."

Bad news meant Emilio was having trouble with his prostitution ring.

Which means I get the opportunity to help him remedy that issue.

"I've got a girl you might be interested in."

"That's what I was told, yes." I was more eager than I wanted to let on. "Tell me about her? Bad news first, if you don't mind."

"Of course. The bad news is that she's been...troublesome. She's shown disrespect to my men. I'm working on correcting that behavior right now, but that brings me to another predicament. I've always been upfront with you, Mr. K, and I don't plan to stop now. This girl, she's been noticed by the Feds."

My eyebrows shot up. "The Feds? Well, that really is a predicament, isn't it?" *Maybe for Emilio, but not me.* Still, I didn't need to let Emilio know the cards that were in my hand. "What makes you think I'd be interested in a girl with Federal heat on her?"

"I know, I know." Emilio sighed with deep frustration. "I realize that she comes with baggage. But let me send you a few pictures of her. She's very, *very* pretty. I think she's just what you've been looking for."

I stood as my excitement grew. "Describe her."

"She's on the thinner side. About five-six or five-seven. Sixteen years old, with a healthy set of tits and clear skin. She's got those full, pouty lips and a porcelain complexion. Her eyes are blue, and her hair is naturally black. Hasn't been dyed."

Maribel.

I reached down to readjust myself as I sat up straighter.

"Really? That sounds wonderful. You know what? Go ahead and send me those pictures."

"I'll send them right now." The faint clack of a keyboard followed. "There. I sent them to this number."

"Perfect." I pulled the phone away from my ear just as the message notification flashed across the screen.

Emilio's description hadn't done her justice, and I suspected the low quality of my flip phone hadn't, either. I growled in deep appreciation as I scrolled through each picture.

"Did you get them?" Emilio asked.

My pulse rushed in my ears as I raised the phone back to my face. "I did, thank you. How much do you want for her?"

"Well." Emilio paused, making a show of considering his options. "I might have a couple other interested buyers, especially considering the fact that I'm going to knock a little off the price since the Feds are looking for her."

His deviousness was to be expected. Still, I couldn't help the surge of anger his threat of *interested parties* created. Whether they were real or imagined, it was the oldest and lamest play in the book. But this new girl reminded me of Maribel, and dammit, if that wasn't my weakness. "Of course. Explore all your options."

"I'm having my physician take a look at her tomorrow." Emilio sounded like he was describing the sale of a horse. "I ought to have the results by Monday. That's when I'll send word to my other clients."

I almost laughed. "An auction, huh? Not a bad move with a girl like that." The comment was sincere. Had I been in Emilio's position, I'd have done the exact same thing. Maybe the man wasn't as hopeless a businessman as I'd once thought.

"I'll get a few more pictures to you tomorrow." I could hear the grin in Emilio's words. "I'm going to make this a quick one, though. I'll start accepting bids for her after I have her medical results, and I want to push everything through within a few days."

"Of course. I'll look forward to the pictures."

Though neither of us said the words aloud, both Emilio and I knew who would win Monday's auction.

She would be mine, and once she was mine, there was no way the FBI would ever find her. Mine until the day she died. Maybe, just maybe, she'd even bear my children.

The possibilities for pretty little *Mirabel Two* were endless.

16

L eila was in the dark, literally and figuratively. Unlike the basement in the shabby old mansion, the dungeon in this new house had no windows. She was locked in the last cell in a series of six, three on either side of a concrete walkway. Pulling her knees to her chin, she bit back tears as she considered the small blessing of no longer being crammed in a dog kennel.

Though Adrian hadn't elaborated when they'd left the old house, Leila had gathered from the tense postures of the soldiers and the skittish demeanor of the girls that they'd fled the mansion because the cops were closing in on them.

The second house had been in even worse shape than the first. The wood floor was splintery and cracked, and the air-conditioner was either broken or nonexistent. She'd been certain she would be thrown in the basement, and she'd braced herself for the worst.

Instead, she'd been ordered into another car with her meager belongings, blindfolded, and then driven to a new location. The men who had accompanied her hadn't removed the bag over her head until the iron of her cell door clattered shut. A little while later, one of the men returned to take her for a shower.

With no idea if it was day or night, she was here, curled in the fetal position atop the thinnest mattress she'd ever seen. Where the floor of the old house had creaked beneath the footsteps of the upstairs occupants, here, however, she heard nothing. Well, aside from the occasional skitter of a bug or mouse, the painful groan of her stomach, or the beating of her heart.

Beyond exhaustion, Leila was finally ready to let sleep claim her. Her eyelids drooped until a sharp clamor jerked her from the tentative slumber.

With a gasp, she sat bolt upright, looking desperately for the source of the movement in the gloom beyond her cell.

Nothing.

Had the sound been in her mind? Was she finally losing it?

She snapped her head in the direction of a light click. A sickly glow from old fluorescent tube lights flickered a few times before fully illuminating the overhead light fixture. Until that moment, Leila hadn't even known there *were* lights down here.

The buzz of a second fixture followed the first, and despite the weak illumination, she squinted at the sudden change.

"Wh-who's there?" Her voice sounded like a dying frog.

"How do you like your new accommodations?" The Captain stood just beyond the glow of the lamps, but she didn't need to see him. His voice turned her blood to ice.

Adrenaline pumped through her veins. The sudden surge was like fire licking at each nerve in her body. Her heart thundered, beating against her chest as if it meant to punch a hole straight through and escape. If only she could. Even without the sudden rush of lightheadedness making the room spin, she was still trapped in this damn cell.

Blinking repeatedly against the meager light—though to her, it might as well have been a supernova—she forced herself to focus on the shadowy figure of The Captain.

Leila opened and closed her mouth as she willed the words to her dry lips. "I-I'm sorry." This time, she sounded less like a frog and more like a mouse.

He clucked his tongue and slowly shook his head. "I know you are. But my question is, how sorry are you? Because something tells me you aren't sorry enough."

She swallowed against the lump in her throat. "I am. I mean it. I swear. Please."

A light metallic click was followed by the creak of hinges as the cell door swung inward. "Please, what?"

Looking up to meet his gaze, she bit her lip to stifle a sob. "I'll do whatever you want. I'll work the streets, I'll make you money. And I'll be nice to all the men. Anything. Please, just let me out of here."

With a sigh, he closed the door and dropped down to sit at her side. "You know something that my father always used to tell me? He used to say that actions speak louder than words. You know what that means, right?"

Leila nodded weakly.

He rested a hand just below the hem of her black running shorts. "I'm sorry, sweetheart. I'm sorry I had to do any of this. You're much too pretty to be sitting down here in a basement, but your actions left me with no choice. You know I wouldn't have let Giorgio hurt you, right?"

Another spike of adrenaline urged Leila to run, but she was too tired, weak, and hungry to do any of that. Besides, that would just piss him off and earn her an even worse punishment. She dropped her head submissively. "I know. But you weren't there."

He squeezed her thigh. "No, but Adrian was."

At the mention of Adrian, the hairs on the back of her neck stood on end. She felt the heat of The Captain's stare boring into the side of her face. Licking her lips, she forced herself to turn to him.

"Adrian looks out for you girls when I'm gone. You know that, right? You don't think he'd have let Giorgio hurt you, do you?"

Tears stung the corners of her eyes. "No, I don't."

A slow smile spread across his face. "That's better."

"Are you going to sell me?" The words spilled from her lips like blood from a wound. "Adrian said that if I-I wasn't good...then you'd sell me. But you don't have to. I'll be good, I promise."

He looked surprised, almost curious. "Adrian said that, huh?"

She didn't have the mental capacity to lie. Not right now. "Yes. He said that I needed to behave. That I needed to be nice to you and your men."

His expression softened. "Well, he's right. He was telling you that because he's looking out for you. And he's looking out for me. Adrian's a good man, don't you think?"

Biting down on her tongue, Leila nodded.

He patted her thigh. "Actions speak louder than words, sweetheart. I believe you when you tell me that you're going to be better behaved, but I want you to show me."

Her fingers began to tremble. "How do you mean?"

As he rose to his full height, he dropped both hands to his belt. With a light clink, he undid the clasp. Bile threatened to claw its way up the back of her throat and into her mouth.

But by now, she'd learned better. There was no point in protesting or making an effort to show these men the error of their ways. All they wanted was obedience. They wanted her to be still and complacent so they could fulfill the sick desire that drove them to run this despicable place to begin with.

She licked her dry lips, trying to bring some moisture back to them. "Okay. What do you want me to do?"

His mouth twitched in victory. "Take off your clothes. We don't have much time left together, but I intend to make the most of it."

Even in her disoriented state, Leila didn't miss the implication of his cryptic statement.

Maybe, just maybe, if she did as he asked, he would feel compelled to keep her here.

As she'd once heard her brother say, better the devil you know.

She could only hope that her situation wasn't beyond salvaging.

17

I took in a deep breath, savoring the salty tinge in the air as the *Equilibrium* set off to open waters. With a contented sigh, I leaned against a rail that overlooked the deck below. The waning sunlight glittered off polished glass as I took another sip of wine. I couldn't honestly recall the name of the aged red, but I knew it cost at least four figures.

No matter how hard I applied myself, I could never commit the names of different wines to memory. And if I was honest, there was a good chance I couldn't even tell the difference between a fifteen-dollar bottle and a six-hundred-dollar brand.

However, the wealthy socialites and politicians with whom I kept company couldn't get enough of the bitter drink. They'd ramble on about vineyards, fermentation techniques, historical wine aficionados, and I'd smile and nod.

More often than not, they had no intent to educate me. They merely sought to make themselves sound official and important.

As much as I enjoyed charming and manipulating the powerful men and women who attended the elaborate fundraising celebrations I hosted aboard the *Equilibrium*, I was always struck with a certain sense of relief when they left.

That wasn't to say that I was worried about them discovering any of my secrets. In fact, there were plenty of regulars who indulged in the same taboo pleasures I so enjoyed.

Fortune 500 CEOs, American and foreign politicians, and the occasional celebrity, nearly all of them had skeletons in their closet. The fact that they banded together to celebrate money they'd raised for a charity that combated human trafficking was an amusing irony.

Sure, some of them were unwitting, but I doubted their backgrounds were clean, either.

Everyone had their secrets. Everyone sought to hide the dark part of themselves for fear the outside world would shun them if they knew the truth.

Me? I didn't care what others thought of me. I only maintained my appearance because it made my life easier. But at the end of the day, none of it really mattered.

Tonight, however, my good spirits were unrelated to the celebration that had ended a half-hour earlier. Unbeknownst to any of the attendees—save Mark, of course—I had been informed my bid had just bought me my lovely Maribel Two.

I couldn't help smiling at the possibilities. Over time, perhaps she might even eclipse the original.

I'd spent the last week negotiating with Emilio Leóne to outbid the handful of other potential buyers who had made offers for Leila Jackson. The price had ended slightly higher than I anticipated, but money was of no concern to me.

All that mattered was that she was mine. And the day after tomorrow, she'd be here.

Mine to do with as I pleased.

Movement drew my gaze sideways, to a tall man with a neatly styled crop of chestnut brown hair and steel-gray eyes. The years had been kind to Stan Young. Even with a five o'clock shadow, he looked closer to his mid-forties than his mid-fifties.

I raised two fingers from my glass. "Evening, Senator Young. I trust you enjoyed yourself?"

Loosening the pale green tie around his neck, Stan shrugged. "I doubt I enjoyed it as much as my wife did. She loves these damn things."

I chuckled quietly. "Cynthia sure seems in her element when she's at these events. Danielle never really cared for parties."

Stan nodded at the reference to my ex-wife. "Cynthia used to say the same thing about her, actually. I think she felt bad for her."

I took another sip of my expensive wine. "Well, Danielle's happier now, I'm sure."

Believe it or not, the statement was true. I'd gone out of my way to treat Danielle like a queen, and I knew beyond a shadow of a doubt that she'd never had so much of an inkling that anything was amiss. Though she'd join me on the *Equilibrium* while we were docked or close to shore, she never cared to travel too far out into the water. And at the end of the day, she and I decided that the paths for our respective futures were just too different to reconcile.

The decision had been amicable, and I'd ensured the divorce process was as painless for her as possible. Even now, neither of us harbored any ill will toward the other.

Stan leaned against the railing at my side. "So, what's this gift you said you've got for me? If it's another watch..." His mouth curved into a scowl as he adjusted the silver band around his wrist. "I swear to god, it better not be another watch."

My mood was too pure to be offended. "Definitely not a watch." I beckoned him to follow me as I polished off my wine. "A little something to help with the stress of your re-election campaign. Didn't you say that there was someone challenging you in the primary this year?"

Stan's lip curled in disgust. "Yeah, some Army vet named Ben Storey. He's been a real pain in the ass. Blue collars in Illinois sure love to see a vet running for office."

"Well, if you need any help with it." I left the offer open-ended.

Devious amusement washed over his face. "I've got it under control for now, but if that changes, you'll be the first person I get ahold of."

On the way to the set of steps that led to the lower decks, I deposited my emptied glass on the wooden bar in the center of an enclosed dining area.

I waved, acknowledging a member of the ship's crew, as Senator Young and I descended the three floors to the deck that was just above the lowest. A short hall off the landing ended in a heavy metal door that was guarded by a handful of state-of-the-art monitoring devices. Whenever I hosted a party or entertained guests aboard the *Equilibrium*, one of my trusted security staff manned the desk. Otherwise, I let the expensive surveillance system do the bulk of the work.

The crew of the ship knew to avoid the second-lowest deck, but I was fairly sure they thought the floor contained material wealth or sensitive data. And in some respects, they were right.

I knelt for an ocular scan before swiping my access card over an electronic lock. With a faint click, the magnetic locks disengaged.

After pushing past the heavy door, I blinked to let my eyes adjust to the artificial light glowing overhead. We made our way past another security station. The guard looked up, past the trio of monitors on his desk.

As he raised a hand in greeting, the sleeve of his gray

jacket slid down just enough to expose the start of the military tattoo on the inside of his forearm. Devin Childress was a veteran of the Special Forces, and his appetite for pretty young girls was unrivaled by all but a few. The man had been the perfect selection to head up security for my more sensitive endeavors.

Once we returned Devin's greeting, Stan and I passed through another round of locked doors and into a room that served as a foyer. The second set of doors weren't as imposing as the first, but I liked the privacy they offered.

We each deposited our phones, wallets, and any other accessories into a locker before we set off for a well-lit hall. Almost every door at this level of the *Equilibrium* was sealed with a biometric locking mechanism. Only those I granted permission to could access the area. The installation had cost a small fortune, but based on the number of close calls I'd had over the years, it had been a worthwhile investment.

On one side of the hall was a series of cells, each walled off from the other with a waist-high concrete ridge and a pane of bulletproof glass. Like the previous areas, the rooms here were sealed with magnetic locks. A sturdy concrete pillar separated the fronts of the cells and housed the locking mechanism for the doors.

I gazed out at my play space, six individual rooms. All but two were occupied. Just like any standard prison, each section sported a bunk bed, a steel toilet, and a sink.

Stan crossed his arms over his chest. "Only four right now? That's unlike you, Brian."

I settled my gaze on a familiar brunette and shrugged. "Hard times, I guess." I kept the bit about my newly acquired Maribel to myself. No one would touch her but me.

"I'm guessing one of these is for me?"

When I turned back to the senator, he lifted an eyebrow.

Rapping my knuckles against the glass of the brunette's

cell, I returned his curious expression. "I know you like the girls with a little more experience. This one's Russian, one of Ivan's girls."

Stan fixed his gaze on the girl as he uncrossed his arms and stepped forward. "Russian, huh?"

"Thought you'd enjoy that." I entered in a six-digit code and pressed my thumb to the bottom of the keypad beside the brunette's door. Panic flickered in her eyes as her gaze shifted between Stan and me.

With a light click, the magnetic lock disengaged, and the girl's body went rigid.

She'd been jumpy since I first brought her to the *Equilibrium*, but the anxiety today was different. The unabashed fear to which I'd grown accustomed had been tamped down, replaced with a sentiment I couldn't immediately identify.

As I crossed the threshold, I could feel Stan's curious gaze on the back of my head.

The air in the cell was all wrong.

I caught a whiff of perspiration mixed with the fresher smell of the bar soap the girls used when they showered. Normally, the light scent faded not long after the girls washed up, but inside the Russian girl's cell, citrus and cedar cut a swath through the usual musk.

A faint hiss accompanied the door as it started to swing closed. When I turned my gaze to the young woman huddled in the center of the room's twin-sized bunk, time froze.

Her eyes—a pristine shade of pale blue—were bloodshot. Wild. Even from that distance, I could see the tremor in her thin shoulders. Though my first thought was that she had consumed a stimulant, I dismissed the idea as soon as it formed.

Anyone near this part of the *Equilibrium* was trustworthy. No one so much as approached the area unless they'd been under my direct supervision for five years or longer. I made exceptions occasionally, but those were mostly for paying guests. There was no one on board who would have dared smuggle drugs to my girls.

As I neared, my feet felt as though they trudged through molasses. The air was still wrong. The scent was too fresh, too *sharp*.

The rush of movement started in my periphery as I spared a glance to where Stan stood outside the cell.

Through my never-ending consultations with optometrists, I'd learned that the corners of the human eye were the most receptive to changes in light and movement. An evolutionary adaptation that had served the ancestors of modern humans well when they were lower on the food chain.

A surge of adrenaline rushed through my bloodstream as I took a swift step backward, pivoting to face the Russian girl as I moved. A blur of mint green and white whipped in front of me. Had I not moved, the swipe would have severed my carotid artery.

Within minutes, I would have bled out on the pristine concrete floor.

Before she could retract her arm to attempt a second strike, I snapped my hand forward, clamping down on her wrist. I squeezed until I thought the tips of my fingers might break skin.

As I shifted to the side, I kept hold of her wrist. The faint snaps of popping cartilage and her subsequent cry barely registered as I twisted her arm behind her and up between her shoulder blades. A light clatter told me that her makeshift weapon had fallen to the floor.

Good. Best to get this over with quickly. I appreciated a spirited girl, but I had my limits.

With my free hand, I took hold of a chunk of her dark hair and shoved her with tremendous force.

Her yelp of surprise was cut short, replaced by the echoing thud as her head slammed into the sturdy glass. She made a noise, a squeak maybe, or a gasping breath, and I smashed her head against the window once more to silence her.

I'd tuned out her pained cry right along with the unpleasant sensation of the force of the blow reverberating up my arm. I still hadn't made note of her weapon. My focus was singular, my purpose clearly laid out.

Until I noticed Stan waving to get my attention and knocking on the glass.

The sight of my friend and colleague of nearly two decades ripped me from the tunnel vision with the force of a Mack truck.

"Brian!" He waved a hand to ensure he had my full attention.

Tightening my grip on the Russian girl, I blinked a couple times before I glanced down to the floor. There it was, beside the doorway, the bar of green soap that had been carved to resemble a handle. The harsh fluorescence caught the polished shine of the triangle-shaped piece of ceramic tile that had been diligently molded to the top of the soap.

A shiv. The little bitch had tried to cut open my throat with a damned shiv.

The two heavy blows had left her breathless, dazed, and bloody but still alive.

Good. Now that I'd returned to my senses, I knew her departure from this world wouldn't be a pleasant one.

As if he could read my mind, Stan rapped against the window again. "Hey, you said you only had four girls, right? Three others aside from her?"

I didn't realize mathematics was your strong suit, Senator.

I bit back the irritable remark. Stan was my good friend,

and I meant him no ill will. But I could feel the sting of rage as it clawed at me.

Clearing my throat, I finally responded, "Yes. That's right."

Stan's expression turned devious. "And this one was mine, right?"

My anger faded as I caught onto his meaning. "That's right."

Stan rubbed his hands eagerly. "With this whole election cycle, especially with Ben Storey breathing down my neck, I really could use a night to blow off some steam. The last thing I need is to make a smartass comment to a reporter that's getting on my nerves." He waved a hand at the Russian. "You've still got the room with the binds that hang from the ceiling?"

With a pitiable moan, the girl thrashed against me. But my grip was iron, and I outweighed her by close to eighty pounds. I wasn't passionate about fitness, but I made a point to stay in shape.

I tightened my grip on her hair and shoved her face into the window, but the force behind the motion was nowhere near what I'd used for the first two blows.

The power was heady. "Yes."

"Perfect." Stan clapped his hands together as if he'd just finished speaking to a room full of his constituents. "If it's not too much trouble, I could use some pliers and an icepick."

I do like the way that man thinks!

"Let me see what I can do."

18

A s Amelia slipped through the narrow opening in the doorway, the blinds clattered softly against glass. For a split-second, she thought she was late to the scheduled briefing. When three familiar faces turned to regard her, she glanced reflexively at the clock.

On a normal day, she arrived alongside Zane or Joseph, but both men had beaten her to the conference room today. Even the Organized Crime Division's Supervisory Special Agent Spencer Corsaw—who was notoriously late to meetings—had beaten her to the briefing. As had Jasmine Keaton, who was studying something on her iPad.

No, Amelia was on time. *They* were early.

Amelia shuffled the manila folder to her other arm and nodded a silent greeting. For the past week, she'd unearthed any and every piece of information she could find about Giorgio Delusso. According to the Department of Motor Vehicles, Giorgio stood six-foot-one, weighed approximately one-hundred-ninety pounds, and had first obtained a driver's license at eighteen years old.

He'd lived in Chicago for almost all his life, and though he'd been affiliated with the Leóne family since birth, his criminal record was clean. Aside from a fistfight outside a bar, which had been reduced to a misdemeanor for disturbing the peace, and a couple parking tickets, there was no official indication that Giorgio was a career criminal.

However, the databases to which the FBI had access encompassed more than official convictions. From the FBI database, Amelia had learned of the numerous investigations into Giorgio's involvement in drug trafficking and prostitution. In several of the cases where he'd been a suspect, his cousin Emilio appeared as well.

The more she learned about Giorgio, the less she liked him. With any luck, she'd be able to kick him square in the balls before she placed his ass under arrest.

Once she'd been satisfied that she could pass a public records quiz on Giorgio's behalf, Amelia had taken to the streets.

For four-and-a-half days, she'd been Giorgio Delusso's shadow. And after all that work, Amelia knew where the Leónes' underage prostitution ring had moved. She'd seen plenty of girls come and go, several of whom looked to be in their mid-to-late teens.

Diligent as ever, Amelia pushed her telephoto camera lens to its limit, taking photos of each girl from as far a distance as she could manage.

After a week of combing through evidence from the house and trying in vain to identify any of its former occupants, their murder board had filled out. For the most part, the new photos and notes were strictly to rule *out* potential suspects, not to narrow in on any one person or group.

Though Amelia was conflicted about lying to her colleagues at the FBI, she hadn't divulged the source of her information about Giorgio. Instead, she'd told SAC Keaton, in a private meeting, that she'd been given Giorgio's identity by a confidential informant.

The explanation was technically true. The only problem was that Amelia's CI wasn't real.

There was no way in hell she'd ever add Alex Passarelli's name to a piece of FBI paperwork.

The taste in her mouth turned bitter as a sense of unease wriggled down her spine. Pushing the sensation to the back of her mind, she strode to the front of the room. With a quick glance over the murder board, she flipped open her manila envelope.

"Hope everyone had a nice lunch break." Amelia tucked a wayward piece of dark hair behind her ear. "I heard there was a pretty nasty accident on the interstate. Palmer, were you driving around on your break today?"

Crossing his arms, Zane let out an indignant huff.

The sarcastic response was enough to drive away Amelia's lingering feelings of uncertainty. She winked, earning an eye-roll from Zane, along with an amused grin.

Amelia cleared her throat. "Okay, now that I got that out of the way. We have a press conference scheduled in a couple days to give an update on where we are with Leila's case, right?"

SAC Keaton groaned softly. "The Bureau is starting to take some of the heat that was on the Janesville PD. By the end of the week, I'd guess we'll bear the full brunt of the media circus."

Plucking out a photo of Emilio Leóne, Amelia dropped the manila folder to an office chair in the corner of the room. Without speaking, she headed straight to the picture of Giorgio she'd taped onto the whiteboard at the start of the investigation.

In the interest of maximizing their efficiency, she, Joseph, and Zane had split the legwork of Leila's case amongst themselves. As the media scrutiny increased over the past couple days, SSA Spencer Corsaw and the newly returned Fiona Donahue had lent their assistance.

Zane had posted up around the area in West Garfield Park where they'd first spotted Giorgio and where Gabriella Hernandez had identified Leila. According to Zane, none of the regular working girls had returned, including Gabriella and their person of interest, Giorgio.

Gabriella's absence had piqued Amelia's suspicion, but a phone call had assured her that Gabriella and her mother were safely out of town.

Due in part to the sense of urgency that permeated Leila's case and Amelia's good old-fashioned paranoia, she hadn't divulged the pertinent information about Giorgio and the Leónes to anyone other than SAC Keaton.

Amelia rapped a knuckle on the board below a DMV photo. "This is Emilio Leóne. He's a capo in the Leóne family, and word has it he's next in line to be the underboss." She pointed to Giorgio's picture. "This is his cousin, Giorgio Delusso."

Joseph lifted an eyebrow. "You figured out who he is? How?"

With a coy shrug she hoped was convincing, Amelia suggested, "A little elbow grease."

As she launched into the rundown of the Leóne family she'd been given by Alex, all four sets of eyes in the room were glued to her.

She went through the research she'd done on the two houses Giorgio was known to frequent, including the fact that they were both owned by the same corporation. A shell corporation, as best as Amelia had been able to tell—a shell corporation that she had loosely tied to the Leóne family. The ownership of the two houses removed all doubt as to whom they truly belonged.

Spencer Corsaw cocked his head sideways and glared at Amelia. "Have you been sitting on all this?"

Just as Amelia opened her mouth to offer a sarcastic reply, Jasmine cut her off.

"No, Corsaw, she hasn't. She's been working with me."

Amelia smiled pleasantly, thankful for her boss's support. "It's been a lot of work keeping up with Giorgio without him noticing me. We didn't exactly have time to sit around and bring everyone up to speed before now."

Spencer's jaw clenched, but he remained silent.

With a light creak, Zane leaned back in his chair. "So, the same shell corporation owns both houses, and that corporation has some ties to the Leóne family, and you've seen some Leóne guys and some working girls in one of them."

Amelia and SAC Keaton nodded at the same time.

Zane scratched the stubble on the side of his face. "Don't take this the wrong way. What you did here was damn impressive, but are we sure this is enough to get us a warrant? I get that Leila was working the streets in an area controlled by the Leónes, which makes sense, but is it enough for us to raid the place?"

Amelia raised her hand to stave off any more questions, turned to the office chair, shuffled through the photos still in her folder, and made her way back to the whiteboard.

All the while, Zane's scrutiny was unwavering. The keen edge in his eyes was all at once captivating and unnerving. Maybe he was skilled at observing human behavior, or maybe he was a mind-reading alien. Amelia wasn't sure she'd ever learn the truth.

After fixing a piece of tape to the top edge of the newest

photo, Amelia slapped the picture onto the whiteboard, just below Emilio and his cousin.

Joseph's eyes widened, and Zane muttered a handful of four-letter words.

Amelia scrutinized the paparazzi style picture of Emilio and Leila. "I took that yesterday. It's the only time I've seen Leila leave the house, and the fact that she's accompanied by Emilio Leóne himself is telling. I don't know what they've got in store for her, but whatever it is, it's not pleasant."

Jasmine reached for her iPad. "We'll have a warrant for both houses by the end of the day."

"Damn." Joseph ran a hand through his dark blond hair. "That was fast."

Amelia fought against a sigh. "You know, I doubt you'd say that if you were the one who'd spent the last few days crammed in a car in the middle of June."

Joseph's mouth twitched with the hint of a smile—an odd gesture for the typically stoic man, especially within the confines of the FBI office.

SAC Keaton was scowling at the iPad screen as her fingers flew over the glass. "We carry out the raid tomorrow. Right now, we've got cameras on the place, so we'll know if anything unexpected happens. With any luck, Leila Jackson is still in one of those houses. We can't let the press get hold of this. If they do, the Jacksons might hire an army of private investigators with all the money they've raised online."

Amelia glared at Emilio's image, wishing the man into the depths of hell. "We're dealing with one of the most powerful criminal organizations in the city of Chicago. The Leónes have been in this city since the days of Al Capone, and the last thing we need is a couple overconfident PIs rolling in thinking they're going to get their big break by outdoing the Bureau."

Joseph's expression went rigid.

Amelia lifted a finger before he could argue. "If we want to get these people, we have to treat it like it's a bomb removal. We go in once. No mistakes, because with the Leónes, we don't get a second chance. If we mess this up, they'll all disappear into the woodwork, and Leila will be as good as dead."

19

A humid breeze rustled the pages of Alex's paperback novel, carrying with it the scent of freshly cut grass. Alex took a deep breath, relishing the opportunity to enjoy air that wasn't tinged with car exhaust from the ever-bustling traffic in downtown Chicago.

Even in the relative shade of the circular gazebo, the midafternoon temperature had risen high enough to make his exposed forearms feel sticky. He liked the fresh air, but the humidity was just short of stifling.

An unbidden memory floated to the surface of his thoughts. Years ago, on a day quite similar to this one, he'd been with Amelia at a park in an upscale Chicago neighborhood. He'd pilfered a bottle of wine from his parents' newly installed wine cellar. The vintage merlot had likely cost close to three grand, but he'd known neither of his parents would miss it. They'd drank like fish, even back then.

Despite the fact that the wine was ritzier than the average person would ever experience in their lifetime, he and Amelia had passed the bottle back and forth like cheap beer.

They'd been sprawled out on the merry-go-round for less

than ten minutes when Amelia sat up, fanned herself, and declared that it was "fuzzy outside." He'd lapsed into a fit of laughter until tears stung his eyes, and the mirth wasn't due to the booze.

All these years later, Alex still used the term to describe oppressive humidity.

Brushing at the light sheen of sweat on his forehead, he flipped to the next page in his newest science fiction novel. He'd never read much of the genre until a fellow D'Amato capo, Giancarlo Forcelli—or John, as he preferred—had hounded him to read *Dune*.

Though Alex still wasn't sure if the genre was for him, he had enjoyed the epic sci-fi classic, and now he was working his way through the second in the series.

The quiet hum of a car's engine drew Alex's attention to the gravel parking lot in front of the picnic area. The Leóne lieutenant was right on time. He watched Adrian park the car, keenly aware of the weight of the forty-five holstered behind his back.

Adrian seemed on the level, but Alex doubted he'd ever relax in the presence of a Leóne lieutenant.

Especially one of Emilio Leóne's lieutenants.

Alex closed the book and set it on the wooden bench at his side.

Adrian approached, clad in another patterned button-down t-shirt, dark jeans, and boots, walking a fine line between *dad* and *mafioso style*. With a couple more gold chains and a pair of track pants, he'd be solidly in the latter category.

Alex straightened and smoothed out the front of his pastel blue dress shirt. "Afternoon."

"Thanks for showing up on short notice," Adrian replied, though his expression was pinched.

Alex stretched his legs. "It's fine. You're impatient, huh?"

"A little, yeah. It's been a week." Adrian sat across from him. "I told you this was time sensitive."

Propping both elbows on his knees, Alex leaned forward, all his attention focused on the Leóne lieutenant. "You did, but you still haven't mentioned *why* it's time sensitive."

To his credit, Adrian didn't falter at the increased scrutiny. Unperturbed, he met Alex's stare before saying, "I don't expect you to get it. But they, Emilio, he's selling an Italian-looking girl. She's only sixteen. Black hair...blue eyes...fair complexion. She reminds me of my daughter. My wife and I are both Italian. Most of *the Family* are."

Pain took a swing at Alex, landing a sucker punch to his gut. Gianna had blue eyes, just like their mother.

At the remembrance of his sister, another image flashed in Alex's mind. An image of Amelia holding a flier with a computer-generated photo of a teenage girl who matched the description Adrian had just given him.

"Hold on." He raised a hand. "That girl, do you know her name?"

Adrian turned his gaze out over the expansive grassy hill that led down to the lake. "I know her first name's Leila. Don't know her last."

Alex clenched and unclenched his hands. Dammit. He did. "Jackson."

Adrian frowned. "What?"

"Leila Jackson. That's her name. Have you heard of that new Netflix show, *Vanished*? It's one of those crime documentaries, kind of like *Making a Murderer*."

Adrian turned his focus back to Alex. "Yeah, my wife is obsessed with it. She loves those kinds of shows, but I can't stand them. They hit a little too close to home, you know what I mean?"

"Closer than you think. Leila Jackson was the subject of an episode on *Vanished*. That complicates matters."

Harnessing his irritation, Alex took in a long breath. "Here's the thing. When we first met here, you said you'd give me information about the Leóne trafficking ring. And I said I'd take that information and do what I could to interrupt the... supply chain."

Adrian nodded.

"That's not something that happens overnight, you follow? Everything you've given me, I've passed on. We're ready to raise hell when the time comes, but we aren't the Feds. We can't just storm the place and lock up all those assholes in charge. Not unless we want to start a war in our own city."

Raking a hand through his hair, Adrian heaved a sigh. He opened his mouth to reply, but Alex cut him off with an upraised hand.

"But...with the added scrutiny this Leila girl brings through her Netflix debut, I might know just the sources to alert."

Using law enforcement against the D'Amato family's enemies wasn't unheard of, nor was it out of bounds during an outright war. During a ceasefire like the one the Leónes and D'Amatos had maintained for the past several years, however, the maneuver was fraught with risks.

But those risks only reared their head if the Leónes found out that the D'Amato family was responsible.

Alex still wasn't sure how well he should trust Adrian, but he could trust in the worry he'd witnessed in Amelia's eyes when she'd shown him Leila's flier.

He was under no illusion that he and Amelia could be anything other than secretive allies in their respective lines of work. Hell, by now, she'd likely already figured out where the Leóne family had imprisoned Leila.

But tonight seemed as good a time as any to check in on the progress of her search.

When Adrian cleared his throat, Alex wondered how long he'd been silent.

Blinking away the image of Amelia, Alex rubbed his temple. "It's unorthodox, but I know someone who can take them on face-to-face."

Adrian looked genuinely curious if a bit skeptical. "The Feds?"

Alex bit back a knee-jerk sarcastic retort, replying with more constraint than he felt. "Yeah, I've got a contact."

"Make it quick if you can." Tapping a finger against his knee, Adrian pursed his lips as if hesitant to say more. But, after a breath, he added, "Emilio's selling Leila to The Shark."

Revulsion and surprise crawled down his back, and all Alex could do was stare.

He'd been truthful with Amelia. Neither he nor anyone in the D'Amato family knew The Shark's identity. Alex had gone as far as double-checking with all the family's commanders.

They didn't know the man's name, but they knew he was no ally to the D'Amatos. A decade ago, when Gianna had been kidnapped, rumors—just whispers at the time—had surfaced that suggested the man might have been involved in her disappearance. But as the years rolled on, the idea seemed more and more farfetched. Still, the D'Amato family kept their distance.

Alex swallowed as he shoved the thought aside. "Do you know who The Shark is?"

Adrian shook his head. "No. I don't even know if Emilio knows his real name."

"When is it happening?"

"Tomorrow morning at nine. The sale went through yesterday. Emilio took her to one of The Shark's people, and they," Adrian scrubbed his face with his hand, "made sure that Leila was 'as advertised,' I guess."

Alex growled low in his throat. This wasn't good. "Tomorrow morning? You're sure she's still there right now?"

"I brought her a granola bar before I left." Adrian nodded. "She's still there."

Urgency was essential. If Alex wanted to give Amelia a way into the house where Leila was kept, he needed to ensure she had probable cause for a warrant. Moreover, he needed to ensure that the warrant was expedited, and that the FBI was ready to knock down the Leónes' door within the next sixteen hours.

A distant laugh carried on the wind, breaking Alex's concentration. He looked around to be sure no one was sneaking up on their meeting, and once satisfied with their privacy, he returned to analyzing the angles he could work to leak the right information to the Feds.

He'd given Amelia the information about Giorgio and the Leónes days ago. Even though she was bound by certain legalities during her search, she also had the resources and the might of the FBI at her back.

He was sure she already knew about the house. More than likely, she'd followed Giorgio to the location where Leila was held. But did she know Leila was there? Had she seen Emilio and the girl leave the house?

For now, Alex had to assume the answer to all the above was a resounding *yes*.

But she didn't know when Leila would be taken to The Shark.

Without speaking, Alex pushed to his feet. "Okay. I'll get ahold of my contact with the timeframe."

Adrian lifted an eyebrow. "You trust this contact?"

"Yeah. It's an old friend. They're trustworthy, don't worry."

Adrian seemed to be struggling with some type of internal debate. After nearly a full minute, he raised his head.

"I don't doubt you, but there's something you ought to know about the Feds. Emilio's got someone on the inside too."

"That doesn't surprise me." Grating his teeth together, Alex grabbed his book. "I'll do what I can from my end. If it works, you know what's coming, so it would be in your interest to call in sick for a few days." His mission clear, Alex took his leave without waiting for Adrian to reply.

As he strode away, he processed his possibilities. He had two pieces of information for Amelia. Not only would she have to pull off a raid on Emilio Leóne's prostitution ring with little to no advanced notice, she also had to do it with a rat in her midst.

As stressful as the situation was for Alex, he said a silent *thank you* to anyone who might have been listening.

At least he wasn't Amelia right now.

20

One hand on the cat in her lap, stocking feet propped up on the recliner, Amelia could easily fall asleep here —if she hadn't been so hungry. The scent of roasting meat wafted by her, carried on the faint breeze of the central air-conditioner, and her stomach growled in response.

She wasn't sure when her father had obtained furniture that was more comfortable than hers, but she made a mental note to look into upgrading the clearance couch she'd bought for her living room.

Then, maybe she'd get cable so she could fall asleep to evening baseball games. And maybe she'd get a cat to curl in her lap. And she'd pester her dad for his pot roast secrets.

At the thought of pot roast, Amelia stretched both arms above her head, and blinked a few times to clear her vision. The orange tabby in her lap made a sound closer to a squawk than a meow as it stretched both front paws over the side of Amelia's legs.

Patting the cat on the head a couple times, she glanced from the modestly furnished living room to the arched doorway that led to the dining area and then the kitchen.

Waning sunlight caught the polished glass of a panoramic photo of Wrigley Stadium that hung in the dining room. The print was the only non-family picture on any of Jim Storm's walls, and it was only there because he'd won it in a raffle at a work Christmas party the year before last.

Any time Amelia brought up the lack of décor, her father reminded her that she'd taken almost an entire month to unpack all the boxes she'd moved from Boston to Chicago. Even now, all she'd done was slap a couple movie posters on the walls.

Amelia didn't think she'd fallen asleep, but the golden shade of sunlight filtering through the windows told her otherwise. Her father was out of view, but she caught part of his quiet muttering.

"No, you can't have any of this. This is people food. You're a cat."

On cue, both ears of the feline on her lap perked up. With one more lazy stretch, the orange and white tabby leapt to the floor and trotted off toward the kitchen.

Amelia used both legs to push down the recliner's footrest. "I think Cheese heard you talking to George in there."

Along with Jo, Nolan, and Hailey, Amelia's father volunteered at an animal shelter that was within walking distance of his apartment. Jim Storm had been the first to volunteer a couple years earlier as part of his journey in sobriety.

After he'd taken Hailey and Nolan to help him one weekend at the shelter, the two preteens had begged their mother to let them spend Saturday mornings with the cats and dogs.

Well before Nolan and Hailey joined him at the shelter, Amelia's dad had adopted a pair of five-year-old cats. For the past few months, her dad had mentioned how much he wanted to add a dog to his furry family. Ultimately, he'd decided that the pup would have to wait until he landed a place with a yard.

Amelia caught the shadows of movement near the kitchen doorway. With one ceramic plate balanced on each hand, her father's green eyes flicked down to the floor as one cat and then another bounded past his legs.

With an elbow, Amelia pushed herself to sit upright. "Wait, you made me a plate? Since when do I get waited on when I'm over here?"

Between trying not to step on the cats and balancing the food, her father shot her a grin that revealed white, straight teeth. He did work in reception at a dentist's office, after all.

"You and Cheese were both asleep. I would have just woke you up, but I didn't want to disturb Cheese."

Amelia snorted. "Of course. Cheese has a hard life as a pampered house cat."

Her dad shrugged and extended a plate of steaming roast, carrots, and potatoes to her. "See, I knew you'd understand."

Chuckling, Amelia accepted the food. Both cats leapt up onto the center cushion of the overstuffed couch, but Amelia dared them to get close to her scrumptious dinner.

The television drew their attention as the commercial break ended. Aside from the occasional comment about the baseball game or reminding the cats that they couldn't have human food because they were cats, they ate in silence.

Amelia didn't have to be an investigator for the FBI to pick up on the weight that hung in the air between them. Though she had cleaned more than half her plate, her father had hardly touched his.

She could only hope he'd speak before she had to prod him for the reason behind his unease.

She never had a problem asking suspects a million and a half personal questions, but when it came to open communication with her blood relatives, she was at a loss. More than likely, her inability to carry on a conversation that might leave her vulnerable was a product of the seventeen years her father had spent as an alcoholic.

He'd never been cruel to Amelia or her siblings, but he hadn't been pleasant, either. More often than not, he had simply been *absent*. Amelia had found her personal connections elsewhere—through the other girls in her neighborhood and, of course, Alex Passarelli.

At the thought of the D'Amato capo, the potatoes and gravy lost their flavor.

To her relief, her father's voice drew her from the brief contemplation. "I heard from Lainey a couple days ago."

Amelia's relief was short-lived. Rather than vocalize a response, she shoveled another bite of food into her mouth.

Normally, her father appeared young for his age. He was almost always clean-shaven, and even after nearly two decades of heavy drinking, his genetics had kept the wrinkle lines to a minimum.

But whenever he talked about Lainey, he looked about fifteen years older.

He stabbed a carrot with his fork. "I take it you heard from her too?"

Another heaping spoonful of potatoes kept Amelia from having to respond.

Balancing the plate on one knee, Jim ran a hand through light brown hair that had only recently been sprinkled with silver. "You know I'm proud of how far I've come. Of this place, and how things are going now that I got rid of the booze. But…" jaw clenched, he shook his head, "there's part of me that says I shouldn't be able to feel that way about anything as long as your sister is…well, you know."

A junkie.

Amelia kept the term to herself, shrugging as her gaze shifted between her father and the television. The bitter taste had returned to her tongue, and her heartbeat rushed in her ears.

She didn't know how to reply to his concern. Sure, she worried about Lainey too, but there was only so much mental bandwidth she could reserve for her youngest sibling. In the event, however unlikely—and it *was* unlikely—that Lainey came to Amelia and expressed a sincere desire to pursue change for herself, Amelia would welcome her with open arms.

But as long as Lainey only reached out to try to manipulate her surviving family members into donating their cash, Amelia would continue to ignore the calls and texts. She knew better than to fall for Lainey's sob stories, and she could only hope that her father's experience in battling addiction had given him the same wisdom.

Amelia cleared her throat and reluctantly turned to her father. "There are some things you can't control, and I hate to say it, but Lainey's one of them. We've done everything we could, and it's up to her now. You can be glad for where you're at and still care about where she's at."

God, she hoped that made sense. Discussions about matters of the heart weren't Amelia's forte.

Holding the plate out of reach from the cats, her father sighed and slumped down in his seat. "Yeah, I guess. You know, I got a two-bedroom apartment because I figured the extra storage space would be nice. Plus, there's a room and a bed for Hailey or Nolan if they want to spend the night." He slowly pushed his food around on the plate. "But what I was really hoping was that Lainey would get rid of that asshole boyfriend she's with and come home."

Though Amelia's knee-jerk response was to tell him not to hold his breath, she swallowed the remark and glanced down to her plate. "We've done everything we can, Dad. It's up to her now."

"Yeah, it is. I know that." He sighed, looking defeated. "She won't change unless she wants to."

What Amelia had never said aloud to another living human being was that she, like her father, blamed herself for Lainey. If she hadn't been in such a rush to get out of Chicago after the end of her and Alex's relationship, if she hadn't joined the military, if she'd just stayed in Chicago, maybe her little sister wouldn't have fallen in with the group of kids that ultimately introduced her to her current drug of choice—heroin.

But the fact remained that Amelia had been *told*, threatened even, to leave Alex, even to leave Chicago. At the time, she'd been a naïve eighteen-year-old fresh out of high school, but Luca Passarelli was an imposing figure even to seasoned career criminals.

She fought to keep the scowl from her face as images of Alex's father surfaced in her thoughts.

On some level, Luca was responsible for her sister's path. Then again, she could tell herself to blame Luca, but she was never successful.

If she'd just been braver, *stronger*, and stayed in the city, she could have helped Lainey.

Pulling herself from the contemplation, she scooped up more potato and took a hefty bite. The silence that had settled over Amelia and her father was so complete that she could have fooled herself into thinking that they'd fallen victim to one of the supernatural entities in a Stephen King novel.

Amelia's appetite was gone, but she forced herself to finish the food she'd stabbed with her fork. From the corner of her eye, she watched her father as he pushed meat and potatoes around on his plate. He looked so stressed and downfallen, that just looking at him broke her heart.

She should have asked him what was on his mind—that's

what a good daughter would have done—but she continued to munch, though she could hardly taste the food. Maybe she would get lucky, and the Cubs would make a surprise defensive play that would steer their conversation toward a topic that didn't make Amelia break out in a cold sweat.

Her father cleared his throat, and Amelia's stomach dropped.

Lowering her fork, she lifted an eyebrow and turned her head. "Yeah?"

He dropped his chin to stare at his plate. "I talked to Joanna the other day. She told me about all the payments that were hitting her salon before Trevor died. And about how Hailey and Nolan have six-figure college funds."

Whatever remained of Amelia's appetite fell away. She hadn't wanted Jo to tell her father about the curious financial statements, but at the same time, she hadn't wanted to send her sister-in-law into a spiral of panic by swearing her to secrecy, either.

Dread curling into a knot in her stomach, Amelia set the plate on the end table at her side. Cheese moved to cross her lap to get to the food, but she swept the orange tabby up in her arms instead.

"Look." Her father held up a hand to stave off her protest. "I know what you think. I know you think that Trevor was in the wrong place at the wrong time."

Amelia wanted to scream, to lash out at the unfairness of her brother's death. Instead, she kept her voice calm even as her pulse rushed in her ears. "He was. I've been through that case seven ways from Sunday, and I've talked to the two detectives who conducted the investigation. They're good police, Dad. Everything they did was by the book."

He set the plate in his lap and spread his hands. "I'm not saying they're not. But…you have to admit, there are a lot of coincidences. And if Trevor was *working* for someone. Someone like, like—"

"If that was what happened, the detectives would have found something." She took a breath, to soften the angry edge her voice had taken, and set the squirming tabby on the floor.

Even she didn't believe the words as they came out of her mouth. She'd long suspected there was more to Trevor's death than met the eye—more than the investigating detectives had unearthed—but she had no substantiating evidence for her suspicion.

She'd warred with herself over the feeling more times than she cared to count. Trevor had been an integral part of her father's sobriety, and he'd even brought Lainey home for a year before she relapsed.

But Amelia had dealt with death in one way or another for her entire adult life. She never got used to losing a friend or family member, but grief had become something of a routine. Trevor had been special to Amelia and her family, and so it made sense for them to believe that the circumstances that surrounded his death were just as unique. That if they looked hard enough, they'd find an answer that would give them closure.

In reality, obsession only prolonged grief. Loss was complicated, and there was no shortcut to overcome it.

Her father's pleading gaze drifted in her direction once more. "Shouldn't we tell them about this? Tell them that we think something was going on? I mean, they didn't know about Jo's salon, right? It'd be a new lead. Maybe they could find something."

Amelia had started shaking her head before he even finished. "No. No, we don't do that. If we do that, then the IRS will audit Jo, and if they find anything off, it won't be a stretch for them to hold her responsible. She'd lose everything. She could even be arrested." Straightening in her chair, she jabbed an index finger in her father's direction and then to herself. "*We* deal with this by keeping our damn mouths shut."

Combing a hand through his silver-specked hair, her father slumped down in his chair. "Yeah, you're right."

The steely determination melted away. Amelia hadn't meant to sound so mean. She softened her voice. "There's nothing they'd find from it, anyway. Besides, that's not the type of memory Trevor deserves."

Her father looked as if he were holding back tears. "You're right. On all accounts."

She wasn't so sure she agreed, but the suspicion would fall on her and her alone.

If there was more to Trevor's death, then she would deal with it herself. She was no stranger to this grim world, but her father and her sister-in-law were. Their lives were stressful and complicated already. They didn't need to add constant paranoia to their routines.

The clatter of her phone buzzing against the end table jerked her from the glum line of thought. As her gaze met the white glow of the screen, an invisible hand seemed to squeeze her throat. The number wasn't one she'd saved to her contacts, but the area code was local.

Casting an apologetic glance to her father, she scooped the phone off the stone surface of the end table.

With a slight smile, Jim held up a hand. "Don't worry about me. If that's the FBI calling, you'd probably better answer it."

Amelia swiped the green answer key. "Agent Storm."

"Hey," a familiar voice greeted.

As she felt the color drain from her face, she was glad for the low light of the living room. Her father had drawn the dark curtains over the picture window behind the couch so light wouldn't glare off the television screen.

Plate in one hand, she rose to stand. "Hey. What's...what's up?" She cringed at how stupid the question sounded.

With an outstretched arm, her father waved his fingers in a silent request for her plate. Wordlessly, Amelia handed over the dish before she turned to make her way down a nearby hallway.

On the other end of the line, Alex Passarelli cleared his throat. "I've got something important. I need to talk to you."

She leaned against the drywall beside an old family photo. "And not on the phone, I take it?"

"That's right. Can you meet me?" There was an unexpected note of urgency in his voice.

"Where? And when?"

"I'm at home, but I can meet you somewhere else if that's convenient."

Amelia almost laughed at the politeness of his offer. "No, that's okay. I can be there in," she pulled the phone away from her face to check the time, "fifteen minutes?"

"That's good. The sooner, the better." His cadence was rushed, and she picked up on wind whistling in the background.

"Okay. Fifteen minutes."

"See you then."

After bidding him farewell, she jerked the phone from her cheek and swiped to end the call as if the device might bite her.

The sooner, the better was not a phrase she ever wanted to hear from someone like Alexander Passarelli.

Worry swirling through her, Amelia slid the phone into the pocket of her slacks and turned to make her way back to the living room.

Even though her father smiled and reassured her that he

understood the need for her to leave, guilt still gnawed at her.

Though her first thought was that Alex's interruption of her evening had better be for a damn good reason, she already knew he wouldn't have called her without precisely that.

21

As the swig of bourbon burned its way down Alex's throat, he leaned against the granite countertop. With a glance over the breakfast bar to the wall-spanning windows at the other end of the living area, he sighed. On a normal evening, the brilliant hues of orange, gold, and blue that painted the horizon would have brought him a measure of contentment.

Today, the sunset served merely to remind him that the clock was ticking.

Another D'Amato capo might have wondered why Alex was so invested in the search for Leila Jackson. Until his meeting with Adrian that afternoon, he'd been sure that Leila was a lost cause. He'd already pictured the outcome of the FBI's investigation.

Amelia would, at least, try her hardest. He couldn't speak for the rest of the agents. They might even be successful in knocking over Emilio Leóne and a handful of his degenerate flunkies. However, Leila would most likely be long gone by the time they got to her. Because, at the end of the day, finding a person after they'd been sold into human trafficking was almost always a lost cause.

She wasn't gone, though. According to Adrian, she was still locked in a house, under the protection of Emilio and his people.

He took another swig of his bourbon. The entire scenario was eerily familiar. This was Gianna all over again.

His throat tightened at the thought of his little sister, and he took another gulp of the caramel-colored liquor. The alcohol warmed his stomach and soothed the stiffness of his muscles.

Scrubbing one hand over his face, he pushed back the stray strands of dark hair that had fallen into his eyes. He didn't like to make a habit of drinking after a stressful day, but the situation with Leila—specifically, how much he'd been reminded of Gianna—warranted an exception.

He'd only just refilled the glass when a light knock jerked him out of the uneasy memories. Though he'd been expecting her, his heart still slammed against his ribs when he met Amelia's eyes through the peephole. Glass in one hand, Alex flicked the locks and yanked open the door with the other.

Amelia offered him a quick smile as she stepped over the threshold, but the look didn't reach her eyes.

Without speaking, he led her through the foyer and back into the kitchen. The sunset had waned, and the brilliant pinks and oranges had taken on a heavy blue tint. A mass of clouds neared the horizon, almost as if the oncoming storm was chasing away the daylight.

Alex held up his glass. "Can I get you anything to drink? Bourbon?"

Her head was shaking before he finished. "No, thanks."

With a slight nod, he took a long pull. The burn in the

back of his throat wasn't as noticeable now, but the sensation was still comforting.

After a short spell of silence, Amelia fixed him with an expectant glance. "Well? I'm here. Why couldn't this have just been a phone call, though?"

Alex raked a hand through his hair and leaned against the counter. He still wasn't sure how to word the explanation without coming across as a condescending ass. "I just wanted to make sure our conversation wouldn't be overheard."

Amelia jammed both hands into the pockets of her zip-up hoodie. "Because you think the FBI's listening to my calls?"

"Wouldn't be the first time they tapped someone's phone without consent."

Amelia gritted her teeth. Anger flashed across her face for a brief moment before she let out an exasperated breath. "Fine. Do you have a cocktail shaker? Preferably stainless steel." She held her phone out to him.

Alex attempted to process the odd request. "Thought you said you didn't need a drink?"

"Not for me. I'll put my phone in there if that will make you feel better about being listened in on."

He opened his mouth but then bit off a sarcastic response. "I'd just rather not take my chances." Her suggestion, odd as it was, made sense. Stainless steel should work as a shield and prevent signals from getting in or out. That would ensure their conversation remained between the two of them. He mentally filed that away for future use and walked around the counter, drink in hand, to the bookcase and retrieved the shaker. While he was there, he topped up his drink, just for good measure.

Amelia stared at him, still holding the phone out. "Please, take your time." She tapped an impatient foot, staring unflinchingly as he meandered back in her direction with the cocktail shaker in hand. "This better be good."

Alex narrowed his eyes as dread and anticipation pricked at the back of his neck. "You forget that I'm the one doing you a favor here."

Amelia heaved a sigh and dropped the phone into Alex's open hand. "I'm sorry. I'm in a bad mood, and I shouldn't bite your head off. You are helping me, after all."

Now it was Alex's turn to sigh. "It's okay. I'm not exactly thrilled myself to have to be the one sharing this kind of information, given our respective positions and all." He closed the smartphone inside of the cocktail shaker and set it on the counter.

To his relief, some of the irascibility left her features as she shrugged. "Yeah. We're both in precarious positions. Truce then. Cards on the table. What did you want to talk to me about?"

He broke away from her gaze and took in a long breath. Ever since he'd left Riverbank Park after his meeting with Adrian, he'd debated how much information he should give to Amelia. Old friends or not, they were still on opposite sides of the law, and someday, the FBI's scrutiny might fall on the D'Amatos.

But for the moment, the heat was on the Leónes, and taking them down a notch was well worth the effort.

Alex launched into an edited explanation of the information he'd been given by Adrian. Amelia's expression, as she listened, might as well have been carved from stone. First, he advised her of the scheduled appointment for the sale of Leila the following morning. Then, secondly—more reluctantly—he regaled Adrian's assertion that the Leónes had a connection deep within the FBI's ranks.

"Who gave you that information?"

Alex stiffened. Surely she knew that question would push him too far.

Rubbing the bridge of her nose, Amelia waved a hand.

"You don't have to answer that. What I really want to know is how reliable they are."

The tension in his muscles melted away as quickly as it had come, and he scratched at the stubble on his chin. "Honestly? I wasn't sure at first, but I've been working with them for a little while now, and they haven't led me in the wrong direction yet. And yes, the information comes from within the Leóne family. I can't say who, but they're as trustworthy as you get in this business, you know?"

Amelia rested one hand on the counter as she clenched and unclenched the other. Though her face was still carefully blank, her posture was about as relaxed as a marble statue.

A leaden silence descended over the kitchen. Amelia's eyes were fixed on the blue and gray glass tile backsplash, but Alex doubted she saw it. All the while, her nostrils flared as she pumped her fist, digging her fingernails into her palm.

Alex kept his thoughts to himself. He'd just dropped a bombshell on her—revealing that one of her FBI colleagues worked for the Leóne family. Someone, who she might think of as a *friend*, was as sleazy and despicable as Emilio Leóne himself.

He didn't doubt she needed a moment to process.

When her gaze finally shifted back over to him, he almost jumped in surprise. It might have been the booze, but for a split-second, he'd convinced himself that she was a figment of his imagination.

The spell broke as she let her head loll back to stare at the beams and pipes that crisscrossed the ceiling. She spat out a series of expletives before returning her attention to Alex.

He silently raised an eyebrow.

"The house. The first house. We thought someone made us when we were at that nightclub, but they didn't, did they?"

Her question was rhetorical, but he didn't dismiss or confirm the possibility. Either scenario seemed plausible.

He'd never been to one of the Leóne affiliated clubs, but he was sure they had their fair share of security measures designed specifically to pick out agents of the law.

After another spell of quiet, he flashed her a quizzical glance. "What's your next move, then? Now that you know there's someone in that office who's working for the Leónes, I mean."

Slowly, Amelia shook her head. "Well, I still don't have any idea who they are. But if I assume that they're responsible for the first house being evacuated, then it has to be someone who's involved in this investigation in one way or another."

Alex clasped his hands behind his back. "Best to treat it as a worst-case scenario, right? Just assume that there's a traitor in your midst and plan accordingly."

He didn't mention the intimate familiarity he had with sniffing out potential traitors in his circle of allies. No matter how far the D'Amato family strayed from conventionally violent lines of illegal work, the world of organized crime was treacherous. It would always be treacherous.

Her expression darkened. "You're right. I should assume they know everything that I know. Which means." She straightened. "They know when we're going to hit the new Leóne location."

As she muttered another slew of curses, Alex drank deeply from his bourbon. The adrenaline and anxiety from his and Amelia's interaction had chased away his buzz.

She raised a hand and pulled out her car keys. "Okay. Okay. I need to deal with this. We can try to figure out who the rat is some other time. Right now, I need to make sure that bastard doesn't give the Leónes another way out."

We?

As much as Alex wanted to know if she had truly meant *we*, he merely smiled.

Amelia took a swift step in his direction, and in that split-second, Alex thought she meant to reach out for an embrace. Midway through the motion, she stopped herself. Embarrassment, though brief, flickered through her eyes as she offered her hand instead.

With a light chuckle and a reassuring smile, he clasped her hand and shook. "Old habits, huh?"

Her laugh was equal parts nervous and relieved. "Yeah, you could say that."

"Be careful, okay?"

She kept her hands at her sides and took a step backward. "No promises."

"Fair enough." Alex stuffed his hands into his pockets so that he wouldn't reach for her. "Be alert, then."

She nodded. "I can do that."

Don't trust anyone.

He left off the reflexive thought, locked the door after she was gone, and threw back the rest of his bourbon.

This was going to be a long twelve hours.

22

M y flight from Virginia Beach into Chicago had been forced to land early in Indianapolis due to a series of thunderstorms sweeping up from the South on through to the Midwest. Though I was eager to return to Chicago tomorrow morning to pick up my prize, the stopover didn't bother me.

Better a night spent in an Indianapolis hotel than a plane crash. Besides, we'd be back in Chicago before seven the following morning. I'd posted up at a familiar hotel, one I'd stayed at on a previous trip to the city. I ordered a late dinner via room service and settled in.

I had just settled in to watch a rerun of a documentary about the Unabomber when the muffled buzz of a phone caught my attention.

Frustrated but curious, I leaned over to pull open the drawer of the matte black nightstand to retrieve the buzzing phone. Like the rest of the furniture in the pricy hotel room, the nightstand was understated, functional, and modern.

Flipping open the prepaid phone, I squinted at the unsaved number that flashed across the little screen.

If Emilio tells me something's going wrong with this sale, I swear to god.

I took in a steadying breath and pressed a key to answer the call. No, I had Emilio's number memorized. My night-time caller was someone else.

"Yes?" Though I made an effort to displace some of my irritability, I wasn't entirely successful.

"It's me."

As soon as Red's familiar voice grated out the two words, I sat up straight, surprised. "It's been a while, friend. How are you?"

Red let out a quiet chortle. "Fine. Been better, but I'll make it."

I leaned against the cushioned headboard, forcing my body to relax. "I'm sorry to hear that. If there's anything I can do, just say the word."

"Maybe. I'll let you know." Red chuckled again. "This isn't about that, though. I've got something, and I wanted to bring it to you first."

Tension knotted my shoulders. "I'm listening."

"I know you and the senator have been doing business with the Leóne family."

"That's right. They've been a good business partner so far. They're much more," I glanced around the room as I searched for the word, "*amenable* than some of the others, especially the D'Amatos."

"That's part of their problem, I'd say. Their...amenability tends to land them in the spotlight more than it should. The D'Amatos are smart, and they stay in the shadows. But..." he blew out a breath, "I digress. That family isn't part of this conversation."

"Good." I'd dealt with them in the past, and the arrangement hadn't ended well for any of us.

Red hesitated before he spoke again. "It's the Leónes' prostitution ring."

My blood turned cold; my mouth devoid of moisture.

"I don't know all the specifics of *how*, but the Leóne prostitution ring is going to be taken down tomorrow night. That includes the girl you plan to purchase."

I was on my feet in an instant, rage and disbelief fueling the action. "Tomorrow night? I have it scheduled to meet up with one of Emilio's men to pick up my new prize at nine tomorrow morning."

"I can give them the heads-up, and they can disappear. It might take an extra few days for them to get her to you, but it would still be possible."

"No." I was shaking my head before Red finished. "No, if the Leónes abandon the area and the Feds find nothing, they'll be suspicious. They'll know that someone tipped them off, and that won't be good for anyone."

If the FBI was slated to take down Emilio's prostitution ring tomorrow night, then I was left with a wide window to acquire my new prize and avoid FBI scrutiny.

Red was right. I *could* give the Leónes a warning, but the sudden evacuation would raise more than a few eyebrows. The likelihood of compromising Red's identity was slim, but I wasn't willing to take any chance with a connection this valuable or my new prize.

I didn't realize I'd lapsed into silence until Red spoke again. "You still there?"

I paced to the window. "I am. I'm just thinking."

"I think you're right. Notifying the Leónes is too risky. There are a limited number of people at the Bureau who know about this raid right now. There'll be more tomorrow when we bring in the rest of the tactical team, but the pool of suspects is a little too small for my liking."

"I was thinking the same thing. We let the Feds hit the Leónes this time. The buck stops at them." Pacing back to the door, I gave myself a moment to think. "The Feds get their arrests, and that's the end of that. They know that their odds of finding a girl who's left the country are slim to none."

"You're still going to get her?" Red's tone was polite but surprised. He and I had a mutual respect that neither of us extended to many others in our business.

"Of course." I needed my Mirabel Two. "A deal's a deal, and Emilio won't be able to make good on it once he's in prison. But the less you know about my plans, the better."

"Right. You know what you're doing. I'll leave you to the rest of your night. If you need anything else, you know how to get ahold of me. And if I hear anything else, you'll be the first person I contact."

"Perfect. Have a good night, my friend."

"You do the same."

With a quiet snap, I closed the flip-phone and returned it to the nightstand.

While I often sent Mark or Devin to conduct business with the Leónes and their ilk, I had measures in place for more volatile situations. And picking up my new prize had the potential of being a very volatile situation.

I'd ask Devin for a couple of his most loyal men, and I would merely send them to acquire my new prize. I wouldn't tell them the reason for the errand, the name of the girl, or even the fact that I was personally involved in the exchange.

In the unlikely event that Emilio and his men were tailed by the Feds, my people wouldn't have any information to give them. With so many safeguards in place, the risk to me was minimal.

If I had to throw Emilio Leóne to the wolves to obtain my prize, then so be it.

She was mine. Plain and simple.

23

Between the conversation about her sister, the persistent air of awkwardness with her father, and then the news from Alex, Amelia figured she was doing well to avoid spitting out a four-letter word with every step.

Her sister was a heroin addict. She and her father would never have a normal relationship. And there was a rat in the Chicago field office of the FBI.

She barely registered the manicured lawn and the neatly planted flowers of the two-story house as she stalked up a few steps to the sidewalk.

Though she'd never been to SAC Keaton's house, Amelia had always pictured the neighborhood as a cookie-cutter suburb where well-off people moved to escape the city. Jasmine Keaton's husband was a college professor, and one of her two kids attended an Ivy League school.

To her surprise, the Special Agent in Charge lived in an older Chicago neighborhood. Tall trees lined the street to block out the light and noise from the city. Though the gray stone houses were built close together, each sported a modest front yard.

If she hadn't been so preoccupied by the slew of what-ifs whipping through her mind, Amelia would have been impressed by the area. The houses were smaller than what was found in the suburbs, but the old trees and Victorian-inspired architecture gave the neighborhood a certain charm that couldn't be found in newer construction.

Amelia swallowed any remaining trepidation as she came face to face with the tall door. Before she could slip back into the vortex of paranoia, she rapped her knuckles against the dark wooden surface.

"It's Storm."

A muffled voice replied, but Amelia couldn't make out the words. Before she could ask the woman to repeat herself, the door swung inward. Amelia expected Jasmine to be bleary-eyed and tired, but the SAC looked as sharp and alert as always. But rather than the pajamas Amelia had expected, Jasmine wore a pair of dark jeans and a t-shirt.

They made their way through the dim foyer and down a short hall to reach the kitchen and dining area.

Jasmine retrieved two mugs from one of the cherry wood cabinets and lifted an eyebrow as she faced Amelia. "Based on that look, we're going to need some coffee."

Amelia leaned against a marble counter. "I was thinking hard liquor, but that works too."

SAC Keaton cracked a smile as she poured them each a cup from a freshly brewed pot of coffee. "No, no booze, I'm sorry. We've got work to do, Storm. What exactly did you hear from this CI of yours?"

Whether the twinge of disbelief in Jasmine's voice was real or merely imagined as part of Amelia's ever-present paranoia, she wasn't sure.

She ignored the notion and accepted the blue-gray mug of steaming liquid. "The Leónes know about the raid we're executing tomorrow night. My CI says that they've got someone in the FBI tipping them off."

Jasmine's gaze dropped to her coffee as she narrowed her eyes. Amelia had expected an outburst of disbelief or shock, but SAC Keaton seemed...disappointed.

Tucking away her own surprise, Amelia resisted the urge to fiddle with her hair or tap her finger against the mug.

After a tense spell of silence, SAC Keaton finally glanced back up to Amelia. Determination had replaced her disappointment.

"This isn't the first time I've picked up on something like this, but this is the first time I've had an outside party confirm my suspicion."

Amelia drew her brows together. "How long?"

SAC Keaton blew on her coffee. "I'm not sure. Until tonight, I haven't been completely sure whose payroll they're on, either. I figured it was either the Leóne family or the drug cartel."

"Not the D'Amato family?" Amelia blurted out the question before she could think twice.

To her relief, SAC Keaton was unperturbed. She shook her head, her eyes fixed on the breakfast bar at Amelia's back. "No. I ruled them out a while ago. If they've got connections in the Bureau, I doubt we'd find out like this."

Ignoring the phantom hand that clamped down on her stomach, Amelia moved to sit at the table. "So, what's the plan? If we wait until tomorrow to raid the Leóne houses, there's a good chance they'll all be gone. And that means Leila will be gone too. Sold to whoever this Shark guy is."

Jasmine toyed with the handle of her mug. "I don't know nearly as much about him as I feel like I ought to."

Amelia shrugged. "From the sounds of it, no one does."

"We can work on that after we take care of this." Jasmine lifted her mug but just held it under her nose, not yet taking a sip. "The Leónes think we'll be knocking on their door tomorrow night. Or, at least, that's the assumption we're operating under, right?"

"Worst-case scenario, yeah. Something tells me that this and the other house are connected. That Zane and I weren't made, but someone tipped them off."

SAC Keaton took her first sip. "I wouldn't rule it out. We have the no-knock warrant for the two Leóne houses."

Relief weakened Amelia's entire body. "Then we do the raid tonight?"

SAC Keaton checked the time. "Tonight, yes. In two hours. I'll call everyone in under the pretense of a credible terrorist threat. That way, our rat won't have an opportunity to reach out to the Leónes."

Couldn't have said it better myself.

After a quick sip of coffee, she raised her mug. "Do you have something I can pour this in?"

She was ready to go take these bastards down.

*Z*ane checked the time. Though he wore the pricey yet understated timepiece more for looks than anything, he was glad he remembered to put it on before he left his apartment thirty minutes earlier. As soon as he'd arrived at the field office, SAC Keaton had demanded that each of them, including the members of the tactical team, hand over all potential communication devices.

Keaton's request raised the hairs on the back of Zane's neck. There was only one reason a Special Agent in Charge would strip their agents of phones and other electronics— they were worried about information falling into the wrong hands. SAC Keaton had assured them all that the precaution was normal when dealing with a criminal organization as well connected as the Leóne Family. She'd given the disclaimer with such a confident and reassuring tone that Zane almost believed her.

But he knew better. That's why he'd been assigned to Chicago in the first place.

He wasn't here just to investigate suspected criminals, but

to sniff out corruption like a cadaver dog searching for a corpse.

Zane pulled himself from the thought and turned his attention to the man driving the black SUV.

As if sensing Zane's piercing glare, Tom Harris shot him a quick glance. "We're just circling the neighborhood a few times before we all roll in."

Zane double-checked the rearview mirror, making sure no strange cars tailed behind. "Right, we surround the smaller house at the same time SSA Corsaw and his team hit up the big house."

Harris grunted.

Zane wanted to take that as an acknowledgment but needed verbal confirmation. "Was that a yes?"

"Yes," Harris barked back at him.

"Three minutes now." A deep voice came through Zane's earpiece.

In the back seat, Amelia cracked the knuckles of one gloved hand and then the other. The soft staccato pops pulled Zane's attention toward her.

Thanks to the meager light that penetrated the heavily tinted windows, Amelia's bangs created eerie shadows over her face. The rest of her dark hair was pulled back in her trademarked braid that swept past her shoulders.

Agent Emily Wilson sat next to Amelia. With an M4 Carbine resting against one knee, Wilson's mouth was set in a hard line as she scanned the houses they rolled by.

Six agents had been assigned to the smaller of the two Leóne houses, and nine to the larger house. There were other field and tactical agents stationed around the block to guard the perimeter, and Joseph Larson had been stationed with SAC Keaton in a surveillance van to monitor both teams.

Anticipation stretched the three minutes it took to pull up behind a second black SUV, making each moment last for an eternity. And yet, at the same time, Zane could have sworn he'd only just blinked and Harris was throwing the gearshift into park.

Harris's gaze shifted from Zane to the two women in the back seat. "It's go time."

Wordlessly, Amelia shoved open her door and leapt to the asphalt.

Zane followed suit, smacking the bolt release on the side of the rifle as he elbowed the passenger side door closed.

From their spot across the street, the split-level ranch was unassuming enough. Zane drove by similar houses on a daily basis. He'd never stopped to consider that any of the residences might house an operation as perverse as the Leónes' human trafficking ring. It was no small wonder the place had been overlooked for so long.

A breeze rustled leaves overhead, and the branches of the larger tree scratched against the roof like the nails of a creature. The air carried with it the telltale scent of ozone that preceded a storm.

"Weather is getting bad." As if she'd read his thoughts, Amelia's voice snapped him away from the diligent observation of the house. "I think we might even be in a tornado watch."

He turned to flash her a curious glance. "A tornado watch? In Chicago?"

Amelia's shrug was noncommittal, as if the idea of a raging funnel of destructive wind and debris that flattened anything in its path was nothing new.

She turned to face him fully, and he decided that a tornado wouldn't have been able to compete with Storm's fury in that moment.

Her eyes were shifty as she peered across the street to their target. Almost as if she were counting all the windows and doors of the structure, making a mental tally of the entrance and exit points. "The lights are on. They might actually be here this time." Her mirthless voice had a slight tremble, but Zane wouldn't dare call it fear. It was as if she had gone into a state of hyper-awareness.

Zane grated his teeth in an effort to tamp down his moment of weather-related anxiety. He'd spent the majority of his life on the east coast, so he was familiar with hurricanes and their devastation in a very personal way. A tornado, on the other hand, was something new.

If they weren't about to head into a conflict situation, Zane might have laughed at the way a tornado—even an imagined one—made him more nervous than raiding a mob boss's secret lair. But this was not the time.

Centering himself with a deep breath, Zane fished a handful of folded blue papers from the inside pocket of his jacket. He and Amelia followed Agents Harris and Wilson as they skirted around the SUV and across the street. Though they made an effort to stick to the shadows, the hairs on the back of Zane's neck stood on end.

All it would take was a casual glance out the window or a conveniently timed departure. They'd lose the element of surprise, and the men inside would have the opportunity to flee the area before the remainder of the tactical team had a chance to set up a perimeter.

He looked from one glowing window to the next. Drapes or blinds blocked out the majority of the light inside, and he couldn't tell if there were shapes moving behind the barrier or if his overactive imagination was playing a trick on him.

As he stepped over the curb to the strip of grass in front of the sidewalk, Zane glanced to Amelia. Even in the low light, determination was evident in her steely gaze. A far cry from the trepidation he'd seen at the previous house.

Her focus shifted, almost as if she could sense the sudden

scrutiny. "What?" She turned her narrow gaze on him with a look that made him want to take a step back.

He shook his head. "Nothing. Just thinking about tornadoes for some reason."

She smirked, but before she had the chance to say something snarky, Agent Harris beckoned them forward.

Harris pointed to the paper in Zane's hand. "That's the warrant, I take it?"

Zane nodded. "Sure is."

"All right, you three know the drill." Harris tilted his chin at a familiar dark-haired man who held a compact battering ram. "We've got Agent Wilson with another two agents out back to make sure no one tries to run off into the night. Lopez breaches the door, and then we take point. You two follow, announce the warrant, and make arrests. Then, we'll give the signal to Agent Wilson. She'll take backup and head down to the basement to secure it."

Amelia readjusted the rifle against her shoulder, barrel pointed at the sidewalk. "We don't expect them to get violent, but the Leóne family is cagey. Best to prepare for the unexpected with them."

Agent Harris scowled at the mention of the prominent crime family. "You're right, Storm. We go in fast and quiet, at least until we're actually inside. We've got backup standing by and ready to roll in if things happen to get messy. When I heard who we were dealing with, I made sure we pulled out all the stops. Any questions?"

Zane and Amelia both shook their heads.

Orange streetlight reflected off the glass of Tom Harris's watch as he turned his wrist to check the time. "Sixty seconds, exactly. Let's go."

They advanced silently, the grass muting their steps as they headed toward the door. The porch, though technically covered by an awning, had clearly been neglected.

As they drew closer, taking the few concrete steps up to the porch, Zane picked up on more evidence of the house's state of disrepair. Little imperfections in the house's exterior like cracked siding, tree roots pushing up the concrete at the edge of the porch, and windowsills that looked like they belonged in the 1980s. Whether the front door was beige or just dirty, he couldn't quite tell.

One thing was clear, this was not a family residence. Old places like this, when kept up by their owners, retained their value. But for those who used them merely as investment properties, the upkeep and maintenance were afterthoughts only focused on when something broke beyond use. That, to Zane, was a good sign that they were, in fact, at the right place.

Amelia and Tom flanked the right-hand side of the door. Zane and Lopez took the left. Harris checked his watch one last time before raising his free hand.

Time slowed to a crawl as the man lifted three fingers. Though Zane's pulse rushed in his ears, his grasp on the Carbine was steady.

They had no idea what awaited them on the other side of the dingy front door.

Maybe they'd walk into a den of heavily armed men, or maybe they were about to rush headlong into another dead end. The surveillance of the house had been constant over the past twenty-four hours, but maybe they'd missed an angle. An exit.

Overhead, the drooping branches of an old oak scraped at the roof. The smell of incoming rain was stronger now. Zane thought he spotted a faint flash of light against the orange-tinted night sky.

As soon as Harris's gloved hand closed into a fist, the quiet shattered like a pane of glass in an action movie.

A crack followed the dull thud of Lopez's battering ram

as metal smashed into cheap wood. In one blow, the door blew backward into a pint-sized foyer. It crashed against drywall with a second quieter crack and came to rest awkwardly on one hinge.

Zane shoved the warrant back into a pocket as he followed Agent Lopez through the doorway. Just past the foyer, a short hall opened into a galley kitchen, and an arched doorway on one side revealed a dining room.

A thin haze of smoke drifted toward the bronze-finished light fixture that hung a few feet above a circular wooden table. Aside from a couple smartphones, all that adorned the tarnished tabletop was a heavy glass ashtray.

Only seconds had elapsed from the time they'd breached the door to the time they arrived at the dining room, leaving scarcely any opportunity for the men in the house to react.

Four sets of eyes went wide as Zane and Agent Lopez stepped through the doorway.

Zane tucked the stock of the rifle tighter against his shoulder. "Hands! All of you, hands where we can see them! Slowly!"

The white light caught the faint shine of one of the men's ebony hair as he nodded. Without breaking his scrutinizing glare away from Zane and Lopez, he flattened both palms against the table.

Zane recognized him from Amelia's series of paparazzi photos.

Emilio Leóne. The man was actually here.

Lopez sidestepped to make room for Amelia and Agent Harris. "How many more are in here?"

Emilio's dark eyes flitted to the older man at his side and then to the two others. None of them made a move to answer the query.

Though he kept his finger on the frame of the rifle, Zane settled the red dot sight over the center of Emilio's chest.

"Hey, asshole. How many more are in here? We've got a warrant to search this entire house and another one to arrest whoever's in it. If you want to make us go through here room by room, let me tell you…it won't end well."

Even though Zane wasn't sure what he meant by his own threat, he let the words hang in the smoky air. They'd go through the house no matter what Emilio told them.

Emilio exchanged glances with the older man. "It's just us."

As much as Zane had come to dislike the Leóne capo over the past week, he had to admit that the man's cool veneer was impressive. The older man—Emilio's number two, if Amelia's research was correct—was almost as calm as Emilio. If not for the bead of sweat running silently down number two's temple, he'd have sold the completely calm veneer.

Agent Harris pointed to Amelia, and she and Lopez skirted around the edge of the room, disappearing through another doorway to begin the search.

"Here's what you're all going to do." Zane kept the red dot on Emilio. "You're all going to keep your palms flat on that table, just like your boss, you got it?"

The men exchanged nervous glances before dropping their heads in acknowledgment and palming the table.

Based on their casual attire—a white dress shirt for Emilio, a polo for the man at his side, and a couple button-down t-shirts—it was clear none of them had expected the FBI to knock down their door.

Once arrests were made and suspects were charged, Zane would have to sift through the differences in the two raids. The SAC might not have come out and stated plainly that there was a rat in their midst, but her emergency gag order on the team had proven successful. She had to know that someone in the FBI office was in the Leónes' pocket, but that wasn't the kind of knowledge to be shared in a department-wide briefing.

To his chagrin, there had been so many people involved with both houses that he would need months to sift through every field agent, every tactical agent, and every crime scene technician.

He shoved the thought aside. First, they had to get through tonight.

The silence in the cramped dining room was oppressive. Aside from a faint crack of thunder and the muffled sound of voices from deeper in the house, the air was still. From over the clamor of his heartbeat, Zane could swear he heard Emilio Leóne breathe.

Each Leóne man had taken to diligently staring at their hands, but none made a move to disobey Zane's order to remain still.

Zane barely stopped himself from jerking the rifle around when Harris's voice sliced through the silence.

"Roger that, Alpha Team." Tom lowered the barrel of his rifle and pointed to his earpiece. Along with the leading tactical agent at the second house, the agents guarding the perimeter were the only members of the raiding party who had been outfitted with communication devices.

Zane spared a quick glance to Tom, but he didn't lower his weapon.

"Well, Mr. Leóne." Tom's voice was laden with condescension. "I've got some bad news for you. All those girls you were keeping in your other house are on their way to the FBI office. So are all your guys from that location, but they'll be in a different part of the building, not to worry."

Harris's methodical version of sarcasm was impressive. More often than not, Zane couldn't even tell if the man was *being* sarcastic.

Though slight, Emilio lifted a shoulder. "I've got no idea what you're talking about."

Tom chuckled quietly. "Sure, sure. Well, just so you know. My colleague told me that your cousin Giorgio tried to take off as soon as the door was breached."

The muscle in Emilio's jawline popped. For a split-second, his eyes narrowed before he painted an impassive expression on his face. "I don't know nothing about Giorgio. He's his own man. You got problems with him, you do what you gotta do."

"Come now, Emilio. We know how your family operates. Don't play dumb with us."

Emilio lifted his head, sending a haughty sneer in Zane's direction, refusing to answer the agent's taunt.

"Don't worry, Giorgio will be fine." Tom flashed Zane a grin. "Corsaw clotheslined him with the stock of his rifle before he even made it to the backyard. Knocked him out cold, but no serious injury."

Before Zane could get in another verbal jab, movement snapped his and Tom's attention to the open doorway at the other end of the room. Amelia emerged from the relative darkness.

Zane lowered the rifle but kept the stock tucked against his shoulder. "Did you find her?"

Her worried gaze slowly shifted from Tom to Zane, and then the men seated at the kitchen table.

As her eyes settled on Emilio and his companions, a sneer curled her lip. Zane had never seen such a hateful look cross Amelia's face. She could be downright scary with a look like that. And he was glad he had never been on the receiving end of that kind of death glare. Her grip trembled as she held her weapon at the ready. Zane wondered if she might be considering something outside the scope of their mission. He cleared his throat and drew Amelia's attention back to him.

She let out a heavy breath. "Agent Wilson has her. They'll be headed to the FBI office soon. The rest of the house is clear."

With his free hand, Tom Harris gestured to the four men. "What are we doing with these four knuckleheads?"

Amelia's scowl returned as she tilted her chin at the four Leóne men. "As for these guys, they're all under arrest. We'll Mirandize them and load them up. All of them except Mr. Leóne, here. I've got a few questions for him."

Emilio's mouth was a hard line, but indignation flickered in his dark eyes as he regarded Amelia. "I've got nothing to say to you."

As Amelia offered the man a sarcastic smile, Zane finally let go of the laughter he'd suppressed since Tom's assessment of Giorgio Delusso.

"Yeah, okay." Zane shouldered his rifle and retrieved a set of cuffs from his back pocket. "We'll see about that, bud."

The cunning undertone in Amelia's voice insisted that she knew more about the Leóne operation than she'd let on. And if she still had an ace up her sleeve, then Emilio was in for a long night.

25

Amelia felt like a snake shedding its skin as she stripped her Kevlar vest off. With a sigh, she tugged on the hem of her gray t-shirt to let fresh air circulate over the sweaty part of her chest where the vest had covered.

The green glow of the stove's clock told her they'd been at the house for close to an hour, but with the way time was moving, she could have sworn half a lifetime had passed her by in the rundown split-level.

The three men with Emilio Leóne had been read their rights, bound with industrial-strength zip ties, and loaded into the back of an unmarked van. All the rooms had been cleared multiple times over. As soon as she was through with Emilio, the crime scene techs would move in to collect physical evidence and search for other clues that would tie the occupants to the crimes of which they'd been accused.

She should have felt a measure of satisfaction at the fact that their raid had resulted in the arrests of almost ten Leóne soldiers and a Leóne commander. But when the consummation edged its way into her mind, all she had to do was picture Leila Jackson's gaunt, hallowed face.

The girl's eyes, once a sparkling shade of vibrant blue, had seemed dull. Haunted.

According to Agent Wilson, the poor girl had shrunk back in her makeshift cell even after she had explained that she was with the FBI. Amelia figured the only reason Emily Wilson got through to the girl at all was because she was a woman.

Even then, Emily had to repeatedly reassure Leila before she would so much as budge. Apparently, Leila had been convinced that Agent Wilson's appearance was a test of her loyalty to someone she called The Captain.

Amelia didn't need more than one guess to figure out the identity of the man who'd struck such a debilitating fear in the depths of Leila's psyche. Worry for the child sat heavy on her shoulders as Amelia stepped away from the laminate counter and made her way to the halo of light that shone through the arched doorway.

Emilio Leóne's dark eyes flicked up from where they'd been fixed on the silver handcuffs that bound his wrists and ankles, effectively cutting off any hope he had of escape. Strands of black hair fell over his forehead, and stubble darkened his cheeks, but despite the shadows beneath his eyes, he remained alert.

Amelia didn't let her gaze linger on the Leóne capo. Crossing both arms over her chest, she leaned against the doorway.

Zane had disappeared into the house, searching for any electronics or monitoring devices that could prove useful. In the meantime, Amelia had been left to oversee Emilio.

The perimeter of the house was still heavily monitored, and even more FBI personnel had posted up at certain points along the streets leading to and from the residence.

Though the agents involved in the raid were still under a communication lockdown, SAC Keaton hadn't wanted to risk being caught unaware. If any unwitting Leóne soldiers were headed to the house, they'd be spotted well before they reached their destination. At a quarter after three in the morning, anomalies weren't difficult to spot in the quiet neighborhood.

So far, Amelia hadn't mentioned the information she'd gotten from Alex to anyone aside from SAC Keaton. They still didn't know the location of the meeting to sell Leila, and as the minutes ticked away in relative silence, Amelia wondered if they'd even find out.

She'd sized Emilio Leóne up over the past couple days—ever since she'd first spotted him with Leila—and she was certain his loyalty to the Leóne family was unwavering. The Leónes might not have been as organized and disciplined as the rival D'Amatos, but they were just as loyal.

Not all of them.

Alex's information about Leila Jackson had *come* from a Leóne soldier, after all. Then again, selling out to a rival syndicate hardly compared to cooperating with law enforcement.

She couldn't help but wonder what had inspired Alex's informant to turncoat. Had he grown a conscience, or did he just want Emilio out of the picture so he could have a larger piece of the pie?

If Amelia was a betting woman, she'd put her money on the latter. The idea that anyone who worked for a sex trafficker had a conscience was as laughable as it was naïve.

But if there was one common goal shared by all members of the Leóne crime family, it was the pursuit of power. The desire to paint themselves in a favorable light so the men who ran the family would take note.

As Amelia moved to tap an index finger against her elbow, she froze in place.

The Leónes were loyal to a fault.

That was how she could get to Emilio. If she threatened to ruin his image of steadfast loyalty, he would crack. The tactic was unorthodox, and the only method to employ the strategy was likely illegal, but she was out of options.

At the start of the investigation, the enigmatic figure referred to as The Shark wasn't part of her plan. But now, he was the *only* part of her plan.

Movement drew her out of the contemplation as Zane appeared in the doorway across the room.

Was he the insider working for the Leónes?

A knot formed in her stomach as she considered the possibility. She'd started to think of Agent Palmer as a friend and enjoyed their pretend spats and sarcastic banter.

Growing up, one of the few pieces of good advice she'd received from her father during his days of heavy drinking was to trust her instincts.

Instinct had served her well when she was in the military, and as far back as she could remember, there had always been a feeling. Like a sickness in the pit of her stomach, her own personal warning when someone was truly shady. Even as a kid, it had been there.

She thought back to her sixth-grade teacher, Mr. Johnson. The man had been in his mid-thirties, was married, and had two daughters of his own. He'd always been regarded as the cool teacher who treated his students more like adults than the children everyone else viewed them as. He'd approached her with an offer. She could stay after school to help him with a project, and she'd earn extra credit.

Amelia's grades had been in the toilet at the time, and the only aspect of parenting that seemed to interest her father was to chew her out for the poor marks on her report card. She could have accepted the teacher's offer to get her father off her case.

There had been no logical reason for alarm bells to be

going off in her head, but she couldn't shake the unease. So, despite his reputation and the fact he was her teacher, Amelia couldn't bring herself to take him up on the offer for extra credit.

Six months after she rejected Mr. Johnson's offer, the FBI had knocked down the door to the man's house as part of a coordinated raid against a child exploitation ring. For years, he'd lured unsuspecting students to his home, where he filmed himself as he took advantage of them.

When Amelia mentioned the incident to her father, he praised her for having that gut instinct.

Blinking away the memory, she met Zane's steely eyes. The internal alarm was nowhere to be found.

Her personal assessment wasn't an end-all be-all for determining the motivations of those around her, but for now, she would heed her father's advice. Her gut told her that Zane's motive was the same as hers—to break apart the Leóne trafficking ring until it was an unsavory stain on the collective memory of the city.

She tilted her head toward the kitchen. "Agent Palmer. Can I talk to you for a second?" She glanced to Emilio. "Alone."

A ghost of a sarcastic smirk passed over Zane's face. "Sure thing, Storm." He waved a hand at Emilio. "You. Just stay there."

Mumbling something she couldn't hear, Emilio slumped down in his chair and stretched his legs.

Boards creaked as Zane made his way across the tarnished wooden floor. With one more glance at Emilio, he stepped over the threshold and motioned for her to follow him farther into the shadowy space. As he backed up to stand beside the stainless-steel sink, his gaze flitted from Emilio to her and back.

"There." He crossed his arms and leaned against the

counter. "I can still see him, but as long as we keep our voices down, he can't hear us."

Amelia looked over her shoulder. Emilio was again focused on his handcuffs.

She lifted an eyebrow. "You're sure?"

With a knowing grin, Zane reached out to the side and turned on the faucet. "Positive."

A portion of Zane's amusement made its way to Amelia's face. "Okay, then. You remember when I told you and Larson that Leila's captors might sell her?"

Zane's smile faded. "Yeah. We got to her in time, though." His tone indicated the statement was more question than comment.

Amelia leaned in closer until she caught a whiff of the mystery product in his dark blond hair. "We barely got to her in time. If we'd kept to the schedule and knocked down the door tomorrow night, we would have been too late."

His concerned expression bordered on suspicion. "How do you know that?"

She gave him a flat stare. "My CI. SAC Keaton knows about it too. That's why we were here tonight."

Her explanation seemed to smooth some of the creases in Zane's expression, but she still picked up a hint of questioning behind his eyes. Maybe that was just his general scrutinizing look. Maybe she was just being paranoid. Since learning about the Leóne man in the bureau, Amelia had her hackles up, wondering who she could really trust.

The edge of Zane's lip quirked up. Not quite his trademark grin, but congenial all the same. "Okay. Well, it's a good thing we changed the time."

Amelia held up a hand. "Yeah, but that's part of the problem. We don't know where the sale was supposed to take place, and all we know about the buyer is that his moniker is The Shark."

"Is he a lawyer?" Zane's eyebrow arched curiously.

If only she knew. "I've got no idea. Larson said that he's like the boogeyman or some kind of urban legend, but my CI says otherwise. My CI says that he's got a kink for torturing women and girls, and he's loaded. But beyond that, they didn't know much about him. But…" she raised a finger, "that's who Leila was being sold to."

Lips pressed tightly together, Zane crossed his arms again, turning his eyes skyward as if searching for an answer. After a few moments in awkward silence, Zane shook his head. "But we don't know where they're going to meet him, or even if they're going to meet him at all. If he's remained anonymous all this time, chances are he's sending someone in to do his dirty work so he doesn't get caught."

Amelia's heart sank. Zane had come to the same dead end. And he was right.

Even if they coaxed the location out of Emilio, the odds that they'd actually come across this Shark were slim. If they wanted any chance at getting to the man himself, they would have had to stalk Emilio and his men as they met with The Shark's errand boy. Then, they'd have to follow the errand boy and hope he or she headed straight to their boss's lair.

To accomplish such a feat, they'd need Leila, and Amelia wasn't willing to so much as broach the idea of using the girl as bait. The poor girl had been through more than enough already.

Like swirling gas and debris came together to birth a star, all the little pieces of information coalesced into a plan in Amelia's mind.

Though slight, he shook his head. "No. That's stupid, Storm. There are too many variables we can't account for."

Had he read her mind? The realization was there in his worried gaze. She hadn't said the thought out loud. How could he possibly have figured it out?

"Hear me out here." She held up her hands, palms out, trying to look as passive as she could. "How else do we get to him? Do we wait for some other poor girl to go missing so we can follow the clues and hope we find him then? Hell, we don't even have a first name. All we've got is his damn moniker."

Zane let out a growling breath and pinched the bridge of his nose as if that might ease whatever tension he was feeling. "Just so we're on the same page here...you want to pose as Leila so we can follow the people away from this meeting, right?"

She squared her jaw.

He growled low in his throat. "We don't know who Emilio was supposed to meet. For all we know, they might know him, and they'll realize right away that we aren't him. They might just turn tail and run, or they might try to fight. We don't know. There's way too much that we *don't know*."

Amelia crossed her arms. "If they recognize that something's wrong, then we arrest them. We question them, and then at the end of the day, we're better off than we were before. At least then, we'd have *something* to go on. We could use the names of the people we arrested and go from there."

Zane blew out a long breath. "True."

Amelia sensed her opportunity and pressed on. "That's the worst-case scenario. We've got bigger guns than they do, and we'll have more people than them. Despite what Hollywood likes to portray, there aren't many people willing to start a Wild West shootout with the FBI. And best-case scenario, well..." she shrugged, "we get to this Shark character and come away with a major arrest."

"But this is all assuming that we get the location of the meeting from our friend in the other room." To her relief, the doubt had vanished from Zane's tone.

Meeting his gaze, she offered him a half smile. "I've got an idea for that too. But…"

His stare intensified. "But?"

She shoved a piece of hair behind her ear. "It's not exactly…ethical."

Zane let out a snort. "You're worried about ethics with Emilio Leóne? You shouldn't be."

There was more to that statement; Amelia was sure of it. And though she wanted to take it at face value, suspicion wormed through her mind as she scrutinized his face for any sign of deception. Until this case, she'd only had brief opportunities to work closely with Zane.

Sure, they had their office banter, but they'd both only been in Chicago for a few months. Though Amelia had never taken issue with bending rules, she'd grown accustomed to Joseph Larson's by-the-book attitude.

Was this a glaring clue that Zane was the inside man, or was he just as eager to get to the bottom of this case as she was? Too many questions needed answers, but at that moment, finding the Shark beat out her need to investigate Zane's motives.

Before she could open her mouth to say as much, Zane's grim expression softened as if he had sensed her unease. "I worked in D.C. before I transferred out here, remember? A few years before I left, one of the Mexican drug cartels started to set up shop in the city." He lifted a shoulder. "Between them and the Russians, there was only so far you could get when you were doing things by the book. I don't want to say that we did anything illegal, but…"

She studied the man beside her closely, getting a whole new view on Agent Zane Palmer. "The gray area. Bending the rules, but not breaking them. Right?" Maybe he was just as eager as her to get this Shark.

"Something like that, yeah." That trademark grin of his

returned, disarming her the moment it flashed across his face. "As long as you don't start breaking Emilio's kneecaps with a tire iron or waterboarding him, it won't be anything I haven't seen before."

"Well, that leaves me with nothing fun to do," she teased, feeling a little more confident about her partnership. "I guess I'll just have to leave the tire iron out in the car."

He chuckled silently as amusement broadened his smile. "Perfect. I'll follow your lead."

With a wink, Amelia turned off the faucet. "Okay. Let's go."

Emilio snapped to attention as soon as they passed through the doorway. Wordlessly, Amelia pulled out a wooden chair and dropped down to sit across from the Leóne commander. From the corner of her eye, she saw Zane stretch both arms above his head before he leaned a shoulder against the doorframe.

Though his gaze shifted between Amelia and Zane suspiciously, Emilio remained silent.

Wood creaked as Amelia leaned forward to prop her elbows atop the table. "Mr. Leóne, sorry to keep you waiting for so long. We've got a few questions for you."

Emilio laced his fingers together. "I've got nothing to say to you people. Not without my lawyer present."

Amelia had expected the rebuff and enjoyed taking him farther down the rabbit hole. "Why would you need a lawyer? You've done nothing wrong, right?"

His expression darkened.

Waving a dismissive hand, Amelia chuckled. "We're not asking you about anything you've done, anyway. It won't take a rocket scientist to figure out all the shady shit you were doing here, and it won't take an expert interrogation, either."

Emilio's venomous stare faltered for the briefest of

moments before he snarled, "What the hell are you talking about?"

Amelia tapped a finger against the tarnished wooden table. "Well, I'll tell you what we're *not* talking about. We're not talking about you. In fact, you can think of yourself as a witness right now. And..." she gave him a playful wink, "witnesses don't need lawyers, do they?"

With both hands clenched into fists, Emilio narrowed his eyes. "I don't know what kind of game you're playing. And I don't have to tell you people anything."

Keeping her tone playful, Amelia leaned back in her rickety chair. "No, I don't suppose you do. There's not a lot I can do to make you spill your guts, short of, well, I don't know..." she added steel to her voice and countenance, "breaking your knees with a tire iron?"

A little of the color left Emilio's face. He held on to his stony expression, but the way he seemed to find anywhere to look except at Amelia said his defiant streak had waned.

Zane chortled behind her. "Let me know if you need me to grab it from the car."

The muscles in Emilio's cheeks vibrated as he clenched and unclenched his jaw. A spark of fury flared to life in his gaze, but next to the anger was the sentiment Amelia sought.

Emilio Leóne was nervous. He was used to ignoring society's rules and playing by his own, so he didn't have to stretch his imagination to believe that a couple unsupervised federal agents would be more than willing to do the same.

Truth be told, his assertion wasn't far off the mark. Every time Amelia pictured Leila's hallowed cheeks, she wished she could forgo legal formalities and smash Emilio's chiseled face into the table until he gave her the information she wanted.

Instead of reaching for a handful of Emilio's hair, Amelia painted a deceptively pleasant smile on her lips.

Shaking his head, Emilio looked from Amelia to Zane.

"This is bullshit. You can't do this. I don't have to talk to you without my lawyer. This is ill—"

Amelia smacked her hand against the table. The sharp slap shattered the quiet atmosphere with the force of a cannonball.

Emilio jolted back, and metal clattered as he retracted his hands to assume a defensive posture.

As soon as he realized he wasn't in danger, the Leóne capo attempted in vain to return to the cold impassiveness he'd worn before.

"Illegal?" She pinned Emilio with a hard stare. "You were going to say that this is illegal? I'm sorry, Mr. Leóne, have you passed the Bar?"

Emilio opened and closed his mouth a couple times before he spoke. "That's not relevant, I—"

"Yes or no!" Amelia's voice cracked through the air like a whip. "Have you passed the Bar, Mr. Leóne?"

Shadows danced along his cheeks as he gritted his teeth, but he didn't respond.

Amelia straightened in her seat. "No, I didn't think you had. Now, if you're finished with your little…outburst, let me tell you what's going to happen here tonight."

She could hear the elevated cadence of his breathing in the silence that followed. Her goal so far hadn't been to get Emilio to crack but to make him realize she wasn't bluffing.

When he didn't vocalize a reply, she allowed her amusement to show. Smiles were all part of the process—the more unhinged she appeared, the better.

"That girl in the prison cell in your basement is Leila Jackson, but I'm sure you knew nothing about that." Amelia propped both elbows on the table and laced her fingers together. "You were going to sell her, weren't you?"

Emilio's expression mimicked surprise.

Before he could speak, Amelia lifted a finger to silence

him. "I'm not done yet. You were going to sell her tomorrow. Well, today, technically. And you were going to sell her to someone who you people call The Shark."

A faint sheen of perspiration became visible on Emilio's brow. His breathing, too, seemed to have grown labored. "I don't know what you're talking about."

With a snort, Amelia waved a hand. "Right. Of course you don't. Remember how I said that there's more than enough in this house to hang you? Well, that's true. But..." she made a show of weighing her hands, "with that taken into consideration, we have nothing to point us to this Shark character that you all seem to hold in such high regard. Now, I'm a big picture kind of person. I'm sure you can relate, right, Emilio?"

He clenched his jaw and shook his head. "I'm not going to make a deal with you people. Just send me to prison with the rest of my guys."

Amused, Amelia's smile was genuine this time. "You'd like that, wouldn't you?"

Emilio blinked but remained silent.

Draping one arm over the back of the chair, she turned to Zane. "Kind of weird when you run into someone who asks to go to prison, isn't it? Why on *earth* would you *want* to go to jail, Mr. Leóne? You said yourself that you had no idea what we were talking about. Do you think you deserve to be in prison for some reason?"

Zane matched Amelia's expression with a sly grin of his own. "It is weird. I bet all your friends are wondering why you stayed behind, aren't they?"

This time, Emilio took longer to temper his shocked expression. "No. They know I wouldn't talk to you. They know I'm no *rat*."

Zane's stare didn't waver. "Do they, though? That's the

thing about traitors, Emilio. If they know what they're doing, you never see their betrayal coming."

With an appreciative nod, Amelia turned to Emilio. "And it looked like you were being investigated a while back for an unrelated venture. Something about drug trafficking, if I remember right. Drug trafficking in Milwaukee, wasn't it? All those charges were dropped, and our colleagues in Wisconsin said it was due to lack of evidence. But was it *really*? Or was it something else? Maybe. I don't know." She twirled her finger in the air to make a show of searching for the right word. "Maybe you cut a deal. Let someone else take the fall, so you didn't have to."

Emilio bared his teeth as his face flushed with anger. "They'll know you're lying. I'm a *Leóne*."

Amelia almost laughed. "But you did. You cut a deal, and some poor shmuck is rotting away in the prison cell that was meant for you. It all comes out eventually."

"That's bullshit. You got nothing!"

"You sure about that?" She leaned in close, dropping her voice to a whisper only he could hear. "I got plenty of friends in low places. You'd be surprised by the things they'll be happy to dig up if I happen to look the other way on occasion. I know where all of your skeletons are buried, Leóne. Do you?"

He exploded backward so hard he almost lost his balance and tumbled from his chair. "You're lying! You got nothing. My family knows I'd never turn on them."

"Do they, though?" She rose to her full height with a cackle that would have done Cruella de Vil proud. "Because your reaction right now says something entirely different. Right, Palmer?" She turned her gaze to her partner, trying to communicate with her eyes for him to back up whatever she said.

He didn't let her down. "If you're starting a death pool, give me twenty-four hours. I'm feeling lucky with this one."

"That's generous of you. I would have guessed, for an in-house job, maybe eighteen, tops." She rounded on Emilio, curiosity opening her eyes wide. "Tell me. How long does the Leóne family usually need to take care of a problem?"

"This is bullshit. I want a lawyer."

"I wouldn't do that." Amelia's grin drooped into an exaggerated pout. "Be mad all you like, but deep down, you know there's truth to what I'm saying. Once word gets out you've been working with Feds and rolling on your own people, you'll be dead by sunrise. That's the price in your family, right? The expectation of loyalty is paramount."

Amelia let silence be her friend for a few moments as she rounded the table to stand behind the man who'd begun to stink of sweat.

She leaned in close to his ear. "I'm sure you're intimately familiar with the policy, Leóne. It's all there in your eyes. The suspicion and paranoia. How many times have you personally 'dealt with' one of your people because one little thing was off about them?"

Through the shroud of silence that descended, Amelia could have sworn she heard Emilio's heart trying to break free from his chest. She moved back to her chair, shifting it even closer to him this time.

Strands of ebony hair fell across his face as he let his head droop and again stared at his handcuffs. "You're just messing with my head. You got no proof. Nothing. Try to call me a rat. Go ahead. They'll never believe it." As he lifted his chin to meet her stare, she offered him a sly smile.

"No proof. Is that what you think?" Zane chuckled quietly. "I don't think they'll be interested in *proof*. Your family isn't a courtroom, Emilio."

Amelia covered her mouth to cover a yawn that was only

a little fake. She was tiring of this game. "Besides, we've still got Wisconsin. And once you walk out of here today, I dare say your family might sense a pattern."

Emilio's jaw went slack. "No. You can't do this. You can't do *that*."

"Can't do what?" Amelia laughed, though the sound was mirthless and condescending. "Can't let you go? Weren't you just telling us about how this was all illegal? You never called your lawyer because you didn't *need* one!"

His head was shaking before she finished. "You can't do that. They'll kill me."

"Put me down for twenty on a three-hour spread," Zane offered eagerly, nodding toward the door like he couldn't wait to strike up a bet with his fellow agents. "I think I'd better hedge my bets. Fifteen, sixteen, or seventeen hours 'til they whack him."

She turned and winked at Zane's well-timed play, letting the silence become anxious before she rounded back to face Leóne. "And after you're dead, Emilio, you'll still be branded a rat. That's a stain that can't be washed away, isn't it?" She tapped her lip. "How long do you think they'll let your fiancée stay so pretty?"

Emilio raised his cuffed hands to push the hair out of his eyes. "What do you want?"

Though the question was laden with vitriol, the words were music to Amelia's ears. Casting aside the game they'd been playing, she turned serious. "I want your buyer. I know they're not coming here, and I know you were supposed to drive Leila to the meeting location. I want the time, the place, and any other details you can give me."

She already knew that the meeting was slated for nine in the morning, but the question would be a good gauge of Emilio's propensity for telling her the truth.

Emilio's heavy gaze shifted between her and Zane. In the

past fifteen minutes, he might as well have aged ten years. "And if I tell you?"

Amelia tilted her head in feigned contemplation. "You tell us everything you know about that meeting. I don't care about anything else, that meeting is all I want. You do that, and we'll say that we pulled the information from your phone or from one of the computers in the house. Then, we'll send you off to prison with all your friends, and we can forget about this unpleasant conversation."

The Leóne capo fixed his blank stare on the drywall to Amelia's side. She let the wheels in his head turn for a beat before she spoke.

"You can think about it for a little bit, but we don't have all night. Pretty soon, the crime scene techs are going to roll through this house. The second one of them walks through the door, we're done here."

His eyes drifted back to her, but the indignation was gone. It was replaced by defeated resignation. "You'll say you got it all from my phone? And no one will know it was me?"

Amelia kept her expression blank. "That's right. We can say it was part of your deleted browser history, something that was permanently deleted before we could log it as evidence."

With a shaky sigh, he swiped at the sweat on his forehead. "Fine. The meeting was supposed to happen at nine tomorrow morning, or today, technically."

Leaning forward in her chair, Amelia glanced at the digital clock above the stove. "So, about four-and-a-half hours from now?"

Emilio nodded. "Yeah. Some park north of Oak Brook. Timber Park. The southern parking lot. We were just supposed to say, 'I'm here for the drop-off,' so they'd know it was us."

As she tapped her finger against the tabletop, Amelia let the room lapse back into silence.

Zane cleared his throat. "Who are you supposed to meet? Do you have names for any of them?"

"No names." Emilio shook his head. "The buyer, I've never actually met him. He just goes by Mr. K. They call him The Shark, but he prefers Mr. K. He said he'd send a couple of his boys from security. Guys we haven't met before."

Amelia didn't like this at all. "Any reason for that?"

Emilio shook his head. "He didn't say." The Leóne capo lapsed into silence, but the muscles in his jaw shifted as he gritted his teeth. Finally, he lifted his head and met her questioning gaze. "You people have no idea who you're dealing with. This guy is connected. He's got cops on his payroll, *Feds* on his payroll. If you go after him, you're both as good as dead."

Studying Emilio carefully, Amelia picked up on his genuine fear. "You just said you don't have any idea who he is. Now, you're trying to scare me by telling me he's going to track me down if I arrest him." She glanced to Zane, who nodded. "I don't think you're really qualified to make that assessment, Mr. Leóne."

"Just because I've never met him doesn't mean I don't know what he's capable of." He looked around the room as if unable to find a thing to focus on. "He's got more money than God, and he's got friends in high places." He looked down, picking at the nail on his right hand. "When your loved ones start to turn up dead, don't say I didn't warn you."

Flattening both palms, Amelia pushed against the table and rose from her chair.

She pinned Emilio with a withering stare, and this time, he was quick to look away. "Maybe someone like that frightens *you*, Mr. Leóne. Maybe you think that this Mr. K is the absolute worst that humanity has to offer, but trust me when I say this...I've seen the devil, and he doesn't wear a suit and tie."

As she straightened, Amelia turned to her partner.

"We need anything else from him?" Zane asked with more uncertainty than he'd had in the last few moments.

"I don't think so." She spared another glance to Emilio and rapped her knuckles on the table. "Thank you, Mr. Leóne. Your cooperation in this matter is *greatly* appreciated."

He shot her a petulant glare, and she countered with the widest of smiles.

The sheer defeat in his eyes gave her a measure of satisfaction that an arrest alone wouldn't so much have touched.

She'd beaten Emilio Leóne at his own game, but now she had to hope she could do the same to Mr. K.

26

Though the sun had risen more than an hour earlier, the parking garage at the FBI office was still as shadowy and dim as it had been at night. Zane stifled a yawn and glanced out the tinted passenger's window at his side. The car's engine hummed quietly, but between the sound and the closed doors, he couldn't make out what Spencer Corsaw was saying to Joseph Larson and SAC Keaton.

After hearing about the potential of a rat among the agents, he paid extra attention to the subtle interactions and movements of each agent on the team. As soon as the case was finished, he'd have a closer look at each person's reports and logs.

Humid air blew through the back seat as Amelia Storm pulled open the rear passenger side door, shocking Zane from his focused observation.

When Amelia's eyes—vivid blue instead of forest green— met his, Zane blinked a few times to anchor himself in reality. He'd had a few sets of colored contacts from a Halloween party he'd attended two years ago. He could have passed as

Thor with his natural eye color, but at the time, he and his then-girlfriend had sought authenticity.

He'd thought the details were silly back then, but now he was glad that he'd gone all-out in his depiction of the Norse deity turned superhero. In fact, he'd been the one to make the suggestion to Amelia and SAC Keaton. Leila's blue eyes stood out in striking contrast to her fair skin, and such a feature was difficult to miss.

In order to save some cash, he'd bought a total of four pairs of reusable blue contacts. Between his stash of colored contacts and Amelia's hairstylist sister-in-law, they had enough costume accessories to put on a play.

A pair of worn track pants and a baggy zip-up hoodie completed Amelia's disguise. The transformation wasn't jarring, but Zane, Joseph, and SAC Keaton all agreed that she could pass for Leila at a cursory glance. Amelia was only an inch or so taller than Leila, and the baggy clothes hid much of her figure.

Plus, the hoodie offered more than enough space to conceal a trusty Glock and a badge.

In an effort to emulate the appearance of a Leóne soldier, Zane wore black slacks and a neatly pressed white dress shirt. Though admittedly not a far cry from his usual attire, he would have added a gold chain if he'd found one.

Most people with Italian lineage didn't have dark blond hair and gray eyes, but he could only take the disguise so far on short notice.

As Amelia slid into the back seat of the Town Car, Zane reached down to the bag at his feet to retrieve a couple coffee energy drinks. No one at the Chicago field office had managed even a short power nap, and now they were headed to a meeting with a potentially hostile counterparty.

Zane stifled a yawn and handed one of the coffees to Amelia.

She took it with an enthusiasm that made him smile. "Thanks."

Zane leaned back in his seat as he cracked open the can. "So, what do you make of the buyer sending two new guys to this meetup?"

She scratched her temple with one hand while lifting the drink to her lips with the other. "Could be standard for him. He sends people who aren't aware of what they're actually doing, and then they've got plausible deniability if anything goes wrong. Are wigs supposed to itch?"

Zane laughed into his drink. "I think it's normal. I don't know. I wore a wig when I was Thor for Halloween, which is where those contacts came from. But I'd been drinking all night, so if it was itchy, I don't remember."

Amelia's face brightened as she turned to him, curiosity filling her expression. "Why did you buy four pairs of blue contacts?"

He lifted a shoulder and took a quick sip. "Free shipping."

She continued to scratch, this time at her nape. "Didn't take you for the bargain shopping type."

"Is there any other way to be?" Zane's tone bordered on insulted.

"For me. Yeah. But you had Mommy Warbucks."

"Hey." He lifted a finger from his drink in feigned outrage. "Just because my mom made lots of money doesn't mean she just bought us whatever we wanted. We had the necessities covered, but we had to work for all the other stuff. When I was sixteen, she told me she'd buy me whatever car I wanted, but I had to pay the insurance."

Amelia's grin widened. "How'd that turn out?"

"Not quite like sixteen-year-old me expected." His angry façade dissipated as he chuckled at the memory. "I didn't know much of anything about car insurance at the time, and I figured, hey, how bad can it be? Well, as it turns out, car insurance for a sixteen-year-old boy is pretty damn expensive. I'd already gotten a job bussing tables so I could have a few extra bucks, and according to my calculations, I would have had to work eighty-hour weeks just to pay for the bare-bones insurance for the car I really wanted."

Lifting an eyebrow, Amelia sipped her drink. "Did you?"

Zane laughed. "Hell no. I got a ten-year-old Toyota Camry on Craigslist. It was a solid car, though. Lasted me all the way through college."

"Toyotas last forever." Amelia wholeheartedly agreed. "I bought one when I got my signing bonus from the military. I didn't replace it until I got out of Quantico."

As their side discussion drew to a close, Spencer pulled open the driver's side door and dropped down into the seat. Once the door was closed, he heaved a relieved sigh. "I didn't think it was supposed to still be this damn hot at seven in the morning."

Zane shrugged. "It's mostly the humidity right now." Reaching down to the plastic bag at his feet, he grabbed a coffee drink for Spencer and passed it over. "Here. Figured we could all use a little pick-me-up."

"Oh, thanks, Palmer. I love these things. My wife buys them in bulk at Costco." He set the can in the cup holder before he dropped his hand to the gearshift. He turned his tired eyes back to Zane. "We've got about an hour drive to get there. I figure we can find somewhere nearby to park and scope the place out. We could circle the park a few times, but I don't want to do that if I can avoid it. They might be staking the place out too."

"That's true." Zane had been thinking the same thing. "Best to look over the place from a distance. Drones are probably out too."

"Exactly." Spencer's attention shifted to Amelia. "We'll have Harris and the tactical team on standby, as close to the meeting spot as we can get them. Harris said they'd be in a FedEx van and a couple unmarked cars. If everything goes according to plan, you'll be getting in a car with these people by yourself. You sure you're okay with that?"

She smiled. "I'm fine. Just make sure Harris and the cavalry are ready to roll in if something goes off. I'll be wearing a mic, so they'll have more than enough of a heads-up."

Spencer lifted one dark eyebrow. "The distress call?"

"I'm not feeling well." Amelia patted her side. "Don't worry. I've got the Glock."

Zane scratched at the stubble on his chin. "We aren't expecting much from the guys we're going to meet now, but this Mr. K is a different story. We have no idea how he'll react once he realizes he's been set up. We know he's well connected and that he's wealthy, but we don't know the lengths he's willing to go to keep himself that way. Might be that he thinks it's better to commit suicide-by-cop than go to prison."

Amelia's eager gaze settled on Zane. She didn't have to speak for him to know she'd be happy to oblige Mr. K if he decided to commit suicide-by-cop.

And if he was honest, he couldn't say he felt any differently.

Spencer continued the short briefing. "Harris will follow close behind. Wherever you wind up, he and his people will surround the area, and they'll alert the local cops. They've got a couple snipers with them, so you'll be covered from a distance too. You'll need to buy a little time at the start so they can get into position, but they won't need longer than a minute or two."

Amelia and Zane both nodded.

Rubbing both hands together, Spencer fastened his seat belt, popped open his drink, and shifted the car into gear.

The drive to Oak Brook took a little over an hour in morning traffic, but they still arrived thirty minutes ahead of the nine o'clock scheduled time. Though they'd discussed some potential strategies and what-if scenarios on the trip, the drive itself was uneventful.

Aside from Spencer spitting out expletives any time someone cut in front of him without using their blinker, it had been a relatively smooth drive.

Parked on the south side of a two-lane road that separated the park and forest from the start of a neighborhood, they scoped out the area through binoculars and familiarized themselves with the park's layout. Aside from a hiking trail that circled a breadth of trees and relative wilderness, amongst which was nestled a couple small picnic sites, the park didn't boast much in the way of landmarks.

It didn't take Zane long to realize why Mr. K had selected this location. Despite the lush greenery and the plentiful space, the park was vacant. In the fifteen minutes they spent observing the area, they hadn't even spotted a lone jogger.

When Amelia ran an internet search on Timber Park, they'd been provided with their answer.

For the past two decades, the wooded area—including a small lake—had been a popular location for killers to dump their victims' bodies. Local urban legends even insisted that the park was haunted.

Zane and Amelia asked Spencer how he hadn't known about Timber Park, and the SSA merely shrugged. According to him, none of the murders had been Federal jurisdiction. Before Amelia and Zane could give the man too much grief for his oversight, they spotted a flicker of silver amidst the distant trees.

Passing the binoculars to Amelia, Spencer glanced at Zane. "It's a car. Headed to the southern parking lot."

The first wave of excitement greeted him like an old

friend. "Guess they wanted to make sure they got here with plenty of time to set up before anyone else arrived."

After Spencer notified Tom Harris and the tactical team via radio, they pulled away from the convenience store parking lot they'd used for reconnaissance.

Every stop sign and red light on the roundabout route back to the park was agonizing. He didn't anticipate much in the way of volatility from the men they were about to meet, but the sooner they finished the meeting, the sooner Amelia could head toward Mr. K, and the sooner the whole ordeal would be over.

But even though the light traffic felt as if it had taken forever, when the gravel lot came into view, he wished he'd had a few minutes more. The sentiment was the same for almost any nerve-racking event, and Zane would be surprised if his two companions weren't filled with the same sense of impending unease.

As Spencer pulled into a spot across from a sleek silver sedan, Zane realized he wasn't nervous about the meeting itself. He was nervous about what came after. Despite all their planning, there was always an element of uncertainty. The chaos effect that had the potential to ruin the best laid plans. And of course, there was also the rat. Whoever that was. He knew he could rule out Amelia at this point, but what of Spencer, Harris, or Larson?

The hum of the engine ceased as Spencer shut off the car. "Show time. I'll open Storm's door, and you walk with her over to that car." His gaze flitted to the rearview mirror. "They're getting out now. They must be our guys."

Using her hands to tussle her hair, Amelia looked like an actor sinking into her character's mindset. She slumped her shoulders and tilted her head down, and with those two movements, the transformation was incredible. Gone was the confident FBI agent. In her place was a young girl. Exhausted, meek, and subservient.

Zane gave the command to Spencer. "Let's go."

After pulling down the aviator sunglasses resting on his head, Zane and Spencer shoved open their doors in tandem. At least with sunglasses, his light-colored eyes wouldn't be visible.

As Spencer strode around the front of the car to make his way to Amelia's side, Zane eased the door closed and turned to the pair of men and their silver car.

An Infiniti. Classy for a couple errand boys.

The two men stood in front of the rear fender of the luxury vehicle. The taller of the duo sported caramel-colored hair that took on a reddish tint in the morning sun. To his side, the second man was as bald as a baby. Both wore slacks and dress shirts, but neither man had a visible weapon. In all honesty, they looked more like chauffeurs than gangsters or goons.

Zane tried to covertly study the men's facial features as Spencer pulled Amelia out of the back seat. Taking hold of Amelia's upper arm, Zane nodded to Spencer. The SSA stepped back to wait beside the passenger side door.

Though Zane kept his grip on Amelia's arm, he didn't think a display of callousness was necessary. If the bald man and his friend were unaware of the nature of the meeting, then they wouldn't expect any such behavior. If the men were *truly* in the dark, then they might have been under the impression that Amelia was here of her own volition.

As they closed the distance, Zane greeted them as if conducting a normal business transaction. "We're here for the drop off."

The taller man's face lit up with recognition, even a hint of relief. "You're Emilio, then? We were told you had black hair."

He could lie. He could say that their boss's description had been off, or even that he had dyed his hair in anticipation of summer.

But the lie had the potential to be costly. The errand boys might have been oblivious to the fact that they were aiding in the sale of an underage girl, but their suspicion could still be piqued.

Instead of lying, Zane laughed. "No. Emilio's my boss." He turned to point at the black-haired, dark-eyed Spencer Corsaw. "That's Emilio. He doesn't ever deal with this shit, and he never lets me drive the damn car."

His heart thudded against his chest, but he kept his expression amiable.

As the bald man's mouth curved into a grin, he glanced at his companion. "Hey, that sounds familiar, doesn't it?" His words drawled out with a thick Southern accent.

The taller man snorted out a laugh. "Yeah, it sure does." He extended a hand to gesture to Amelia. "Could you have your girl there look up at us? I doubt there was a mix-up, but we ought to be sure."

"Sure thing." Zane nudged Amelia's upper arm. "Baby doll, be a good girl now, and look at the man."

Wringing both hands in front of herself, Amelia hesitated before lifting her chin. As she glanced from Zane to the pair of men and back, the bald man nodded.

"Yeah, okay. That's our girl. We'll take her from here. Thanks for being on time. That ain't always a luxury we get."

Zane flashed his trademark grin.

Clueless henchmen.

Now, whether their obliviousness was a positive or a negative, they would have to wait and see.

27

A s Amelia eased into the back seat of the silver sedan, she caught a hint of stale cigarette smoke and mint. She glanced around the interior in the hope that she might find a clue as to who these men were or where they were taking her, but the gray upholstery was spotless. Even the carpeted floor had been vacuumed.

Chances were good that the car would be detailed again to remove any trace of Amelia's presence.

Well, it *would* have been detailed, but the end of the two men's day was about to undergo a dramatic change.

Back at the FBI office, SAC Keaton and Joseph Larson had agreed with Amelia's team that the likelihood of violence at the meeting to drop off Leila was minimal. A couple of lackeys had a far better shot at beating criminal charges than the person who oversaw them.

Part of Amelia hadn't expected the impromptu operation to succeed as far as it already had.

So far, the obliviousness of the two errand boys had worked in her favor, but their ignorance was a double-edged sword. If the case ever went to trial, they would be useless as witnesses, and plausible deniability would give them each a solid legal defense.

The sound of the driver's side door opening pulled her away from the contemplation. Fiddling with the drawstrings of her hoodie, Amelia lowered her head and fixed her gaze on the floor. She might have fooled them at a casual glance, but she wasn't willing to push the disguise much farther. Besides, she was supposed to be a frightened teenager right now.

By the time the bald man took his seat, the chill of adrenaline had become a stranglehold.

With a long, silent breath, Amelia clenched and unclenched her hands to ground herself in reality. If she was overcome with such a strong sense of trepidation, she could hardly imagine how Leila would have felt if the actual meeting had taken place.

Leila wouldn't have had a microphone hidden in the collar of her shirt, nor would she have had a badge and a Glock.

Still, as they pulled away from the gravel lot and the circle of tall trees, Amelia felt more and more like a lost diver being swept out to sea. But instead of endlessly shifting water, she was being propelled toward a monster.

Swallowing in an effort to chase away the cotton balls that had been stuffed in her mouth, Amelia dared a glance up to the rearview mirror, looking straight into the predatory gaze of the driver.

A malevolent smile stretched his lips.

An involuntary shudder worked its way up from the base of her spine, and her stomach clenched. If she hadn't been after a much bigger fish, the expression alone would have been enough to make her whip out her gun and badge. Amelia could just imagine the kind of thoughts that inspired a lecherous look like that on a criminal's face.

Rather than narrow her eyes to shoot the creep a steely glare, she dropped her chin and averted her gaze. The men might have been ignorant of the fact that they were aiding in an underage human trafficking deal, but they were far from innocent bystanders.

Though she expected the pair to discuss the music on the radio, the ongoing baseball season, or even the damn weather, the bald man wasted no time before launching into a story about one of his more recent sexual conquests.

"Hey." Scratching his dark beard, Baldy turned to his friend. "You know that new girl the boss hired to clean back at the house?"

The other man nodded. "The one with the ass like..." Amelia caught the flicker of movement as he gestured, but she wasn't quite able to make out his hand motion.

Baldy clapped his hands together as if he were issuing himself a high five. "Yeah. That's the one."

The driver laughed as he replaced his hand on the wheel. "Dude, isn't she like seventeen? She's jailbait, isn't she?"

His buddy joined in the laughter as if the comment had actually been funny. "Age is just a number, you know? And that's the great thing about high school girls. I get older, but they'll always be the same age."

Amelia pressed her lips together to avoid a resigned groan. If he was going to quote from a movie, he could at least get the wording right.

Baldy went on to describe in detail how he'd used his position of authority as a member of the security team to manipulate the poor girl into having sex with him not once, not twice, but three separate times. Grating her teeth together to keep from pulling out her service weapon to pistol whip the sick bastard into a coma, Amelia made a mental note to circle back to the recording of the men's conversation. If she made it out of today in one piece, she would make it her personal mission to ruin the two men's lives.

As Amelia scowled, she combed a little more black hair in front of her face to further obscure her expression.

The pair went on to swap similar stories, each more graphic than the last. Whoever they thought Amelia was, they didn't care enough about her presence to censor themselves.

For the first twenty minutes of the journey, they traveled north. As the driver merged onto a freeway that would take them east, Amelia breathed out a silent sigh of relief. At least on the interstate, Amelia didn't feel like she'd been left completely alone with the two rapists. She didn't doubt she could take them both on regardless of whether they were armed, but if they tried, she would lose her opportunity to make it to their infinitely more depraved boss.

Once they exited the freeway to turn north again, Amelia knew they had to be close to Lake Michigan. Without fully lifting her head, she made an effort to pick out street names and landmarks. Problem was, she'd never been to this part of Illinois. As far as she was concerned, the lakeshore areas north of Chicago were reserved for the wealthy. Amelia had written off ever visiting the area before she'd even finished grade school.

As the car slowed to a stop in front of a red light, Amelia tilted her head to the side to rub her eyes. She'd never worn contacts before, and Joseph Larson—who had worn contacts since he was a freshman in high school—had spent close to twenty minutes teaching her how to put in the lenses and adjust them until they were comfortable.

Thanks to his patient tutelage, she had hardly noticed the contacts so far that morning. But as she rubbed her eye, the lens shifted away from her pupil. At first, she assumed that the lens had drifted beneath her eyelid, so she blinked repeatedly to usher it back into place.

Instead, a wet tear fell from her lower lashes. Or, at least, she thought it was a tear until she looked down to the back of her hand.

To her chagrin, an ethereal circle of blue peered back up at her.

Squeezing both eyes closed, Amelia gritted her teeth together to keep a string of expletives at bay.

"How much time we got left before we get there, you think? We're almost there, right?" Baldy's question came after a solid five minutes of silence.

"'Bout ten, probably a little less. Why?"

"I've got to take a leak. I'll be good for ten, though."

For the last forty-five minutes, Amelia had been praying to whatever god would listen, begging for the agonizing journey to finally come to an end. Now, the announcement came as abruptly as a punch to the gut.

She moved slowly and carefully, pinching the contact lens between the thumb and forefinger of her free hand. With a steadying breath, she closed her eyes and pictured Joseph's lesson.

Gritting her teeth, she followed along with his instructions to position the lens on her finger. With a quick glance through the semi-opaque curtain of her hair to ensure neither man was watching her, she lifted her hand and pressed the contact to her eye.

The dry lens felt like a shard of glass. Her vision blurred as tears flooded her eyes, bringing much needed moisture to soften the contact and allow it to adhere. Every instinct told her to blink hard to sweep away the offending intruder to her sensitive eyes, but she fought to maintain control.

Breathing slowly, she closed her eyes, counting to three before opening them. With another breath, she closed again and counted. Each time her eyes opened and closed, the lens shifted until, eventually, she got it to slide into its place. By that point, her tears and nose were running like a faucet, but at least she could see, and her identity remained intact.

Amelia made no attempt to hide her sniffles as she wiped her cheeks and brushed away the matted strands of hair. Being frightened played right into the role she was playing, not that the men escorting her seemed to pay any attention. Still, her heart hammered a relentless cadence against her chest as she clasped both hands together on her lap and regained composure.

When she looked out the window, she realized with a start that her assertion about their proximity to Lake Michigan had been spot-on. As the car cruised past a speed limit sign marked with a forty-five, the morning sunlight sparkled along the water like so many sequins.

Unlike the marinas of Chicago, the docks this far north seemed to be reserved for personal use. Amelia had never been all that interested in boats, but if she had to guess, most of the larger vessels moored to the docks were worth a small fortune. Though she spotted the occasional fishing boat, most of the space was reserved for a crowd with plenty of zeroes in their bank accounts.

The road curved inland, and a cluster of tall trees all but obscured Amelia's view of the lake. When the car came around the bend, the driver slowed the vehicle and flipped on the blinker.

After a short stretch of asphalt between trees, they emerged in a long, rectangular parking lot. A two-story building, likely used as a storage facility for the owner of the marina, cast a shadow over the driver's side of the car.

Aside from a sleek Mercedes coupe and a gunmetal Audi, the lot was vacant. Amelia hoped the lack of vehicles meant she wouldn't be forced to square off against a damned army.

As her gaze bounced around the immediate area, she hoped she looked more like an awestruck girl and less like a soldier conducting reconnaissance. She spared a glance to the men in the front seats, but they were oblivious to her presence.

For most of the drive, she'd been worried about how long Tom and his team would take to secure the vicinity. The wooded area that separated the marina from the main road was a stroke of luck. The trees provided ample coverage for Tom Harris and the rest of the FBI to approach without giving themselves away.

She would have to trust that her colleagues would set up their perimeter quickly. Amelia assured herself that the GPS tracker, hidden along with her microphone, was the most accurate in the industry. That meant her team could keep their distance and avoid piquing the two men's suspicion but still be close enough to get to her should any trouble arise.

As they pulled up to park beside the Mercedes, Amelia turned her attention to the docks. The farther of the two housed a couple motorboats and a jet ski, but when she swept her gaze over the closer dock, she froze in place.

A modest yacht cast a shadow over the two men who stood about halfway down the length of the dock. Even from a distance, Amelia could tell that the taller man's rapt attention was fixed on the car. Through the tinted window, she met the unyielding stare until he turned back to his companion.

The hairs on the back of her neck stood at attention like a regiment of little soldiers, and she clenched and unclenched her fists as the cold creep of adrenaline resurged. As much as she wanted to keep her attention on the pair of men on the dock, she swallowed and forced her chin down.

She didn't much care for the man's position on the dock. If she whipped out her badge, there was a chance he could sprint to the nearby yacht and sail off into Lake Michigan. Though the FBI could have a chopper in the air at a moment's notice, Lake Michigan was a massive body of water. Even if they reacted immediately, there was a chance the man could slip away.

"Okay. We're here."

The bald man's voice snapped Amelia to attention.

The driver and his bald passenger shoved open their doors. With her eyes averted downward, Amelia reached for the handle to let herself out into the sunlit parking lot. When the door didn't budge, she was unsurprised. Enabling child safety locks was Kidnapping 101.

A rush of salty, humid air greeted her as Baldy pulled open the door. Amelia hugged herself as she set a tentative foot on the asphalt, giving the impression of a nervous teenager all while enabling easy access to her Glock and badge.

Baldy waved a hand at the two distant men. "Come on, Mr. K has been waiting for you." His tone was so upbeat, he might as well have been dropping her off to meet with a beloved friend instead of an enigmatic sex offender.

Keeping her head bowed, Amelia followed Baldy's lead. From the corner of her eye, she watched the taller man cross his arms and lean against the rear fender of the Infiniti.

The parking lot was well maintained and clean, but Amelia felt as if she was dragging her feet through knee-deep mud. She hated walking so slowly, but her sluggish gait was purposeful. Though she was sure Harris, Zane, and the others were preparing to close in, she still wanted to afford them as much time as possible.

As she and the bald man stepped onto the boardwalk, she went through a mental checklist for the seven-hundredth time.

They'd been parked for close to three minutes, maybe

longer. Her fellow agents had followed her GPS signal—just far enough behind to avoid being spotted, but close enough to be of use if the situation deteriorated. Three agonizing minutes should have been plenty of time.

Her footsteps became hollow as they passed over onto the dock. After she'd kept her focus on the ground, Amelia took in a long breath and tilted her head to take stock of the two men.

The taller of the pair had a serious five o'clock shadow darkening his cheeks, but the tight set of his jawline was clearly defined. The hair on top of his head was dark as well, but the occasional silver strand betrayed his generally youthful appearance.

A mature man would be slower and more experienced, whereas youth tended to have more speed and power. Based on the way his shoulders filled the shirt he wore, it was obvious the man took care of himself, probably worked out too. Amelia weighed everything she saw, considering her options and the probability of success if she had to get into a physical altercation prior to her team swooping in.

As soon as Amelia met his pale green eyes, she knew he was Mr. K. The second man was an imposing figure with his muscular frame too, but his eyes didn't have the same spark of viciousness, of *hunger*, as his companion.

Part of Amelia—the part she tried to ignore now that she was no longer in the military—secretly hoped that Mr. K would try to run, or that he'd try to fight. After all the stories she'd heard, and after witnessing the abject terror in Leila's eyes, she wanted a reason to put a bullet in his ass.

She slipped one hand beneath the zip-up hoodie as she returned her attention to the ground. In the last few steps, she brushed her fingers against the textured grip of the Glock. Closing her hand around the weapon, Amelia breathed in deeply and held it.

If any of the three men perceived her as a threat, the motion would set off alarm bells in their heads. No man in their right mind conducted an illegal meeting with another man who approached with one hand tucked into his jacket.

Her pulse rushed in her ears, but what she could see of the men's posture was relaxed.

Apparently, the same paranoia didn't ring true for trafficked teenage girls.

"Thank you, Ryan." The taller man stuck out a hand.

Sunlight caught Ryan's bald head as he nodded. "No problem, Mr. K. Uneventful trip, just like you said."

"Glad to hear that. Thanks for coming to work on your day off."

Amelia snuck a sideways glance at Ryan, catching him as he grinned. She turned away before the scowl could form on her lips. She still wished she'd had the opportunity to pistol whip the creep.

As Ryan's hollow footsteps grew quieter, Amelia clenched her teeth together.

Tom Harris had plenty of time. He and the tactical team *had* to be out there. If they weren't, then Amelia would just pretend they were.

"Hello, Leila. It's nice to meet you." The man's voice was smooth, but the definitive tinge of hunger permeated each word.

Still clamping one hand around the grip of her Glock, Amelia kept her gaze low, maintaining the guise of submissiveness. As soon as she tilted her head up, the façade would be over.

"Are you Mr. K?" Her voice was light and airy—a practiced tone she often used with customer service reps.

"That's me." He nodded, and even from where she angled her gaze toward the ground, Amelia didn't miss his smirk. "Look at me, dear."

For the split-second that followed, she tried to think of a cheesy 80s-style action flick one-liner. But between her lack of sleep and the same hyper-awareness she'd previously reserved for a war zone, she came up blank.

Tilting her chin up until she met those unsettling pale green eyes, Amelia pulled her Glock from its holster and retrieved her badge with the other hand.

Smug satisfaction gave way to disbelief as the so-called Mr. K opened and closed his mouth.

Amelia didn't give him time to react. She flipped open her badge and glanced to the shorter man and then back to Mr. K.

"I'm Special Agent Amelia Storm with the Federal Bureau of Investigation." She stepped back and leveled the Glock at Mr. K. "Don't make a move. Don't even breathe. My team has this area surrounded." Amelia caught a shadowy movement at the edge of her vision. Without turning to face the would-be runner, she added volume to her voice. "There are snipers in the woods, so don't expect to get far. If you want to try running, know this, I *will* shoot you, and I don't miss."

The fluttering shadow at the edge of her vision stopped. Amelia allowed a smile to break the stony, commanding exterior she had been radiating. As much as she kind of wanted one of them to test her and make a run for it, she enjoyed how nicely all these big burly and abusive men were snapping to attention at her order.

All except Mr. K, who looked ready to argue.

Amelia wasn't about to let him. For the depraved things he'd been planning for poor Leila…no. He didn't deserve a voice.

"Everyone here, listen up." Again, she used her loudest, most commanding voice. She'd have made a good drill sergeant if she'd wanted. "You boys are all under arrest. We've got a nice long list of felonies to charge you with.

Kidnapping, sex trafficking of a minor, transportation of a minor with intent to engage in criminal sexual activity." She let out an exaggerated whistle as she met Mr. K's heated glare.

The fire of indignation in Mr. K's eyes could have warmed Amelia's apartment building for an entire winter.

She matched the intensity of his expression with her own amusement. He could glare all he wanted. Where he was going, he was likely to be on the receiving end of a few unwanted sexual encounters himself.

"If even one of you assholes gets any ideas to try my patience, we can add resisting arrest to the litany of charges. We've already got enough on you to make sure you never see the light of day, so the more paperwork you make for me, the worse it will be on you."

At his unabashed ire, her smile only widened.

Try to run, Mr. K. I dare you.

"Do we all understand each other?" When Mr. K's head dropped in defeat, Amelia pocketed the badge and grasped her service weapon with both hands. "Now, put your hands on your heads and get on your fucking knees. You have the right to remain silent, and I suggest you do. I don't wanna hear a peep."

28

As a streak of lightning arced across the muddy gray sky, Zane wondered if he should regret his offer to drive Amelia to DeKalb. The late July storm had come out of nowhere, and he hoped that meant it was one of the Midwest's scattered thunderstorms.

They'd told the Jackson family that they would be in DeKalb by four, but if Zane had to drive through a storm, they'd have to amend the expectation. A late arrival would be no issue under normal circumstances, but Amelia and Zane's visit had been arranged via a United States Marshal. The Marshals' Witness Protection specialists were some of the most uncompromising, by-the-book people Zane had ever met.

Blowing out a sigh, he leaned against the driver's side of his silver Acura as he glanced from the cloudy afternoon sky to the glass double doors that marked the third story entrance to the Chicago FBI office. In the past five minutes, the darkening of the sky had brought the orange lights of the parking garage to life.

Before he could check his watch, he craned his neck as he spotted a flicker of movement from just beyond the double doors. Amelia's focus was on her phone as she shouldered the first set of doors open, followed by the second. As the glass and metal door swished shut behind her, she returned the phone to the fashionable tote bag slung over her shoulder.

Her black flats made little more than a whisper of sound against the concrete, unlike the rock-hard soles of Zane's dress shoes.

She smoothed a hand over her black button-down shirt as she approached. "Hey. How long have you been out here?"

Straightening to face the driver's door, he lifted a shoulder. "Only about five minutes." He dropped one arm to rest along the roof of the car as she circled around to the passenger's side.

"What? You have that look on your face." She patted her cheek for emphasis. "That guilty look, like when you told me the other day that I didn't need to go to Starbucks for the second time in one day. But then you went and got a Frappuccino on your lunch break."

What was it with women and them remembering everything? With a sigh, he pulled open his door. "I had a free drink, okay? I had to use it in the next few days, and it was a pretty shitty day, so I made an executive decision."

With a sarcastic grin, Amelia rolled her eyes. "Okay, whatever. But that's the look I mean, and you didn't finish what you were about to say."

"Yeah, that." He sighed again as they fastened their seat belts. Wordlessly, he reached across Amelia's lap to pop open the glove compartment. After he shuffled past the registration and insurance papers for the car, he pulled out the object of his search—a half-full soft pack of Camels.

Amelia looked ready to throttle him as he held up the smokes. "When did you get those?"

He dropped the cigarettes into the cup holder and started the car. "I bought them off Spencer. I didn't smoke any of them yet, but I was really tempted to light one up while I was waiting for you."

Her expression was a mix of surprise and guilt. "Hey, I—"

He waved away her concern before she could elaborate. "Sorry. I didn't mean it like that. Not because I was waiting for you, just that I happened to be in a place where I could probably get away with smoking a cigarette."

Amelia gave him a nod of solidarity. "It's been a hell of a month and a half."

"That's one way to put it."

Once they exited the parking garage, Zane turned to a side street that would lead them to the interstate.

None of the trials over the past forty-five days had gone as expected. Or perhaps they'd gone exactly as expected, provided the expectation was for them to go as poorly as possible.

Though Emilio Leóne and his direct co-conspirators had been remanded without bail, Brian Kolthoff—also known as The Shark or Mr. K—had posted bail the day after his arrest. Zane had been under the impression that locating and arresting the Leónes and Brian Kolthoff was the most difficult portion of the investigation, but he realized now how naïve the assumption had been.

Kolthoff's lawyers had postponed the grand jury hearing with one legal motion after another, and as Zane and Amelia drove down the rainy freeway to visit the sixteen-year-old girl who had almost become the man's victim, he was lounging in the lap of luxury. He'd been ordered to remain in Chicago unless he was required to travel by his work as a Washington, D.C. lobbyist.

Zane wasn't so sure the decision to keep Kolthoff in the same state as his almost-victim was wise.

Would have been better if they'd thrown him in a cell with Emilio and let the two of them hash it out.

At least for Emilio and the other Leóne men, the wheels of justice had turned more quickly. Zane could only assume that their lawyers had sped them toward a trial because they were remanded to the detention center, unlike Brian Kolthoff.

But despite the hefty sentences that the U.S. Attorney had hung over their heads, not a single one of them had been willing to provide information in exchange for leniency. Then again, Federal sex trafficking charges already came with a ten-to-fifteen-year mandatory minimum sentence, so there was only so much they could have bargained for in the first place.

Mandatory minimum sentences were tricky, and Zane didn't envy the position the U.S. Attorney had to navigate.

However, in the lengthy trial of Emilio Leóne, even the mandatory minimum seemed shaky. Though the FBI had come across fifteen other girls in their raid, none of the young women had been willing to testify against Emilio or the Leóne family.

Leila had been the only one.

Zane couldn't blame the girls, and he hadn't done much to convince them to change their minds. More than half of them were addicted to one illegal substance or the other, and five of them were under eighteen.

Still, despite the number of aggravating factors that should have added to Emilio's sentence, the prosecutor's case was largely circumstantial.

Emilio's lawyer had an answer for every question that surfaced, an explanation for every inconsistency in his client's story, and a rebuttal for every claim made by the U.S.

Attorney. In the end, with only some physical evidence to back up her testimony, the trial had boiled down to Leila's word against Emilio's.

And today, the verdict had been handed down.

"A nickel." He shook his head and checked the blind spot. "Emilio's doing a nickel for forcing underage girls into prostitution."

Amelia blew out a sigh. "I guess that's what happens when your family keeps one of the best law firms in the city on retainer. It's a hard five years, at least. No good behavior, no time served, just a solid five-year sentence."

Zane flexed his grasp on the steering wheel. "How did the jury believe *any* of the shit he said about not knowing how old these girls were? Or about them using fake IDs? Did they *really* think he carded all those girls?"

With a groan, Amelia rubbed the bridge of her nose. "I don't know. You saw the same trial I did. You saw the guy claim that all the girls came to him looking for work, and there was no one there to dispute it other than Leila. That's only one out of the sixteen that we know of. I guarantee there are others, but there's no way they'll come forward."

As they lapsed into silence, the steady cadence of raindrops against the windshield faded to a light sprinkle. Well, at least one thing had gone right.

"It's just the way it is, though, isn't it?"

Zane fixed Amelia with a curious glance. "What is?"

She leaned back in her seat and shrugged. "Organized crime. Groups like the Leónes, the Russians, the Irish, the cartels. They're always going to be there, more or less. The cops thought they knocked down all the dominoes back when they got Capone, but look at the country now."

He nodded but couldn't shake the sense of deflation that came with Amelia's dose of reality.

She gestured to the cigarettes in the cupholder. "We can get pissed and slowly kill ourselves with whatever we want. With stress, booze, cigarettes, whatever. And I'm not saying that anger isn't warranted here, but the sooner we accept that this is the world we live in, the better off we're going to be when the next case pops up. We control what we do, but that's *all* we control, you know?"

He looked to the cigarettes and then to Amelia. Her gaze was fixed on the windshield, hands folded on top of her black slacks.

"That…is a really good point, Storm. You know," as her eyes shifted to him, Zane released his trademark, disarming grin, "if the FBI doesn't work out for you, I think you might have a career as a motivational speaker or something."

She snorted, but the easy smile returned to her face. "Hey, I'm not saying we live and let live with the Leónes, okay? We've got their number now. They're on our radar, and now that Emilio's trial is over, we can pull together the start of a RICO case. We've got patterns of behavior, and I'm sure we'll uncover more criminal behavior."

He raised his eyebrows. "RICO, huh?"

The Racketeer Influence and Corrupt Organizations Act was a method for the Bureau to collect a number of cases to establish a pattern of organized criminal behavior. Once they amassed enough evidence, the penalties for those convicted were severe. Utilizing RICO was a laborious task, and it required extensive planning and communication on their end.

"Well." She weighed both hands. "I don't know for sure. But it's always there if we get enough evidence."

He nodded. "True enough."

For the remainder of the drive, their conversation took a turn closer to something that resembled normalcy. They were both glad to be done with the constant court appearances that had been required over the course of Emilio and the other men's trials.

When they pulled into the driveway of the Jackson residence, he wouldn't have guessed that all the occupants of the house were about to move. Then again, that was the point, wasn't it? In order to relocate without piquing the interests of the neighborhood, they had to be discrete.

As he and Amelia stepped onto the concrete, sunlight pierced through the clusters of clouds and reflected in the wet asphalt. Though the air had cooled since their departure from the FBI building, the humidity was oppressive.

Wrinkling her nose, Amelia rapped her knuckles against the front door. "It's fuzzy outside."

Zane opened and closed his mouth a couple times. "It's…what?"

"It's fuzzy." She offered him a noncommittal shrug. "The air feels fuzzy."

Though he wanted to ask her more about her bizarre observation, the wooden door swung inward to reveal a familiar woman. The gold star and badge proclaiming her a U.S. Marshal were tucked away, but she carried herself with an authoritative air.

The corners of her golden-brown eyes creased as she smiled. "Agent Palmer, Agent Storm. Nice to see you again. Come on in."

"Nice to see you too, Agent Goodman." Zane acknowledged her with a tip of his head. He followed Amelia into the air-conditioned foyer. After he closed and locked the front door, the U.S. Marshal led them to the living room.

Any mirth that might have remained between Zane and Amelia vanished at the scene before them. Leila sat in the center of the couch, flanked by both parents. Her blue eyes were bloodshot, and the vivid color had become ethereal.

Offering Amelia and Zane a strained smile, Joy Jackson passed a tissue to her daughter. On Leila's other side, Wendell sniffled as he scratched the head of a familiar long-haired calico cat.

A young man with dark brown hair and the same blue eyes as Leila—Pierce Jackson—pushed himself to stand. He gestured for the agents to take the love seat. "Please, sit."

Zane shook his head. "I'm good. Been sitting for more than an hour on the drive here."

Pierce retook his seat.

Amelia knelt down at the coffee table and reached a hand out to squeeze the girl's arm. "What's wrong?"

Blotting her tearstained face with the tissue, Leila glanced from Amelia to Zane and then back. "Thanks for coming, Agents. I was worried you'd be too busy, and I just wanted to say thank you for everything you've done."

Zane shook his head. "Of course. We'd never be too busy to come see you off."

Joy's lips curved into a wistful smile. "We know the sentence wasn't quite what anyone wanted, but we're grateful for everything you did to make it happen." Her expression faltered as she looked to the cat in Wendell's lap. "That's not what's bothering us. We know we're headed into witness protection, and we can't really take anything with us. We're going to be starting over completely, and I honestly think that's for the best, but…"

As the woman trailed off, Zane filled in the remaining blanks. "But that means you can't take your cat, right?"

Joy tried to hide her sniffles behind her hand. "Yeah. It sounds silly, doesn't it? We're leaving so we can hide from this powerful crime family, but we're all here crying because we're going to miss our cat."

Leila squeezed her eyes closed and shook her head. "It's not just that. We don't have time to find anyone to take her, so she'll just go to some shelter." Golden light from a nearby floor lamp caught the tears as they streaked down Leila's cheeks.

Kneeling at Amelia's side, Zane shot the marshal a quizzical look. "Which shelter? Is she just going to the pound?"

Goodman sighed. Her pinched expression told him that she hadn't eluded the weight of the decision. "It's the best we can do on such short notice."

"I can take her." Amelia jumped in with hardly a moment's pause. "I've wanted a pet for a long time, and I was never really able to have one while I was in the military. I've been so busy over the last couple months that I haven't really had the time to look around shelters in town or anything. But cats are super low-maintenance."

Even though the offer came out of nowhere, Zane wasted no time seconding it. "That's true. They sleep for sixteen hours a day."

Leila's expression brightened. "Really? You'd take Hup?"

In that moment, Amelia looked happier than Zane had seen since before they took on the investigation into the Leónes. "Yeah. My niece and nephew love cats, but their mom is allergic, so they have a dog instead. But they'd be stoked if I had a cat they could come hang out with."

The tears that slipped down Leila's face this time were from an entirely different source. "I'll still miss her like crazy, but I'll feel so much better if I know she went straight to a good home."

Zane elbowed Amelia's shoulder. "Hey, we're going to work out some kind of visitation here, aren't we? I want to hang out with Hup too."

As Leila and her mother laughed at his silly joke, the hopelessness faded from their eyes. It was a small thing, sure.

Cats were easy, but being able to lift that one small burden seemed to make all the difference to them. And with the way things had gone, any win was worth celebrating.

29

Flashing a quick smile to the security officer behind the metal detector, Red strode to the nearest elevator. He jabbed the "up" arrow, and before he could even step back, the silver doors slid open with a cheery ding. At six on a Friday evening, the twenty-story business tower was sparse.

With one more glance over his shoulder, Red stepped into the pristine elevator and pressed the button for the nineteenth floor. He'd been to the office plenty of times before, but for the past month and a half—ever since Brian Kolthoff had been arrested—he'd kept his distance.

The man he was here to see, Senator Stan Young, was a hands-off type. If he could send someone to complete a task in his stead, he wouldn't hesitate. In some ways, the senator's philosophy was impressive. He knew there were people better suited to specific jobs, and he never got caught up in the twisted web of pride that had led to the downfall of so many before him.

Brushing both hands along his black suit jacket, Red leaned against the handrail and watched the floor indicator rise. The senator spent much of his time at the Illinois state capitol building in Springfield, but he returned to the corporate headquarters of his agricultural empire regularly.

Another ding sounded overhead, and Red turned his attention to the sliding doors. Most of the office lights had been turned off after the staff left for the day, but sunlight streamed in through the tall window at the end of the hall.

To his right loomed the shadowy entrances to a series of conference rooms and shared offices, and to the left, a pane of glass separated a cluster of cubicles from the hall.

Stuffing both hands in the pockets of his suit jacket, Red strode down the carpeted hall in almost complete silence. The corridor split off in both directions when he reached the window, but he hardly had to think about the direction in which he was headed.

A frosted glass door had been propped open with a stopper, and the sleek waiting area was cloaked in shadow. The blinds had been drawn to block out the sunlight from the full wall of windows that took up one side of the office. The chair behind the reception desk was empty, and Red was struck with an amusing thought. Without sunlight or employees, the entire floor felt like a level in a survival horror video game.

Chuckling to himself, he strode past the reception desk to another open doorway. Before he could announce his presence, Senator Young glanced up from where his attention had been fixed on a sheet of paper.

The corners of Senator Young's gray eyes creased as he smiled. Muted daylight caught the edge of his white gold wedding band as he swept a hand at the two plush chairs in front of his desk. "It's been a while, Agent. Please, have a seat. Do you want anything to drink?"

Red shook his head and took the offered seat. "No, thanks. I'm good."

Stan nodded. "Okay, then. I appreciate you coming on such short notice."

"It's no problem. I figured with everything that's happened with Brian and the Leónes, we'd need to meet up to set everything straight and figure out where we go from here."

The senator tipped his head thoughtfully. "Right. Well, as you know, it's an election year. Which makes this doubly annoying."

"There's someone challenging you in the primary, isn't there?"

Stan's expression turned grim. "Ben Storey, former military, happily married to his high school sweetheart, two honor roll student kids. He's Captain America, and he's a pain in the ass." He waved a hand. "But that's my problem right now, not yours."

"Well, just let me know if anything changes on that front."

A devious smirk played across Stan's lips. "Of course. But for now, here we are. I'm still in the dark on some aspects of what happened last month. Emilio Leóne was sentenced a couple days ago, but Brian hasn't even been indicted by a grand jury."

"That'd be his lawyers earning their retainer."

Senator Young chuckled. "I wouldn't expect anything less. But how did the FBI even get to him? I know how careful he is when he's dealing with the Leóne family." Concern darkened the senator's expression. "What the hell happened in your office? What went wrong?"

"I told Brian about the raid, and we both agreed that it was in our best interests to leave it alone and let the Leónes take the fall. Like you said, Emilio's been sentenced already, but Brian hasn't even been indicted. And at the rate things are going, he *won't* be indicted."

Stan tapped a finger against his clean-shaven cheek. "No, he probably won't be. And even if he is, the likelihood that he's charged with anything other than solicitation is slim. Who was behind this, though? Who led the charge? Do you think they'll be a problem going forward?"

He paused to consider the question. "She might be."

Young lifted an eyebrow. "She?"

"Amelia Storm. I don't know how she did it, but it seemed like she was one step ahead of us at the end. She claims her information came from a CI, but I haven't heard her mention a name. The name wasn't even mentioned in court."

Malevolence flickered in the senator's eyes. "Storm? Isn't that…"

"Yes, Trevor Storm's sister," Red finished for him.

Stan leaned back in his office chair and brought his hands together, pointer fingers touching his chin, and silently gazed up at the ceiling as if praying to the tiles for answers. The moment of silent contemplation ended with a malevolent smile cooling the room.

"Stay close to her. Monitor what she's doing. Throw her off the trail if she picks it up again. You know what needs to be done. As for that CI. Well…" Young's eyes narrowed, "find out who the asshole is and take care of him."

❄

HUP HAD ONLY LIVED in her apartment for a couple days, but Amelia was already certain that she'd been destined for cat parenthood. The long-haired calico had been frightened at first, but after Amelia fed her some treats and a can of wet food, the cat wouldn't let her out of its sight.

In a video call with her sister-in-law the day before, she'd held Hup up to the camera and lifted one white paw to wave at Hailey and Nolan. The children had been thrilled with the new member of their family.

Stretching both legs along the chaise of her sectional couch, Amelia pulled her attention from the television to where Hup was curled up in an orange, black, and white ball on the center cushion. Amelia settled back in the pile of pillows and returned to half-watch the animated series she'd seen a hundred times over.

Today was her first full day off in ages, and even though she'd been dedicated to knocking out housework and errands, all she'd accomplished by nine that night was a load of laundry. Otherwise, she'd been almost as lazy as the cat at her side.

As her eyelids grew heavier, Amelia pulled the microfiber blanket up to her chin. Her thoughts blurred with the dialogue from the television show, and each scenario was more bizarre than the last.

Before she could drift off to sleep, a familiar buzz jerked her back to full consciousness. The transition could only be described as violent.

Sitting bolt upright, Amelia took in a panicked breath and forced her bleary eyes to find the source of the sound. Gold light from the fixture above the oven provided an ambient glow, but it barely made it to the couch. And in her half-asleep state, it took longer than usual to make the connection between the noise and her phone.

When the second ring rattled her nerves, Amelia had it figured out. She groaned and pawed at the wooden coffee table, reaching for the smartphone.

"Work call." She looked at the cat in disbelief. "It's a work call, Hup. At nine-thirty on a Saturday."

Hup, apathetic to her whining, was already too busy with nightly grooming to *mew* in reply.

Amelia stifled another groan as she swiped the green answer key. "This is Agent Storm."

"Agent Storm?" The woman's voice was cool, confident, and...familiar. "I'm not sure if you remember me. We met at a nightclub at the beginning of June."

"The beginning of June?" Amelia squeezed her eyes closed and ran through her mental calendar. "Nightclub."

"Evoked," the woman rushed to offer.

Amelia froze as she finally placed the woman's voice. "Vivian. Mind if I ask how you got this number?"

Vivian sighed. "Of course. My name *is* Vivian, but I wasn't at Evoked because I'm part of that...scene. If that's what you want to call it. I was there working. I'm a PI, and I'm based in Chicago. I can send you whatever information you need to prove who I am. As for your number, I got it from the FBI."

She'd double-check all that tomorrow. "Working? What were you working on at Evoked?"

"Those two that you and your husband were talking to. Elijah and Sara. Elijah's ex-wife hired me to get evidence for an upcoming custody battle. When she told me where she thought Eli had been going, I knew right away that I'd be in for a ride."

Amelia tried to connect the dots. "So, you need my help with a divorce case?"

Vivian chuckled. "Not quite. You know, this city has many secrets, and it's not all that uncommon that I dig up three more when I'm just trying to get to the bottom of one."

Grating her teeth, Amelia swung her legs over the side of the couch. "What does that mean?"

When Vivian sighed again, she sounded tired. "I saw the FBI press conference about Emilio Leóne's conviction. The Leónes are slippery, so I knew that whoever did the legwork to get to a *capo* had to have done a damn good job. And I knew that person would be trustworthy. Not any Tom, Dick, or Harry knocks down a Leóne kingpin, you know?"

Vivian wasn't far off the mark. Ever since Emilio's arrest, Amelia's hyper-awareness had returned in force. Any time she went outside, she felt like she was walking into the blistering sun of the Middle East. She half-expected to see convoys of military vehicles on her way to work or to wake up to discover she'd never even left the Army.

Maybe the Leónes would come for her, but she was confident she'd see them coming from a mile away.

Amelia cleared her throat. "Okay. Yeah, but Emilio only got a nickel. His right-hand guy got more time than he did."

"It's the principle of it all. But I'm sorry, I digress. I'd really like to meet up with you soon. We can meet at the FBI office, I'm fine with that. But the long and short of it is that I need your help. I know you're familiar with the Leónes and their trafficking operation now, and I've got a lead that's spiraling into more than I can handle."

Tension eased away from Amelia's shoulders. "Another sex trafficking ring?"

"Forced labor, among other things." Vivian's tone became stony. "From what I can tell so far, this operation is huge. Chances are good there are some big agricultural businesses involved. I still don't know how deep this rabbit hole goes, which is why I think it's time I pass the torch on to someone with a little more authority than me."

As Vivian mentioned the trafficking ring, Amelia was reminded of her and Zane's conversation on the way to DeKalb. Another criminal investigation against the Leóne family was another step toward a RICO case.

Amelia reached for the television remote. "What time do you want to meet?"

The End
To be continued...

Thank you for reading.
All of the Amelia Storm Series books can be found on
Amazon.

ACKNOWLEDGMENTS

How does one properly thank everyone involved in taking a dream and making it a reality? Here goes.

In addition to our families, whose unending support provided the foundation for us to find the time and energy to put these thoughts on paper, we want to thank the editors who polished our words and made them shine.

Many thanks to our publisher for risking taking on two newbies and giving us the confidence to become bona fide authors.

More than anyone, we want to thank you, our readers, for clicking on a couple of nobodies and sharing your most important asset, your time, with this book. We hope with all our hearts we made it worthwhile.

Much love,
Mary & Amy

ABOUT THE AUTHOR

Mary Stone lives among the majestic Blue Ridge Mountains of East Tennessee with her two dogs, four cats, a couple of energetic boys, and a very patient husband.

As a young girl, she would go to bed every night, wondering what type of creature might be lurking underneath. It wasn't until she was older that she learned that the creatures she needed to most fear were human.

Today, she creates vivid stories with courageous, strong heroines and dastardly villains. She invites you to enter her world of serial killers, FBI agents but never damsels in distress. Her female characters can handle themselves, going toe-to-toe with any male character, protagonist or antagonist.

Discover more about Mary Stone on her website.
www.authormarystone.com

Amy Wilson

Having spent her adult life in the heart of Atlanta, her upbringing near the Great Lakes always seems to slip into her writing. After several years as a vet tech, she has dreams of going back to school to be a veterinarian but it seems another dream of hers has come true first. Writing a novel.

Animals and books have always been her favorite things, in addition to her husband, who wanted her to have it all. He's the reason she has time to write. Their two teenage boys fill the rest of her time and help her take care of the mini zoo that now fills their home with laughter…and yes, the occasional poop.

Connect with Mary Online

- facebook.com/authormarystone
- goodreads.com/AuthorMaryStone
- bookbub.com/profile/3378576590
- pinterest.com/MaryStoneAuthor
- instagram.com/marystone_author

Made in the USA
Monee, IL
05 July 2021